S.A. Jones is a Melbourne-based novelist, essayist and reviewer with a PhD in History. Jones' previous novels are *Red Dress Walking* and *Isabelle of the Moon and Stars*. She has authored dozens of opinion pieces and essays on politics, history, sexuality, public policy and theology for *Kill Your Darlings*, *The Age*, *The Guardian*, *Overland*, *The Toast*, *Regime*, *The Drum* and *Page Seventeen*.

THE
FORTRESS

S.A. JONES

echo

echo

A division of Bonnier Publishing Australia
534 Church Street, Richmond
Victoria Australia 3121
www.echopublishing.com.au

First published 2018
Reprinted 2018

Printed in Australia at Griffin Press.
Only wood grown from sustainable regrowth forests is used in the
manufacture of paper found in this book.

Cover design by Alissa Dinallo
Cover image © Elisabeth Ansley / Trevillion Images
Page design and typesetting by Shaun Jury
Typeset in Perpetua

A catalogue entry for this book is available from the
National Library of Australia
    ISBN: 9781760407940 (paperback)
    ISBN: 9781760407957 (ebook)
    ISBN: 9781760407964 (mobi)

🐦 bonnierpubau
📷 bonnierpublishingau
📘 bonnierpublishingau

In memory of Madge Hunt (1928–2015) who knew that words matter.

Work. History. Sex. Justice.

A moving body is a creative body. It produces the food on our plates, the walls that protect us and the art that delights us.

We created and recreate ourselves by standing apart. We honour they who won us our solitude, but we are not petrified.

Pleasure consists in the freedom to, and the freedom from, and every Vaik will herself determine in what measure these things are best.

We are instruments of the sovereignty of all women, and do not shrink from the sacrifice this entails.

Work. History. Sex. Justice.

We are Vaik.

CONTENTS

| ANIN

JONATHON BRIDGE pressed the buzzer beside the imposing
iron gate and waited. He had never been so near to The
Fortress before. For most of his life the white, glittering structure
on the hilltop had simply been a historical fact. There, like his
mother had been there. In the glare of sunlight it shimmered and
levitated above the city. Now, up close, Jonathon saw that the
whiteness of the exterior wall was created by a mosaic of mother-
of-pearl and mirror. The tiles fractured his face and reflected it
back, in pieces.

'Mr Bridge?' A voice crackled through the intercom beside
the gate.

'Yes.'

'We've been expecting you. One moment, please.'

There was a wheeze, then a groan, as if a mighty machine were
firing up. The gate unlatched and opened an inch or two.

'You may enter.'

Jonathon hesitated. He turned and looked back down the steep
hill to the city. Somewhere out there in the tangled motherboard
of freeways and skyscrapers, bright lights and cubicles was his
office. And his home. It would be a long time before he saw
them again.

He shouldered the gate wider and entered a small grassed
enclosure. The gate clanged shut behind him, making him start.

A few birds pecked at the ground, undisturbed by his presence.

'Walk towards the door directly in front of you,' said the disembodied voice.

Jonathon looked for its source but could find nothing.

The door opened before he reached it, and a slim, androgynous figure bowed in greeting. *This person*, Jonathon thought, *must be an electii.*

'Welcome.' The figure stood aside to let him enter the hallway, which was long and high and lit only by muted globes set into the ceiling. The dense air seemed to part as he inched forward, re-forming behind him. He heard a *blip* and looked around.

'Metal detector,' said the electii. 'Keep going.'

The closed doors on either side were black slabs cut deep into the wall. Jonathon passed maybe a dozen doors until he came to an open room. He stepped inside, squinting into the gloom.

The electii entered, softly, behind him. 'Once your eyes have adjusted, you will observe that there is a wicker basket in the corner. Place your clothes, jewellery and personal effects into the basket. When you have disrobed, I will position you for examination. Take your time. There is no rush.'

It took a moment for Jonathon to make out the basket against the wall, then he slipped his silk-inlaid jacket from his shoulders. He flinched slightly at the recent memory of five women arrayed against him, his jacket hoisted before them like a standard. He folded the jacket gingerly, as if it might bite him, and placed it in the basket. Cufflinks, wallet and keys followed, then his belt, shirt, underwear and pants. Lastly, his shoes and socks. He placed the shoes sole-upwards on his bespoke trousers.

Naked, he returned to the centre of the room and waited. The electii came towards him and Jonathon noticed the peculiar sound — something between the clinking of ice in a glass and the rustle of brown paper — made by his (or was it her?) gown.

An outrush of breath and a vigorous rubbing of hands, then

the electii took Jonathon's elbow and guided him to the wall. 'I need you to stand spread-eagled, taking your weight in your fingers.'

Jonathon listened closely to the electii's voice but could not say whether it was male or female. It bothered him, the not knowing. He spread his long, elegant fingers against the wall and tipped himself towards it.

The electii probed at Jonathon's ankles and moved upwards; thorough and practised hands searched for contraband, weapons or messages. Jonathon heard the stretch and slap of a rubber glove being forced onto a hand and braced himself. The questioning fingers eased down the moist slice dividing his bum cheeks.

'Take a deep breath, Mr Bridge.'

Jonathon exhaled and clawed at the wall a little as the electii's finger probed his rectum.

'That part is over,' said the electii, as if Jonathon were a small child at the dentist, 'but stay still.' There was the stretch and slap of the glove again as it was removed and discarded. Jonathon breathed in and out as soundlessly as he could. The electii squeezed his balls and turned them in half-circles one way and then the other. What, Jonathon thought, could possibly be hidden in there?

The hands moved upwards, probing his abdomen, his underarms, his shoulderblades.

'Excuse me,' the electii said, pinching Jonathon's nostrils four times in rapid succession then delving into the folds of his ears.

Jonathon had many questions for the electii and if he wanted to ask them it had to be now. He knew from his reading that there were no electii beyond The Veya Gate and, even if there had been, questions were forbidden past that point. But somehow the very intimacy the electii had forced on him just now made him uncharacteristically shy.

'Thank you,' the electii said formally. 'Please stand at ease.'

At ease? Jonathon nearly laughed out loud. *Mate, you've just been knuckle-deep in my arse.*

'Here.' The electii removed a gown from the wall and handed it to Jonathon. 'Run it through your hands, get used to the feel of it.'

This was masjythra, a fabric made and worn only at The Fortress. It felt like the glomesh of a purse his wife had once owned, but incredibly light. It also felt strangely animate, as if it might slither away if he dropped it.

'Let me help you,' the electii offered.

A head taller than the electii, Jonathon bent down so that the garment could be dropped over his head. The electii smoothed the fabric across his back and shoulders. Nothing happened for a moment or two, and then the gown pulsed and slid across his torso, melding to his folds and hollows. Jonathon swore in surprise under his breath.

'You get used to it.'

The gown stopped mid-thigh. Jonathon tested his range of movement, stretching his arms above his head and raising up on the balls of his feet. He bent to touch his toes — or his knees, rather. The garment moved with him like a skin, emitting the clinking-ice sound he'd heard earlier. He turned away and gave his balls an experimental scratch. He felt strange outside the confines of his underwear. Untidy. He scratched himself again.

'Reach around behind your neck,' said the electii, 'and locate the hood.'

Jonathon pinched the material where it met the base of his skull and pulled it away from his body. It yielded after a microsecond and he slipped his hand beneath it. He pulled out a length of material and draped it over his head. The metallic squares twitched then traced his skull, leaving his face exposed.

'If you are ever in Her presence,' the electii said, 'you must immediately place the hood on and leave it on unless She tells you otherwise.'

Jonathon turned his head sharply. 'When will I see Her?'

'Impossible to say. Maybe soon. Maybe never.'

A wild violence flashed through Jonathon's blood. He wanted the definitive. A yes or a no. AC or DC. *You chose this*, he reminded himself.

'I'm sorry, Mr Bridge,' an apologetic clearing of the throat, 'but I'm going to have to take your wedding ring, too. No personal effects are permitted.'

Jonathon placed a protective hand over the gold band. *You chose this*, he reminded himself again. Not too long ago he'd thought choice was a straightforward proposition. Now he knew better. He circled the wedding band with his thumb and index finger but couldn't pull it past his knuckle. From the shadows, the electii offered him a small saucer. He dipped a finger in. It was oil, probably the same oil the electii had used to ease his (or her?) finger into Jonathon's rectum.

The oil loosened the ring, and he was able to pull it over his knuckle and slip it off. The white strip on his ring finger glared in the darkness.

'Give the ring to me, please.'

As Jonathon handed the ring to the electii he couldn't help saying, 'Take care of that.'

'I will,' the electii said kindly.

When Jonathon and his wife had first discussed having a baby, Adalia said she thought the electii were lucky, in a way. 'At least they get some choice in the matter instead of having male or female foisted on them.' Jonathon hadn't wanted an argument so he'd just shrugged.

'This is where we say goodbye,' the electii told him. 'I can't accompany you into the second chamber. Go back to the hallway and continue walking away from the entrance. Enter the next open door you find, which will be directly in front of you. Good luck, Mr Bridge.'

'Thank you. Goodbye. And good luck to you, too,' he said, though he didn't know what the electii would consider lucky.

Jonathon returned to the hallway, turned left and shuffled towards the chamber. The doors continued on either side of him, locked and completely silent. Did they house other supplicants, come like him to make a clean breast of things? He'd read all the literature he could find on Vaik civilisation, but it was scant on practical details. Ahead of him he saw a chink of light around a door. He pushed it open (it was surprisingly heavy) and was dazzled by the brightness on the other side. He held his hand between his eyes and the light for a few seconds, then lowered it, slowly.

He was in a rectangular room where swirls of red and blue tiles chased each other across the walls. Large windows the shape of bishop's hats framed the lapis lazuli sky. The room was perfumed with something sweet and grassy. A brass samovar and red glass goblets stood on a table beneath one of the windows.

'Would you like tea?'

Jonathon turned towards the voice. A woman gave a slight nod in greeting then poured from the samovar. She gestured towards one of the plump cushions dotted across the floor.

'Please, sit down.'

Jonathon lowered himself awkwardly to the ground, monitoring the stay of his hem. He wasn't as limber as he'd once been. Long lunches and immobile hours in front of a computer screen had reeled in his joints. The woman watched him coolly. When he was seated on the cushion, she passed him the goblet of tea.

'Should I keep the hood on?' Jonathon asked her hopefully.

She smiled, amused. 'I'm not The Woman, so you may remove the hood if you so choose. How is your tea?'

He took a sip. It was hot and sweet with an aftertaste of aniseed, nothing like the bitter black coffee he usually drank.

'I tend the gardens between The Dryans coast and the eastern buildings. You are assigned to me.'

Assigned?

She wasn't Jonathon's type; that is to say, she wasn't pert-breasted and young with burnished salon-skin. Her long auburn hair fell in messy waves down her back and she was pale, almost reflectively so. Jonathon vaguely wondered how she kept her skin so white under the sun in the gardens. He found it impossible to guess her age. Perhaps late thirties, perhaps early forties. Around his age. He couldn't imagine fucking her.

'Lift up your masjythra.'

'What?'

Her brows arrowed above her flinty green eyes. Jonathon rested the goblet on the ground beside him and lifted the robe to his upper thigh.

'Higher.'

He kept lifting until his cock and balls were in full view. He had a strong urge to stand up so he could suck his stomach in and flex his thighs. The way he did with the poodles. Instead he sat there obediently, holding up his gown for a stranger's forensic observation.

'You can lower the masjythra now.'

Was she impressed? Disappointed? Bored? Her impassive face gave nothing away.

'We take very few supplicants, and those we take we have to be sure can adapt to life here. I've read your file.' She paused to take a sip of tea, then held his eyes with her level gaze. 'Your wife is pregnant.'

This didn't seem to be a question, so Jonathon didn't reply.

'Your wife is five months pregnant. You will miss the birth of your first child. Does that trouble you?'

'Yes.'

'Does that trouble your wife?'

'Yes.'

'So why are you here?'

You have my file, he thought. *You probably know the reasons better than I do.*

'I want to be a good father,' he said. 'I don't know another way of doing that. Becoming that. Better I miss the birth than the rest of her life.'

She inclined her head to one side. 'Her? Your file doesn't specify a gender.'

'We don't know the baby's sex. For some reason I think of her as a her. Anyway, it sounds much better than "it".'

'You want to be a good father. Why don't you go to antenatal classes? That's what most men would do.'

'I'm not most men.'

'That's what most men say.'

Jonathon grew impatient, as he always did when people were cryptic. He reached up to adjust his tie, his habit when annoyed, then remembered he wasn't wearing one. The masjythra shifted around his collarbone.

'My wife wanted me to come,' he said flatly. 'It was the only condition on which she'd take me back.'

The woman gave a dismissive wave of her hand. 'A poor reason. It lacks conviction on your part. Acting on someone else's wishes won't be enough to sustain you here.'

'I've been accepted, haven't I?'

'Yes. You have. But this is your last opportunity to reconsider. Once you pass through The Veya Gate and into The Fortress proper, there's no going back. You see out your time. One year. I urge you to think better of it.'

He shook his head.

'Your relationship to the Vaik and your status here will

be unlike anything you have experienced before. It is almost impossible to give you an accurate analogy of your relationship to us. I *can* tell you what you, and we, are not.

'The Fortress is not a jail, although you will be held under guard if you break our laws. You are not a prisoner, but your movements, your time, your labour will be almost entirely regulated. The Vaik will direct when and what you eat, when you sleep, when you rise. Every eleventh day you will have half a day to spend according to your inclination and wishes. This is known as "the half". You are free to roam around a prescribed area of the grounds. On all other days the spaces you inhabit and what you do there will be directed by us.

'Perhaps the most difficult thing to grasp about your relationship to us is the nature of your submission. While you stay with us you are to obey all Vaik commands and you are forbidden to ask questions of us unless explicitly authorised. But we are not in a master-serf relationship. You are not chattel, and our obligations to you are as strong and binding as those you owe to us. When you come to us it must be in a state of willingness to empty yourself out and entrust yourself to us. Without that trust your supplicancy will be futile. You may as well return to your life right now. Your subjectivity must be given to us freely and entirely. We will keep it until you return through The Veya Gate. We will not return it beforehand under any circumstances.

'You will see and experience things that will be strange to you, that may offend your notions of what is good and right. But you have offered your will up to the Vaik, and you are our vessel. You must learn to hold yourself in a state of suspension, which is not at all the same thing as apathy. Some men think they can come here and close themselves off for a year, fold into a pocket deep in their souls and then unfold again at the end of their time. This serves no one. It is a trick, a deceit to hold power while pretending to cede it.

'Whatever your male friends may have told you, we are not in a relationship of subordinates and dominants. Our authority over you is real and entirely tangible. There is no safe word you can utter that will make the power flow differently between us. We have dungeons here. Whips and chains. But they're not props and The Fortress isn't a sadomasochistic theatre.'

Her mouth twitched slightly. 'We have had supplicants in the past who were,' she paused, '*misinformed* about our culture. The reality came as rather a shock.'

'Well,' he said, 'to be fair, there's not a great deal of credible literature on the role and place of supplicants in Vaik culture. I went looking for it. Almost no one who's been a supplicant writes about it afterwards. I assumed that silence was part of the contract.'

She shook her head. 'We impose no prescription on what supplicants do or say once they leave The Fortress. How could we? We have no jurisdiction outside the perimeter wall and would have no way of enforcing it if we did. I suspect the silence derives from the difficulty of translation. I have lived in your world, so I know how difficult it is to draw comparisons. I can't tell you "life here is like x or like y", because it's not. You will find the same thing when you leave. You'll meet very few people capable of understanding what you will understand in a year's time.

'That's probably the most difficult thing for you to grasp: the Vaik way of seeing is not your way of seeing. You are not a tourist and this is not a cultural exchange. You will learn to see through our eyes, but this will take time and experience. Until then, you must let us inhabit that place where your will would otherwise be. Even when it grates against what you believe and what you think you know. Our relationship to supplicants has been codified over centuries. What you now enter is an ancient rite, recognisable in one form or another for more than a thousand years. It will be helpful to remember this history, to trust it. The Vaik are dependent on this tradition, too. Without it, we could not reproduce and our way of life would be gone after a generation.'

Ah yes. Reproduction. As a teen, Jonathon had been like other spotty boys whose glands were spurting new and strange urges into his body. They had fantasised about life in this world of endless oestrus and ceaseless yes.

As if summoned by some secret signal into which he had not been initiated, two women entered the room. Unlike the Vaik to whom Jonathon was assigned, both were what Jonathon thought of as prototypes: tall and lithe, brown-skinned with hay-coloured hair and high, wide foreheads. They looked at him intently, almost accusingly.

'Are you ready to begin?'

Jonathon nodded.

'I will recite the terms of your confinement at The Fortress. These Vaik bear witness. At the close of each question I will ask you if you consent. Your answer will be "I consent". You will then be required to sign a written contract. Do you understand?'

He nodded.

'You remain in full possession of your will until you enter The Veya Gate. From then on you will be a vessel of submission to me and to all the women of The Fortress. You will obey every command, request and direction given by a Vaik once you pass The Veya Gate. The only circumstance in which you may question any command, request or direction so given is where two or more commands, requests or directions contradict each other. You consent to this?'

'I consent.'

'You are forbidden from having any contact with the outside world. Any attempt by you to send unauthorised communication outside The Fortress by any and all means, including through other residents and inmates, will be severely punished. Persons beyond The Veya Gate are free to write to you provided that the letters are written in ink. No typed or printed material will be allowed. All letters will be security screened and read by the Vaik. They will be passed on to you at our sole discretion. You consent to this?'

'I consent.'

'You will remain at The Fortress for one year. This timeframe is non-negotiable, regardless of any change in your circumstances. Do you consent?'

'I consent.'

She gave a barely perceptible frown at his answer, as if she had expected better of him. 'You understand that if your wife dies in childbirth or you are diagnosed with a terminal illness the period of your tenure does not change?'

The two Vaik who were bearing witness glanced at each other then back at Jonathon. He had the distinct impression that his interlocutor had veered off script.

Adalia had seen him off that morning, her hands pressed against the just-rounding belly that contained their daughter. 'I'm proud of you,' she'd whispered. How he'd hungered to hear that.

'I consent,' he said.

'Your records indicate that your sexual health is sound. We undertake that you will leave The Fortress in the same state of sexual health. Once you pass through The Veya Gate your body becomes our responsibility. We will meet all your physical needs: food, clothing, bedding, hygiene and medicine, should it be required. We direct the uses of your body at all times. You consent?'

'I consent.'

'There are limits to the uses to which your body will be put. You will be subject to no immoderate physical force. You will not be exposed to substances that could permanently imperil your health. You will not be required to labour beyond fourteen hours in a twenty-four-hour period. Do you consent?'

'I consent.'

'You are permitted no sexual contact with non-Vaik inhabitants of The Fortress unless expressly requested by the Vaik. You consent?'

'I consent.'

'You understand that among the inhabitants of The Fortress are men who have been declared isvestyii. They may be part of your assignment, may sit at the same table with you – in short, will pass their days with you. You are expected to show them the same courtesy you extend to others. You are forbidden from raising your hand in anger to any inhabitant of The Fortress, including Vaik, isvestyii, national servicemen, residents and supplicants. Do you consent?'

'I consent.'

'You relinquish all parental rights to any child or children you conceive in The Fortress. You have no right to a confirmation of paternity and should you suspect paternity you will seek no contact with any such child or children once you vacate The Fortress. You have no responsibility – pecuniary, legal, filial or moral – towards any such child or children. You consent?'

'I consent.'

'Once you pass The Veya Gate, all questions to the Vaik are forbidden unless expressly authorised. The use of questions to elicit information, initiate conversation or seek direction is not permitted. What you need to know, we will communicate to you. Do you consent?'

'I consent.'

'You are to address the women of The Fortress as "Mistress" unless they give you their name. If a Vaik gives you her name, it is generally a sign of great favour. My name is Mandalay. I tell you this because you are assigned to me. You will obey every woman in The Fortress, from the smallest girl-child to The Woman.'

Jonathon immediately looked up. 'When will I see Her?'

'I suspect you're going to struggle with the prohibition on questions, Jonathon Bridge. That's not for me to say. Drink your tea.' Mandalay took a sheaf of papers lying next to the samovar and signed. Jonathon had half-expected a quill and ink but she passed him a simple silver ballpoint. 'Take your time. The contract is a faithful representation of what we have discussed.'

Jonathon scanned the contract, then signed and handed it back to Mandalay. Something velveteen and warm slipped through his blood. *They're drugging me?*

Mandalay appeared to have read his thoughts. 'It's only temporary. For security purposes. You will remember nothing from the point of The Veya Gate to entering your quarters. This is your last opportunity to ask questions.'

'The electii I met earlier.'

'Yes?'

'Man or woman?'

'Yet to be decided. Perhaps both. Neither. Anything else?'

He wanted to know how the question was decided, but this required a turn his mind couldn't make. Instead he asked her how long she had been at The Fortress.

'Twenty years.'

'And where,' his tongue and head were growing heavy, '... where were you from?'

'The Green Sea Isles.'

He used to be good at geography.

'That's a long way,' he said.

'Yes.'

'Have you seen The Woman?'

But Mandalay didn't answer, or perhaps he didn't ask.

When he woke he had no memory of emerging from The Veya

Gate and arriving at his quarters. The last thing he remembered was taking the final oath at the imposing white obelisk.

I submit.

I submit.

I submit.

When he woke it was dark. The only light came from the moon pouring through the arched window open to the night air. His room was small and bare and dominated by the large square bed. The bed was built into the wall on two sides and easily large enough for three or four people. It was soft and warm, inviting him to slip back into the luxuriant siren call of the drug. For a minute more, Jonathon yielded to the floaty blankness, then he hurled himself upright and swung his feet from the bed to the floor. The sudden movement made him dizzy. He dropped his head to his knees and took deep breaths.

His tongue felt furry from the aniseed tea. Someone, perhaps Mandalay, had placed a jar of water on the rustic wooden table next to his bed. He drank it greedily. His masjythra had been removed; he saw it glinting from a hook on the wall. Jonathon counted slowly backwards from twenty then stood up and shuffled the few steps to the window and looked out.

His quarters were several floors above the ground. He could hear, though he could not see, the seabirds cawing beneath. To his right he made out a curve in the perimeter wall – still pearlescent in the moonlight – before it disappeared into the darkness. Beneath the birdsong was the rush and gurgle of the tide and the low murmur of air through the small vents in the floor.

He turned from the window to the four square metres that would house him for the next year. On the table was a laminated card that appeared to contain a map and some instructions. Beside the bed and the table, the only other furniture was a low, three-legged stool. The walls were white-washed stone; the floor was timber, smoothed by the years and the polish of bare soles. He dropped to his knees and explored the room with his fingers, familiarising himself with the lee of the boards, the placement of the vents and the hollow thud of cavities in the wall. He didn't know, exactly, what he was looking for. A power point, perhaps. A secret tunnel chiselled by the previous inhabitant that might lead him to the outside world.

He sighed, then drew himself back onto the bed. He closed his hand on his cock and gave it a perfunctory tug. He didn't feel remotely aroused but wanted to pretend that his life would go on as normal, his routines undisturbed. He pictured a breast. A thigh. Tight round buttocks. But the images shimmered and dissolved. Frustrated, he tugged harder. Jureece, naked and supine, flew across his mind. Jonathon's hand fell onto the bedclothes, his cock limp. He curled like a sea urchin and buried his head in his hands.

One year. Your choice.

He fell asleep then woke to a chime peeling through The Fortress and a low bustle of activity coming from somewhere below his quarters. He rose from the bed, took the masjythra from its hook and threw it over his head. The tiny metallic squares pinched the hairs on his chest and arms as they cinched to his body.

His water jar had been refilled. It unnerved him: the idea that someone, probably a man, had come into his room while he slept. He took the jar and stood at the window.

The sky was still pink-streaked in the post dawn. Far below him men in different-coloured masjythra walked in single file in the direction of the chime. When they'd passed, Jonathon leant out of the window and tipped the jar over his head. It took him a moment to recognise the tang in the air as salt. It had been years since he'd been this close to the open sea. He'd forgotten the way it left a film over his skin. He needed coffee, badly.

He picked up the laminated card on his bedside table. It told him where to find the toilets and water stations. Jonathon followed the directions to the urinal and released a stream of pungent, greenish urine – probably the drug. Like his quarters, the bathroom was clean and spare. There were no mirrors.

Out in the hallway he paused, homing in on the chiming noise then turning towards it. At the end of the corridor he came to a staircase that zigzagged at a gradient just sharp enough to make him concentrate on his footing. He followed it to the level ground and fell into step with another man wearing the same coloured masjythra as him.

Mandalay had told him not to ask questions of the Vaik, to wait to be addressed, but did that apply to the men? He looked at the man next to him, ready to nod a greeting if given the opportunity. But the man kept his eyes on the ground. Jonathon peered closely at him. He was younger than Jonathon, no more than thirty. Why was he here? It occurred to Jonathon that he might be isvestyii. What had he done so bad, so young, to warrant that kind of punishment?

The ground-floor corridor opened onto a wide, sunlit verandah. The young man turned and, in the sudden flash of light, Jonathon saw the other half of his face. He sucked in his shock. The man's face appeared to have melted on one side, his milky eye dull.

As if sensing Jonathon's gaze, he turned his other eye onto him. 'This way,' he said.

Jonathon followed him into a long, low building filled with the sound of clanking cutlery. Men in masjythra sat in rows on rough-hewn benches at wooden tables. Most were intent on the steaming blue bowls in front of them.

Jonathon flexed and balled his hands by his sides. Coffee. He needed coffee. He looked around for a percolator. An urn. Sachets of low-rent fucking instant.

On their last holiday Jonathon had taken Adalia to a resort high in the mountains. It was a two-day drive. Their oak-panelled room overlooked an orchard and in the afternoon it was suffused with the scent of cherries. There was a plunge pool and sauna on their balcony. At breakfast they had two dozen types of coffee bean to choose from. The beans spilled luxuriously, dark and glossy, from labelled sacks. Vanillin. Chocolate-infused. Brandy-simmered. Macerated-in-pear. He scooped measures of the hotel's signature cherry-coffee and took it to the waiter for grinding. He walked carefully back to their table with the steaming mugs, milk and sugar in both. He'd asked the waiter to coif Adalia's froth into a heart.

In the dining hall, the scarred man directed Jonathon to a spare seat at one of the benches. As Jonathon sat down, he tugged the masjythra as low as he could, so low it pulled tight at the front of his neck. A blue bowl was placed in front of him, and a smaller bowl to the left. He picked up the small bowl and sniffed it hopefully. Tea. He took a sip. It tasted grassy, not like the sweet aniseed tea. From behind him someone ladled porridge into the larger bowl. He had little appetite, and even less for this sticky concoction of oats and milk.

'Eat,' urged the scarred man, although he didn't look up. 'You'll need it.'

Jonathon spooned the mixture to his mouth between sips of tea. He made a rough calculation of how many men were in the hall: fifteen tables, ten or eleven seated at each, plus the dozen or so servers. A hundred and seventy odd men, some of whom had to be isvestyii. The rest were a mixture of supplicants like him, national servicemen and a few – a very few – men granted permanent residency. Could they take The Fortress if they wanted to? Had anyone ever tried?

The Vaik sat outside on a large terrace at round tables, enjoying the mild spring sunshine. Men in ochre-coloured masjythra delivered platters of fruit and pastries to them. Did they get coffee? Jonathon saw Mandalay among them, conspicuous by the long red hair spilling from under her hat and by her pale, reflective skin. She was peeling an orange and laughing at something one of the other women had said.

Jonathon shifted on his chair. The rough wood chafed his balls. Just what he needed. No internet. No coffee. Splinters in his dick. He half-choked, half-snorted his spoonful of porridge. Next to him, the scarred man shot him a warning glance.

'Sorry,' Jonathon spluttered, pressing his balled fist into his chest to dislodge the porridge.

'Eat,' the man said again.

Jonathon moved the food mechanically from bowl to mouth, bowl to mouth. It wasn't that it was bad, but he hadn't eaten breakfast in years. He subsisted on black coffee in the mornings. Maybe a doughnut if a poodle brought him one.

The gardens, Mandalay had said. That would make Adalia laugh – him, who could barely keep his office cactus alive.

He looked again at the Vaik. Mandalay wore a loose, white diaphanous gown that ran to her wrists and ankles, and a floppy green hat. She and her companions were cut sharp against the blue sky, as if they'd been superimposed on it. No girl-children were among them, but other than that they were of all ages. The very oldest had wiry white hair in braids down to her waist. She sat in a wheeled chair decorated with brightly coloured patches of silk. Most of the Vaik had the brown skin and straw-coloured hair of the first women of The Fortress, the natives of this place. But there were others, foreigners like Mandalay.

Were any of them The Woman?

Jonathon studied them surreptitiously. She was said to be ancient. Ageless. Perpetually youthful. Dark. Light. Slender as a reed and the embodiment of voluptuous. There were so many stories about The Woman that she could have been all or none of the women taking their breakfast on the terrace.

Mandalay caught his eye. He dropped his head and reached for his tea. His hand shook slightly.

Midway through breakfast, one of the women came into the hall and took up position on a podium. She wore white like Mandalay, so perhaps she was gardens too. She leafed through a leather-bound volume on the lectern and began to read out loud. When Jonathon was younger, much younger, he'd had a gift for languages. There was a time when he would have understood a lot of what the woman was saying; before the numbers took him. Now, he picked out the odd word. Sea. Woman. Work. Sex. He'd always liked the sound of the Vaik language – its sonorous, long vowels that dipped suddenly into a sibilant rush. It made him think of a soprano who broke off mid-song to swear vengeance against a dozing audience member.

Another chime signalled an end to breakfast. The men in the blue masjythra moved through the hall collecting bowls and placing them on trolleys. The women disappeared.

'Follow me,' the scarred man said to Jonathon. 'I'm gardens, too.'

'How did you know I'm gardens?'

'Silver masjythra all work outdoors. You're too tall for the quarry and your hands shake too badly for masonry.' The man nodded towards Jonathon's hands. 'Cigarettes?'

He shook his head. 'Coffee. Black coffee.'

'You're in for a rough few days.'

Yes, he thought, *three hundred and sixty-five rough days, to be precise*. 'I'm Jonathon.'

'I'm Daidd.'

On leaving the dining hall they continued along the verandah in the opposite direction to the sleeping quarters. The outside wall was decorated with the same pearl-and-mirror mosaic Jonathon had noticed when he'd entered The Fortress. Glossy ferns spilled from multi-coloured glazed pots along the timber walkway. After a few hundred metres the verandah dropped away to an orchard. Daidd reached up and pulled a handful of cherries from a tree. He chewed them then spat out the pips.

'Five more days. Maybe six. Then we'll pick them.'

At the close of the orchard they met six men in silver masjythra.

'Let's go,' said Daidd. They shouldered heavy canvas sacks between them; gardening tools, Jonathon guessed. The ground sloped downwards past neat rows of grapevines. They were travelling east, away from the sea. The gardens stretched all the way to the horizon in front of him. He had always known that The Fortress was vast; everyone knew that. But now that he was within its walls, the sheer scale of it amazed him. They trudged on for an hour, and the horizon came no closer.

At a signal from Daidd they dropped the sacks. The men fronted a large rectangular field overrun with weeds. Along three sides were low stone walls in need of repair.

One of the men bent down and gingerly examined the weed. 'Goosen's Trial. You're fucking kidding me.'

'We're clearing it,' Daidd said.

'With what?'

Daidd raised his bare hands then pointed to the sacks. Mandalay appeared from behind him, silent as a cat. The men picked various implements from the sacks and set to work.

'Jonathon,' said Mandalay, 'come with me.'

He followed her to the wall flanking the field on its far, long side. She reached for a canvas bag hanging from the stone masonry, fluted at one end and fed from a coiling white tube that disappeared over the wall. She unstopped the cork and water trickled to the ground.

'Drinking water, pumped straight from the aquifer. Drink plenty of it, especially during your first couple of weeks. Dehydration can creep up on you. Come this way.'

They walked to a square window cut into the wall. Jonathon

peered out then stuck his head through. A vast chute connected the window to the quarry beneath.

'At the end of the day,' said Mandalay, 'all of the Goosen's Trial you've picked needs to be thrown down this chute for incineration. If you leave it out, even overnight, it will take root again and the day's labour will be lost. Any large boulders can be thrown down here too.' She removed a smooth blue stone from the pocket of her billowing white dress and dropped it into the chute. It clattered earthwards. 'The tunnels run directly to the east quarry. We re-use the boulders. Some are used to fortify the wall, others are crushed for cement or ceramics.' She turned back to face the field. 'As it gets warmer out here, the snakes become more active. If you disturb one, keep your footing and slowly raise your left hand. Can you whistle?'

Jonathon pursed his lips and made a tuneless whistle.

'It will do. Hold your stance and keep your hand raised – this makes you look like the aggressor. A Vaik will come and remove the snake, or Daidd will do it if we're not available. Understood?'

He nodded.

'There's sunscreen in the sacks. Put it on at least three times a day. Okay, get to work.'

Jonathon lathered himself with sunscreen then fossicked through the tools left in the sacks. All his life he'd been surrounded by beautiful gardens, but he didn't have a clue what it took to make them so. He chose a gaff and a trowel and joined the men in the field. The day was mild, but within minutes he was drenched in sweat. It ran in small rivers from his dark hair along his temples and into his eyes. No sooner had he swabbed it than it was back, stinging his eyes and loosening his grip on the tools. He tried placing his hood on but it just made him hotter.

'Here.' Daidd rummaged in a sack and threw Jonathon a rag. Ignoring the black looks from the others, Jonathon crossed the field to where the water bags hung on the wall. He released the cork, drenched the rag and ran it across his face, noticing how white and delicate his hands were. Office hands. He manoeuvred himself underneath the water bag, took a long drink then tied the wet rag around his head. It dammed the sweat, a little.

He returned to his post, wedging the hook under the weed, trying to find the angle from which he could lever it out of the ground. He pressed on the handle of the gaff but misjudged the weed's resistance. He overbalanced and went sprawling forward.

'Fuck,' he muttered, spitting out dirt. He rose onto his haunches. The man in front of him was bent over, exposing the *I* branded onto his upper thigh. Instinctively, Jonathon recoiled. The man stood up, sucking at the tender flesh between thumb and index finger where the sickle-shaped thorns of the Goosen's Trial had embedded themselves. He sucked at the bitter poison and spat it onto the ground. He turned and caught Jonathon's eye.

He knows, Jonathon thought, *He knows that I know.*

Jonathon returned to the weed. Goosen's Trial was notoriously tough. It could run for kilometres in one direction then double back like a diabolical ball of yarn. It curled around large boulders and tree roots and stuck tiny spikes into anyone foolish enough to try to uproot it. Jonathon altered his footing and attacked the root again, acutely aware of the isvestyii standing metres away. 'Isvestyii' was the Vaik word for the unredeemed, literally 'self dissolving to nothing'. Jonathon did not want to think about what the man had done.

The gaff was useless; it kept bending under the ropey shoots. He threw it down and decided to copy some of the other men who were pulling at the weeds with their hands. He curled the coarse vine around his palm, trying to avoid the thorns and their slow-burning poison. He thought of Adalia and their unborn child floating in her belly. He'd left them alone – unprotected – against men like the isvestyii. He tightened his grip on the vine, ignoring the hot rash flourishing from his fingers to his elbow. Not that he'd offered much in the way of protection. He was almost never there. Long hours. Long lunches. The poodles.

Maybe *he* was what Adalia needed protection from. He pushed back against the thought, tugging on the root. It yielded unexpectedly, and he fell backwards onto the soil. He saw himself as if from above, an upturned turtle. Adalia's great protector.

Daidd extended a hand to pull him up. Once upright, Jonathon tugged his masjythra down. He watched how the other men were tackling the weed. Some favoured digging it out; others tugged and pulled, pivoting to find the angle of least resistance. All had fiery red welts on their forearms.

After a few hours Daidd told the group, 'Enough. We eat now.'

Daidd picked up a sack and walked towards some fruit trees in an adjacent field, brushing dirt from his arms. He gestured for the assignment to follow. Jonathon straightened and kneaded the small muscles in his lower back, which were in spasm from their sudden, insistent use. His wrists were inflamed and his legs shook. Trying to mask the trembling in his body, his weakness, he followed Daidd.

He joined the men under the leafy canopy as they made seats of the knuckling tree roots, his back against the trunk. The isvestyii sat a little apart from the group on a patch of scrubby lawn. Daidd opened the sack and handed around chunks of bread and cheese. Something rumbled, low and insistent, in Jonathon's stomach. It took him a moment to understand that the sensation was hunger. Real hunger. He tore the dark bread apart and wedged the cheese inside. The bread was chewy and the cheese sharp.

He surveyed their progress. Between them they'd cleared perhaps three or four square metres, if that. The Goosen's Trial they'd ripped up was piled onto a bed of rocks. Already the roots were nosing downwards, seeking the soil.

Soundlessly, Mandalay appeared over the rise with a woman Jonathon hadn't seen before. She was a tall blonde, as black as

Mandalay was white. They reminded him of opposing pieces on a chessboard. Mandalay stepped towards him and without a word turned his hands over in hers. His palms were puckered and blistered. The small holes where the thorns had bored were weeping a gelatinous white substance he hadn't known his body could make. His hands shook; underneath the morning's exertion his body still remembered coffee.

'Make sure you tend these tonight,' Mandalay said. 'I'll have some mistaelnet ointment left on your table. Heat it with a candle, then rub it on. It will sting, but it will stop the bores becoming infected.'

Jonathon nodded. He was aware of his own smell, keen and acrid. He wanted to upturn the water flask on himself. Mandalay dropped his hands and turned to the rest of the group. She said something in Vaik, and two of the men – Daidd and a strapping dark-haired man – stood and followed her and the other woman. Jonathon thought they would go to the edge of the field to assess the morning's work but instead they disappeared over a rise in the grasses.

'Where are they going?' he asked, forgetting himself. Four pairs of eyebrows raised themselves for answer. Feeling foolish, he took another piece of bread and cheese and settled himself on a gnarled root.

Lunch was finished in silence. The only sounds were the flutter of birds come to eat the bugs upturned in the field and the occasional mewl of pleasure from beyond the grasses.

The afternoon brought the sea breeze and the salt gnats. They nestled into the hairs on Jonathon's legs, arms and pubis, and gorged themselves on his sweat. Once bloated, they fell to the ground, leaving behind an unbearable itch. He scrabbled at the air, trying to catch the little fiends, but for every two he swatted, ten found the moist folds of his scrotum. He tried to resist, knowing that scratching would just make it worse.

Sweat and dirt formed a grimy carapace over his skin. Bending and digging had shocked his long-dormant muscles awake. His sores and his rash burned. He wanted to scream. And claw at his hair and upturn the pile of weeds and swing a punch at the isvestyii. He thought longingly of his air-conditioned office. His ergonomic chair that felt like a second, more perfect spine. The poodles who would happily trip away to make him a coffee if he asked for one in his smiling, sorry-to-be-a-bother way. Instead he was here, broiling and itching and reeking like a shagged goat with no relief in sight. He walked away from the group to compose himself. It wasn't even the end of the first day and he wanted to renege, recant.

Daidd was beside him, saying something in Vaik that Jonathon didn't understand.

'What?'

'Aeraevest.' Daidd placed his fists in front of his chest. 'It's the word for the sentry posts at The Fortress that face the sea. The first line of defence. It also means watchfulness of self. You need to learn it if you're going to survive here.'

It was on the tip of Jonathon's tongue to say 'Don't you know who I am?' or to issue some threat about what he would do when he got out. Only a dim understanding that this would be a fatal display of weakness held him back. The effort of silence from a man used to being heard sent the blood hammering through his head.

'Come with me,' said Daidd.

Jonathon trudged after him across the field to where a section of the stone wall had collapsed. Daidd pointed to the tumble of stones. 'Pick those up.' He took four deliberate steps to the side and pointed to the ground. 'Put them here.'

'You can't be serious.'

'Move them. Now.'

Jonathon felt, rather than saw, Mandalay watching him. He picked up a smooth white boulder – hard and tangible in his wounded hands – and stumbled with it to the spot Daidd indicated. He could barely see for the red mist across his eyes. He turned back to collect another stone, and another. He didn't feel his feebleness or his caffeine addiction or the itching bites or the sweat that menaced the weeping sores on his hands. There was just his rage spending itself between the slow transference of rocks from one pile to another.

The sun was going down by the time the men packed their tools and trekked back towards their quarters. Jonathon plodded along, dazed with exhaustion. His feet mechanically kept time with a long, low chant sung by a couple of the men. When the seabirds whirled overhead, he knew that they were close.

Just before the final approach they stopped to let a crocodile of schoolgirls pass. One of the girls, perhaps thirteen or fourteen years old, reminded Jonathon of Adalia. She had the same impish grin and ruddy cheeks. To his surprise the girl smiled, showing her dimples, and raised her hand in greeting. Delighted, he smiled and waved back.

'You know what they do with the boy-children?' The isvestyii had sidled up to him. 'They slit their throats as a sacrifice to their god.'

'The Vaik have no god.'

'Then where are they?'

'Where are what?'

'The boys.'

Jonathon turned so he was looking the isvestyii full in the face. 'Fuck. Off.'

Daidd led the men to a roofless wooden building at the far end of the cherry orchard. Each of them removed his masjythra and handed it over to men in red at the entrance who in return provided each worker with a large cup, a ball of soap and a nailbrush. Inside the bathhouse they stood three men to a barrel of fresh water. Jonathon plunged his cup to the bottom then upturned the water over his face and neck. It was cool and crisp and immediately, deliciously, salved the itch of the salt-gnat bites. He dipped his cup again and again, oblivious to the men around him. When his body was dripping he set to it with the brush and soap.

The brush shredded the little blisters that had formed on his skin like bubble wrap, and the soap stung the bores left by the Goosen's Trial. Still, the feel of the water, flushing away the filth, was ecstasy. He dissolved the tracks of mud and salt winding through the hair on his arms and legs and attacked his earth-packed nails, the rind around his ankles.

Wordlessly, Daidd handed his brush to Jonathon and indicated that he was to scrub his back. Jonathon hesitated.

When he'd moved back in with his parents, after Adalia had thrown him out, he'd whiled away his days at their kitchen table, drinking. His father had entered the kitchen, seen Jonathon, and panicked. The urge – writ large across his face – was to step backwards into the hallway and pretend he and his stricken son hadn't made eye contact. But they had. Jonathon's father walked towards him and reached awkwardly for his shoulder. He rested his hand there for a second or two, then turned and left the room. That was Jonathon's last memory of physical contact with a man – aside from the electii, potentially.

For some reason, Jonathon then recalled earlier in the day when Daidd and the dark-haired man had followed Mandalay's summons over the rise in the grasses, the sounds that had reached back to the resting men. Jonathon's cock stirred at the memory. Hurriedly, he threw cold water on his groin and devised a complex mental equation.

Daidd was tall and wiry. If he'd had any fat when he entered The Fortress, he'd long since lost it to labour in the fields and the sexual demands of the Vaik. His stark tan line followed the dip and weave of his masjythra. The contrast between the dark and light parts of Daidd's body brought Mandalay and the other woman, her black complement, striding towards Jonathon again. *Seven sevens are forty-nine. Forty-nine times seven . . . carry the six.* Jonathon ran his brush along Daidd's shoulders, the skin shivering at the cool water and the bite of the soap. He cut the surface of the barrel again, frothing now with bubbles and soap scum. *Three hundred and forty-three.* Jonathon tried to remember the words Mandalay had issued to Daidd and the other man. Shi veistai? Shy vestyi? Would he recognise them if Mandalay, if any of the Vaik, issued them to him? Daidd and the other man had followed the two women, expressionless. Did this happen every day? Was it always Daidd and this man, or did Mandalay choose differently every time? *The square root of thirty-six is six.*

Some of the men here, a few at least, must be gay. Were they also 'assigned'? Or left to their own devices?

Daidd turned a little so Jonathon could scrub the other side of his back. His waxy scars coursed from his face down his neck and into his clavicle.

'Does it hurt?' Jonathon asked. 'If I scrub it?'

Daidd shook his head. Jonathon ran his brush over the melted skin that even the salt gnats had no taste for, then rinsed it with water from his cup.

Daidd turned. 'Thanks.' He raised his brush as if to scrub Jonathon.

Jonathon's instinct was to refuse, but would that be thought suspect? A case of protesting too much? He couldn't help but notice how large Daidd was. His long penis hung slackly, even insouciantly, from his body. Was that why Mandalay had chosen him?

Jonathon's face was completely blank as he turned around and yielded to the cold water and hard bristles. He shuddered as the brush shredded a fresh hive of blisters.

Mandalay had been inscrutable when she'd examined his groin. It was hard to imagine that she'd remained so when scrutinising Daidd.

For as long as Jonathon could remember, The Fortress had been the subject of smutty boys' locker-room jokes. 'Pussy Prison,' they called it, but quietly. The laws against Vaikray — speaking ill of the Vaik, and criticising or usurping Vaik laws and ways — had been repealed for a long time and had not been enforced for even longer, but Jonathon had still thrilled to the jokes. Sometimes, when drunk and emboldened, his friends concocted farcical schemes to be declared isvestyii and locked inside Pussy Prison forever. *If that's punishment, I've been a bad, bad boy.* But for all that, few male citizens elected to do their national service within The Fortress. What man, after all, wanted to serve women?

Jonathon winced as the soap met his weeping skin.

'You're done,' Daidd said, dousing him with water.

You chose this, Jonathon reminded himself.

'What do you know about choice?' Adalia had demanded during her inquisition. 'These women. The — what do you call them? Poodles? You think they're sucking you off in the photocopying room because they can't resist you? Do you know what it takes for these girls — and they're not much more than girls, Jonathon — to be accepted into a program at a firm like yours? Years of slog and study and luck. Some of these girls, the ones from poor neighbourhoods like The Dryans, are carrying the weight of their whole family's expectations on their shoulders. So tell me, when you and your cronies let them know what's expected — what's *required* — how much choice do you think these girls have?'

Adalia's anger, like her happiness, like all her moods, was intensely physical. He could smell the salt weltering in her eyes.

She went pale from fury, making the natural rouge on her cheeks stand out like muddy boot prints across her face.

Daidd, Jonathon and the others left the barrels and walked outside to a tiled area where they were hosed down by the men in red. At the end of the walkway, one of them handed Jonathon a rough towel and a laundered, silver masjythra that snaked around his body until it fit. He felt good, unbelievably good, to be clean.

From the bathhouse they proceeded to the dining hall. As soon as he sat down Jonathon was overcome by fatigue. It moved over him like a warm, irresistible wave. He jerked awake just before his head hit the bowl of stew in front of him. For a second, before the sleep rolled back from his head, he was in his chair at work. Pleasantly drunk, waiting for his brain fog to clear before he went home to Adalia.

'You'd better eat,' Daidd urged him.

Jonathon thought he wasn't hungry, but after the first spoonful his belly stirred, then roared. He dropped his chin to the lip of the bowl and gobbled up the strings of meat and the dumplings. Then he upturned the bowl and drank, gravy trickling down his chin. Daidd pushed a plate of bread towards him; he ripped a piece off the cob and wiped the bowl clean with it.

Were the Vaik sitting outside on the terrace? Did one of them read from the leather-bound volume on the lectern again? He couldn't have said. His world had compressed to a pinpoint of exhaustion and hunger.

By the time the serving men began collecting the bowls it was dark. The rest of the men scraped the benches back from the tables and trudged towards their quarters. They walked shoulder to shoulder but didn't speak; each man was intent on the square wedge of downy luxury waiting for him before the chime signalled the start of another day.

Mandalay had left a small jar of green balm on Jonathon's bedside table, beside a stub of candle and a single long match. The mistaelnet. He struck the match on the dry stone wall and held it carefully against the candle. He gouged a ball of balm from the jar and held it next to the flame, then rolled it, softening, into his palm. It stung, as Mandalay had said it would. He worked it into the weeping holes on his palms and fingers and the soft webbing between thumb and index finger. It smelt vaguely familiar. Of camphor and something minty. Perhaps his mother had rubbed something similar onto the bruises and scrapes of his childhood. But no. His mother wouldn't have done that.

Jonathon blew out the candle, pulled the blanket against his chest and was asleep.

Before he'd come to The Fortress, time had been a tangible entity. It was a commodity he could measure and cost. Time roped one thing off from another so each meeting, each deadline felt quantifiably different. At The Fortress, days and nights bled into each other. Jonathon woke to the same chime each morning and sat at the same rough pew at the same rough table next to Daidd for breakfast. He used the same tools he'd picked from the canvas sack that first day, preferring their known limitations to the effort of familiarising himself with something new.

Every day he tussled with the Goosen's Trial. Its stubborn refusal to yield, or to yield only at the point where his toppling over was a certainty, seemed personal. Vines would converge from opposite directions of the field, bringing the men close enough to collect each other's sweat. If the isvestyii was in the cluster, the others would wordlessly fall back, leaving him to it. Otherwise they'd swear and elbow and tantrum, Daidd often taking men to one side to move rocks a short distance and then move them back again. The close of the day was marked by the foul smell of Goosen's Trial burning in the quarry below, and the slow trudge to the bathhouse. Washing Daidd, and being washed by him, became routine by dint of repetition. Remarkably quickly, Jonathon lost the capacity to say whether a thing had been yesterday or a week ago.

Pain was a constant companion. Bending down to uproot the weed meant there was an auger at every joint boring through bone and muscle. His back was the worst: standing upright released a hundred little fireworks across his spine as each muscle failed to compensate for the weakness in the others. He was constantly adjusting himself in search of perfect, painless equilibrium. The only time he was pain-free was when he lay perfectly still in bed at night and exhaustion rushed him. He had never known such swift and perfect carriage to sleep.

Sometimes, when he was elbow-deep in a tangle of weed and the sweat stung his eyes, his mind wandered to names for his child. He would like for her to have a Vaik name. Later, when the child was old enough, he would tell her that as she had been forming in Adalia's womb he too had been enclosed and reshaped. He'd tell her how he'd learnt to clear fields and drunk water from a sack hanging on a high stone wall. How he'd gone to The Fortress to learn to be her father. It pleased him to think that he had a story he could tell now. His own story, and the baby's. Adalia's too.

But no. Adalia had her own story.

One day he stood up from the dirt to stretch his back when he noticed that the white band on his ring finger had turned the same colour as his limbs. He raised his hand and stared. His forearm was tanned and dirt-matted and his fingers almost the same colour as the soil. Mesmerised, he turned his hand to study his palm. It was crosshatched with scars from the thorns. The pads under his thumbs were calloused and rough. He lifted his hand so close to his face that he smelt the faint menthol from the mistaelnet ointment under the dirt. He brushed the grime from his fingers and blinked to focus his eyes. All trace of his wedding ring was gone.

What he looked forward to most was the close of the day when they sometimes crossed the schoolgirls on their way back to quarters. The ruddy-cheeked girl always waved to him.

'Hello there!' she'd say. 'Did you have a good day in the garden?'

'A very good day, Mistress, thank you,' he'd say, as if they were playing a game in which she was his feudal overlord and he a tenant farmer. In some ways, he supposed he was. She'd wave again and move off. The men stood still to let the girls pass. Jonathon watched them for as long as he could, before returning to his assignment, trudging slowly along the road.

He was never the last man to turn, though. That was the isvestyii, and the expression he wore as he followed the girls with his eyes over the horizon made Jonathon's stomach lurch.

'What did he do?' Jonathon asked Daidd one day when they had both made for the water bag at the same time.

'I don't know what you're referring to. And you need to get out of the habit of asking questions.'

Jonathon jerked his head towards the isvestyii, who was standing a little apart from the rest of the men in the nearly cleared field.

Daidd hesitated, then pulled the stop on the bag and tilted his head to the water. 'I don't know.'

You do know, thought Jonathon. *You know very well. You're just not telling me.*

Every eleventh day was the half. They'd leave the field after lunch, before the salt gnats blew in, and return to quarters to bathe and eat. Then they were free to wander about the grounds as long as they didn't venture further than the orchard at one end and The Veya Gate at the other. The red masjythra were stationed at both points, just in case. A few of the men spent the half clustered beneath the shade in the orchard playing board games. Some dozed nearby. Most, like Jonathon, lay on their beds listening to the seabirds cawing below. The half made him anxious. The sudden cessation of order and routine felt like running into a barrier at top speed. Thoughts crept into the vacancy. Fears.

One half when he returned to his room there was an envelope on his bed. It was a sharp, white rectangle against the green of his blanket. His name was scrawled across the front in Adalia's distinctive, swirling hand. He stood still, staring at it. His limbs were leaden, so heavy they might break through the floor to the foundations and down, down to the slow-pulsing magma beneath. He stood like that for a few minutes then extracted himself, finger by finger, from his inertia. Once in motion, he couldn't stop. He paced between the doorframe and the open window, never taking his eyes from the envelope. Panic made his hands clammy. He wiped them on his masjythra, which had become restless too, and prowled the stone floor in his bare feet.

Jonathon knew he could pick it up and throw it out of the window unopened. Let it sail down the soft blue air to beneath the perimeter wall where a curious bird might collect it and carry it out to sea.

Only Adalia could break him. Only Adalia could tell him that – after all, after everything – she did not want to be reconciled. She would raise their baby alone. Without Jonathon's, what had she called it? *Corrupting influence.*

He saw it all now.

She'd already had the locks changed before his bizarre interrogation at The Arbour Room. His stuff was still in boxes at his parents', ready for a return trip to his marital home that was never going to happen. It would be easy to effect the paperwork in his absence. His mother had tried to warn him.

He backed against the wall, as far from the vile envelope as he could get. He would go mad, locked in here for another ten months, without the promise of Adalia and the baby waiting outside the gates. Did Adalia know that? He could hardly blame his wife if she had become vengeful. Her lack of jealousy and malice seemed to him now not the response of a woman who had known her own worth, but a strategy. She had lulled him to security, pushed down her rage until he was imprisoned and powerless to arm himself against it.

He took a deep breath and crossed the room in two steps. He sat on the bed and tore the envelope open. His breath came in ragged bursts.

The envelope contained a card. He screwed his eyes tight shut, then opened them. The card was a photograph of sorts. Against the green-black background a little human floated towards him. Underneath, in her swirling, looping hand, Adalia had written 'stay strong, my love' and alternating crosses and zeroes. Four of them. The pressure in his chest released, drawing the breath and the tears out of him. He pressed the ultrasound to his chest and closed his eyes in relief.

After a moment or two he opened his eyes and studied the photograph. The first time he'd seen a scan he'd struggled to believe that the prawn-like creature, barely discernible against the static, would become a child. It was a featureless blob arrested in a white sack. But this photograph he held in his hands was undeniably of a baby. His baby. The foetus faced straight onto the camera, holding a thumb to its lips. The eyes, nose and fingers were clearly visible. Jonathon pored over every detail. Was he foolish to imagine he traced a likeness, something of Adalia's grin on the child's face?

He was foolish. Decidedly foolish. But he didn't care. He laughed aloud and the sound echoed along the hallways. He tucked the ultrasound under his pillow and left the room. He needed to be under the big dome of the sky to make room for this big feeling in his chest. He tripped along the corridor, past the rooms of dozing men and down the zigzag ramp to the huge wooden doors that opened onto the verandah. He knew the way to the dining hall, and from there to the fields and the bathhouse at the end of the cherry orchard. He'd explored no further than that.

Now, he felt exhilarated. He strolled along the verandah in the opposite direction to the one he usually took. The glossy green ferns overspilt the pots and trailed across the timber floor. The verandah ended in a row of steep steps from which a cobblestone path branched out in three directions. Nearby but unseen, a Vaik was singing, low and sonorous. He wheeled around but couldn't find the source of the song.

He decided to follow the middle path. It snaked beside some small, squat buildings of pearl and mirror. He walked on until he came to a group of buildings that looked like slabs of butter piled on top of each other, the higher ones slightly smaller than those below. The slabs had the same bishop's hats for windows he'd seen in the room where he first met Mandalay.

The schoolgirl poked her head out of a window on the topmost floor and hollered down to him, 'Hello there.'

'Good afternoon, Mistress.' He shaded his eyes to look up at her. He wished he had a hat so he could doff it. She was leaning far out of the window. He worried she might fall and wanted to tell her to go back inside.

'What are you doing?' she asked.

'Just wandering about the grounds.'

'Oh yes,' she said, leaning even further out, 'it's the half, isn't it?'

He nodded and instinctively raised his arms to catch her, lest she fall.

'Wait there. I'll come and let you in.' She disappeared and after a moment opened the wooden door for him. 'Come in, then.'

Jonathon hesitated. Was he permitted in this building? Was it the girl's home? Mandalay's words came back to him: *You will obey every woman in The Fortress, from the smallest girl-child to The Woman.* He stepped across the threshold into a wide hallway.

'This way.' The girl led him up two flights of stairs. On their way he glimpsed rooms empty of furniture but with the walls entirely covered in murals. He wanted to stop and look at them but the girl took the stairs two at a time, her feet flashing white under her skinny legs. He smiled to think he would have struggled to keep up just weeks before. 'In here.' She walked into a broad, sunlit room much larger than it had seemed from the outside. It had murals like the others. The floors were of polished oak and strewn with sketchpads, crayons and pencils. 'This is a Story-Keeping House. Let me show you what I'm doing,' she said, taking his hand and leading him to one of the sketchpads. 'Sit down.' He lowered himself to the floor as she held a picture up to her chest. 'See.'

He looked at the picture and then at the mural directly behind it. In the mural, a sentry post sat atop a long slice of wall dividing the sea. What had Daidd said they were called? Aeraevest? The sentry wore an ankle-length green dress, dark like the sea beside her. She was intent on the horizon, her slender fingers folded around the barrel of a spyglass. In the far distance, a sailing ship was just visible. Whether it was friend or foe was impossible to tell.

'I may have taken a few liberties,' conceded the girl. In her picture she had accurately rendered the sentry post and the Vaik, but her sea was alive with brightly coloured fish and coral. 'Historian Teacher says I need to be faithful to the murals if I'm to be a Keeper of Stories. But who's to say that underneath the dark water we can see, there aren't starfish and anemones and seaweed that we can't?' She dropped the picture to the floor and looked earnestly at Jonathon. 'I mean, they could be there, couldn't they?'

'They could indeed, Mistress.'

She grinned, making her dimples look like quote marks around her mouth. Then the sunshine disappeared and her face darkened. 'Historian Teacher says just to paint what's there.' She affected a snooty, authoritative air. 'A Keeper of Stories sublimates her own desires to the story. She recognises in herself a responsibility to the past and to the future. She opens herself up as a conduit between these two points.' The girl was a great mimic, and Jonathon fought the urge to laugh. She picked up a pencil and made some corrections to the sentry's dress. 'Can you draw?'

'No, Mistress.'

'Paint?'

'No.'

'Don't you like to?'

'I don't know, Mistress. I'm not sure I've ever really tried.'

'Well, try now.' The girl ripped a crisp sheet from her sketchpad and wheeled it across the floor to him. 'Use this.' She handed him a thick lead pencil.

Immediately when he held it in his fingers, he began to tingle with the urge to write Adalia's name. Maybe he could even write to Adalia. He glanced at the girl, her hair falling over her forehead and covering the light spray of freckles across her nose, as she concentrated on her drawing. Could she get a letter out for him?

Jonathon drew a line. The lead was silky over the smooth paper. He attempted a fish, open-mouthed and blowing bubbles. Then the prow of a boat, so he could have the pleasure of writing Adalia's name along it.

'Do you know this story?' Without looking up from her drawing, the girl pointed to the mural behind her with her spare hand. Jonathon looked again at the dark water and threatening skies. 'The sentry is Eshtakai. She lived a long, long time ago, back when only the Vaik could be sentries and The Fortress was much smaller than it is today. The sentries lived in tiny rooms dug into the perimeter wall underneath the lookouts. They watched the sea all night and most of the day, sleeping in forty-minute shifts. Eshtakai was looking across the ocean when she saw a ship on the horizon. She climbed the ladder to the top of the lookout and lit the warning pyre. Soon, there were lots of ships on the horizon, coming faster and faster. When they were within range of The Fortress they dropped anchor and started firing lighted arrows over the wall.

'The Vaik still used thatched roofs in those days so their houses caught fire and burnt down. The men on the ships came ashore in small boats, looking for places to set their ladders and get over the wall. They laid siege to The Fortress for days. More ships came, ships with canons. They punched holes in the perimeter wall, and the Vaik worked around the clock to patch them up.

'But Eshtakai had a plan. When the men came to the wall, trying to find a way over, she slipped into the sea and swam out to the fleet. She swam from ship to ship until she found the supply galley. She pulled herself over the ropes and hid behind a barrel until she could make her way to the kitchen. The supply ships were crewed mostly by women. Young women and girls from villages far across the sea who kept watch over the preserves and doled out rations to the soldiers. Some of the women had been snatched from their homes and pressed into service. So night after night while the ships assaulted The Fortress, Eshtakai braved the cold water and came aboard the supply ship to talk to the women. Those women whispered to the women onboard the other ships, the ones who emptied chamber-pots for fat admirals and trimmed beards and picked seaweed out of the nets – and worse.

'One night there was a terrible storm. The sort that happens every ten or twenty years here. The ones the Vaik call sestyatesh. The seas were roiling and the men thought that was why their stomachs were heaving. Even the men who hadn't stood on dry land in years were bringing up their stomachs. They barely noticed the servant women urging them to take the tonic they'd prepared.

'The women tossed the dead men overboard for the sharks. The ones who survived into the next day were declared isvestyii and taken into The Fortress. Those women were the first foreigners to come to live at The Fortress. We still have one of their ships in the playground near my school. I love to pretend that I'm Eshtakai prowling around the deck looking for the women.'

Jonathon had a hundred questions for the girl: did she live with her mother? What happened to her brothers? Did she know who her father was? Instead he said, 'That's an interesting story, Mistress.'

'Eshtakai was very brave, don't you think? I mean, with the sharks and the cold water and the canon fire?'

'Very brave, Mistress.'

'My name is Ulait.' She sat up, very straight and solemn. 'I give you permission to call me by my name, which is Ulait.'

'I'm honoured to know your name, Mistress,' Jonathon chose his words carefully, 'but, begging your pardon, I would prefer to keep calling you "Mistress".'

Ulait spun her drawing away from her on the wooden floor. 'I don't mind,' she said. 'Let me see your drawing.' Jonathon pushed his scribble towards her. She turned it the right way round and pored over it. 'Well,' she said brightly, 'it's really very good for a first try.'

'Thank you, Mistress.'

'Fewer dolphins and treasure chests than mine. Historian Teacher would be pleased.'

'I think your teacher would have her work cut out with me.'

'What did you do – before you came to The Fortress, I mean?'

'I was an executive for a large software company.'

'What did you execute?'

'I was in Strategy, which is all about setting the direction for the company. I decided which products to develop, which markets to pursue. What kind of workforce we needed.' He thought, guiltily, of the selection panel he'd sat on for the poodles – junior analysts, he corrected himself.

Ulait wrinkled up her nose in thought. 'So if your company was at war, you'd be one of the officers who looked at maps and moved models of tanks and soldiers around on it and then told everyone where and when they had to go and fight.'

'I guess so.'

'Did you have to do a lot of studying to get your job?'

'I did, Mistress.'

She sighed. 'Historian Teacher says no worthwhile endeavour comes free of hard work.'

'I think she's probably right.'

Ulait looked up from his drawing to the murals wrapped around the walls. Her face was elastic, a dozen expressions telegraphing her fast-moving thoughts. 'I work hard. At least, I think I do. I know every story in this building and all the buildings in the north-eastern sector. I can draw most of them from memory. But, I don't know.' She bit her lip and thought for a moment. 'It's like my mind picks up the story and takes it somewhere it isn't supposed to go. Like the wind blew it away and set it down in a place I hadn't been before. So before I know it, Eshtakai is swimming with dolphins or The Fortress is on a spaceship and I,' she sat up straighter and mimicked her teacher again, 'have not been faithful to the story.'

'You have imagination,' said Jonathon. 'Perhaps you'll paint your own pictures or write your own stories.'

'Hmm. Historian Teacher says that's all very well. But if all this is destroyed, who will recreate the stories about who we are?'

Jonathon began to ask why all this would be destroyed, then corrected himself. 'It's very unlikely that this would be destroyed. No one has attacked The Fortress in three hundred years. Chances are everything here will outlive me and even you by several centuries at least. Anyway, there's always room for new stories. Look.' He pointed out a bare rectangle on the wall. 'One of yours could go there.'

Ulait laughed at him. 'That *is* a story,' she said. She stood up and positioned herself before the painting immediately to the left of the blank space. It was of a naked man, his back to the viewer, strapped to a post. Black cord bound his hands behind him. His body was rigid; he seemed intent on the dark water creeping up the beach towards him, and the hint of darker shapes within.

'The man is isvestyii and The Woman has decreed that he will be put to death. He drowns. Or the sharks eat him. Then,' Ulait moved in front of the bare rectangle, 'he dissolves to nothing.' She waved her arm at the space. 'That's what this is. Nothing.'

'Nothing,' Jonathon repeated. 'It's a difficult concept to get your head around. Even nothing has to be made of something.'

A cloud moved across Ulait's face. 'One of the men in your assignment is isvestyii.'

'Yes. I know.'

'He makes my stomach go cold.'

Jonathon felt a soft blow of air straighten the hairs on the back of his neck. 'He cannot hurt you, Mistress.'

'I know. But I don't like him. I wish The Woman would call him, like the man in the painting.'

Jonathon stared again at the painting. He entered through the back of the man's head and looked through his eyes. He heard the rush of the waves up the shore and their ever-lessening retreat. Heard the seabirds squalling from their posts on the perimeter wall, preparing to spar for the juicy scraps left by the sharks.

'I wish she would too, Mistress.'

Jonathon returned to the residential quarters just before the gong sounded for dinner. He washed his hands and splashed his face, then took the zigzag path down to the verandah. There was a subtly different energy among the men on the half. They weren't as dulled by exhaustion as they normally were. They'd had time to look about them. To think.

The dining room was louder than usual. Something like

conversation had broken out above the clatter of the serving bowls and the low rumble of the trolleys delivering food to the tables. Jonathon directed his steps towards his table and the rough wooden pew where he sat next to Daidd. He very nearly walked into Daidd who was standing stock-still in front of it.

Only one man was seated at the long table. The isvestyii, his hands clasped in front of him on the table, was staring straight ahead. The men who usually sat at that table, who Jonathon knew by sight, were banking up behind and around him. The blue masjythra pushing the trolley of food had stopped too, uncertain what to do. He ladled stew into a bowl but placed it on the table opposite the isvestyii, then worked his way down the empty side of the table.

Wordlessly, Daidd took up position at the narrow end of the pew where the isvestyii was seated and gripped the plank. Other men followed.

'On three,' said Daidd. 'One, two, three.'

As one, the men lifted the heavy pew and tipped out the isvestyii. He banged his chin on the table then fell to the floor. Jonathon heard a scuffling noise, then the isvestyii crawled out from under the table and took off, scuttling among the tables.

Daidd, Jonathon and the other men sat down and ate.

Jonathon pulled at the weed, sensing for the slight give that meant he was attacking it from the right direction. He'd been in the field since just after sun-up. Summer was nearly upon them and they had to get the seed in the ground. They had a matter of days to clear what remained of the Goosen's Trial and the boulders, plough the soil and repair the stone walls.

He eased off, gently testing the vine with his index finger as a man would test for weight on the end of a hand reel. Satisfied, he tightened his grip. The thorns ate into the back of his hand, but his skin had become tougher and he barely winced. There was the satisfying *thud-thud-thud* as the vine punched from the soil. He wound it round his hand and kept pulling until its green turned white. He unwound it and picked up a shovel, digging for the dense, matted bulb that followed a few feet from where the vine changed colour. He found the bulb easily, then took a trowel and dug around it, careful to lift out the ball in its entirety.

Daidd and one of the other men were heaping up the threads of vine on a wheelbarrow and ferrying them to the wall to tip into the quarry. The burning tyre smell was heavy in the air and would not shift until the afternoon breeze. Jonathon collected up his strands of Goosen's Trial and walked directly to the quarry chute.

He'd been looking for an opportunity to speak to Daidd all morning, but they were paired in different groups. Mandalay had put Jonathon with the isvestyii. They barely spoke or looked at each other, but Jonathon was acutely aware of his presence and tried always to position himself to the other man's back. But sometimes the Goosen's demanded a change of direction, and Jonathon couldn't be sure where the isvestyii was. It gave him the same sick feeling of claustrophobia he'd had as a child when, playing hide-and-seek with his older brothers, the darkness in the cupboard would close in on him and he could never be sure if he wanted to be found or not.

Every time Jonathon took the ultrasound into his hands and traced the outline of the growing form, Ulait's words recurred to him: *He makes my stomach go cold.*

The other men didn't speak much to the isvestyii, but then, they didn't speak much as a general rule. The field absorbed the bulk of their energy and most habituated quickly to not speaking unless spoken to.

Daidd tipped the barrow of weeds down the chute then paused to wipe the sweat from his face and stretch his back. When he made for one of the water bags, Jonathon followed. He glanced quickly at the rest of the men, making sure they were out of earshot.

'The isvestyii. He likes little girls.'

Daidd wiped the water from his mouth and said nothing.

'He's dangerous,' Jonathon said.

Daidd shook his head. 'The Vaik have been handling his kind for centuries. They know what they're doing. Anyway, there's no opportunity for him to be alone with the schoolgirls. Besides, it's not worth the risk. Death, for certain.'

'The Woman already has the power of life and death over him. You may as well get hung for a sheep as a lamb.'

Daidd looked across the field to where the isvestyii was trying to haul a boulder from the ground. He sat on his haunches and pulled, the strain showing on his face. His balls hung slackly through his masjythra.

'He broke into a school.' Daidd's voice was low. 'He broke in armed with a gun, a rope and a jar of vaseline. He found a classroom of ten-year-old girls. Shot the teacher dead. He tied up and raped three girls. One died of her injuries.' Daidd spat onto the ground. 'Hard to imagine anything worse than that. If The Woman was going to have him executed, she would have done it already. If he so much as puts a foot wrong, it's the stake on the beach and he knows it.'

'You're assuming he's capable of making a rational deduction and controlling his impulses.'

'He is. Everyone is. It's what The Fortress teaches.'

'What about the girls?' It was the first question Jonathon had asked in a long while. It sounded harsh and abrasive, as though he was waving a knife in the air.

'There's no opportunity to be alone with them.'

'Not true.'

Daidd raised a questioning eyebrow. Jonathon was about to

tell him how he'd met Ulait alone in the Story-Keeping House but decided against it. 'We cross the children at the end of the day.'

'Yes. *We* cross them, the whole assignment. He'd have to manoeuvre to be alone with them.'

'I don't think we should wait.' It was only when the words were out that Jonathon realised what he was proposing. He looked down at his brown, thorn-pocked hands, startled. Could he really kill a man? Did he have it in him?

'Be careful,' Daidd whispered. 'Only The Woman has that power. You steer close to Vaikray.' Daidd turned and walked back to the field and the remaining clumps of Goosen's Trial.

Mandalay came at lunchtime to check their progress. She spoke briefly to Daidd then strode out, barefoot, into the field. She scooped up a handful of earth and picked through it, then smelt it, before crumbling it between her fingers. She dusted her hands off, placed them on her hips and considered the wide expanse of field.

Jonathon chewed his bread and cheese as she paced. She must know about the isvestyii. The details Daidd had given him were enough to jog his memory. The man had been married, with three children. He'd lived out in The Dryans – the sprawling, working-class mess on the other side of The Fortress wall – held down a job and had no prior criminal history. 'He was a plumb normal guy,' the neighbours said (don't they always say that about monsters?). 'He'd come over for barbecues on holidays. His kids played with our kids in the backyard. He cleaned his car, followed football. There was nothing odd about him. Nothing at all.'

Jonathon remembered the vaseline: a single grotesque detail that made the story stand out from the procession of violent sex crimes reported in the press. The isvestyii had left for work in the morning with the gun and the rope tucked into his backpack. He stopped at a shopping centre along the way and bought a flat white to go and a tub of vaseline – large. For my eczema, he told the shop assistant. The school he chose was in the good part of town. Jonathon's part of town. That was probably why it was such big news.

One of Adalia's colleagues had written a series on sex crimes in the city, around the time Adalia and Jonathon first talked about having children. Adalia wept when she read about the case. 'You have to be so brave to be a parent,' she said. 'So brave.' Jonathon found the case repugnant too, but he let go of it easily enough, replacing it with other transitory bits of news. It didn't lodge in his gut and give him a sick feeling in his throat. Make him want to claw at his skin till he drew blood. The way it made him feel now.

The isvestyii sat not three feet away, eating bread and cheese and idly plucking at the grass. He looked up to find Jonathon staring at him. They locked eyes. Jonathon wanted to find that behind the man's eyes was an abyss: a rank, dark cesspool. But he looked like any other man.

The isvestyii glanced away first.

Jonathon lay awake that night. It was the first time since he'd come to The Fortress that sleep hadn't claimed him easily. Despite the day's exertions he felt restless. Wired. He got up from his bed and moved to the window. It was moonless, so the perimeter wall was a dark slice against the night. The seabirds slept. Somewhere along the corridor came the occasional cry of climax. That and the rush and retreat of the ocean were the only sounds.

Staring out into the darkness, he thought of the second story Ulait had told him. About how an isvestyii, once put to death, dissolved to nothing. The Vaik had no god and worshipped no supreme beings, but they did believe in the infinite nature of life. For them death was simply a transubstantiation of energy, not its end. The same way boiling water will turn to steam, each passing life was absorbed into new lives, the trees, the air.

But for isvestyii, death was not just an end, it was a reversal.

Isvestyii passed nothing on, transformed nothing, were absorbed into nothing. Where there had been energy there was less than nothing: a negative. Isvestyii were allowed no burial, monuments or obituaries. Their wives could expunge the marriage from the official record, censoring the years by fiat. Children could nominate a new father or apply for a fresh birth certificate, the name of the offending parent blank.

Jonathon tried to think it through. The isvestyii in his assignment had three children. Each one was a unique splicing of their parents' genetic material, their parents' parents' genetic material and a chance soupçon of the freefalling energy of the deceased. What happened, then, when a parent was declared isvestyii? Did those cells turn themselves off? Blank out like light bulbs, leaving airy spaces in the soul? Jonathon had always feared there was something insubstantial about himself, as if half his descendants had been declared isvestyii and he was so light he could float away. He'd felt a vague discontent for as long as he could remember. It made him snarky, even aggressive. 'Edgy,' his friends said. 'Arsehole,' said others. He'd played up to it, dropping sardonic bombs into conversation to see which fuses would take and where the glass would shatter.

Looking into the answering darkness, feeling the salt carapace re-forming on his skin after the late-afternoon scrub, Jonathon confronted the possibility that he had no self to dissolve, and that being declared isvestyii would make no difference.

No difference at all.

There was a carnival atmosphere out in the field. Mandalay and seven of her companions had come to observe the last of the planting. 'Mallow-root,' Daidd had told him: the sugary, spongy fruit with large purple flowers. Adalia liked it with jam and custard.

The cleared and fresh-ploughed field gave Jonathon a bodily satisfaction. It hummed in his muscles and through his blood. His exertion had produced the apple-crumble earth, picked it clean of the choking weed and forged the shallow holes for the mallow-root seeds. In a few days the seedlings would wend their way up through the soil, and in a few months the mallow-root would be on plates and in bellies. It gave him a feeling of accomplishment unlike any he'd felt before, and he was – by most standards – an accomplished man.

Two blue masjythra had accompanied Mandalay and the other women to the field, heaving a large wooden basket between them. Jonathon's stomach had groaned when he'd seen it. Although there was ample food at The Fortress, it was unvaried. Sticky porridge and tea for breakfast. Wedges of cheese with chewy bread for lunch. Stew and cob for dinner. Jonathon was beginning to forget the bitterness of coffee, the astringency of wine. As for chocolate, he half-wondered if it was something that really existed or if his mind had conjured it in the twilight between asleep and awake.

'Come.' Mandalay handed out hessian purses and watering cans. The purses were divided into two pouches. She showed them how to clip the pouches around their masjythra, then took a seed from one pouch and held it up for them to see. 'This is a mallow-root seed. A healthy seed has an unbroken husk around it like this one. Discard any seeds where the husk is broken. Take three seeds and drop them lightly into a hole. No more than four seeds in any one hole because the roots will strangle one another. In each hole also drop one of these tablets.' She held up a small green pill from the other pouch. 'It helps to combat the salt. You need to pair up. One for the seeds and pills, one for the water.'

Jonathon immediately turned to Daidd, who nodded his agreement. Jonathon strapped the pouch around his waist, the way Mandalay had shown him. It cinched his masjythra, making it ride up an inch so he felt the silky air against his groin. A surge of blood ran to his cock.

The pairs of men took up position at the bottom of the field and began methodically working their way upwards towards the wall where the water bags were hung. Jonathon picked out seeds and an anti-saline tablet and dropped them into the shallow holes. Then he covered them with a thin layer of soil, pressed lightly on it with his foot and moved on. Daidd paused and upturned a slow trickle of water onto the seeds.

Mandalay and the women threaded through the dual lines of men, Mandalay explaining aspects of the planting to the other Vaik. Apprentices, Jonathon thought. They wore brightly coloured diaphanous gowns that fluttered about them as they moved. A couple of them took their shoes off and held them, dangling, by their sides as they followed Mandalay. They wove in and out between the men, pressing close to observe the drop of the seeds, the position and depth of the holes. They were so close that Jonathon felt the brush of their hair on his arms. He caught at the scent of sandalwood that trailed them and was grateful that the vile smell of burning Goosen's Trial was gone from the air.

A sudden gust of wind, unusual for the morning, blew Jonathon's seeds away as he dropped them. They landed a few centimetres wide of the hole.

'You missed,' said one of the women. She bent to retrieve the seeds, picking them carefully from the soil. Jonathon was acutely aware of how close she was to his cock. She smiled up at him, a knowing smile, as if she'd divined his thoughts. She stood, dropped the seeds into his pouch then reached under his masjythra. 'Scattering seed,' she said playfully. 'Tut. Tut. Tut.'

Jonathon froze. He felt himself bulge in her warm hand. She moved it up and down his shaft, alternately gentle and insistent. The lines moved on around him. He felt Daidd hesitate. The woman's eyes held Jonathon's. She was brown-eyed and honey-haired with square, strong shoulders and dark skin. Her translucent yellow gown gave her a golden glow. If there was a Vaik prototype, it was she.

Jonathon entered a sensory echo chamber where all his thoughts and feelings were amplified. He felt the warm sun on his face. The salt rind thickening on his arms. The still figure of Daidd by his side. The absurdity of it all: a man, frozen in a field, forbidden to move while a beautiful stranger played with his cock. All the while lines of men planted seeds as if nothing about this were out of the ordinary.

But nothing about The Fortress was ordinary and Jonathon had no psychological reference point for what was happening. Given the choice, would he stay here to be fondled by this woman? Or would he dash her hand away, pull down his masjythra and storm off?

'Come here.' The woman summoned Daidd. She dropped Jonathon's cock and addressed herself to the other man. 'Take off your masjythra.' Daidd did as he was told, lifting the garment above his head and dropping it onto the freshly ploughed earth. The woman forgot about Jonathon and stared at the naked man beside her.

Daidd looked like two different men who had been carved up then pressed together. There was his poor, shattered half-face and shoulder with its candle-wax surface; he was a man children would stare at and adults would pretend not to see. But downwards ... He could have been a sculptor's masterwork. He was interconnected lines and indents, angles and arcs: a study in human geometry. His tan line served to focus the eyes on his taut abdomen, the blur of his pubic hair and the long, thick penis stirring against his thigh.

'You're magnificent,' said the Vaik, and it was as if she'd casually upturned the contents of the watering can onto Jonathon's groin. His cock slunk back between his balls. 'Untie me,' she commanded him, gesturing to the strings on her gown. He fumbled at her throat, waist and wrists. 'Take it off.'

He lifted it over her head, then, unsure where to put it, folded it in front of his groin.

'Come here.' She circled his head with her hand and clamped him to her breast. He opened his mouth for her nipple and sucked. 'Good,' she whispered. 'That's good. Daidd, play with that magnificent cock of yours.'

She knows his name, thought Jonathon. He flicked her nipple lightly with his tongue, then closed his teeth over the erect point. Not hard, just enough for her to feel their imprint.

'Go down,' she said, breathlessly, pressing her hands against his shoulders. He lowered himself past her large brown nipples and soft abdomen. He dropped to his knees, brushed her hair back with his fingers and parted her upper lips. As he brought his tongue towards her clitoris he noticed the rest of the assignment approaching from the other direction. They had reached the upper end of the field and were planting another row on their return.

He clasped his hands around the woman's buttocks and drew her closer. He smelt her desire through the scent of sandalwood.

As the lines drew equal with them, some of the women stopped to watch. Mandalay and the men continued on, dropping seeds and anti-saline tablets into the soil.

The woman gasped as Jonathon's tongue probed her. She clutched his hair between her fingers, giving him instructions. 'A little slower ... Hard for a few strokes, then pull back ... Good.' She moaned, then addressed Daidd: 'You're to fuck me now.' She straightened Daidd's masjythra on the ground and settled on all fours. 'Slow at first, the way I like it.'

'Yes, Mistress.'

Jonathon stood up and joined the other women, watching. He'd seen people fucking before. A few times he and one of the other guys from work had wound up in a hotel suite with a couple of pood– junior analysts. Once, he'd even shared a girl with a colleague after a hellishly boozy night at a conference. They were cocaine-fuelled binges he'd gotten off on. This was different. Daidd moved in and out of the woman, doing as he was instructed, his knees in the soil. She tossed her honey-blonde hair over one shoulder and played to the gallery, arching her back, pouting and mewling. The women around him were intent on the scene. Some stroked themselves through their gowns. Jonathon felt ancillary. It was a strange and unsettling feeling for him, who was used to being at the centre of things.

'How is it for you, Daidd?' The Vaik turned her head towards him.

'Good, Mistress.'

'Reach around and play with my clit.'

Daidd eased all of his considerable length into her, laid his stomach flat against her back and reached for her, his hand disappearing behind her thigh. She closed her eyes, concentrating on her own pleasure now. The gallery could take care of themselves. After a few moments of stillness she began thrusting her hips backwards.

'Sit up, Daidd. Grab my hips. Fuck me hard.'

Daidd moved in and out of her, the unscarred profile facing Jonathon. He was concentrating. His jaw was set, his eyes unfocused in the way of people carefully monitoring some internal mechanism. What was he thinking about, Jonathon wondered. Not coming? Staying hard? Or did he think only of the Aeraevest?

The woman cried out, shuddered, then dropped to her elbows. Daidd held himself perfectly still, his big hands lightly draped on her hips. She drew her long hair back from her face, winked conspiratorially at the collected Vaik and eased herself off Daidd. He continued to kneel, his large, twitching cock pointed towards the end of the field like a weathervane uncertain which way the wind was blowing. She stood up, shook herself and then stretched tall, her cheeks flushed.

'Thank you, Daidd,' she purred.

He nodded slightly, still not moving.

'Oh, Daidd,' she cried suddenly, 'you're in the dirt!' She gave him her hand and he rose to his feet. She bent and dusted his knees off. 'Sorry, Daidd. I didn't realise.'

'It's nothing, Mistress.'

'You should have said something.'

'I was,' his mouth twitched a little, 'preoccupied.'

She smiled. 'Oh, Daidd, what would we do without you?' She threw her arms around him, then kissed him gently on the cheek. Jonathon felt a stab of something very like envy. She retrieved her gown from him and dropped it over her head. 'Come,' she said to him, 'we've got some planting to finish.'

When the seeds were tucked away in the ground, they opened the baskets and set the food out on blankets near the knotted trees that had served them as seats for the season. The mere sight of the food made Jonathon feel drunk. There were fat bunches of dark cherries and slabs of cured meat. Roasted chicken drumsticks, a leg of ham and wedges of cheddar. A chocolate cake with cream (he hadn't imagined chocolate after all!) and – perhaps most incredibly – draughts of apple cider made at The Fortress. It fizzed on Jonathon's tongue and tickled his nose. The bubbles were aerating his brain. He might float away.

The Vaik shared in the feast, sitting among the men and discussing the progress of the planting. Root vegetables were growing in the western gardens, corn and maize in the north. Leafy greens and beans were going into beds in the south. Now that the mallow root was in, Jonathon's assignment would be moving on. It was becoming too hot to labour out in the field, and they would be given summer work; though none of them had yet been told what. The uncertainty made Jonathon feel slightly anxious.

He shaved some more ham from the leg then, utterly sated, leant his back against the tree trunk and closed his eyes. His eyelids reflected the dappled light of the canopy. His limbs felt heavy and liquid, as if he'd been drinking Mandalay's aniseed tea. One of the women began to sing, a low dirge in Vaik that the others took up. He drifted off to sleep, lulled by the tune and Daidd's softly spoken explanation of the words. It told of a field that refused to sprout no matter what the women planted or how carefully they tended the soil. Eventually they stopped trying to coax anything from the field and used it as a cemetery, the final resting place for the stillborn, the miscarried and the babes who didn't live past two moons. Overcome with sadness, the field began to grow trees that no one had ever seen before: slim, silvery birches with bowed branches that trailed blue-green leaves to the ground. The Vaik called them weeping trees.

When Jonathon woke it was to the afternoon breeze and the salt gnats. The Vaik had decamped. The men were picking over the last of the food and trying to rouse themselves to collect the gardening tools and begin the long march back to their quarters. Jonathon massaged a crick in his neck.

The isvestyii was holding a mug of cider and staring out at the field. His eyes were cold and hard. 'Why do we do this?'

No one answered.

He turned from the field towards the assignment. 'Why do we do this?'

'Do what?' said Daidd flatly. Jonathon winced under so many question marks.

'Play at being serfs for these girls. There are enough men to take The Fortress and put an end to this bullshit. We could do it. Or are you all too pussy-whipped to see how pathetic you are?'

'There's no "we",' Jonathon said. 'There's us,' he gestured towards the assignment, 'and then there are cunts who rape children.' The rest of the men murmured their assent.

The isvestyii looked down at his feet.

Jonathon closed his eyes to return to the peaceful state brought on by the food and the cider. It took him a moment to understand that the isvestyii was addressing him.

'… hiding out from a debt? Or one of your secretaries finally make a complaint about your extracurricular expectations?'

'Shut it,' said Daidd, 'before it gets shut for you.'

Jonathon nestled further into the tree roots that cradled him. 'Let him ramble, Daidd. No one's listening.'

There was silence for a time. Jonathon was on the edge of sleep when the song the isvestyii was singing crept around his torpor and fingered the nerve underneath his breastbone.

I got a job I can dangle
I got long lines of coke
I know the people you need to sleep with
I got rich man's rope

Jonathon was on his feet and barrelling towards the isvestyii, the red mist so thick across his eyes that he didn't see Daidd intercept him and plant his shoulder into his solar plexus. Daidd held his palm against Jonathon's chest, his arm straight as if he were directing traffic.

'Stop,' he commanded.

'You're protecting that? That —' But Jonathon didn't have a word contemptuous enough.

'I'm protecting you.' Daidd held Jonathon's gaze. 'You took an oath. You swore not to raise your hand against anyone at The Fortress. Even that.' He jerked his head at the isvestyii.

The other men were stirring. They'd caught the scent of blood.

The isvestyii raised his hands, mock innocent. 'I didn't do nothing.'

Jonathon pushed Daidd's hand away and tried to shove past him, but Daidd blocked his way. 'Don't do this. He's not worth it.'

'Just minding my own business and he comes at me wanting to start something,' mumbled the isvestyii.

'Aeraevest,' said Daidd. 'Say it with me.'

'Aeraevest. Aeraevest.'

Jonathon moved the rocks in his mind until he felt the anger slip from his body. Slowly, Daidd loosened his grip on Jonathon's arms. During the long march back to their quarters, Jonathon incanted the word in time with his steps.

Until he met Adalia, Jonathon didn't know that most of the women he knew tittered rather than laughed. He heard Adalia before he saw her.

He was at a party, crowded into the kitchen with some of his cronies, beer in hand. The light was low, so low that you couldn't be sure if the person leaning against the opposite wall was someone you knew well or not at all. Black-and-white clad waitstaff shouldered through the clusters of people, bearing trays of canapés and vol-au-vents. Jonathon's friend broke off his long and rather dull story about a new account he'd acquired to pull some nibbles from a circulating tray, and that was when Jonathon first heard Adalia. Even in the throng of people and with loud, pulsing bass throbbing in his ear, he heard her. Her laugh was utterly infectious. It rumbled through her and poured out like a flock of joyful, cheeky birds. He heard the laugh and it made him smile.

'Who *is* that?' he asked his friend. His friend, also smiling, didn't know. 'Excuse me.' Jonathon pushed his way out of the kitchen and set out in search of the laugh. Soon enough the peal rippled through the house again. Jonathon followed, homing in on it.

'Jonathon!' One of the poodles accosted him. She threw her arm around him and planted an extravagant kiss on his cheek.

He surreptitiously wiped her raspberry lip gloss away. 'Hi. How are you?' What was her name?

'Good. Really good. Isn't this a fabulous party? I almost didn't come. I've been nursing a hangover for most of the day. Work drinks got a bit out of hand last night. But,' she raised her flute, 'hair of the dog and I'm right as rain. Oh look, there's Andy. It's so dark in here I didn't see him before. Must go say hello,' and she was off.

Jonathon waited for the laugh but it didn't come. He felt suddenly murderous towards the poodle. Maybe the laugh had gone home. Or was sad. Or kissing someone. *I'm being ridiculous*, he thought. But still he had a keen and unnerving sense that he'd missed a key assignation and his life would now continue on a different – fundamentally wrong – trajectory. Later, much later, he would wonder if the feeling had more to do with the square blue pill his friend had given him and that he was unfair to hold Adalia responsible for his later disappointment. But for that moment he stood still in a crowded apartment, listening intently. Then there it was again. He followed.

In his memory she was standing in a pool of light. Rationally, he knew that this couldn't be right because the apartment was so dark. Still, that was how he remembered it.

The laugh was neither tall nor short, fat nor thin, pretty nor ugly. She was wholly and utterly herself. He watched her from across the room. She took a canapé from a tray, nodding vigorously at her companion as she ran the cheddar and kransky through her teeth then idly poked at her gum with the pick. At one point she drew her arm across her body and scratched her elbow, her pleasure in the dissipating itch writ large on her face. Everyone around her looked as posed and cold as a mannequin.

Jonathon approached her and the man she was talking to. As he entered their personal space the man raised a quizzical eyebrow.

'Hello.' Jonathon thrust his hand towards her; she took it. 'My name's Jonathon. Jonathon Bridge. I understand if you have reservations about "Bridge" and want to keep your own name. But I'd like for our children to have hyphenated surnames. I'm thinking two girls and a boy. No cats, though. Everything else is up for negotiation but I'm hopelessly allergic to cats.'

She looked at him, nakedly evaluating whether he was funny/charming or arrogant/alarming, then she burst out laughing. That laugh. It trilled through him.

'My last name's Draw,' she said. 'How's that for a max-power surname?'

'Draw-Bridge? Really?'

'Not really,' she sighed, 'though I'm beginning to wish it was. My name's actually Fullbright. Adalia Fullbright. This is —' But the man she'd been speaking to was gone.

'Fullbright-Bridge. Or Bridge-Fullbright. They both sound pretty good, don't you think?'

They danced. Somehow in that cramped apartment with chattering people standing shoulder to shoulder and waitstaff turning side-on to squeeze through, they contrived a space to dance. Her dress was backless and when Jonathon put his hand on her bare skin he felt a sympathetic current.

The filter between Adalia and the world was large-grained. When amused, she laughed. When sad, she cried. Even her sloth was magnificent. The days that she decreed to be 'pyjama days' were spent propped up on the voluminous pillows that covered her bed watching old movies on her enormous television. She kept boxes of expensive chocolates for just such occasions, so by the end of the day they were rolling around on silvery wrappers. They drank amaretto – a pyjama day drink, according to Adalia – and ordered takeaway, even answering the door to collect the pizza in their pyjamas. They'd break off the movies to make love, the foil fluttering around them.

Adalia gave the most lascivious blow jobs Jonathon had ever known. She liked to make him stand up, then throw a cushion on the floor. Then, never taking her eyes from his, lower herself to her knees. She'd lean back slightly, and slowly, very slowly, unbutton her shirt. Her skin was creamy white most of the time, but flushed red when she was turned on. Or angry. She removed her bra then leant back even more so he could enjoy the roundness of her gorgeous breasts with their large brown nipples. He'd never experienced anything as erotic as Adalia's gaze as she took him in her hand and guided him into her mouth, all the while locked onto his eyes. It was intense, unsettling and filthy. Sometimes, he had to close his eyes and gather the pieces of himself back together. When he opened them again, her knowing brown eyes would be there, unblinking.

He'd first told her he loved her when she had him in her mouth. He hadn't realised he was going to say it, hadn't even considered what it meant. Her gaze simply extracted the words from him the way cyanide will separate dirt from minerals. When he said it, a smile played at the corners of her otherwise occupied mouth. She ran her tongue between her upper lip and him, her eyes powerful, self-satisfied. Hungry. He came immediately and she drew back, releasing him from her mouth so he blew all over her waiting face.

The experience had been strange, even faintly troubling. He'd come on women before in that way, a couple of times through misfire and once or twice deliberately with the poodles. But he'd never felt so powerless before. It was like Adalia drew something from him that he wasn't sure he wanted to hand over. She led, and he followed. Or was towed. In those utterly unguarded moments of his purest pleasure, when she locked onto his gaze, he knew that he could conceal nothing. Adalia looked through and into him. Her psychic sonar bounced off his inner walls, transmitting the cavernous spaces inside him.

The absence.

When Jonathon took Adalia to his brother's wedding, his friends and family half-suspected him of playing a joke.

Adalia has sashayed out of her bedroom wearing a shiny black gown. It was fitted around the bust where drawstrings barely contained her ample bosom, clung tight to her generous hips and belly, then flared out into a fishtail at her ankles. Iridescent blue sequins sewn onto the underside of the fishtail glowed like scales. She didn't say 'Does this look all right?' or 'How do I look?' but 'How awesome is this?' Then she performed an unpartnered tango up and down her hallway, teeth clenched against the stem of an imaginary rose. When she turned, her skirt flashed in a shimmer of pearl and indigo.

He introduced her to the wedding line-up as 'My partner, Adalia', enjoying the flicker of disbelief in his mother's eyes as she'd taken Adalia's hand and said hello. 'We'd hoped to meet you before now, Adalia,' his mother added, her tone implying that, had Adalia been vetted, she would not have made it onto the guest list.

Adalia, unruffled, had subjected his mother to her bone-crushing handshake and said, 'Yes. I've been remiss. Terribly so. I work all hours. But that's no excuse, is it? I'll invite you to lunch soon, I promise.'

'That would be lovely,' came from his mother's mouth, but her eyes said something different.

The guests were bunching behind them, gifts under their arms, eyeing off the trays of champagne on the other side of the pleasantries. They were waiting to shake hands with the bridal party, make their offerings and sink under the evening's anaesthetic of free-flowing wine, rich food, and expansive grounds with their little grottos and groves where – who knows – a pretty girl (or pretty by candlelight) might take a tumble with you before you poured yourself and your wife into a taxi and fought the city traffic for the oblivion of your own bed.

Jonathon felt all this pressing into his back. The stone that had been fattening, hard and pitiless, in his gut since boyhood grew colder and weightier.

'Jonathon, are you all right?' His mother's cool fingers reached out and pressed his hand.

He looked at her face, all sharp angles and pink flesh needled taut. He reached for Adalia's hand. 'I'm fine. Better than.' And he stepped out of the line across the smooth wooden floor to their seats, never loosening his grip on Adalia's hand.

Her eyes darted over the room, drinking it all in. 'I want to know everything,' she said, 'all the sordid family secrets. Spare me nothing.'

'You see that man over there? The one with the purple flower in his buttonhole and the cummerbund trying to give him a waistline?' Adalia nodded. 'That's my Uncle Jaspar. My mother's brother. I caught him in bed with one of the cleaning ladies when I was thirteen or fourteen.'

Adalia turned her bright liquid gaze on Jonathon. 'You're joking?'

'No. They were going at it in one of the guestrooms. I can show you the room if you like.'

'What did you do?'

'There was a long pause where they looked at me and me at them. Then I reversed out of the room, closed the door and went about my business.'

'Did you tell your mum?'

'God no. She'd have had a fit.'

'So what did you do?'

Jonathon's fine mouth twitched. 'I told my Uncle Jaspar I was short on cash. He gave me two hundred dollars. Told me to spend it wisely. I said it would do. For a start.'

Adalia blinked. 'You blackmailed him.'

'I said I was short on cash.'

'And how long did this cash-flow problem persist?'

'Till college.'

Adalia burst out laughing. 'You're an extortionist. I've fallen in love with an extortionist.'

Jonathon hailed a waiter and relieved him of an open bottle of champagne and two flutes. He filled them, then clinked his against Adalia's. 'I'm a maximiser of opportunity.'

'You're shameless.'

'That, I concede, is true.'

He watched Adalia watching him. He knew she was half-horrified. Panic flickered in her eyes even as she laughed and shook her head at his confessions. But the part of her that loved stories, that made her a good journalist, was hooked.

'Let's dance.'

The doubt lifted from her eyes as they moved to the dance floor. Adalia loved to dance. She threw herself into the music, seemed to know every song. A bubble of people formed around her, bobbing like corks in her energy.

'Come on,' she pleaded, when Jonathon collapsed in his chair, 'get up and dance with me.'

'I'm done for.' He loosened his tie and wiped his brow with a napkin. 'Let me recuperate. You go. Rejoin your admirers.' And she was off, twirling and grinding under the glittering lights. He'd lose sight of her, then catch a flash of blue and there she was, bringing up a conga line or waltzing with one of his uncles — though not, thank god, Jaspar.

His mother lowered herself into Adalia's seat. She sat, straight-backed, wineglass in hand, surveying the dance floor. Jonathon studied her profile. She seemed to him to have barely changed from when he was a boy. The same smooth, inscrutable face beneath her finely plucked eyebrows. The same tawny hair, shampooed to a high sheen, dried and straightened to an effortless bob. He knew that the wine in her hand was warm. She wouldn't relax until the speeches were done, the cake cut, the official photographer finished for the night. Till then she would glide about the room, repairing uncomfortable silences and administering water to the sots who couldn't be trusted not to rekindle old arguments.

'Are you pleased, Mother?'

She tapped her shell-pink nails on her glass and considered. 'She lacks ... gravitas.'

Jonathon followed his mother's eyes to where Adalia was dancing. 'I wasn't talking about Adalia.'

'Oh. You meant?'

'The wedding.'

'The wedding. Yes. It's all gone off remarkably well. If we can keep your Uncle Jaspar from groping the waitstaff, I think we can claim it as a success.'

'Do you think he'll be happy?'

'Who?'

'My brother.'

'Oh, Jonathon. The things you say.' She shook her head and took the tiniest sip of her wine.

'Would you like me to get you a fresh one?'

'No. I'm fine with this.'

'So do you?'

'What's that?'

'Think he will be happy?'

She turned her slate-grey eyes on him, looking very much as if he was a hand of cards she could do nothing with. 'Jonathon, please. Don't start.'

'Don't start what? I'm genuinely curious to know what you think.'

'Yes,' she said, as though through a mouthful of shards, 'yes, I think he'll be happy.'

Jonathon looked over to where his brother was dancing with his new bride. He seemed happy enough.

'I hope you're going to behave tonight, Jonathon. This is not the time to play your favourite role of family malcontent.' She smiled brightly, patted him on the knee and threaded her way through the tables, scattering greetings and compliments.

'I hated summer camp,' Jonathon said to her retreating back, the shimmer of her perfume. The armful of roses on the table.

II ANNOD

THE NIGHTS were stifling. Even breathing was an effort. Jonathon lay as still as possible on the bed, waiting for the late-evening sea breeze. He listened to the hum of the mosquitoes that swarmed through the open window and hovered above his bed. Like all the other men, Jonathon was coated in a repellent issued by the Vaik. It worked, but it smelt of swamp water and you had to cover every inch of yourself in it. The smallest patch of unprotected skin would send the mosquitoes dive-bombing from the ceiling to gorge on his blood. He kept a sheet over his body as protection from the little fiends, but even the touch of the light cotton was too much in the heat.

He threw back the sheet and raked his fingers through his hair. He hadn't seen his reflection since the day he'd entered The Fortress and the tiles on the perimeter wall had scrambled his face. He vaguely wondered what he looked like with his stubble and shaggy hair and skin chastened by sun, wind and salt gnats. He had lost his fat to the fields, so the masjythra clung to the bulge and indent of muscle and sinew. If he'd been with a poodle now, he wouldn't have had to suck his stomach in. He dismissed the thought with a growl of disgust.

A squabble erupted beneath his window but was quickly resolved, the seabirds rendered docile by the heat. He dropped his head over the side of the bed to feel cool air from the vent blowing on his face. He flicked water from the jar by his bed over his body. At one point he considered walking to the bathhouse to immerse himself in a barrel of cool water but it seemed like too much effort. Eventually he drifted into sleep.

When the figure of a woman appeared, silvery in the doorway, he thought he was dreaming. She lingered there for a moment, then slipped across the floor to the window. She leant out and breathed deeply. 'The sea breeze has finally come in. It's late tonight. Tomorrow will be unbearable.'

Her profile was distinct in the moonlight. She had the long, sloping forehead and aquiline nose of the Vaik. Her hair was caught loosely in a clasp at the back of her head. It shimmered in the darkness against her straw and honey hair.

She perched on the edge of the bed and gently lifted his hand. 'You've been using the mistaelnet ointment. Good.'

She slipped off the loose straps of her dress, letting it fall to her shoulders. When she placed Jonathon's hand lightly against her breast, he knew he wasn't dreaming. His dreams these past years were always different, but always the same. Dreams of stalking and pursuit. Of flimsy hiding places and footsteps drawing ever nearer.

The woman trailed her hand along his leg and thigh. 'You are called Jonathon, yes?'

'Yes.'

She closed her hand around his cock. 'Jonathon Bridge.'

'Yes.'

The blue-black water of sleep flowed away. He was awake. Alert.

'The Vaik don't trust bridges.' She cupped his balls and rolled them gently in her palm. 'Things of difference should keep their own kind. Bridges make mischief.'

She stood up and wriggled out of her dress, catching it with her toes and flicking it into her outstretched hand. She folded the dress and dropped it onto the table. Her movements were loose and elastic and entirely unconcerned with whether Jonathon watched her or not. She was tall and rangy, with the spidery limbs of a long-distance runner. Only her stomach was soft and yielding, shot through with stretch marks that glimmered a little in the moonlight. Jonathon thought of Adalia. She was close to term now. The idea keened him with grief. He wanted to hold his wife and rest his hand on her belly. Bar their door against isvestyii. He wanted to lay his lips close to his unborn daughter and talk to her, tell her stories. What stories exactly, he didn't know. If he'd been told stories as a child he didn't remember them. He could tell her that the Vaik were suspicious of bridges.

'Get hard now,' the woman said. She said it casually, as if she'd asked him if he'd seen where she left her car keys.

I submit, he'd said. *I submit.* But how to make his body obey the words his mouth had spoken? It was easier for women, he thought.

The Vaik scraped some ointment from the jar and moulded it to her thumb. 'Relax,' she said.

He held his hands towards her for the balm. Instead she reached under him and wriggled her thumb into his rectum. He cried out in pain and outrage. The cry echoed along the doorless corridor, but nobody came. The balm set his anus on fire, like a thousand salt gnats biting into the puckered skin.

'There,' she said, as his cock sprang up out of the darkness.

She straddled him, took his cock in one hand, then lowered herself onto the length of him. He wanted to push her off. To strike her face with a closed fist. Instead he lay there, rigid, tears prickling the back of his eyes. He hadn't known that he could feel this way.

She took his hand, wet his index finger in her mouth and placed it against her clitoris. 'Like this,' she said. He concentrated on holding his finger the way she had shown him. She found her own rhythm, moving up and down, pausing now and again to sit still against him. She was taking herself to the brink, then pulling back. Her eyes were closed, her face intent on some goal he couldn't share. He'd never seen such absorption before, so much concentration of self.

Vest. Vest-ness.

He was the vessel of her self, the ship mainstay on which she was riding out to sea.

Adalia kept her eyes open during sex. *I want to see you*, she'd say, *really see you*. When she gave him a blow job she held his gaze. It sent him instantly to the edge. (*And the poodles?* Adalia asked in his head. *Were their eyes open or closed?*)

The woman shuddered and a wetness rushed over his crotch and thighs. She sat perfectly still, her chin tucked against her chest. Then she opened her eyes and looked at Jonathon. He let his hand drop to his side. She smiled.

'Jonathon Bridge,' she said softly. 'Jonathon Bridge.'

She eased herself off him and sat on the edge of the bed again, her feet on the floor. She reached for his water jar and took a long drink. She offered him the jar. He shook his head. She moved again to the window and leant out. He heard in her slow intake of breath the intonation of satisfaction.

'The seabirds are so quiet tonight.' She ducked her head in, scooped her gown off the table and dropped it over her body. 'Good night. Sleep well,' she said over her shoulder as she left.

The chime was sounding. He placed the pillow against his head to block out the sound. He needed to sleep. He'd lain awake long after the Vaik had left his quarters and had slept for perhaps three hours. But the chime went on. He threw back the pillow and that was when he saw it.

He was thick with blood. It was matted through his pubic hair and coated on his penis. It ran in sticky patches down his thighs and stained the mattress and the sheet. He cried out and sprang up, looking for the source of the wound. He pressed his hands against his stomach, checked his thighs.

Perhaps the woman had punctured the lining of his colon and he was bleeding from his small intestine. He had no mirror. Nothing with which to check that most private, hidden part of himself. He didn't feel damaged. The sting of the balm had worn off. The chime clanged on. What would happen if he was late? How did he get someone's attention? He heard the shuffling of the men below and was about to cry for help when he realised that the blood wasn't his.

'Fucking bitch.'

He clamped his hand over his mouth as if to net the words from the air and stuff them back inside. He waited, for a strike of thunderbolt or for his room to sink into the earth. Those found guilty of Vaikray had been strapped to a post at low tide. Small incisions were made on their nipples with a delicate blade wrought by the Vaik especially for the purpose. The blood was left to trickle down the abdomen, along the legs and onto the feet. The creeping waves took the first, tantalising sniff of blood out to the deep water. The sharks would begin circling before the prisoner's calves were wet. Drowning was considered a blessing.

A ferrous tang hung in the air and on his tongue. He smelt like prey. He looked down at himself, trying to figure out what to do. His masjythra wouldn't stretch to cover all the blood. He didn't stop to ask himself why he was afraid to pass another man on the way to the bathroom.

He poured some water from the jar onto his hands, then rubbed it onto his crotch. It seemed only to spread the blood further. Dampening a corner of his sheet he wiped at the blood, amazed that there was so much of it.

'Shit. Shit, shit, shit, shit.'

He picked up the empty jar and hurled it against the wall. The jar dissolved when it hit the stone, sending a fine spray of glass through the air. Jonathon was in a fury. He followed the glass against the wall, smashing his knuckles into the stone. The shards embedded themselves in his bloody fingers. He wanted out. Wanted to return to his life as Jonathon Bridge: a man whose corner office looked down on the sprawl of the city. Whose clothes were expertly tailored. Whose CEO sought his counsel and clinked a whisky glass confidentially against his, late on a Friday night. A man desirable to young women, whatever Adalia said.

He didn't hear Daidd enter his room. Daidd caught him in mid-flight, gripping both arms in his and holding them behind Jonathon's back, forcing his head towards the ground.

'Stop,' Daidd commanded. 'Enough.'

Jonathon tried to fight Daidd off but he was too strong. Jonathon's back couldn't break the deadlock. Tears and snot clogged his nose so that, held upside down, he felt as if he was drowning. He stopped struggling in order to gulp mouthfuls of air.

'Enough,' Daidd said again, then, 'Aeraevest.'

Daidd slowly released him, then took a couple of wary steps backwards. He looked at the massacre spread across Jonathon's crotch and thighs.

'What happened to you?'

'The woman who came here last night. She – she fucked me and left this behind.'

Daidd didn't speak for a moment. 'Menstrual blood,' he said flatly. 'You're having a meltdown over menstrual blood.'

'Look at this.' Jonathon spread his arms wide in front of him, stupefied that Daidd didn't seem to understand.

'You're a married man.' Daidd shook his head. 'Anyone would think your wife had never had a period. Wait here.'

Daidd left the room, still shaking his head slightly. Jonathon looked down at his blood-spattered knuckles. When the scabs formed they'd tighten the flex in his hands, making it harder to pull the Goosen's Trial from the soil.

Daidd returned with a bucket of water, a bandage and a sponge. 'Here.' He handed the bucket and sponge to Jonathon. 'Wash yourself. Then I'll bind your hand.'

Daidd turned and walked to the door, keeping his back to Jonathon's ministrations.

'We're going to be late,' said Jonathon as he dipped the sponge into the bucket.

'Yes.'

'I'm sorry about this.'

'Don't worry about it.'

'I don't know why it freaked me out so much.'

'You know, on some level you ought to be flattered.'

'Why's that?'

'A Vaik who comes to your bed when she's menstruating is unlikely to conceive. She's operating from desire alone. Of all the men here.' Daidd gestured towards the rest of the quarters.

Jonathon tried to find something in this that gratified his vanity, but he felt only … incidental.

'You done back there?' Daidd asked.

Jonathon peered into the pink-stained bucket. 'Yeah, I'm done.' He took his silver masjythra from the peg on the wall and threw it over his head.

'Hold still,' said Daidd. He squeezed the shards of glass from Jonathon's knuckles with his nails while Jonathon moved a pile of rocks a short distance in his head.

Jonathon's assignment was broken up. Some men were issued new masjythra and assigned to masonry. They would spend the summer patching up buildings in the grounds. Others were dispatched to garden maintenance, keeping the vegetable beds moist in the summer heat. Others disappeared with the cattle in search of feed at the furthest recesses of The Fortress. To Jonathon's relief, he was to remain in his silver masjythra with Daidd in the gardens.

'Not just any garden,' Daidd explained on their first day, 'the shaenet. It literally means "body garden". It's a place of tremendous significance. Most of the medicinal and recreational plants are grown there.'

'Where I come from, "recreational plants" has a very specific meaning.'

'Here, too.'

Jonathon's mouth fell open in surprise.

'You know, the Vaik aren't saints, Jonathon. And they're sure as hell not aesthetes.'

'They just seem so clean-living and worthy. They're like, I don't know, good-looking churchgoers.'

Daidd paused, as if considering whether to speak what was on his mind. 'The Vaik aren't innocents. You're like a piece on a chessboard to them, and they have a very specific idea of what the endgame looks like. Nothing here is spontaneous. Nothing.'

Behind an iron gate, half-obscured by shambolic ivy, was the shaenet. Daidd forced the gate open and ushered Jonathon through. The smell was overpowering: sweet and deep and utterly intoxicating. Jonathon tried to isolate each scent. There was bergamot. Lime. Something like rose, but a rose stripped back to its essence and amplified. Fresh-cut grass and churned earth. Cinnamon and wood-smoke. Jonathon filled his lungs with it, exhaled, then breathed again.

The shaenet was ranged into plots, some square, some rectangular, that banked upwards against the high walls. Each plot was bounded by a low stone wall and accessed by a strip of mossy path. The plots, though small, were dense and fecund. Each was tended by two men in silver masjythra. They worked with trowels and stakes and skeins of twine, finer work than in the fields. Jonathon looked for the isvestyii and was relieved not to find him. Ancient trees bordered the garden on all sides, their massive canopy spreading across the sky. Jonathon looked up to see the ribbons of blue sky shimmering through the leaves.

'This is old,' he said.

'Yes. Hundreds of years old. Maybe older.'

'Excuse me.' A man nosed his wheelbarrow past Daidd and Jonathon. He was carting straw.

'This way,' said Daidd. Jonathon followed him along the path that led to the back of the shaenet, away from the gate. The ground was on a slight incline, and as they walked, dropping lower, Jonathon heard the distinct sound of running water in the distance. He gave Daidd a curious look.

'There's a stream that runs from a source in The Dryans. It opens out into a small bay west of here. The Vaik use the water to irrigate this garden. I've heard, though I don't know if it's true, that in some myths the stream is said to have mystical properties.'

'I thought all the Vaik myths were catalogued. In the Story-Keeping Houses.'

'The Vaik keep the Story-Keeping to themselves. Mostly. Maybe even here they have sects. Maybe it was just some nonsense that the men made up to amuse themselves.'

'The things you do when you don't have PlayStation.'

Daidd led Jonathon to the far end of the shaenet. The shade deepened the further they went on, deliciously cool, and the sound of rushing water grew louder. The garden hummed with bees and the close concentration of the men. They came to a halt in front of a large shed. Peering through the open door, Jonathon saw what looked like a greenhouse and several men ranged at high tables. They wore safety glasses and gloves and held fine blades; they appeared to be dissecting plants. Daidd gestured for Jonathon to take a seat at one of the large blocks of wood dotted around a long rustic table outside the shed.

Daidd picked a contraption up from the table and sat down next to Jonathon. 'This might not be familiar to you.'

'It's not.' It looked like a laboratory microscope, but it was larger and had a hefty lever attached.

'It's a press. For mistaelnet.'

Jonathon took it from Daidd's hand and looked it over. 'Mistaelnet. They make a balm out of it. Mandalay left some for me when I first came here, for the sores on my hands. You heat it up with a candle and rub it into the bores. It's good stuff.'

'It's an extraordinary plant. Extract the oil and you can turn it into that balm. You can also distil it into a tincture for indigestion and dyspepsia. But,' Daidd's face broke into a wide grin, 'you can also dry the seeds, crush them up and put them in water. This prompts an incredible reaction, almost as if the water becomes animate. It starts swirling like it's going down a drain.'

'What is that used for?'

Daidd's grin grew wider. 'You drink it. The Vaik call it sterysh. It means "dragon sweat".'

'So, what ... it's like an ale? Or a wine.'

'It's like liquid weightlessness. Like anaesthetic but you're very much awake and alert.'

Jonathon laughed. 'So it's a party drug.' He turned the press over in his hands. 'If this gets out there'll be men lining up outside The Fortress to be supplicants.'

'Hardly. The Vaik like to get high and fuck as much as the next person, but they're regulated about it. I've only been offered sterysh a couple of times. The penalties for drinking it without Vaik sanction are high.'

'They must trust me, then. To assign me here.'

'Perhaps. Or they're testing you.' Daidd took the press from

Jonathon and placed it on the table. 'Or, more likely still, you can't conceptualise what they have in mind. Let me show you our plot.'

Jonathon bristled at the inference that he was witless compared to the Vaik. He'd been the head of Strategy at a tier-one company, after all. Daidd had been at The Fortress so long he wouldn't know what that meant.

Jonathon decided to let it go and turned his attention to the patch of earth that would occupy him for the next three months. It was the size of the desk in his office and about midway between the entrance to the shaenet and the shed. Guided by Daidd, Jonathon learnt the subtle, secret language of Vaik horticulture.

Mistaelnet was unprepossessing: stubby and coarse-leaved with no obvious smell. It was only when the tough, oval-shaped leaves were crushed that their pungent menthol aroma was released. It sent Jonathon's nostrils a-tingling and made him feel that his windpipe had been wiped clean. It took skill and practice to recognise when the leaves were ripe: they became slightly rubbery and squeaked when folded between thumb and forefinger. He collected the plucked leaves in a large woven basket and took them to one of the rough-hewn pews and tables at the far end of the garden. He sliced the leaves with a fine scalpel that was given to him by Daidd each morning and pocketed by Daidd each evening. By slicing the leaf down the middle, Jonathon was able to extract the tiny black seed used to make sterysh. When cut, the leaves oozed a slimy gel that made the blade slippery. Jonathon's fingers were crisscrossed with slices and nicks, quickly healed by the mistaelnet's juices.

The seeds, once dug out, stuck to the pads of his fingers. He used tweezers to pull them off and scraped them into glass jars. The jars were collected by other silver masjythra who loaded them onto trolleys and took them for processing. This was closely overseen by the Vaik, who had an almost preternatural sense for how many seeds a plant should yield. Daidd had warned him that the penalty for sampling the seeds was severe, and Jonathon, though curious, was determined not to be tempted. In the months he worked in the shaenet, he saw only one man succumb, dumb with pleasure. His rictus grin never faded as he was hauled out of the garden by the Vaik. Jonathon did not see him again.

He ground the sliced leaves with a mortar and pestle, shaved wax into the mix, then added oil until the mixture had the consistency of a balm. Using a blunt knife, he packed the balm into small tins that made their way through The Fortress to tend cuts, bruises and weeping sores. Watching as the aromatic tins trundled off gave him a satisfaction that recalled the big contracts he'd secured at the firm. That this feeling could be the same when the tasks seemed so disproportionate struck him as odd, at first.

Besides mistaelnet, Jonathon cultivated other herbs and medicinals. Norsling was a shrub that dropped purple bulbs the size of golf balls. Daidd told him it was used to bring on contractions. Fascinated, Jonathon plucked one of the glossy baubles and took it back to his quarters; he kept it on the table next to his bed until it rotted and was removed by an unseen hand. The stalk from the vende plant yielded a smoky, peppery flavour commonly used in the stews that were served in the dining hall. It strengthened the immune system and promoted blood flow to the genitals. The knobbly, fast-growing grass that he had initially thought was a weed was an ingredient in a drink called verrglet. Snapped off and put on the tongue, it barely had any taste; but held over a flame, it became sweet and luscious.

Each man worried for his plot. It was cooler in the shaenet than in the rest of the grounds, but still the plants were thirsty. All irrigation was done by hand, and it was slow and backbreaking work. At the very edge of the shaenet, behind the shed, was a stone well fed directly from the stream. The men spent much of the day ferrying buckets between the well and their plots.

Contingents of Vaik, in twos and threes, wandered the gardens several times a day, checking on the mistaelnet yield and testing the moisture in the earth.

Jonathon searched among the women for the one who had come to his bed and left her menstrual blood behind like a nick on his bedpost. He was never sure whether he'd seen her or not. It had been dark, and she shared the colouring of the vast majority of Vaik. And if he did see her, what then? He was here to submit. Had *chosen* submission. For Adalia, for himself. Still, he wanted a confrontation. Wanted to hold her to account, though for precisely what he couldn't say.

Sometimes, Ulait would visit the shaenet and chat to Jonathon as he worked. She'd spread a little blanket on the ground and sit with her sketchpad and crayons. He enjoyed listening to her prattle about her lessons and her teachers. (*But the boys*, he wondered before he drifted into sleep at night, *where are the boys?*) Ulait would almost always bring a treat of some kind, biscuits or a slab of chocolate. He let the morsels dissolve on his tongue, excavating each ingredient then squashing it on his palate to savour the alchemy of the whole. Out in the world, he could buy whatever he wanted, whenever he wanted. He and Adalia enjoyed all manner of food and drink, but not like this. He felt that his senses were opening up, deepening.

He could detect the lavender in Mandalay's hair on the breeze before he saw her. The hairs on his arms lunged for contact with the flowing gowns of the Vaik as they came past, inspecting his plot. Infinite pink subtleties in the sky telegraphed tomorrow's weather. The sound of Ulait's springing step through the grass pinched the valves in his heart.

His cock, like the rest of him, was sensitive and alert. He woke up to cries of pleasure echoing through the residential quarters. For the first time, he unambiguously wanted the sexual attention of the Vaik. He had a raging hard-on several times a day, no longer bothering to stretch his masjythra over his groin. His breath shallowed in expectation when the women came to the shaenet, but though they coupled freely in the lush patches of grass, he was never chosen. Sometimes, when he woke at night, the mere touch of his bedding became unbearable. His skin was aflame. He craved relief, any relief, and thought about sliding his hand along his body to the dozen or so tugs that would bring it. The Vaik had never told him that self-pleasure was forbidden, but somehow it felt wrong. He kept his hands by his sides.

Jonathon woke to a certainty that launched him bolt upright from the bed: his child would be born today. It was a knowledge that seeped from his marrow, from whatever complex spiral of DNA made him irretrievably and ineluctably himself. He examined the conviction within him. He had never been mystical. Never read his stars or played with the tarot. He'd been derisive when Adalia had tried reiki, so this knowledge seated in his bones unnerved him. Yet he did not doubt it was the truth: his child would be born today.

He sprang from the bed and plunged his head into the dawn air outside his window. The air was soft and warm, the sky pink-streaked. The unseen sea moved lazily in and out of the bay like breath. Adalia would be setting their birthing plan in motion: phoning her sister who was to act as doula and driver, dashing off a note to him care of The Fortress, taking the pre-packed bag from the hallway cupboard and breathing slowly, calming herself. The bag included a CD he had made for her to play during the birth. It was a collection of classical music and all the Vaik songs about childbirth he'd been able to find in the city's cultural archives. He'd also recorded a love letter he'd written to his wife.

The sack of Jonathon's stomach twisted, released and twisted again. He looked down, disbelieving the sensation, yet he wouldn't have been surprised to find he was standing in a gelatinous puddle, blood trickling down his thighs.

Daidd entered his quarters and seemed to immediately register the shock on his face.

'You seem unwell.'

Not knowing what to say, Jonathon shrugged. He braced himself in case the pain came again.

'I think ... I think my wife has gone into labour.'

'How do you know?'

'This is going to sound very strange, but I think ... I think I'm having labour pains.'

Daidd smiled, a broad smile that showed his white teeth and brought lustre even to his milky, dead eye. He extended his hand and shook Jonathon's warmly. 'Congratulations.'

Jonathon smiled quizzically. 'This is freaking me out, but you don't seem very surprised.'

'It's not so strange when you think about it. That child is fifty per cent you. She's connected to you in a way that no one else ever will be.'

'Fucking hippy,' said Jonathon, but he was pleased with the thought. He felt overwhelmed and overfull. He wanted to run laps. Leap from the window then abseil back up the wall.

'Come on,' said Daidd. 'I'll shout you breakfast.'

'Ha.'

They joined the lines of men making their way to the dining hall and took their seats. For the first time in months, Jonathon's body remembered coffee. His hands twitched as badly as they had during his first morning there. He spooned the food mechanically to his mouth, his mind elsewhere. He worried about the pain and the possibility that Adalia would resent him for not being there. The idea that she might call out for him made him desperately sad.

During their long nights talking, in the days before Jonathon was confined, they'd agreed on Adalia's first words to their baby:

Hello little one. I'm your mummy, and I love you very much. Your daddy isn't with us in this room, but he's with us. He loves you and will see you soon.

Jonathon tried to calculate the time it would reasonably take for a message to be couriered from the hospital to the perimeter wall, through The Veya Gate to his room. He looked around the dining hall and outside to the terrace where the women ate, but he couldn't see Mandalay. She would be the one to receive the message. She would be the one to bring it to him.

After breakfast, Jonathon followed Daidd outside into the still air. Could Adalia see the same stretch of blue sky through her hospital window or had she tunnelled so far into herself that nothing seemed real but the pain? The masjythra relaxed to detach its tiny squares from one another, letting the breeze flow across his body.

'One day someone's going to stick these things under a microscope and figure out what they're made of,' he said to Daidd, gesturing to the fabric.

'Only the Vaik know, and I suspect only a few of them. There's a legend that The Woman puts a few drops of her menstrual blood into the weave and that's what makes it come alive.'

'Sounds like bullshit to me.'

Daidd shrugged. 'It's as good an explanation as any.'

They set off past the bathhouse and the cherry orchard then veered left towards the shaenet.

'There's so much we don't know about the Vaik,' said Jonathon. 'How their society is governed. Where the boy children are. Whether The Woman is a real, actual person or a symbol. It must have taken you a long time to make peace with not having the answers.'

'I've wondered about all those things, and more. Ultimately, though, it works. I don't know why, I don't know how, but it works. The rest is just detail.'

Jonathon chose his next words carefully, not wanting to rub Daidd's nose in it. 'Ye-es. But, and I hope you won't mind my saying this, you have to put the best spin on it. I mean, it's not like you can leave.'

Daidd bent to pull a weed from the stony path, shook the dirt from its roots and tossed it into the adjoining field. 'I can leave any time I want. I could walk through The Veya Gate right now and no one would stop me. I'm freer than you.'

Jonathon paused mid-stride and reached his hand to Daidd's scarred shoulder. 'You're free to leave.'

Daidd stopped too. He turned and looked Jonathon in the eyes, one eye brown and alert, the other opaque and elsewhere. 'I've been free to go for three years.'

'And yet you stay.'

'I've chosen to become a permanent resident.' Daidd pursed his lips, thinking. Then he kicked a stone into the field. 'Like I said, it works. More or less. I'm not sure the same can be said for out there. I'm useful here.'

They resumed their walk, Jonathon mulling over what Daidd had said. The idea of being able to find his way to The Veya Gate, walk out through the iron gate that had given him entry and fly, fly down the steep hill to the Women's Hospital ... it made him feel as if a giant was sitting on his chest, compressing his heart and lungs so he had to breathe shallowly. Carefully.

Jonathon was shaken out of his reverie by a burst of laughter up ahead. Walking at right angles to him and Daidd were half a dozen girl Vaik, Ulait among them. Each of them seemed to be talking at once. They turned their heads, bird-like, to dip in and out of the feed of chatter, so intent on their conversations that they didn't notice Jonathon and Daidd.

Jonathon was seized by an impulse. He broke into a run and gambolled for the girls as fast as he could. He pumped his arms and legs, the effort a joy. He felt the grass spring back beneath his feet and the air eddy at his elbows, carrying him along. His child was being born. His child!

He threw his arms out and caught Ulait at the breastbone, intending to swing her off her feet and whirl her around. They would dervish in the soft summer air in celebration. Ulait dropped her head and bit Jonathon's thumb. He cried out in pain and released his hold. There was a ferocious tug at his shoulder and he was cartwheeled through the air. He landed with a sick thud on the ground. Winded and unable to speak or move he looked up into Ulait's cold eyes. Soldier's eyes, reflecting nothing.

The expression dissolved almost immediately and Ulait dropped to the ground beside him, her face a picture of concern. 'Oh gosh, are you all right? Where does it hurt?'

Everywhere, he thought. *I've become pain.*

Daidd caught up and bent over him, feeling among his ribs. 'Nothing's broken,' he said. He bent his head to Jonathon's ear and hissed, 'What were you thinking?'

I wanted to dance. To sing. To celebrate.

But he couldn't speak. He closed his eyes and focused on coaxing breath into his windpipe. One of the girls held a flask to his lips and dripped water into his mouth. Slowly, sensation returned and he was able to sit up. The girls sat by him on the browning summer grass, patient and concerned. Ulait held his hand, stroking it gently.

'I'm awfully sorry,' she said, 'but sneaking up on somebody like that is not a good idea.'

'I wholly agree.' His voice came in a whisper. He imagined that underneath his masjythra he was one massive bruise. Tears leaked from his eyes.

'Oh, please don't cry.' Ulait's face crinkled with concern. 'That's just how we're trained. It's not personal. I didn't mean to hurt you.'

Jonathon didn't have a voice to explain that he was crying

for fear that he would no longer feel the labour pains under his reddening chest.

The girls insisted on escorting Daidd and Jonathon part of the way to the shaenet. Their progress was slow, at first because Jonathon was still winded and then because he was reluctant to part from them. He enjoyed their stories about school and was fascinated by the snippets he gleaned about their lives. About how they would all do sentry duty in the Aeraevest for one year when they turned eighteen and how they were all trained in midwifery. About the combat training they did from when they were five, which accounted for how expertly Ulait had flattened him. Life outside The Fortress didn't seem to exercise their imaginations at all. What, he wondered, were they told about 'outside'?

At the turn-off to the shaenet they parted ways. Ulait hugged him so close he felt enfolded in lavender. She gave him a wet kiss on the cheek. 'I do apologise, Jonathon Bridge.'

'It's nothing, Mistress.' He could breathe freely again and, other than a tenderness in his chest, seemed to be fine.

Ulait and her companions set off for school and their chirruping chorus began again. A couple of the girls bumped shoulders with Ulait, conspiratorially. Jonathon watched them until they disappeared from view on the other side of a hill and only their birdsong remained.

'You're smiling,' said Daidd.

'Yes, because in thirteen years or so I'm going to have one of those.'

Mandalay was waiting for them at their plot. She was inspecting the mistaelnet leaves with her fine white fingers. 'You've done well,' she said, not looking up from the plant. 'These are thriving.' She brushed dirt from her fingers and stood. 'Today, you're coming with me.' She picked up a large canvas bag from beside her feet. It made a clinking sound as she shouldered it. 'This way.'

Jonathon followed Mandalay and Daidd to the end of the shaenet, near the well. They exited through a rickety wooden door fixed into the stone wall and were swallowed by wild, waist-high green. They tracked a slight path of tamped-down grass that released a minty smell under their feet. Jonathon wanted to look about him to savour these new sights and smells. He wanted to record everything about this auspicious day, but Daidd and Mandalay walked fast, sometimes disappearing behind trees as he struggled to keep up. Ahead, he heard a gurgling, rushing sound.

'Not long now,' Daidd called over his shoulder. He was strangely excitable. Usually contained in his movements, he was thrashing the long grass with his hands as he pressed on after Mandalay. Even the milky-wash of his almost-blind eye was astir. His jitteriness unnerved Jonathon. He wanted to call out to him to stop, to turn back. To return to the quarters with him and await the news that would be coming through The Veya Gate.

After fifteen minutes the grassland thinned out into a clearing. Nestled within it were a series of vertically connected pools, all fed by waterfall. The inner pools were frothy from the pounding of the water, the outer pools glassy and clear. The pools were bordered by boulders, all mossy and verdant. Off to one side of the clearing was a table and chairs piled with towels and clothes.

In the pools, four women were chatting animatedly to one another in Vaik. One of them lifted her arm languidly from the water. Diamond-drops hung from her elbow and plopped to the surface. Her skin was threaded with red and blue veins and hung loose and bat-like from her bones. She brought her arm down hard against the water, making a tremendous splash. The other Vaik shrieked in protest.

'Mandalay,' the splashing Vaik called, her voice rich and almost manly, 'what have you brought us?'

'Treats, my darling ones. Treats.'

Mandalay placed her bag on the table and drew out a small, sealed container, a bottle of water and several glasses. She kicked off her shoes and tripped nimbly over the boulders to the pool. She knelt on the spongy moss and dropped a kiss on the older lady's forehead. The lady gave Mandalay a look of great affection then turned her gaze on Daidd and Jonathon. Her grey eyes were unflinching in the wrinkled pockets of her lids.

'Time to unwrap the presents.' She laughed wickedly. 'Remove your masjythra, both of you. Let us see what you are made of.'

Jonathon pulled the garment over his head. A light breeze rippled across his sweat, his penis shrivelled into his body. He pressed experimental fingers to his chest, but the tenderness was almost gone. He had not bruised.

'Turn around.'

Jonathon and Daidd turned slowly before the Vaik in the pool. Jonathon had the feeling that he was goods being appraised at auction.

'Nice. Very nice. And have we drinks, my darling Mandalay? It's not a party without a drink.'

Mandalay began to stand up, but the woman gestured for her to stay where she was. 'No, no. I will do the honours. I'm pruning in here.' She clambered out of the pool and picked her way over the smooth rocks to the table. She reached up and coiled her thinning hair in her hand, streaming out the water, then draped an orange robe around her shoulders.

Jonathon had never seen the naked body of an old woman before. He had never even imagined it. Intellectually, of course, he knew that he and Adalia would age, but the physical reality of it — what those bodies would look like, smell like, feel like — he'd never considered. Those years between the half-century and death were not so much a mystery to him as they were an undiscovered planet. The body moving now to mix a drink from the things Mandalay had lain out on the table simply did not exist for him.

Yet here it was.

She was of middling height and slightly stooped at the shoulders. Long threads of iron-grey hair sprouted in patches from her scalp. Her face was deeply lined but her eyes were sparkling and mischievous. Her slack breasts pointed earthward. In fact, all her skin seemed to crave the earth. Even her knees had a hound-dog expression.

Her movements were sure. She poured water into the glasses, then spooned powder from the container into each one. The water swirled and turned the same verdant green as the moss on the boulders. She ferried glasses to each of the Vaik in the pool, then returned and offered a glass to Daidd, who accepted it eagerly.

The woman turned to Jonathon. 'This is not a command,' she said, raising the glass to him, 'this is an offer.'

He had a strong curiosity to try the sterysh. A drug cooked up by the Vaik would make coke seem like a downer.

He reached for the glass, but something stayed his hand. His arm fell back by his side.

'No thank you, Mistress.'

'As you wish. Now come, Treats, come to the pool.'

Jonathon felt his way carefully over the slippery green rocks and lowered himself into the perfectly clear water. It was like stepping into a mirror. Pebbles, smooth as boiled lollies, twinkled in blue and duck-egg grey on the bottom. He gripped them beneath his toes, and that was when he felt the twist from some previously unknown sack in his stomach. He'd done his reading. He knew how slowly and painfully the womb released what it had nurtured.

Jonathon waited, wanting his body to bend in Adalia's direction again. Opposite him, Daidd sat on a slab of submerged rock, the water line at his nipples. His penis, clearly visible in the crystalline water, was hard and at the ready. One of the Vaik — a woman who wore her hair in absurdly girlish plaits — straddled him, her back to Jonathon, and began kissing him. Jonathon was acutely aware of the suck and drip of tongues and mouths. He watched Daidd's fingers stroke the curve of her back, the raisin-like moles and patches of dried, friable skin. Beside him, the Vaik opened their legs to the cool water, and stroked themselves.

Jonathon was revolted.

He felt physically sick at the idea of parting the grey-pink lips of these crones and pressing his tongue at their withered centres. To smell the decay rising from them.

The woman opposite him was moving up and down Daidd's shaft now. His face emerged and disappeared as she rose and fell, rose and fell. He wore the same expression of concentration Jonathon had seen when he'd fucked the young Vaik in the field. *How does he do it?* Was the sterysh working its magic, transforming each woman into a nymph of the pool? Or had Daidd disappeared far inside himself, running complicated formulas in a panic room in his mind, abandoning his body to whatever was happening to it?

The woman moved faster now, sending ripples out to the rest of them as she rode towards her pleasure. She cried out and threw her head back. Her cry was mistaken by the birds for one of their own, and their answering call filled the clearing. Jonathon wanted to flee, but he didn't.

He stayed, now on his knees in the grass, now prone on the stone shelf in the shallows as the Vaik directed. His cock was obediently rigid. It was partly fear, he knew, that kept him hard. These Vaik were high and they were old, but they were still Vaik — trained from infancy to defend themselves and their civilisation. He had chosen submission, and now he had to honour that choice. Did any of them guess, when his face contorted, that it wasn't with pleasure but pain? The strange, phantom pain that connected him to Adalia and to the tiny, wizened creature she was straining to bring forth.

The message came just before two in the morning. He was dozing, skating over a thin layer of sleep. His dick was chafed and raw, and his chin scratchy and angry. One of the old Vaik's nails had left half-moons in the underside of his wrist. A young man in a red masjythra, grizzled with fatigue, delivered the message: an A4 page folded in half. Jonathon struck a match so he could read in the darkness. And there it was, the ballpoint scrawl that confirmed what he already knew.

> Beautiful baby girl born at 12.04, after eleven hours of labour, 3.25 kilos. Head of dark hair like her daddy. Fingers and toes in all the right places and doing all the right things. Mother and daughter both doing well and expect to leave hospital the day after tomorrow. Both send love to you.

Jonathon read the note through again, then retracted his head and torso. He dove underneath the covers, drew the quilt over and around him, and wept.

It was the last day of work before the office closed for the Christmas holidays, and the final party preparations were in full swing. Jonathon sat at his desk, his tie unloosened despite the warm air purring from the vents in the parquetry floor. He sat upright in his square leather chair, his back to the sheet of glass that broadcast the dipping sun, and watched as two of the poodles moved from partition to partition.

Between them, Clara and Jureece had spent the best part of the week upturning boxes of tinsel, candy-canes, baubles and strings of gaudy beads. Jureece, a tall brunette who dressed like an escapee from a 1950s typing pool, was stringing pearlescent lights from one partition to another. Her pencil skirt and Mary Janes were paired with a tight red t-shirt that said 'Santa, I can explain'. Her pink tongue protruded slightly as she festooned the partition walls.

'Ready?' Clara asked from behind the partition.

'Ready.'

Jureece clapped her hands as the lights blinked on. Clara emerged from the partition, and the two of them stood back to admire their handiwork. Clara was the shorter and more studious of the two. Jonathon had noticed that she wore high collars and turtleneck sweaters to hide a purple birthmark that bloomed up her chest and onto her neck.

'I think it's too low on that side.' Jureece pointed. 'Let's try lifting it up about an inch.'

Clara re-pinned the lights. 'Better?'

'Perfect.'

Most of Jonathon's colleagues had given up any pretence at doing work. They were gathered in clusters around the office, chatting. The bar didn't officially open for another hour but bottles of champagne were already being passed between work stations. Every few minutes Jonathon heard the muffled pop of a cork and the slosh of liquid into a coffee cup. The god-awful muzak that was usually piped into the office had been replaced with god-awful carols. The head of HR, already a bottle of bubbles down, trumpeted a rolled-up wad of papers every time the saxophone blared between verses about chestnuts and sleighbells and snowball fights.

Jonathon swivelled away from his colleagues and rang Adalia's number again. It was still engaged. He swore under his breath. He checked his emails, but there was nothing but the faux-personalised season's greetings sent from office to office and firm to firm like some wispy smoke signal. He stood up and moved to the polished mahogany shelves that lined one wall of his office. His in-tray was just as empty as when he'd last checked it forty-five minutes ago. He sighed and sat down again.

Clara and Jureece had reached his office. They knocked, although the door was open. He gestured for them to come in. Clara placed a box on his table, careful not to scratch the timber that was so glossy it looked like glass. 'Yours is the last office so we're running a bit low on supplies.' She poked around in the box and came up with a bristling rope of gold tinsel. 'Would you like this? Or how about this?' She pulled out a large green wreath: the holly was discoloured and the pine cones drooped from dusty clusters of berries. 'It looks a bit sad but we can fix it up.'

Jureece shook her can of snow. 'Or we could stencil some snowflakes on your window?'

'Not right now, ladies, I've still got work to do.'

Jureece pulled a face. 'No you don't. No one does. C'mon, it's Christmas, where's your festive spirit?'

'Okay then, the wreath,' said Jonathon, figuring it would be the least-fuss item. 'You can put it up on my door.'

Jureece smiled. 'See. That wasn't so hard, was it?' She tossed her hair triumphantly over one shoulder, revealing Christmas tree earrings that dangled from her lobes.

'Have you tried the punch?' Clara asked. 'We put fresh pineapple in it and, like, a gallon of champagne. It's delicious.'

'Not yet. A few more loose ends to tie up and then I'll have some. I promise.'

'Okay.'

They secured the wreath to Jonathon's office door, reattaching the loose cones with superglue and polishing the holly with a tissue. As they were on their way out, Thomas — head of Government and Media Relations — invited the girls into his office, which was next to Jonathon's. Thomas' office had been one of the first to be decorated, so it was already bursting with baubles; nonetheless, he insisted he wanted more. He'd have his hands in the boxes, Jonathon knew, as an excuse to press close to the young women.

Jonathon tried Adalia again.

This time she picked up. 'Hello?'

'Babe, there you are. I've been trying to get through for an hour and a half. What's going on? Are you on your way?' His words came in a rush, and were more accusatory than he'd intended.

'Just give me one second, honey.' She turned her head from the phone and addressed the chorus of voices behind her. 'Not that one, the first photo. The aerial shot. Yes, yes. That one, good. Theresa, did that file come in from The Dryans, yet? The one on the spate of Christmas present robberies? Can you follow that up, please? Thanks – Sorry, darling,' she was back, breathless, 'it's bedlam here. Why is it everything is guaranteed to go to shit the week before Christmas? It's like some inviolable law of print media.'

'What time will you get here?'

'I'll be there as soon as I can. I've got maybe another hour to get this sorted, then I'll freshen up and head over in a cab.'

'So two hours?' Jonathon sounded peevish, even to himself.

'Maybe two and a half.'

He was silent.

'You know, Jonathon, I've been pretty bloody patient with the demands of your work this year. It wouldn't kill you to send some support back my way.'

This was too true for straight-out contradiction, but still it annoyed him. Adalia didn't have to work. None of the other directors' wives worked. What's more, he was actually bucking the trend in *wanting* his wife at the Christmas party.

'Let me know when you're on your way.'

'I will. I love you.'

He paused fractionally before answering. 'I love you too.'

Adalia hung up first. He held the phone a foot above its cradle then dropped it. He enjoyed the crashing sound. He picked it up and dropped it again.

He searched his inbox hopefully for some urgent, overlooked task that would take his mind from the impending blankness of the Christmas break. There was nothing but the annual message from the chairman of the board to the CEO and his directors.

> *Gentlemen, let me take this opportunity to wish you and your families a safe, happy and restorative Christmas break. I think we can all agree it's been a great year. Despite the contraction in the economy and a rise in the unemployment and interest rates, we've acquired more than four hundred million dollars in new accounts. Our organic growth has also continued strongly. Winning new business is one thing, but retaining our existing clients and encouraging them to take up additional service offerings in an increasingly competitive environment is another. I've always said our reputation is good, our delivery is better. And you continue to make that true.*
>
> *It would be remiss of me not to mention the outstanding contribution of Jonathon Bridge and his team over the past six months. Jonathon has exemplified our core values of passion, dedication and commitment to excellence.*

The email went on to mention the contributions of other team members before ending in the customary exhortation to rest up and return in the new year ready for even greater things. Jonathon knew that his colleagues were mentioned largely for form's sake and as a salve to the CEO, who was beginning to feel the hot press of Jonathon's breath on his neck. He – Jonathon – was the reason for the fat dividend cheques and the bonuses bouncing into their accounts. Electricity surged through him. He had done incredible things this year, pushed himself beyond what he'd thought was possible.

He permitted himself a smile. Everything was good. Everything would be fine.

But then, as it always did, the electricity spluttered and spent itself, and the hollows grew darker and deeper. The firm would not reopen for six weeks. Six weeks without the deadlines, targets and milestones that were the coathangers of his life. He had thought that marrying Adalia would magically change it all, but when he let his mind drift towards the next month and a half he felt an incipient panic. Like a man who collapses at the end of a marathon but can't command his legs to stop moving; so he just lies there, upturned and pedalling, like a beetle on its back.

Unlike his brothers and his friends, Jonathon had always dreaded the death of one year and the slow crawl towards another. No school, no sport, no structure. He'd rattled around his parents' house looking for something to do, warding off the feeling that he was slipping out of time. He would slap his hands, hard, against the walls just to feel the sting of it. To remind himself that he was matter; substantial. He apportioned time into tasks to ward off the catatonia: run from the tip of their long, sweeping driveway to the fence line of trees that marked the start of the state forest. Look up and memorise sixty new Vaik words every week. Read all the books on world history in the local library in Dewey decimal order. The tasks were, in themselves, unimportant, and he didn't retain much of what he read. But they sustained him until the new year gathered momentum and the comforting routine returned. Stillness smelt rank to him.

He looked at his watch. Ten minutes had passed. He checked his phone in case Adalia had texted. She hadn't. Irritated, he reached up and loosened his tie. 'Fuck this,' he muttered. 'Where's the punch?' He slipped his jacket from the back of his chair, put it on and strode out of his office, closing and locking the door.

Christmas had vomited all over the office. Baubles dangled from the ceiling, some so low that he had to sweep them aside with his hand as he made his way to the large meeting room. The smell of cinnamon-and-clove air freshener hung thickly in the air.

'Here he is,' said the head of HR, thumping him on the back with his papers/trumpet. 'The man of the hour deigns to leave the office and join us.' There was a muffled snickering from everyone around him.

So they've read the email, Jonathon thought. *Good.*

'I am a man of the people after all, Arie old man.' More snickering. 'So where's this punch I've been hearing so much about?'

Jureece was at his elbow, holding a square glass with plum-coloured liquid in front of him. He noticed that her nails were the same colour as the punch. 'Thank you.'

'You're welcome.'

'Where's Adalia?' asked Arie.

'On her way, apparently. There's some crisis or other at the office. Always happens at this time of year. Or so I'm advised.'

'Then you're at your leisure?' said Thomas, who appeared at his elbow. 'The cat's away and the dog will play. Come. Come along, children.'

Jonathon followed Thomas, Arie and Jureece out of the meeting room and through the maze of hallways to the teleconference room. It was dark. The star-shaped dialups were piled on the table like a UFO junkyard. The imposing glass windows showed a darkening sky. Beneath the first twinkle of the streetlights, shoppers paused at department-store windows and bit into candied nuts still warm from the street vendor's grill.

Thomas sat down and took a small vial from his pocket. He carefully tapped the white substance onto the tabletop and chopped at it with his credit card — his corporate card, Jonathon noticed. He hummed 'Jingle Bells' as he cut and recut, then apportioned the powder into straight white lines. 'Give me some of that paper,' he said to Arie.

'You want my precious trumpet?'

'Just hand it over.'

Arie made a show of peeling one layer away from his 'instrument' and handing it over to Thomas. 'Merry Christmas.'

'Big spender, you.' Thomas carefully tore the paper in half then tore it again. He rolled it into a thin straw and held it in his fingers as if it was a precious relic. 'For you, good sir: exemplifier of corporate values and the reason I was able to buy my kids ski trips for Christmas.'

'You're going skiing for Christmas? Where?'

Thomas shook his head. 'I said the kids. I have, ah, other plans.' He held the thin straw out to Jonathon, who hesitated. He hadn't done much in the way of recreational drugs since he'd met Adalia, but it *was* Christmas. And a party. And she hadn't even bothered to show up yet. He slipped the straw into his nostril, bent to the table and hoovered the fine white powder into his brain. He righted himself, ice crystals sprinkling across his peripheral vision. The crystals multiplied, leaping from neuron to synapse until his nerves and arteries were lit up like a Christmas tree.

Arie methodically arranged another line. 'For you, good lady.'

Jureece bent down to the table, and Jonathon noticed how firm and ripe her bottom was in her grey, woollen pencil skirt. She stood up, was still for a moment, anticipating. Then she giggled like a schoolgirl and tossed her hair over her shoulder, catching it in her Christmas tree earrings.

'You're tangled,' Jonathon said. He reached for her hair and gently pulled the threads of glossy chestnut from the clasp.

'Thank you,' she said, so close he felt the warmth of her breath on his neck.

'Any time.'

The magic glittered through his body. He had done well.

Exceptionally well. His bank account bulged. He had a beautiful apartment in the middle of the city that captured the skyline in three directions. He was a powerful man who would keep climbing. It was clear to him now as he stood in front of the window to the city that all would be well.

He felt Jureece sidle up to him, her shoulder next to his. 'Look at this view,' she sighed. 'I never tire of it. When I first started I'd come in here every day just to watch the city going about its business. It always makes me feel that I've arrived somehow.'

He nodded. 'I know exactly what you mean.'

'I really feel that I have something to offer the company, into the future.'

'Have you applied to stay on?'

'Of course. But you know.'

He didn't need her to finish the sentence. His firm kept on one, maybe two of the poodles each year. The rest were flung out after their internship to second-tier firms or further study or ... Actually, Jonathon had no idea what else they did. He'd never troubled himself to inquire.

She inched nearer to him. 'Do you think I have something to offer?'

He turned to look at her, the warmth of the drug coursing through his veins, fighting off stillness and death. Jureece bent her head slightly, so she looked up at him through her dark lashes. Her gaze was liquid and inviting.

His phone buzzed in his pocket. He took it out and glanced at the screen. Adalia.

He answered it. 'Hi, babe. You on your way?'

There was a crackle of static.

'I can't hear you, you're dropping out. What did you say?'

'... going to take me a bit longer ... late story ... without me ...'

'What? What did you say?'

But she was gone. Or the connection had been lost. He swore under his breath.

'Was that your girlfriend?'

'My wife.'

'Will she be here this evening?'

'Allegedly. At some point.'

'Well,' Jureece reached out and lightly grazed her claret fingernails along his lapel before straightening it, 'I'll just have to do my best to keep you entertained until then.'

He downed more coke, more punch, more flattery. The looming break swam away from him, ceased to exist, had never existed. The Christmas carols rang through the halls and the boardrooms. He tripped over people kissing beneath mistletoe tacked to doorframes and bent his head to tables of glossy jet where piles of fairy dust disappeared and reappeared and disappeared again. He looked at his phone from time to time to see where Adalia was and then, annoyed at himself, returned to his office and dropped his phone on his desk to keep himself from looking anymore.

Jureece and Clara swam at him down a long corridor. Jureece held a bottle of champagne in one hand and was struggling to support a very drunk Clara, who sagged beneath her.

'A little help?' Jureece said, laughing.

Jonathon took Clara's weight on one side and together they made slow progress to The Quiet Room. They paused for Clara to be violently sick into a bucket they found in the cleaner's cupboard. Then, unsure how to empty it, they just left it in there.

The Quiet Room had been a whim of the former head of personnel and resources who'd thought it would be helpful for the staff to have 'a space where they can connect with their creativity'. The room had powder-blue walls and an enormous aquarium running the length of its back wall. The fish swished their tails inquisitively as Jonathon and Jureece lowered Clara onto the soft suede couch. She curled her knees up to her chest, sighed contentedly and promptly went to sleep. Jonathon draped his jacket over her to keep her warm. Above her, a poster was tacked to the wall that read, 'Success comes to those who choose it.'

Jonathon fucked Jureece as Clara slept. She was pliable and theatrical, offering herself this way and that and always – he knew – with one eye on her future. He hadn't been with a woman other than Adalia for a long time. Jureece's body was womanly, with pendulous breasts that he fucked with relish, but still she had left childhood behind so recently you could catch the scent of it on her. She was smooth and perfect in the way that youth is always smooth and perfect.

He had to encourage her with his hands to go down on him. She looked at the ground when she opened her mouth to take him in. Even when he wound his hand around her hair to pull and push her up and down his cock, she didn't look up. Not like Adalia. This thought made him resentful. He couldn't even fuck another woman – privately, furtively – without inviting his wife in to share the experience.

Frustrated, he tightened his grip on Jureece's hair and pulled her away from him. He gestured for her to lie down, then kicked off his trousers and underwear. He left his socks on. He dropped to the floor, planted one hand to the side of her head and gripped himself with the other, probing for the entrance to Jureece.

Clara mumbled something in her sleep, and Jonathon and Jureece froze. She quieted and then began snoring.

'Tilt your hips up for me.'

'Like this?'

'Yeah good.' He moved into her and let the rhythm of it take him over. It was so filthy and so wrong and so good. 'Do you like fucking?' he whispered into her ear.

'Fucking you? Yes.'

'Who else have you fucked here?' It excited him, the idea that she was available to take the notes in their meetings and drop files of background research on their desks and open her legs to their hunger. He pictured her, naked except for her high heels, sitting on his desk with her legs spread, each foot resting on a different chair. Her long dark hair caught up in the French roll she often wore and her spectacles perched on the bridge of her nose. Her arms behind her, hands firmly planted on the desk so her back was arched. Her mouth closed with her lips open and wet, her eyes attentive, waiting to receive them as they needed.

'No one. Just you.'

He didn't believe her, and would have thought less of her if he had. Far better insurance to have offered these luscious tits and warm, tight cunt to a couple of the other executives. It's what Jonathon would have done. He came inside her then collapsed on top of her, breathing hard. 'I hope that was okay.'

'It was wonderful,' she purred.

'No, I mean, that I came inside of you. I hope that was okay.'

'Oh. Oh, um, yeah. That should be fine.'

They dressed, but Jonathon left his jacket behind to keep Clara warm, and rejoined the party. Adalia still hadn't arrived. The outlines of the night blurred and bled. Later he remembered being in a small space at one point – it could have been the stationery store – with someone giving him a hand job. Remembered coming across the CIO and Arie getting it on in the stairwell, their pale, hairy bottoms looming at him. Yelps of disgust as the foul contents of the cleaner's cupboard were discovered.

At some point deep into the night, Adalia finally arrived. He both hoped and feared she'd smell the other women on him. He pulled her to him, daring her to find traces of lipstick, perfume, the distinctive yeasty scent of female intimacy.

Could he push Adalia to perform some feat of magic that would fill him up?

Or would she just leave him?

The fear of it iced him. It froze the follicles at the base of his neck and chilled the very pads of his toes. Adalia loved him. Adalia, who was solid and real and effectual in a way that he was not, loved him. And that meant there had to be a self there to love.

There was some unpleasantness in the new year when they all returned to work. Clara had woken the next morning, sick and churning, to find she was naked from the waist down, her thighs sticky. She'd dressed herself, shakily, and called Jureece. Against Jureece's advice Clara had gone to the hospital, and then the police. It had blown over by the time the working year was in full swing, and nothing came of it. But Jonathon felt uneasy. He wanted to call Jureece to ask after Clara — but, well, that would've been awkward.

His memories of what had ensued after he'd left The Quiet Room were shifting and changeable. Segments of the night rushed at him sometimes, then receded. *Why*, he thought, *didn't I stay with her? Why didn't I at least move her into my office where I could have kept an eye on her?* He repeated the questions to himself but the answers didn't come.

Among his colleagues there was a palpable silence about it, and this silence unsettled him more. The men he worked with were generally boastful or cavalier about their sexual conquests, and sorties with the poodles were an open secret. Keeping mum about a blow job in the photocopy room or a tumble after client drinks would've been considered bad form. But the silence. The silence said that whoever had fucked Clara knew she wasn't up for it.

Jonathon found himself looking sideways at his colleagues, trying to place when and where he'd seen them that night. He wanted to enlist Adalia's help. She'd been by far the soberest person at the party and was more observant of little details than he was. But he couldn't draw too near to his encounter in The Quiet Room with Jureece.

The question of what had happened to Clara attached itself to him like a remora. He sought out little details where he could, asking one of the more effectual HR people to let him know where Clara had ended up. When he found out she'd landed a pretty good job with a reputable firm he was pleased, though he couldn't honestly say whether she'd been a wonderful or indifferent employee.

As summer peaked and began its slow roll towards autumn, Jonathon's sleep became troubled. Gone was the mostly swift and blissful slide to oblivion of his first season at The Fortress. Night after night he woke in the dark, his heart thudding. Dreams folded into other dreams but in all of them he carried a baby; propelled by some nameless force through fields and deserted houses and highways thick with cars, sirens and panic, always he had the baby in his arms. Fear of some stalking blackness meant he could neither rest nor put the baby down. She turned her little face into his neck. He felt her wet breath and inhaled the warm-bread fumes from her downy head. This was his child, of that he was certain. And though his muscles screamed for relief and his lungs threatened to give out, he pushed on.

As the nightmare receded, Jonathon mourned the weight of the baby in his arms. He lay there, unmoving, recalling the impress of her fontanelle against his thumb, her chubby fist pressed to his neck. The surprisingly noisy snuffle and whinny of her breathing. He encouraged the lingering tightness in his arms, unconsciously bundling the bedclothes against his chest and cradling them.

Jonathon's craving for his child was a sensation so new, so wholly without precedent, it shocked him. It was as if, at the age of forty-two, he had been shown a new colour or number. His desires and senses, which had seemed augmented and multiplying, now contracted to a single point. He just wanted to gaze down at the sleeping babe in his arms, to lift her gently to his face and nuzzle her warmth, drink in that heady smell.

Yet 'want' wasn't the right word. It wasn't a desire or a whim or an inclination or an ambition or any of the other things that he had attached to the word 'want' before. It was a cellular howling for his baby that shaded into violence. If Mandalay had appeared to him and offered him his child in exchange for strangling the man — nameless, unknown — who inhabited the cabin next door, he would have done it. Done it without pause. Done it impatiently.

Slowly his heart returned to its familiar, silent work. He plumped his pillow and felt something stiff in the down. He wriggled his fingers into the sleeve and brushed against a piece of paper. It was A4 and folded as many times as it could be folded. Jonathon smoothed it out with the heel of his hand. It was thick and creamy, like the sketchpad used by Ulait. He scratched a match against the wall and surveyed the crudely executed lead-pencil drawing. A man was being hurled through the air by a stick figure with a ponytail and breasts. Underneath, in capitals: 'WAS IT GOOD FOR YOU TOO?'

Jonathon felt nauseated. The drawing was clumsy. The only embellishments were a bow in Ulait's hair, breasts with the nipples coloured so darkly the paper had been indented, and a massive, erect penis on the Jonathon figure.

The long match sizzled out in his fingers. How long had the picture been there? The incident had occurred weeks ago. Only Daidd, Jonathon, Ulait and about six of her friends had been there. He tried to convince himself that it was the work of one of the girls, the product of an overheated adolescent mind. But sex was such a part of the Vaik way of life that it probably wouldn't occur to them to draw smutty pictures. They had no need of it. And Daidd, why would he leave this obscene scrawl for Jonathon to find?

The answer was that he hadn't. Jonathon realised that he knew who was responsible. He'd encountered only one man at The Fortress sick enough to do such a thing.

Still, how had he known? What did he want?

Jonathon was bent low over a norsling. Overnight, the beds had been infested by aphids. These insects were chameleons, transforming from their natural sickly pale green to blend with the plant: now purple along the bulb, now green along the stem. They tunnelled and gorged until the norsling collapsed on itself. The Vaik refused to use any form of pesticide, so the pests had to be plucked with tweezers, placed in a jar and drowned. Jonathon and Daidd had been kneeling in the beds since sun-up, their faces pressed close to the plants and their eyes blurry from concentration.

Daidd's gaze kept wandering from the plants to Jonathon and back again. A couple of times he cleared his throat as if to speak. 'I'm going to the shed,' he said eventually.

'Okay.'

Daidd returned with two steaming mugs of tea. He handed one to Jonathon and sat beside him. He rubbed his eyes, then cleared his throat again. 'You don't look well.'

'I'm fine.'

Daidd sipped his tea. 'You're not sleeping.'

Jonathon didn't reply.

'Talk to Mandalay. She can give you a tonic.'

'I'm fine.'

There was the slight wavering movement he'd been waiting for. He plunged for the aphid with his tweezers and plied its sticky feet from the plant. Trapped, the creature reverted to its sickly green and wheeled its many legs and feelers in the air. Its helplessness provoked Jonathon. He held it under the water in the jar, watching as it cycled its limbs ever faster in its panic, then slowed to a twitch and finally stopped. He loosened the tweezers and the body floated up to join the other dead aphids. They released a frothy white scum. He sealed the lid and shook up the jar, dissolving the scum. The aphids appeared to be cartwheeling in space.

Jonathon had developed the habit, before he fell asleep, of re-reading the note from Adalia announcing the birth of their daughter. Then he would hold the ultrasound photo against his chest, as if to cradle the baby. Finally, he'd wriggle his fingers into the sleeve of his pillow, feel the crisp outline of the drawing and withdraw them. Then he'd read the note again, and try to sleep.

But three nights ago he had inched his fingers into the pillow and felt nothing. He peeled the pillowcase back. Still nothing. He pulled the pillow from the sleeve and turned the sleeve inside out. The drawing – the disgusting, sickening drawing – was gone. He checked the gap between the bed and the wall. He riffled through the blankets. Squeezed himself under the bed and examined the floorboards. The drawing was gone.

Someone had taken it.

The idea that the isvestyii had been in his room, between his sheets, revolted him. That he had seen, touched (please god let him not have touched) the ultrasound of Jonathon's child that he kept on the rickety bedside table was intolerable.

A wave of nausea rolled over him. He closed his eyes and breathed slowly in and out.

'I'm taking you to the sick bay,' said Daidd.

Jonathon shook his head, his eyes still closed. He was counting slowly backwards from thirty, resisting the sweaty heat at his temples and across his shoulders that told him he was going to throw up. His nose twitched at the faint scent of lavender on the breeze. He opened his eyes, but Mandalay wasn't there. Only

Daidd hovered above him, looking uncertain as to whether he should say what was on his mind.

Jonathon woke in a cold sweat. Night after night he was being wasted by these dreams in which he was compelled to carry his baby through ruined landscapes, running from some nameless fear. Unable to take rest. His heart thudded and his palms were clammy. A memory burst in on him, sudden and unwelcome, of ridiculing a colleague who had filed a stress claim years ago. She'd said she was suffering from panic attacks. The claim was rejected, and the woman eventually resigned. Jonathon had thought she was a crank, trying to pull a swift one on the firm. What, after all, was a panic attack but the disordered rambling of an insufficiently regulated body? He had no patience for the undisciplined, yet here he was. His nerves were plugged into the grid, frying him from the inside. His glands were fulfilling orders for adrenaline around the clock.

He swung his feet out from the bed, steadied himself and stood up. He leant his elbows on the windowsill and looked out on the moonless night. The rush and whisper of the waves calmed him a little. He pictured Adalia asleep on their massive bed, their baby next to her. He was nearing the halfway mark of his tenure at The Fortress. He could do this.

Calmer now, he returned to bed. He shook his sheet out and plumped up his pillow.

No. It couldn't be.

Something was in the pillowcase. He reached into the sleeve and drew out a folded piece of paper. He dropped the drawing as if it was hot and stared at it. It had landed perfectly square on a floorboard, as if it had been placed there precisely. He stepped over it and left his quarters. He leapt as quickly as the gradient allowed down the zigzag ramp to the door of the residential quarters. It was unlocked, so he stepped onto the verandah and took the path towards the bathhouse.

He began running. He ran blindly, not caring where he was going. He needed to feel the illusion of freedom, of motion. That he could leave if he wished to. His elbows pumped at his sides and sweat ran into his eyes. Low stone walls flashed in the dark beside him and the owls hooted. A bird, disturbed, swooped low and flew with him for a while. His feet, tough and callused, didn't feel the stones and branches. After a few miles he came to a wide field. He stopped, lifted his head to the vast canopy of stars above and screamed himself hoarse.

He slept out in the open that night, knowing he would not be able to find his way back in the dark. He curled up on the grass, his masjythra stretching itself around him, his head on his arm. He was drenched in sweat, but the summer night was mild. He closed his eyes and listened to the scuffling and settling of birds in the undergrowth. He was not afraid.

The sun woke him. He sat up and watched the gentle illumination of the earth. He was in a little copse of springy grass. Beside him was a broad, cultivated field. Beans, he guessed. That was a good sign. An assignment would no doubt be here at some point today to water the field. He could wait for them and be guided back to his quarters. He stood up and brushed grass and dirt from his legs and arms. He thought back to summer camp, all those survivalist skills he had supposedly acquired as a boy. How to start a fire; how to use shadows and the angle of the sun as a compass. He was terribly, terribly thirsty and his throat was sore. He traced the low stone wall bounding the field until he found the canvas water bags. He drained one and used a sprinkling from another to wash his face.

He sat with his back against the wall, his legs straight out in front of him, watching the last of the darkness dissolve as the sun arced behind him and over the field. He was right: the stalks were fat with bean pods that drooped like chandeliers. This field would be harvested very soon. The grass and stones underneath him were slightly wet with dew. The morning was warm, but the season had palpably shifted.

He felt calm and curiously well rested, as if the night out in the open had cleansed him. The drawing now seemed puerile and not worth his notice. He imagined telling Adalia about how the longing for their child had supercharged his emotions, rendering even silly things portentous. He enjoyed rehearsing these conversations with Adalia, bringing her close. He saw the two of them, naked under their silky sheets, the baby monitor crooning beside them. It was late, the city no more than a slight hum beneath them. They were propped up on pillows, awake but with sleep close and easy, whispering to each other. He told her about the drawing and she laughed that laugh of hers, and he thrilled to the sound. He swept his fingers gently along the side of her face and through her hair. She smiled and closed her eyes.

Jonathon heard the trudge of feet moving along the path behind him and smiled at his prescience. He didn't move until the assignment was close enough for him to hear their talk, then he stood and watched their approach. They were silver masjythra, like him. The pure morning light gave them the look of a school of fish moving as one in a clear pool. There were twelve men, most of them bunched together, a straggler at the back. They carried a couple of canvas sacks between them: one for gardening tools, one for food.

Jonathon raised his hand in greeting as the group approached. The man at the front was vaguely familiar from the dining room.

'Bridge,' he said.

Jonathon nodded.

'Have you any injuries?'

'None.'

'Good. The assignments have all been instructed to be on the alert for you. You're to work with us today and return at close. We have food.' He gestured to the man holding one of the sacks. He unzipped it, pulled out a bread cob and handed it to Jonathon.

'Thank you.'

Jonathon waited for the man to indicate whether he—Jonathon—was in any sort of trouble for running off. But he knew enough of Vaik ways to understand that if they wanted him confined to quarters all night, they would bar the front doors. He tore into the chewy, dense bread.

'Oorsel beans.' The man nodded towards the field. 'We're to cut them and pile them up. A cart is being sent for them this afternoon. You done oorsel beans before?'

Jonathon swallowed his mouthful. 'No. Goosen's Trial, mallow and herbs, mainly.'

'Goosen's? Fuck that. Oorsels this ripe are easy. Don't even need secateurs, they just pop right off.'

Jonathon dusted the breadcrumbs from his hands as the assignment entered the field from the gate. The men acknowledged him with slight nods. A couple of them asked, 'All right?' It amused him to think how different this mode of communication was from the one he was used to: the handshakes, the exchange of business cards, the subtle but laden language of which credit card would prevail at the close of lunch. The man who'd greeted him handed out large cotton sacks and assigned each worker a row.

Jonathon opened his sack and dropped it at his feet. The oorsel pod came loose with barely a twist. He sliced it open with his thumbnail and pulled a green, kidney-shaped bean from the sleeve. He popped it into his mouth; it tasted grassy and slightly sour. How he'd hated oorsels as a boy. They'd been a staple at summer camp at Lake Wykaita, always over-boiled and mushy. He'd been surprised years later when, on a date with Adalia, he'd stabbed one with his knife off her plate and enjoyed it.

The assignment worked fast. When the sacks were full they emptied them into a pile just outside the field near the path. By midmorning a small hill of glossy bean pods had formed.

Jonathon found the work dull after the shaenet. He missed Daidd and the important plants for which he felt personally responsible. He filled another sack and tramped down the row to empty it. Another man followed him, so close he could hear his breathing. The hairs at the base of Jonathon's neck lifted and he sped up. He went out the gate and upturned his oorsels onto the pile.

'Suit,' said the man behind him.

He turned. The isvestyii was standing right behind him. Jonathon was close enough to see how his lower eyelashes were stuck to his cheek with sweat. The isvestyii poked his pink, wet tongue through the gaps in his teeth. The bulging pink flesh glistened.

A wave of revulsion swamped Jonathon. 'Fuck off, paedo.'

The isvestyii laughed. Some of his spittle landed on Jonathon's cheek.

Jonathon's hands flexed and opened involuntarily. He told himself to turn, walk away and return to his row. With some difficulty he did so. He steadied himself in front of the next plant and began plucking, with rather more ferocity than before. He looked around but there was only one other man in his row.

Not knowing where the isvestyii was made it worse. The beans were at head height, so when the men were at full stretch you could just see the tops of their heads shuffling along the row. Jonathon couldn't see him. He took deep breaths and returned to his task. After a while he became aware of a childish, singsong chant coming from the row behind him.

Suit boy, Suit boy
Don't need rope, when you got some coke
Suit boy, Suit boy

He whirled around and crashed through the row, but the isvestyii had disappeared.

'Cunt,' said Jonathon under his breath.

Adrenaline whipped through his body, accompanied by the percussion of his pulse. He squeezed his eyes tight shut, then relaxed them. In his head he imagined standing before a pile of smooth white rocks, taking one in his hands and moving it a short distance. He took a second rock and moved it. Three rocks. Seven rocks. Twelve rocks. *Aeraevest.*

Suit boy, Suit boy
Gave a job to his secretary
She eighteen so it ain't statutory

It was the sort of song you'd hear in a playground as children jumped rope. It was everywhere at once. The oorsels were singing it, their leaves shaking. It rained from the skies and shimmied in the dirt. Jonathon ran to the end of the row, bowling over a man on his haunches. 'Hey!' he shouted to Jonathon's back.

Jonathon stopped at the close of the row and glanced up and down. The men were gathering beside the pile of oorsels for lunch. He clambered over the wall, a couple of smooth white stones crashing after him.

The man in charge of the assignment came towards him. 'Bridge. What's wrong?'

'Where is he?'

'Who?'

'The isvestyii. The paedo.'

'Looking for me, Suit boy?'

He was behind him again. Him and that mocking voice and shit-eating grin. Jonathon took a swing but he was off balance and the isvestyii easily ducked it. Furious with himself, Jonathon centred his weight in his heels, one foot forward, one behind, and drew his fists in front of his face. The isvestyii laughed and made as if to walk off, but the other men wordlessly corralled him. The isvestyii seemed unsure what to do. He laughed again, uncertainly, and took a few steps forward. The assignment huddled closer, linking arms. The isvestyii was trapped between the stone wall on one side and the arc of the men. His only way out was past Jonathon.

Even through the red mist over his eyes, Jonathon was aware that the men were breathing as one, chests rising and falling. He danced lightly, never taking his eyes off the isvestyii. He'd boxed at summer camp and later at university. He had sharp reflexes but had always been let down by a lack of stamina. *Not a problem now.* His palms itched pleasurably.

The isvestyii was swaying slightly, not like Jonathon but as if falling under the spell of the tightening cluster of men. Their breathing was ratcheting up. Pre-verbal, almost a groan. They were enmeshed in a cloud of sweat and adrenaline. Jonathon darted forward, jabbing at the isvestyii's face, not to hit him but to startle him out of his trance. The isvestyii flinched and shuddered a little.

'Come on, put 'em up, you bastard,' said one of the men. A chorus of grunts swelled around him.

Jonathon jabbed again, closer this time. The isvestyii put his hands up to protect his face, and the men cheered louder.

'Come on, bash the bitch.'

The call was taken up by the assignment in low voices. '*Bash the bitch. Bash the bitch. Bash the bitch.*'

Jonathon rolled his shoulders. A right jab to the nose would do it. He imagined the *pop*, satisfying as a plump zit released, and then the burst of blood. He dropped his shoulder and was raising his arm when he was encased from behind. Strong arms immobilised him. He thrashed but knew it was pointless. The assignment saw whoever stood behind Jonathon, dropped arms and stepped back nonchalantly, as if their arrangement were an accident.

'Stop. Enough.' It was Daidd.

Jonathon ceased resisting and Daidd let him go. The isvestyii released something like a sob and pushed his way through the widening circle.

'You fucking idiot,' Daidd whispered to Jonathon.

'You.' Mandalay's voice, clear and cold behind him. 'We go. Now.'

Mandalay marched them over the rise and towards the main buildings. Jonathon, Daidd and the isvestyii walked in single file behind her, silently. Jonathon felt sick from the unspent adrenaline in his body and his growing fear about what Mandalay was planning to do with him. He hadn't broken his vow, he told himself.

You would have, though, Adalia's voice echoed through his head. *You would have if Daidd hadn't stopped you.*

He did stop me.

Remember your vow, Jonathon: 'I will not raise my hand in anger against anyone at The Fortress.' Or are all your vows negotiable?

This isn't about us, Adalia.

Everything's about us. You're here because of us. For us.

He deserved it. I'm protecting Ulait, alone in that Story-Keeping House. Think of the backpack he took with him to the school. The vaseline. The rope. He deserved it. Mandalay will see that. If she doesn't, I'll demand to see The Woman.

You'll demand, will you? At The Fortress? Adalia's laugh ricocheted off his skull.

As they came in sight of the long verandah at the close of the cherry orchard, Jonathon noticed that the nights were drawing in. He felt less salt-rinded than usual. For the first time he turned his mind towards what winter would be like. Would they be given a warmer uniform or transferred to labour indoors? *All your physical needs will be met by us*, Mandalay had said. Anyway, he had more pressing things to worry about.

Three red masjythra waited at the foot of the steps that led to the verandah and up towards the sleeping quarters and dining hall. Behind them were half a dozen grim-faced Vaik. Jonathon's group marched to the stairs where Mandalay gave a signal. One of the red masjythra took him by the arm and directed him to the left of the building, in the opposite direction to the bathhouse. Two Vaik followed; Daidd and the isvestyii did not.

'What are you doing?' Jonathon asked. 'Where are you taking me?'

But no one answered.

The man holding Jonathon's arm was shorter than him, but stockier. Jonathon made a swift and brutal calculation. He could knock the man down if he needed to. He didn't doubt that the Vaik could do him some damage if they had a mind to, but he was pretty sure he could outrun them. But run where? The wall was impossible to scale. Even if he could find his way to the sea he was no Eshtakai; the waves or a shark would claim him before he made dry land or hailed a passing boat. He would need help.

He glanced sideways at the man escorting him. He was perhaps in his mid-twenties, with no visible scars on his face or arms. Jonathon pretended to stumble to his knees so he could scan the man's upper thigh.

'Sorry,' he said, as the man hauled him upright. The man wasn't branded as an isvestyii. A supplicant, perhaps? Or a national serviceman? Jonathon was good at alliances. Somewhere in his network of influence, of favours owed and gifts conferred, there was something this man wanted or required. All Jonathon needed was an opportunity.

They walked for some time, long enough for the night to close in. His masjythra shifted around him, lengthening and tightening to his body. Whether from fear or cold, his arms thickened with gooseflesh. Strange bird calls passed from tree to tree, the branches casting ghostly shadows along the path.

They arrived at a large stone building with a steeple. 'Stop.' The shorter of the Vaik stepped to the wooden door and sounded the brass knocker three times, paused, then sounded it twice more. By the light of two burning torches staked to the entranceway, Jonathon made out a tumble of gargoyles carved into the threshold. Peering closer, he saw that they were leashed by an imposing woman who held a sceptre in her other hand. The Woman?

The door was opened. Even in the welter of his predicament, Jonathon felt the warm, liquid punch of desire land in his stomach. She held the heavy door with one hand, her arm a thick rope of muscle in the firelight. She stood as tall as Jonathon and nearly as broad. Her white gown was cinched at the waist by a leather pouch from which poked the handle of a small dagger. A Vaikray blade. It glinted in the torchlight. Her blonde hair fell, iron-straight, to her shoulders. Something about her was familiar, eerily so, but Jonathon could not say what.

She exchanged a few Vaik words with one of the women. Her mouth was round and full, her eyes calculating. 'Eminently fuckable' was how Jonathon and his colleagues had described the choicest of the poodles. This woman was more statuesque than any of them had been, and it was impossible to imagine her fetching and carrying coffee and doughnuts, but still she brought the phrase to Jonathon's mind. She turned her gaze on him and seemed to distil everything she needed to know about him in a second or two. *Adalia*, thought Jonathon, *it must be Adalia she reminds me of, the same penetration. The same shrewdness.*

The woman issued a command in Vaik and turned back into the building. The red masjythra guided Jonathon up the stairs and into the darkened hallway. He escorted Jonathon to a room on the second floor, opened the door and stepped aside to let Jonathon pass through.

'Thank you,' Jonathon said, as he entered. 'Don't close the door yet.'

The man hesitated.

Jonathon looked calmly around him, the way he might have inspected a hotel room before tipping the bellboy. 'They're fascinating, these old Vaik buildings. You must have seen a few on your travels through the grounds.'

'A few, yep.' The man's eyes strayed back along the corridor.

'I've been thinking,' Jonathon spoke in a leisurely way, 'that it would be fun to remodel my country residence along Vaik lines. When I leave in a few months.'

The man scuffed his feet on the stone floor, as though it were burning his soles.

Jonathon made a show of examining the wall nearest to him, taking angles with his thumb and index finger. 'Trouble is, of course, the Vaik don't keep architectural plans in the local library.'

'S'pose not.'

'I'll need an expert. Someone who's had an opportunity to study these structures up close. Who's seen a variety of Vaik buildings. Like this one, for instance.'

'That will be all.' A female voice spoke from behind Jonathon. The red masjythra blushed, nodded and closed the door. Jonathon turned in the voice's direction.

The room was a long rectangle lit only by two candles burning on what looked like an altar, though he knew that couldn't be right. The Vaik had no church, no god. The earthen floor gave off a low orange glow as if it were slowly releasing stored sunlight. A wooden bench ran along the perimeter of the room.

'Tell me,' she said archly, 'when did you develop such a passion for Vaik architecture?'

Jonathon stared into the darkness, his heart clawing its way out of his chest. Could this be The Woman speaking to him from the gloom?

'Would you like tea?' Mandalay materialised from the shadows with a steaming goblet in each hand. She seemed to misread the anxiety on his face. 'Don't worry. It's not a sleeping tea.'

He took a goblet from her and she gestured for him to sit down. He didn't want to sit. He wanted to pace. Fight. Negotiate his way out of this charade of submission. He shook his head. 'I'll stand. If it's all the same to you.'

'As you wish.'

Mandalay seated herself on the bench and sipped her tea, staring at the far wall where the candle-shadow played charades: now a bunny rabbit, now a tree grown gnarled and monstrous.

'You have ill will towards the isvestyii,' she said.

Jonathon snorted. 'That's an understatement.'

'Very well. You hate the isvestyii. He sends filthy, flesh-eating bugs crawling over your skin. He arouses all of your fears about your child. You worry for the girl Vaik. For Ulait.' Jonathon started at Ulait's name but Mandalay remained transfixed by the candles. 'When he tore the Goosen's Trial from the ground you saw rope. When you think of the girls, what he did to them, you push it away, but it comes back. You think he deserves death.'

'He does. And the Vaik think so too, or you wouldn't have declared him isvestyii.'

'You presume to know what we think?'

'It's not a presumption, it's a statement of fact. The isvestyii can't be redeemed. He'll dissolve to nothing at the end. Leave nothing. His family will wipe his name from the official documents. The Vaik will kill him and not one single fuck will be given by anyone.'

Mandalay was silent, drinking her tea. When she spoke her voice was low and contemplative. 'They're all dead now, you know. Those girls. Essa died of her injuries. Internal injuries. The surgeons tried to save her, but ...' Mandalay trailed off. 'One of the girls, Sarai, was a promising athlete. A champion runner and high jumper. She refused to train, after the rape. Do you know what I think?'

She stared straight ahead at the altar now, tears streaming down her face and onto her gown. 'I think Sarai stopped believing in her body. She'd thought she was fast. Powerful. But when it mattered her body failed her. She was no match for a man three times her size. She wasn't powerful. She wasn't strong or fast or any of the things she had believed. She was just a girl. And she was nothing.' Mandalay dashed the tears from her face with her hand. 'I think that's why – afterward – she punished her body. First she stopped eating. Then, after a few years, she shot herself full of pills and gear. We wanted her to come here. We offer sanctuary to all those wronged by isvestyii, as you know, but her parents refused to let Sarai come. Not that you can blame them. We keep isvestyii well away from their victims, but her parents, they worried about that. She made it to seventeen. Seventeen years, three months and four days. Which I think is remarkable.'

Jonathon didn't want to hear any more. He wished Mandalay had given him the aniseed tea and he was now sitting, head propped against the wall, her words rolling off his warm narcotic bubble. Instead, they lanced him. They wriggled into the empty spaces inside him, growing louder and sharper.

'After they cut Sarai down from the tree where she hanged herself, they did an autopsy. They found that every inch of her skin she could cover up was lacerated. Cigarette burns on her thighs. Razor scars on her wrists and feet. Puncture wounds she made with a compass on her stomach. Track marks. Bruises. Chemical burns. Her whole body was a map of pain and loathing. And that whole time, the isvestyii you fought today was here. Fed. Clothed. Protected by the Vaik from men who think he deserves a different sort of treatment.'

'He does,' muttered Jonathon.

Mandalay drained the rest of her tea. She tapped her nails on the brass. Shadows flickered on her pale, tear-stained face. 'The third girl we know very little about. Her parents moved away after the rape. We followed her progress for a while but there's not much you can do when people don't want to be found. She lasted the longest. She was twenty-three when she was killed by an oncoming car. Seven people and three cars were involved in that accident. Everyone else walked away with superficial cuts and bruises. One man had a broken ankle. But Julia died.'

'The isvestyii was here the whole time.'

'Yes. For thirteen years by the time Julia was killed in the accident. Four women — Essa, Sarai, Julia and their teacher — all dead. Yet he lives. And he lives here, among us.'

On impulse, not even fully aware that he was doing it, Jonathon pushed away from the wall and knelt at Mandalay's feet. Only when he was reaching for her did he check the sympathetic impulse to touch, to commiserate. He froze, his hand midway between them.

'Sorry,' he said, bringing it slowly back to his side.

Mandalay gave a slight smile, and relief flooded his stomach. 'It's all right.' She leant towards him and kissed him lightly on the lips. Then she pressed harder and opened her mouth. He answered, his tongue finding hers. She tasted of salt and lemon and rage.

He pulled away and lightly kissed her forehead, her cheeks. The tip of her nose. 'Mandalay,' he said softly. 'Mandalay.'

'I hate this,' she sobbed, 'this ... this *fury* you can't do anything with.'

'You *can* do something, though,' he said fiercely. 'Tie the bastard to a stake on the beach and stick a knife in his gullet.'

Mandalay blinked, and a fat tear ran down her face. 'That won't bring those girls back. Won't mend them. Won't bind their parents' hearts.' She sighed. '*That's* my fury. The isvestyii, I almost don't see him. He's a matter of near total indifference to me. He can't hurt women anymore, and he's isolated. An object of scorn. We drip-feed him the threat of violence, and that threat, the anticipation of it, is worse than the actuality. But those girls. Those girls.'

Jonathon did not want to think about the girls. Hesitatingly, he reached for Mandalay's hair and ran his fingers gently though it. His arm was tense, ready to retract if she hardened. Slowly he bent towards the soft red hair in his hands and breathed in the lavender and earth smell. Anything so that he did not have to think.

'Tomorrow we take the isvestyii to The Great Hall,' said Mandalay.

'The Great Hall,' Jonathon murmured, continuing to fixate on her hair.

'It's the place where all Vaik decrees are made. It's where isvestyii are declared. Where we decide if an electii can enter The Fortress as a woman. It's also where we decide if men like you, Jonathon Bridge, can come live among us.'

He ran his fingertips along her bare arm, her skin as reflective as the perimeter wall, his touch butterfly-light.

'You will be there,' she said.

'What?' he said, forgetting himself in his confusion.

'As you are so certain in this matter, you will judge.'

He shook his head. 'What? Me? This is crazy.'

'The Woman has decreed it. We will come for you an hour after sun-up. Sleep well tonight. Rest.' She gently removed his hand from her arm, then took him by the shoulders and drew him upright. 'I must go.'

'Mandalay, wait! This makes no sense. I don't understand.'

She gave him a sad, rueful smile. 'You will,' she said. Then she turned and left the room.

The Woman has decreed it.

Jonathon was fourteen years old when The Woman first stamped herself on his consciousness. He was at the Lake Wykaita summer camp, the same one he'd attended since he was eight, his cohort growing taller and deeper-voiced with each passing year.

His parents told him how much he enjoyed the camp and how much he always looked forward to it, which confused him, because that wasn't how he remembered it. 'We practically had to drag you out of there last year, you were having such a good time,' his mother said as she manoeuvred his suitcase from the back of his wardrobe. Preparing for camp was one of the few domestic chores she took upon herself. The rest was left to the help.

Jonathon cast his mind back to the preceding year. What he remembered were slow days and bad food. Tepid showers. And an incipient feeling of threat. There was an undertow of menace in every exchange. A sense that at any moment a look or word or gesture might tip a ball game or canoe ride over into fists and elbows and knees. Although Jonathon didn't mind the physical fights so much: they were tangible, knowable, in a way that other things weren't. Like why they had to get their dicks out and jerk off on the same rock. And why the boy who came last or not at all was therefore a fag. Or what another boy – who'd been, to Jonathon's eyes, unremarkable – had done to deserve having his backpack smeared in human shit.

'I don't like it there, Mum.'

'Of course you do,' she said brightly. She hummed a little as she packed his case.

He went.

His chest was permanently tight that summer, as if he was forever holding his breath. Lights out meant ghost stories and the recounting of rapes, murders and dismemberments that had happened near the campsite. He hated these tales, but they compelled him, too. He'd lie awake afterwards, willing the dawn on, determined that the next phone call would be the one where he made his parents understand – finally – that he *DID NOT* like summer camp.

The story about The Woman was told by Zeb, one of the few boys that Jonathon liked. In the twelve months since Jonathon had last seen Zeb, his adult shape had muscled its way out from puppy fat and brought a new, deep voice with it. Zeb was a gregarious, sporty boy with the general magnanimity of the super-rich and the moderately bright. Most of the boys told their stories with the torch under their chin, funnelling its light over their faces. But Zeb placed it at his crossed knees so the light faced outwards, forcing you to look away at the shadows on the wall, or your own hands in the darkness.

'The Woman lives in the highest turret in the tallest tower at The Fortress,' Zeb began. 'The tower is always shrouded in mist, even in the hottest days of summer. Olöcks roost in the hills near the tower. Some say they serve The Woman, acting as her eyes and warning her of any approach. The Woman is a thousand years old. Maybe even two thousand. But you wouldn't know it if you ever saw her. She has hair the colour of summer straw and clear brown skin. The men who've seen her and lived say she has one blue eye and one brown eye, and that when she looks at you she sees into your very soul. She can tell your past, your future and the whole truth about you. She has luscious tits and an arse so pert you could serve drinks on it.'

'Tell us more about her tits, Zeb,' said another boy.

'They're round and coffee-coloured with enormous pink nipples. They're so big and firm that if you tit-fucked her your entire cock would disappear into her cleavage. She's got long, perfect legs, and sitting right between them is a shaved pussy.'

Jonathon was aware of the quickening breath around him, the concentration of lust and shame in the air.

'The Woman's turret is on the perimeter wall so she can see everything for miles around. One night, a fisherman got lost off The Dryans coast. There was a lot of cloud cover so he couldn't navigate by the stars. He saw the candles burning high in The Woman's turret and set his course by that. He brought his boat safely into the little cove by her tower and scrambled up the beach. The olöcks called to The Woman, telling her about the intruder. She set out from the tower, wrapped up in a golden shawl. She found the man shivering and cold and offered to take him to safety. She brought him to the tower where she ordered the male prisoners to prepare a warm bath for him. She washed him herself, lathering him with the sandalwood soap they make at The Fortress. She fed him bread and cheese and gave him wine. Then she took off her dress and gave him a head job – they teach the women at The Fortress how to give head jobs that'll blow a man's mind. Then The Woman climbed on top of the man and fucked him, her cries so loud they were heard all across The Fortress. It went on for hours and hours.

'They found the man a few days later. He washed up in his fishing boat near an effluent overflow in The Dryans. They couldn't figure out the cause of death. His body was completely unmarked. In the end the authorities issued a statement saying that he'd died of natural causes. But that was just because they didn't want anybody to know the real truth.'

Zeb paused. In the darkness the only sound was the held breath of thirty boys. Finally, one of them exhaled. 'What was the real truth, Zeb?'

'The real truth ... Are you sure you want to know?'

A row of shadows nodded against the wall.

'The real truth,' Zeb's voice fell to a whisper, 'is that The Woman has no ordinary cunt. Deep in her pussy is a long, white fang. A sharp needle that finds its way into the head of your dick and sucks you dry. Drains the life force right out of you. That's how she stays young. She'll fuck you to death. Literally.'

The story stayed with Jonathon. He was sure it stayed with all the boys, but for different reasons. When Jonathon thought of The Woman, it wasn't because of her tits or her blow jobs or the razor-sharp tooth in her pussy, although he'd be lying if he said he didn't think about those things. It was something else Zeb had said. That when The Woman looked at you, she saw into your very soul. Jonathon both craved and feared it: the idea of The Woman looking into him and delivering, whole and inarguable, the essence of who he was.

Jonathon woke with the dawn in the garret where they'd kept him overnight. He hoped the familiar red masjythra would bring him his breakfast of sticky porridge and tea, but it was a different man. Jonathon ate while perched on the windowsill. He watched the sun appear over the horizon, lightening the ocean and the sentry posts on the thick slab of limestone the Vaik had built into the sea. He thought of Eshtakai slipping into the water to unpick allegiances on the warships and douse their volley of fire.

The seasons were in flux. The light was different: weaker and more diffuse than it had been even four days before. He looked down at his hands. His nails were split, some to the quick. Despite the coarse brushes at the bathhouse there was a half-moon of dirt under each nail. His blisters had burst and re-formed so many times that his hands were patched with hard rounds of blunted nerve endings. He remembered how badly his hands had shaken those first few days. How conscious he'd been of his freefalling groin, always resisting the urge to cup himself as he walked; trying to keep his balls and cock from nosing out from under his masjythra. The season had changed, and he with it.

His mind felt clear and certain, as it had the day before when he'd woken out in the open. Essa, Julia, Sarai. His child. That was where his allegiance lay. Eshtakai herself could not change that. Still, he felt light-headed at the prospect of seeing The Woman. Why had she chosen him for judgement in this matter? He surrendered to a profound feeling of gratification. The Woman had singled him out. Recognised his specialness.

There was a knock at the door.

'Come in.'

Mandalay opened it and entered the room.

'Good morning,' he said.

'Good morning. Did you sleep well?'

'I did. Surprisingly.'

'Good. The Great Hall isn't far, but it's a steep climb. You'll need these.' She handed him a pair of shoes.

He looked them over with bemusement: ankle boots made of a suede-like material with crude wooden heels and string laces. 'These must be what all the elves are wearing this season.'

Mandalay dipped her head to one side, quizzical. 'Elves?'

'Yes. You know, little guys with pointy hats and booties that make toys and chocolates.' Jonathon pulled the boots on. 'When you hand me fairy wings, Mandalay, that's where I draw the line.'

She bent, grabbed his wrist and wrenched him to a standing position. She was a tall woman, almost at eye level with him. She held him so close that he noticed her eyes weren't dark green any more than the exterior of The Fortress was white: they were a complex honeycomb of amber, brown and grass-green.

'This is not a joke, Jonathon.'

'I know.'

'Your moral certainty won't serve you here. Once we're in The Great Hall, you'll be beyond the reach of my protection. Keep your wits about you. Assuming you have any.'

He thought furiously to ask what he needed protection from, but he couldn't shoehorn his questions into statements before two red masjythra walked into the chamber. Mandalay dropped his wrist, leaving an angry clench-mark. With her back to the waiting masjythra, she mouthed, 'Be careful,' then she turned and addressed the men. 'We leave now.' Jonathon followed them down the stairs and out the heavy wooden door.

They proceeded south, Mandalay leading the way, trailed by a masjythra in front of Jonathon and one behind him. If Mandalay was following a path, Jonathon couldn't see it. Even though it was summer, the grass was thick and waist-high at some points. It hid sudden drops and swells in the earth, making him stumble. Sometimes the grass gave way to patches of gravel. The tiny stones were smooth and slippery; even with the boots he struggled to keep his footing. Mandalay threaded through the grasses and through boulder outcrops, leading them steadily to the peak of a hill. It was wild country, too rocky and steep for cultivation. The rise above them was not far, but tough-going as Mandalay had warned.

They came to a circle of tall, egg-shaped boulders. Mandalay turned and addressed the men. 'We'll catch our breath here.'

Jonathon leant against one of the smooth purple rocks and closed his eyes. The grass licked at his bare legs. Now that he was stationary, the slight wind on his sweat made him shiver.

'Mistress. Look.'

Jonathon opened his eyes and followed where one of the red masjythra was pointing. Just to the left of the outcrop two improbable black birds were fossicking in the undergrowth. They had swan-like necks and bulbous bodies supported by orange, twig-like legs. Jonathon moved to get a closer look.

'Stay where you are,' Mandalay whispered. 'You'll scare them away.'

He froze. The birds unfurled, elongating their necks and

bristling their feathers at the interlopers. He was fascinated. He'd only ever seen olöcks in the zoo as a young boy. When the pair had died, one of old age and the other of loneliness shortly thereafter, the Vaik had refused the zoo's request for more. No one – except perhaps the Vaik – knew quite how many were left in the wild. Their heads had the prehistoric twitch of lizards, and in stature they were closer to lions than birds. Jonathon breathed in and out as slowly as he could, committing the scene to memory. He would tell his daughter about this.

'We need to keep moving,' said Mandalay.

The party pushed on, the ground rising sharply underneath them. The olöcks fled, their legs flashing orange in the grass as they ran.

'I had no idea they were so fast!' Jonathon said.

'They're remarkable birds. And contrary to popular belief, they can fly. But only when there's a storm coming. We think they do it to gauge the air pressure. Come on,' Mandalay commanded.

The last part of the climb was fiercely steep. Jonathon's breath came ragged and the augers were winching into his muscles again. He noticed small mounds of freshly turned earth dotted about the hill. Curious, he kicked at one as he passed. Something white and hard poked out. He bent lower and brushed the dirt away, then snatched his hand from it in horror.

It was a bone. A tiny, fragile bone.

Jonathon looked up, but no one seemed to have noticed what he'd done. Quickly, he kicked the topsoil over the fragment and tamped it down with his boot. Another bone poked out. *A graveyard*, he thought wildly, *I'm stepping through a graveyard.* He commanded himself to keep moving, to avoid drawing attention to himself, but he seemed to be paralysed.

'Jonathon,' Mandalay called to him, 'why have you stopped?'

Stricken, he looked up. He watched her gaze slide from him to the protruding fragment. She moved quickly from her vantage point, her eyes never wavering from the spot. She bent and upturned soil onto the bone, tamping it down with more force than Jonathon had used.

'Another odd thing about the olöcks,' she said, not looking at him. 'They bury their dead.'

'I didn't know that,' he said mechanically.

'Come, we need to hurry.' She strode away from him, quickly reaching the top of the rise where the reds waited for them. Her hair flew behind her like a flag.

He scrambled to the lip to be level with her, then gazed on the scene below.

'Fuck me,' he said under his breath. His disquiet about the bone flew from his mind.

Mandalay smiled. 'I remember the first time I saw The Great Hall. I'd been at The Fortress for nearly four years when I was summoned here to take my final vows. I was so overwhelmed I couldn't find my voice for a minute or two.'

It wasn't difficult to believe. Jonathon had been expecting a municipal building, something like the town hall or government house in his city. Statues and crests, the emblems of statehood. But this wasn't even a building: it was an almost perfect circle formed by the natural rise of the hills. The circle was divided into quadrants by a stream so narrow that you could step cleanly between the banks on either side. The stream also flowed around the circle's perimeter. In each quadrant an amphitheatre of limestone seats faced towards a wedge of stone slabs. Massive glass circular sectors were erected in each quadrant; they caught and transformed the sunlight so the quadrants were awash in ceaselessly dissolving colour. Now amber, now green, depending on the angle. When the sun disappeared behind a cloud it was as though the air was wiped clean, the clarity almost painful to the eye. The cloud passed, and the kaleidoscope twisted again.

'One quadrant for each of the necessities of Vaik life,' Mandalay explained. 'Work. History. Sex. Justice. We're expected at the justice quadrant. Let's go.'

Jonathon followed her down the winding stone stairs cut into the hillside. People were massing in each quadrant, having approached the circle from different points. Mandalay stepped nimbly over the stream and onto the soft springy turf of the justice quadrant. The clear blue water was surprisingly deep and fast flowing. Jonathon had an urge to throw a coin over his shoulder and make a wish.

'Come,' said Mandalay, 'give me your hand.' He reached across for her white hand and she led him into the quadrant.

A prism of light entombed her in bronze as if she were a statue. The light shifted and she was sentient again.

'Sit here.' She gestured to one of the stone slabs and he lowered himself to it. 'Remove your shoes.' He tugged off the boots. 'Now remove your masjythra.' He hesitated, then drew the garment over his head and handed it to her. His body was sharp-cut: a working, functioning machine. He heaved himself backwards onto the rock, feeling the stored warmth of it against his buttocks and legs.

Daidd, the isvestyii, two red masjythra and four Vaik entered the quadrant, taking seats in the amphitheatre.

The woman he had seen yesterday strode into the quadrant. Again he felt a sense of déjà vu. He had seen her before, he was sure of it. A word on the tip of his tongue just wouldn't become sound. *The best thing to do is not to think about it*, Adalia suggested. *It will come when you're not expecting it.* The woman stood before Mandalay, who was now seated in the amphitheatre, and exchanged a few words. Mandalay was tall, but this woman was a giantess. Her dagger was still cinched at her waist.

She crooked a finger at one of the masjythra. He manoeuvred the isvestyii to the apex of the quadrant, tugged off his gown and shoved him against one of the granite slabs. The isvestyii hugged his arms to his chest.

Jonathon felt no pity for him.

The rock beneath Jonathon was smooth and warm. He flipped onto his stomach and lay like a starfish, embracing the heat. The granite felt molten and inviting, as if it might slip over him and cradle him to sleep. But it annoyed him to feel the isvestyii staring at him. He slowly raised his head. The isvestyii rocked back and forth on the rock, his eyes wide and manic. Jonathon met his eyes with a steady, unreflective gaze.

The dagger-carrying Vaik perched on the edge of Jonathon's rock. She held a goblet of tea in her large brown hands. Remembering Mandalay's caution, he resisted the urge to make a crack about the Vaik penchant for tea.

'For you.' She held the goblet out to him.

He rolled onto his side and took it. 'Thank you.'

'My name is Laliya. I give you leave to name me.'

'I'm honoured, Laliya. I am Jonathon. Jonathon Bridge.'

She tilted her head to one side, as if bemused that he would think it possible she didn't know his name. Didn't know his entire history and have a strong presentiment about his future besides.

'How do you like our Great Hall, Jonathon Bridge?'

'It's magnificent. But then everything about the Vaik is magnificent.'

Laliya sipped her tea. 'You are a fan of our society?'

'Very much so.'

'You don't find it at all strange that The Woman would decree that you judge this matter?'

'Yes. That I do find strange.'

'Why do you think she would do that?'

'I was hoping you might tell me.'

'Hmm.' Laliya looked thoughtful. She turned the goblet

to the left and to the right, as if she might divine something from the tea leaves. 'Let's start by being clear on why we are all here.' She looked up and addressed herself to the assembly, her voice resonant and powerful. 'On his entrance to The Fortress, Jonathon Bridge took the traditional oath. Both in writing and in speaking, he affirmed that he would not raise a hand in anger towards anyone at The Fortress. Mandalay, you were a witness to this?'

'I was.' Mandalay's voice was unwavering, but she was even paler than usual, her jaw set.

'Despite this vow, Jonathon Bridge was observed to move towards the isvestyii in his assignment with intent to strike. Were it not for the intervention of Daidd, it seems certain that Jonathon Bridge would have struck the isvestyii. Daidd, does this conform to your understanding of the events?'

Daidd hesitated. 'It's hard to say with certainty.'

Laliya smiled, as if she were humouring a child. 'Of course. We are talking here, after all, about something that did *not* happen. An absence. But on the balance of probability, do you think that if you had not restrained Jonathon Bridge, he would have punched the isvestyii and thereby violated his vow?'

Daidd swallowed. 'On balance, I think so. Yes.'

'Mandalay. You observed these events, though you were out of earshot. What is your view?'

'On the balance of probability, I think it likely that Jonathon would have struck the isvestyii. With what force and how many times I cannot say.'

'The effect of the impact is not in question. The question is one of intent. Would you describe Jonathon Bridge as angry when you approached the assignment?'

Jonathon felt an incipient prickle of panic crawl along his spine. He rose to a sitting position and crossed his legs, the goblet of tea in front of his genitals.

'I could not hear the conversation until I was within two or three metres of the assignment,' Mandalay said.

'How was the assignment arranged?'

'Arranged?'

'Were they picking oorsels, eating lunch, taking water?'

'They were … They were arranged in a semicircle around Jonathon Bridge and the isvestyii. A tight circle. Jonathon Bridge was in a boxing stance.'

'The mood of the assignment — how would you describe it when you approached?'

'Tense. Hostile.'

Laliya turned from the assembly towards Jonathon. A ray of sunlight struck one of the circular sectors, turning the air around Jonathon the colour of claret.

'Were you angry, Jonathon Bridge?'

'Wait a minute. *I'm* the one on trial here?'

'Did anyone tell you different?'

'I was told I was to judge. That The Woman had decreed I would judge this matter.'

'And so you shall. How do you judge yourself, Jonathon Bridge?'

'I don't know what you mean.'

'Were you angry with the isvestyii?'

'Yes. I was angry.'

'What was the cause of this anger?'

'The cause?' Jonathon nearly laughed out loud. 'He's the lowest form of life.'

'If Daidd hadn't stopped you, would you have struck the isvestyii?'

Jonathon sucked in his breath, then slowly exhaled. He considered lying. He was an expert liar, so expert that his fabrications came to seem real even to himself. 'Yes,' he said eventually.

'In violation of your vow, you would have committed physical violence against a resident of The Fortress?'

'I broke no vow. He's not a resident. He's an inmate. He's locked up here for raping and killing little girls.'

'I didn't kill any little girls,' the isvestyii muttered. Jonathon had almost forgotten he was there. He looked shrunken and pathetic, his knees tucked under his chin, his hands locked around his shins.

'What did you say?' Laliya asked him. 'Speak up.'

'I said I didn't kill any little girls.' He spoke to the ground rather than to Laliya.

Jonathon was swamped with disgust. *Look at him*, he thought. *What a cringing and pathetic creature.*

'What do you say to that?' Laliya directed her question towards Jonathon.

'To his contention that he didn't kill any little girls? I treat it with the contempt it — and he — deserve. He raped a child who died from her internal injuries. He left another so damaged she killed herself after years of self-abuse. And the third one had so little will to live she died in an accident that everyone else walked away from.'

'How is it that you know all this, Jonathon Bridge?'

'I read a bit about the case. Before.'

'You couldn't know all that from reportage. That information is not public.'

Jonathon hesitated. 'Mandalay told me.'

'And what makes you certain that Mandalay told you the truth?'

'What?'

'You forget yourself, issuing a question.'

Jonathon remembered something that Daidd had told him. That he was like a piece on a chessboard to the Vaik, every move planned out. Was it possible that Mandalay had lied to him? That this whole thing was an elaborate set-up? The clouds shifted overhead. Tuning forks of light turned the quadrant sea-blue. Jonathon had a momentary sense of panic, as if he were underwater. He sucked the air into his lungs so fast his head swam.

'I'm sorry. I'm dizzy. A moment.'

Mandalay, Daidd, Laliya. They were all submerged in the ocean. He thought of Eshtakai swimming among them, a blade between her teeth.

He was a good judge of character, he reminded himself. 'I do not believe Mandalay was lying to me. She had no cause to, and she was in some distress about the details. Obviously. She seemed ... sincere.'

Laliya shrugged. 'Perhaps you are not as astute a judge of character as you like to think. Perhaps Mandalay likes to make mischief. Perhaps she gets off on having a starring role in dramas of her own making. Perhaps she's a sadist who wanted to see me do this.'

In one fluid motion Laliya launched herself from the rock, lifted her goblet over her head and swung it in a wide arc into the isvestyii's face. Jonathon heard the crunch of brass on bone. The second of contact reverberated around the echo chamber of the circle cut into the surrounding hills. The isvestyii cried out and rolled into a ball like a slater, his hands covering his face.

'Sit up,' Laliya demanded. 'Sit up *now*.'

Trembling, he pushed himself to a sitting position. He held his hands above his head as protection against further blows. Blood gushed from his temple and coursed down his face and onto his chest.

Laliya calmly bent to retrieve the goblet that she'd dropped after smashing it into the isvestyii's face. She cleaned the rim of blood with the hem of her gown, rusting the white fabric.

Jonathon was shocked. It had been so fast, so brutal and so ... 'unprovoked' was the word that sprang to mind. But that wasn't right, he corrected himself. It was entirely provoked. Entirely justified.

The isvestyii whimpered and cowered as Laliya handled the goblet. She casually seated herself on the granite next to Jonathon. 'Do you think me just?' she asked.

'I, I don't know.'

'Speak up, I can't hear you.'

'I said I don't know.'

'You don't know? Yesterday you were prepared to attack this man, in violation of your undertaking to the Vaik. Now, you don't know?'

'I was unarmed,' Jonathon stammered.

'I see. So it's the goblet you object to?' She held it out to Jonathon, who mechanically took it.

Laliya stood up and positioned herself in front of the isvestyii. He made inarticulate, pleading noises. Blood had pooled on the rock and was now dripping over its lip onto the grass, staining it purple. The isvestyii still held his shaking hands in front of his face, peeking up through his fingers to the woman towering above him. Laliya scratched the tip of her nose, then cracked her knuckles. She looked indifferent, even bored, as she lifted her arm and brought her balled fist down through the sea-blue air to the isvestyii's jaw. Her arm was a knot of rope, her fist a boulder. Jonathon closed his eyes so he didn't see the contact.

But he heard it.

The crunch of bone on bone, then something wet, like a full nappy being dropped to the ground. The man began to cry in earnest: great, slavering sobs. Jonathon folded himself into a ball and placed his forehead on his knees, but he couldn't cocoon himself against the sound of the crying man. The sound of shame, pain and fear was all around him, trapped in the bowl of the valley.

'You seem distressed, Jonathon Bridge, yet I was unarmed.'

Jonathon didn't look up. As a boy, he'd repeatedly dreamt of a winding hallway along which he was compelled to open doors. When awake, he could never remember what was behind them.

But it was something that left him winded and small. The doors were open now. All of them.

He wanted Adalia. Wanted her like oxygen. He ached with homesickness, and only Adalia could be home. With his head cradled in the darkness of his arms and knees, he pictured his wife in the colourful kaftans she'd chosen for when she grew big with the baby. He tried to drown out the man's sobbing with his wife's magical laugh. But thinking of her only made the homesickness more acute. Tears welled up in his eyes.

'Do you still think us fair and just, Jonathon Bridge?' Laliya's voice wended its way through the chinks between his limbs.

'Go away,' he said.

She was silent for a moment. When she did speak, she sounded regretful, even kind. 'I cannot. This is my place. My land. My history. Where would you have me go?'

'I don't know. Just away.'

'You sound like a child.'

'I feel like a child.' He raised his head a little so his eyes were visible above his forearms. He knew he probably looked weary and hunted. 'I've the rights of a child here. You have the arbitrary power of a parent. You can do what you want. Say what you want. Make up the rules as you go. I'm trapped here. For six months more I'm trapped here. Yes, I'm a child.'

'You chose to come here. You're here of your own volition. All the rules and obligations of our society were made known to you. Your consent was informed.'

'I didn't know there'd be this –' He waved his hand in a gesture that took in the isvestyii, the goblet, Laliya and her fist. 'No one told me about this.'

'This,' Laliya retraced Jonathon's gesture, 'was only necessary because you broke your vow. Had you kept your oath, the existence of The Great Hall would never have been known to you.' Her tone was reasonable, lawyerly.

Jonathon raised his eyes to where Mandalay sat, intent on the scene unfolding below her. She held herself rigid, the ropey muscles in her neck taut. The sun shifted, drawing a tide of malachite through the valley. *Six months*, Jonathon thought, *six more months. How am I to survive it? What kind of shape will I be in when I leave?*

'For the record,' Laliya stood up, 'Mandalay told you the truth. The isvestyii killed the teacher with a gun at point-blank range. She stood in front of the children, sheltering them with her body. He nudged the gun into her ribcage and shot her through the spleen. Then he raped three of the girls at the school. Perhaps the same school your own child will attend. The police literally peeled him off one of the girls. Essa. Julia. Sarai. So. What do you think he deserves?'

Jonathon stared at the isvestyii. The blood was drying in crusts along his jaw and temple. It was hard to believe that someone who looked so pitiful, so broken, could have done such a thing. Jonathon shook his head. 'I don't know. I just don't know.'

'You seemed certain yesterday.'

'Yesterday was ...' It was different. Why exactly was hard to explain. Suddenly, a word that Adalia was fond of using came to him. 'Was organic. What happened yesterday was organic.'

Laliya ran her hand over her chin, as if checking for shaving stubble. 'Organic?'

'He,' Jonathon jerked his head in the isvestyii's direction, 'tried to mess with my head. Singing stupid songs about how we're the same. We're not the same. What he did, I can't comprehend it. Not in a million years would I do what he did. I was angry. He was angry. You should have left us to it.'

'I didn't sing no songs,' the isvestyii blubbered.

Laliya ignored him. 'You think justice is best served in anger? In hand-to-hand combat?'

Jonathon shrugged. 'At least it's honest.'

'This isn't honest?'

Jonathon laughed a hard, sardonic laugh. The rock was beginning to lose the heat it had stored from the intermittent flashes of sunshine. Goosebumps were puckering his arms. 'This is a mind-fuck. There's nothing honest about it.'

'And you value honesty do you, Jonathon Bridge?'

He sighed, rubbing his arms against the looming cold. 'Truth. I value truth. Truth runs deeper than honesty.'

Laliya smiled. 'That sounds like something a cheating husband would say. *I was never unfaithful in my heart.*'

Jonathon flushed red. He felt the heat beaming from his face. It coursed down his bare chest and barrelled through his forearms, flattening the goosebumps. His ballsacks blared heat into the air. Laliya kept her gaze on him, her knowing smile hard as a car grille, showing fine-pointed teeth. A sudden wind pressed her gown against the outlines of her body, the skirt whipped behind her like a tail. Jonathon's eye was drawn to the bulge in her underpants. Electii. Is that why she seemed familiar?

'I'm not saying anything more,' he said, half-expecting the words to bubble out of him and float to the surface through the blue-green sea. He curled himself up as tight as he could and hid his blushing head in his arms again. *I am the rock*, he thought. *Earthed.*

When they addressed him, and shook him, and Laliya slapped him – open-palmed – and shouted 'Pay attention!' into his ear, he plunged his hands into the centre of the rock. He dipped into geological time, imagining himself moltening and dissolving into the world's core. Then hardening there, far beneath the crust, untouchable and unreachable.

Eventually, Daidd, Mandalay and Laliya half-carried, half-dragged him out of The Great Hall and down the hill, back to the building where he'd spent the previous night. They sent for a stretcher, and some of the men from his assignment carried him to his quarters, tipping him from the stretcher into his bed. He turned to face the wall. Mandalay ran her hand softly down the side of his face. 'Sleep,' she whispered, but he was stone, and could not hear her.

III ETTËVY

WORK. HISTORY. Sex. Justice.

Of the four pillars of Vaik society it was work that spoke to Jonathon. Justice was an abstraction for which he had no use. Sex, like food and wine, was a sensory pleasure that came easily to him. And what was history but dust and footnotes? But work; work he understood.

Unlike many of his friends he did not play at work. He didn't sit on a board or a charity committee, didn't attend fundraisers or openings and consider himself gainfully employed. Work contained him. Without it he would trickle away to nothing. It was this fear of dissolving that eventually got him out of bed after The Great Hall.

He remained in his quarters for some time after Laliya's court. When the chime signalled the start of another day, he did not stir. He didn't join the men in the dining hall or the bathhouse. Blue masjythra brought trays of food to his room at regular intervals, and no one seemed to care that he wasn't in the shaenet with Daidd. Every time he heard footsteps on the zigzag path during labouring hours he expected Mandalay to sweep into his room and command him back to his plot. Perhaps there was even some part of him waiting for an audience with The Woman, where she would reveal what she'd meant when she said that Jonathon would judge.

When it became clear that no one was coming, he got out of bed and took down the new masjythra that had materialised on the peg. It was longer and heavier than his old one. He slipped it over his head, remaining still as the tiny metallic squares worked their cartography, heat radiating from the mesh. He took the zigzag path to the entrance and made his way to the shaenet. The fields were bare now and resting, while the trees yellowed. In the distance work assignments repaired walls and pavements. All wore the longer masjythra.

In his absence the rampaging ivy had been cut back and the holes in the wall papered over with fresh cement. He unlatched the gate, which had somehow escaped the repairs and still creaked, and stepped into the shaenet. The sharp lime and heady wood-smoke scent enveloped him. He stood at the garden's edge and breathed it in. When he'd first seen the shaenet it was lush, overgrown. Now it wore an air of repose. Most of the plots were sparse, their shrubs pruned and bound. Dead and dying plants had been uprooted and the soil mulched. Overhead, the boughs of the ancient trees were stripping themselves bare. The sky that had barely peeked through the canopy a few weeks back now loomed large and silver. The men were raking up the fallen leaves and carting them to the mulching stations near the shed.

As Jonathon made his way to his plot, a man he knew by sight stopped his barrow and shook his hand. Word of his return carried from plot to plot. The men stood as he passed. Some hailed him from the shed. They had heard about his encounter with the isvestyii, about their fight and about Jonathon's trial at the mysterious hands of Vaik justice. No doubt most of it was rumour and innuendo; Mandalay had said that the existence of The Great Hall was unknown to most. He accepted their display of solidarity with a slight nod.

Daidd didn't stand, he simply handed Jonathon his scalpel. 'Welcome back.'

'Thank you.'

He took the cool, sharp blade and knelt into the dirt. He fell to pulling out the weeds that had nosed through the top cover of straw, thinking how puny they were compared to Goosen's Trial. He gently upturned norsling leaves and dry stalks to check for aphids. He carted water from the well, feeling himself solidifying with each upturned bucket. He rejoiced at the sweat on his forearms and the strain in his muscles. The inertia he'd felt since The Great Hall moved away from him, as did the space the isvestyii had occupied in his thoughts. Whatever had been between them was done. Jonathon thought of what Mandalay had said, that the isvestyii barely crossed her mind but she thought often of Sarai, Essa, Julia and their teacher. His thoughts would bend the same way, to his child, to Adalia and Ulait, and to the women the isvestyii had killed. Between him and the isvestyii there was nothing.

Towards the end of the day, when Jonathon handed his scalpel back to Daidd and the men returned their gardening tools to the shadow-board in the shed, Ulait and some of her friends entered the shaenet. Jonathon heard their chirruping talk and laughter and smiled to himself. The girls collected around the fires burning in drums outside the shed and shouted hellos to the men they knew. The men responded with slight bows. Funny, Jonathon thought, how instinctively they all did this, though no one had told them it was the required form of address.

Ulait saw Jonathon and clapped her hands in delight. She launched herself at him and threw her arms around his neck. Instinctively he caught her, clasping her in his arms, leaving her feet dangling a foot above the ground. She felt deceptively light and fragile, her heart beating wildly against his chest, her cheek warm and flushed against his. He caught a trace of lavender in her hair.

She planted a wet kiss on his cheek and then wriggled free. 'I'm so happy to see you, Jonathon Bridge,' she said, brushing the hair from her face.

'And I you, Mistress.'

'I heard about what happened,' she said in a theatrical whisper, 'with the isvestyii.'

Unsure what, exactly, she knew (or ought to know), Jonathon didn't know how to respond. 'You don't need to worry about him, Mistress.'

'I know.' She smiled then flung herself at Jonathon again, pressing her head to his chest. 'I was worried that you'd be hurt. Or punished for breaking your vow. But you're okay. I can see that you're okay.'

Touched, Jonathon tentatively stroked her hair, a darker, redder shade than was usual with the Vaik. 'I'm fine, Mistress. Thank you for your concern.'

'Come to me on the half. At the Story-Keeping House.'

'The half,' Jonathon repeated dully. He didn't know where he was in the cycle.

'It's in nine days' time,' she said. 'Come immediately after your bath.'

'Yes, Mistress, I will.'

Drawing, crayons, Vaik myths, chatter. Parenting practice, he thought. He looked forward to it.

A week after he returned to the shaenet, Mandalay came to him at night.

He had known this moment would come, had known it since their first meeting when he made his vow of submission. Now seemed as fitting a time as any.

It was moonless and the stars dull, as if The Woman had thrown a web over the sky. Mandalay was a shadow among shadows in the thick darkness. Her gown sighed as it dropped to the floor. 'Move over,' she whispered.

He threw back the blanket and shifted to the other side of the bed. She lay beside him and cradled him in her arms. He felt the soft roundness of her breasts against his chest, the warmth of her exhalation, the wiry interlock of her pubic hair with his.

'What are your thoughts?' she asked.

'I want to go home. I miss my wife. I long for my child. I think about her all the time.'

'I know.' Mandalay spoke softly and gently, as if the syllables might cut him. 'But you're not ready yet. In your heart you know you're not ready. Your child needs you whole.'

'Whole,' Jonathon repeated. He imagined himself at work, among his colleagues at one of the long board tables and asking them: *Who here is whole? What is that like, to be whole?* They would think he was mad.

Mandalay unlaced her fingers from the back of his neck and scratched small circles down his chest. She explored his balls, his cleft, his triangle of hair. Her fingers drew him expertly from his thoughts. His blood began to quicken, and with his pulse came the questions he was forbidden to ask.

'Laliya is a man,' he said, into Mandalay's lavender-scented hair.

'No.'

'Yes. At The Great Hall, the wind pressed his gown against his body. I saw his package plain as day.'

'That doesn't make her a man.'

'It's a pretty definitive clue.'

Mandalay folded her hand on him and squeezed. Blood bulged at the head of his penis. 'This,' she said, 'is this what makes you a man? If I tore it off with my teeth would you then be a woman?'

He flinched at the violence of the image, an ejaculation of blood spraying the walls red.

'Is that what a woman is?' Mandalay asked. 'An absence?'

'Of course not.'

She soothed his startled erection, caressing it against the threat of her bite. 'Without this,' she said more softly, 'would you still be a man?'

'Of sorts.'

He gave himself over to the flood and lull of her hands.

'Laliya was electii when she came here,' said Mandalay. 'She lived in the outer fortress for four years, then The Woman decreed that she could be one of us. Laliya was offered the surgery. She turned it down. Most electii do. Being Vaik is a state of mind.' She turned her face to Jonathon and kissed him.

He folded into her, malleable and warm. 'The Woman could be wrong,' he whispered, as Mandalay's lips glanced his earlobe, his hairline, the bony ridge where his shoulder met his neck.

'Impossible. The Woman is never wrong.'

'But she was,' he said, torn between whether to pursue it or give himself over to Mandalay's body, 'about me. She said I would judge the isvestyii. And I didn't.'

Mandalay pulled away from him and propped herself up on her elbow, looking down at him. Her fine red hair tickled his chest. 'You will, though. At some point you will. Don't kid yourself, Jonathon Bridge. This is just a reprieve.'

He longed to know who or what The Woman was. A flesh and blood oracle? A hereditary position passed from mother to daughter? An elected office? A myth kept alive to sustain a ruling council? He couldn't ask, and Mandalay probably wouldn't tell him.

'It's a good reprieve,' he said, reaching for her again. She draped her arms around his shoulders, binding him. He gave himself to her body as to a map, studying the lean course of her neck, the tight wire of her collarbones, the hollows that fit the purse of his lips. Her arms, strong harbours, were muscular and white. He traced their circle with his cheek from the taut ball of her shoulders to the fine bones of her wrists and back. The earth was present in her sweat; she tasted alluvial. The pads of her fingers smelt of herbs.

He wanted to know her, know about her. Why she had come from the Green Sea Isles to this place. Had she loved a man once? Was it disappointment that had sent her across the sea? How many children did she have? What was it to be a parent? Which, of all the saplings and trees she had tended, did she love the most? Did she really protect him, or was it all a stratagem in pursuit of the endgame, as Daidd had suggested? But to know, he had to ask these questions, and questions were forbidden.

This embargo on inquiry, he thought, as he bent his head to her breasts, was the principle that allowed The Fortress to function. It wasn't the stockpile of weapons in the perimeter wall or the exhaustion that left the men hungry for nothing but sleep and food, but the way that the mind slid around and around the same culs-de-sac. This contraction, the falling out of the habit of curiosity, was what ensured compliance. It turned a man inward, towards himself. What he found there made The Fortress feel just.

Jonathon took Mandalay's nipple in his mouth and sucked. She gave a small gasp of pleasure. He wondered if a baby at the breast felt the same way. He tried to picture his own child suckling at Adalia's nipple. But he saw only himself. The image shocked him, and in his shock he let Mandalay's nipple fall from his mouth. He stared at the cleft between her breasts, faintly luminous in the darkness. She ran her fingers through his hair. He felt their pads marching across his brain, knowing. Knowing everything.

He draped a long line of soft kisses from the nape of her neck to the pearlescent web on her stomach. He laid his cheek against the flesh left spongy by childbirth and closed his eyes, briefly. All men, he thought, were awed by this, this power women held in their bellies. Was manhood no more than a pathetic attempt to compensate for aridity? Growth. Mergers. Acquisitions. Productivity. All of them paltry imitations of birth. He laughed against Mandalay's belly.

'What is it?'

He shook his head and continued his trail of kisses. 'Nothing. Nothing you don't already know.'

He nuzzled into her pubic hair and the ferrous smell of her. The scent engulfed him, the same way the shaenet did. He poked out his tongue and followed the protruding lips of her labia. Mandalay sighed, and opened her legs wider. He found the string of her sanitary product and drew it away from her folds with his tongue. He clamped the string between his teeth and pulled gently till the sponge emerged. He dropped it over the side of the bed and returned to Mandalay's clitoris.

'Come,' she said. 'Come here.'

He wiped his mouth and followed her instruction. She laid him flat on the bed, then put one leg over him. She eased him inside her and folded one hand around her breast; the other she placed against her clitoris, showing him how to pleasure her. She reached her arm around his neck and drew her face close to his. He was acutely aware of the rise and fall of her breath, the little moans she made, the warmth of her against him. He focused on the complex feedback loop of stimulus and pleasure between their bodies. He thought of nothing but decoding all the little signals she emitted, from the sucking in of her breath to the flutter in her fingers against his neck, refining his response until she cried out and pulled so hard on his neck that it hurt.

After a few seconds she loosened her grip. He lay there, listening to her breathing return to normal. He hoped that she would stay, spend the night with him. He wanted to feel her warm body against his, to pretend in the half-light between wakefulness and sleep that she was Adalia. That they were at home in their own bed, and there were hours to go before the accursed alarm clock rang. Hours.

But Mandalay kissed him on the forehead and rose from the bed. He felt bereft. She slipped her gown over her head and left, pausing at the door. 'Goodnight, Jonathon. Sleep well.'

He heard her steps move away from him, down the zigzag ramp and off towards whatever part of The Fortress she considered her home.

On the day of the half, Jonathon tried to remember where the Story-Keeping House was located. He'd found it by accident the last time, cartwheeling on his joy that Adalia remained his and that his baby was safely cocooned in her womb. It was to the north, he was sure of that. He began to walk, feeling the crunch and crackle of the browning leaves under his feet.

None of the buildings looked familiar. Was he on the right path? Occasionally he saw other men moving between fields; some were dozing in patches of tepid sunlight. But the habit of not asking questions had become so ingrained, it didn't occur to him to ask for directions.

Finally, after he had meandered for some time, a square building with bishop-hat windows rose in front of him. He waited to see if Ulait would materialise at the window as she had the first time. He stood, gazing upwards. But she did not appear.

The front door was open, so he walked in. Immediately he felt ill-at-ease. The building contained the tense quietness of a surprise party.

His masjythra kept him warm in the cooling air but his bare feet were cold. He sat on the stairs and cupped first one foot then the other in his hands. He considered returning to his quarters, but a niggling fear of disappointing Ulait led him up the stairs. The silence followed him, so complete he felt he disturbed the shadows in the halls. He slapped his feet down on the winding staircase and tapped his hands on the banister just for the company of sound. All of the doors he passed were closed. He tried one; it was locked.

Would he ever find the room where Ulait had explained the picture of the isvestyii to him? Was she even planning to meet him? Perhaps it was only some idle thought she'd had, just as idly discarded and replaced in the carousel of the teenage mind. He would try one more floor. Then he would return to the warmth of his bed and idle away the time thinking about his daughter.

His daughter.

Those two words thrilled him, reminded him that he was now a fundamentally different person. He was a father. A tiny human being depended on him.

He stopped.

There was an open door further along the corridor. He cocked his ear and thought he heard rustling within the room. He paused in the doorway.

If this was the same room as last time, it was radically transformed. It had been bare then, save for the murals; Ulait had strewn her paper and paints along the wooden boards. The room was now adorned with vases of flowers and plush rugs that made his feet itch with the urge to sink into them. A crimson divan – something Adalia would love – was pushed against one wall, and everywhere he turned were cushions, pillows, ottomans, great swathes of silk. Some of the murals were covered by enormous mirrors. In the far corner an elaborate four-poster bed had been erected. He reached down and collected a glossy yard of material, deep green like Mandalay's eyes.

'Do you like the room?'

He turned towards the voice. It took him a moment to distinguish Ulait from the vast tapestry against which she was almost entirely camouflaged. When she walked towards him, her silky red robe fluttering slightly, it was as if she'd stepped from the picture and into life.

'It's amazing. I had no idea we were celebrating.'

Ulait laughed, as if he had made a clever joke. If he had, the punchline was lost on him.

'Would you like tea?'

He wanted to ask what sort it was, but couldn't frame this into a statement, so he just nodded. Ulait took a brass jug from a table laden with food and drink and poured the tea into a goblet. He felt stunned by the plenty laid out before him. Glossy apples competed for space with fat wedges of cheese. Golden chicken drumsticks were arrayed on platters alongside the upturned bottoms of avocadoes. Grapes, cold meats, oysters. Sauces glistening in silver jugs.

Ulait approached him, holding out the goblet ceremoniously. He forced his eyes from the feast. There was something different about her, some detail he struggled to place. She held the goblet at the stem, reached for his hand and closed his fingers around the bowl. Up close, he noticed the dusting of gold powder on her face, her hair. He remembered reading how Vaik warriors painted themselves gold before battle.

'Thank you, Mistress.'

'You're welcome.' She clinked her glass against his and looked up at him from beneath her long, thick lashes. The gold dust had collected in them too, making the gold flecks in her green eyes stand out. She was familiar, suddenly. Jonathon smiled to himself, wondering if every girl-child he saw from now on would evoke *his* child. Ulait smiled back at him, the white glint of her teeth dazzling against the red gloss on her lips.

'You have a lovely smile, Mistress.'

'Thank you, Jonathon Bridge.'

He raised the goblet to his mouth and took a wary sip of tea. To his surprise it was cold and fruity. It bubbled a little on his tongue and fizzed through his nose. Was there no end to the variety of Vaik tea?

'Do you like it?'

'I do.' Jonathon took another sip, then a gulp. The drink was delicious. 'I really do.'

'It's called verrglet, and it's reserved for special occasions. A Vaik might taste this only three or four times in her life. It's our drink of celebration.'

'I grow it in my plot,' Jonathon said, flushing with pleasure. It had been worth it. It had all been worth it. The Vaik recognised his rebirth. Perhaps they were the only people who could. 'I am honoured, Mistress, that you think me worthy of such notice.'

Ulait took a long drink from her goblet, wrinkling up her nose as the liquid bubbled. Then she bent down, put the verrglet on the floor, rose to her full height and pulled a cord on her gown. The gown slipped to the floor in a breathy rush of red. She was naked, her limbs dusted in the gold powder. She looked as if she was encased in bronze.

Shocked, Jonathon registered her as a series of images disconnected from the whole. Her breasts, small and perfectly formed. Jutting hipbones. Tight mound of pubic hair. Tanned, strong legs. Big toe knuckling into the ground. A scab on one knee.

The pieces of Ulait moved towards him and then spoke. 'I have chosen you, Jonathon Bridge.'

He was frozen in shock; and still she moved towards him.

'Take off your masjythra.'

Then panic punched the shock out of him.

'I said remove your masjythra, Jonathon Bridge.'

She was standing so close she could reach out and touch him. He took a step backwards. She raised a questioning eyebrow. He took another step backwards.

'I issued you a command.'

'I can't,' he whispered.

'What did you say?'

'I can't,' he repeated, still moving backwards.

She began to shake, whether from fury or a sudden gust of frigid air he couldn't tell.

'Remove your masjythra. That's an order.'

He dropped the goblet, the liquid splashing his leg, wheeled around and ran. He ran blindly, almost throwing himself down the stairs. He saved himself more than once by flinging his arms around the banister and holding tight while his legs swung. Ulait was screaming at him to halt. If there were Vaik nearby, and there surely were, they would soon amass at the Story-Keeping House. The idea of what punishment awaited him for this, his second transgression at The Fortress, propelled him from the building and onto the forecourt.

He had no plan other than to keep running. There was so much panic and adrenaline coursing through his body that he ran fast and effortlessly. Sweat filmed his body, wisps of mist coiling from him as his core heat collided with the chill air.

Ahead of him was a rise and on the rise a dense clump of trees. He pelted for it, then launched himself into the undergrowth, burrowing on his hands and knees. His masjythra tightened, folding like a pocket over his bare balls and cock, protecting him from the thorns and rocks. Panting, he used his head as a battering ram through the faggots and vines.

Within the copse was a small clearing. He inched around to face the other way so he could see any attack party as it came storming up the hill. He peered through the undergrowth, down the hill to the buildings. He was reasonably certain that he couldn't be seen. The hood of the masjythra crawled up and around his head, flattened itself to his ears and neck, and settled. He placed his head in his hands and rested his forehead against the carpet of leaves. The ground smelt of damp and rot and the endeavours of worms.

'Fuck,' he muttered to the ground. 'Fuck, fuck, fuck.'

What had just happened?

What *had* just happened?

Jonathon prided himself on picking up on the currents and cross-currents that other men missed. It was one of the things that made him so dangerous. But he had misread this completely. Catastrophically. *You* – Adalia's voice in his head – *Always you at the centre.*

'Not me,' he spoke wordlessly to the damp earth. 'Ulait.' His heart wrenched at the thought of her. Poor child.

But she hadn't organised that room by herself. Jonathon lay very still, his masjythra-clad head still clasped in his hands, his nose pressed to the earth. Understanding came.

This day had been planned well in advance. Ulait had made her choice of him, and the Vaik had prepared the room, the feast, her body paint in celebration. He hadn't just refused a Vaik command, he'd defiled one of their ceremonies. Burnt their flag.

He lay there unmoving for some time, long after he knew he had no choice but to pick his way out of the bushes, dust off the dirt and leaves, and trudge back to his quarters to face what needed to be faced.

He thought of the last time he'd had to answer for his sexual transgressions. He'd walked blithely into that, with all the arrogance of a man who'd never been held to account. It had brought him to The Fortress, and the tangled mesh of boughs and moss that hid him, for now, from the Vaik.

The Arbour Room, Glaxxon docks. Two forty-five. Ask the concierge for The Redeemer. When he asks who you are, you say 'The Fox'. Tell no one.

Jonathon read the note again. Adalia's distinctive handwriting swirled across the crisp, olive-coloured notepaper, her great loops roping him towards an assignation on the other side of the city. He passed his square, clean hand over his chin checking for stubble, then he clicked his mouse and opened his calendar. His afternoon was encased in a large rectangle between the hours of one and five. He clicked the rectangle open and groaned as he read its contents:

Goal setting for maximum efficiency: learn the latest techniques designed to hone your focus on what's really important. Hear from the experts how to 'tune out' the white noise and zero in on the issues with the biggest strategic bang for you and your organisation. Prepare to take your communication skills up a notch as you discover how to reorient the time-wasters towards the goals that work for YOU! In just four hours you will refine your approach to strategic goal setting and planning, resulting in a more disciplined, more focused team. Prepare to unleash change!

Jonathon declined the invitation without explanation. He had his own strategic bang to unleash.

It had been some time since Adalia had issued him one of her missives. He would find them slipped into his jacket pocket or taped to the underside of his briefcase. Just the sight of her notepaper was enough to give him a raging hard-on. The notes were brief and to the point: usually just an address, a time and an (often cryptic) instruction:

Wear your silver-blue trench coat, nothing else. Tell the concierge: 'the swallows shall fly at midnight'. Bring duct tape.

Hours dissolved in the pleasures of Adalia's sybarite imaginings. They'd drifted, masked and fully dressed, through a many-floored, dimly lit building; each room dedicated to the pleasures and pains of a specific historical era or event. He'd seen strapping men in jodhpurs whipping each other with riding crops. Bejewelled, dark-skinned beauties re-enacting an ancient erotic text. The Woman finding the fisherman marooned on her beach and taking him back to The Fortress to feed her monstrous cunt.

Once, Adalia had instructed him to meet her at a city park that was popular with the lunchtime office crowd and mothers' groups. He was a little disappointed at the choice of rendezvous point. Adalia arrived tripping over a long, flouncing skirt and with a wicker basket on her arm.

'Lost your way in the woods, little girl?'

'I came to deliver you this basket, then I must be on my way back to grandmother's house.'

'Stay a few minutes with me at least.'

'We-e-ll ... Okay, then. But you must promise to be good.'

She spread a gingham blanket under the shade of a tree and merrily directed Jonathon to rest his back against the trunk. While nosing through the basket and exclaiming over its contents she unbuckled him, straddled him and settled the voluminous skirt around them both. Then, within metres of the oblivious picnickers, Adalia retrieved morsels of cherry, chocolate and cheese from the basket. She fed him with her fingers as she moved up and down on him.

Jonathon relished returning to work with the secret knowledge of Adalia on his fingers, his thighs, his chin. He enjoyed scrawling on the whiteboard, knowing that beneath his gold and pearl cufflinks were tender half-moons left by her nails. The knowledge gave him a glow of superiority. He and Adalia were not, would never be, *that* couple. The couple who had an obligatory post-anniversary dinner fuck. The couple whose conversation had become so threadbare that a meal out without friends to cover the silence was unthinkable.

Jonathon looked again at her message. He felt something that if he'd bothered to analyse it in any depth, he would have recognised as relief. Since Jureece, things had been different. He was waking up at odd hours of the night, clammy with the byproduct of viscous dreams in which Adalia was outpacing him, just out of reach. He would call to her but too late; she had already been swallowed by a crowd, or an overgrown field, or a door for which he had no key. He would lie awake, his heart slowly resuming normal operations, and watch her sleeping soundly on the pillow next to him. Occasionally, she burrowed her shoulders into the bedclothes as if tunnelling deeper into unconsciousness and further from him. Sometimes when she did this, anger surged through his body. How could she not know what he had done? What he continued to do. Why was she not pulling him back from himself, filling him up? He'd started to sleep in the spare room, about which she said nothing. In fact, she'd been oddly quiet and withdrawn for the past week or so.

The hours between now and the assignation stretched ahead of him. He scrolled through his emails and responded to the most urgent. He pre-empted the colleagues and clients who were most likely to call him that afternoon and dealt with their issues. He made excuses to his team and indicated he would not be contactable during the afternoon. His vagueness about his whereabouts sent a ripple of anticipation through the office. It was from occasions of equal mystery that he plucked plump, ripe corporate fruit seemingly from the ether: the accounts that wended their way to him under the noses of other bidders, and the star recruits that brought their juicy insider information and contacts.

Jonathon took the jacket from the back of his chair and slipped it on. He riffled through his desk drawer and found a bottle of cologne. He splashed it on the undersides of his wrists and the pulse point on his neck. The warm, spicy scent suffused his office.

He locked his computer and flicked the out-of-office messenger on. He set his phone to silent, picked up his wallet, keys and Adalia's note, and left the office, giving Arie a conspiratorial wink as he passed him in the hall. In the basement car park, the headlights of his convertible flashed on and off as he approached. He programmed his GPS and drove out into the stream of city traffic.

Jonathon resigned himself to crawling through the choked streets as he crossed the city, waiting for the lunchtime crowd to pass by with their phones at their ears and their oversized shopping bags on their shoulders. After an hour or so the knot of traffic unwound and he entered Glaxxon; within minutes the jostle and hum of the city yielded to the gritty, close maze of the dockland suburb. The sunlight was tepid in the grey streets but still the paint peeled from the shop facades in shreds like leprosy. The people he drove past didn't look up.

Fifty years earlier Glaxxon had been a thriving community of migrants fresh from the boats. People had come there to re-experience the epicurean specialties of the towns and villages they had left behind, buying the wares from street carts and markets that stretched from the town hall all the way to the sidings at the docks. Glaxxon had a faintly underworld glamour about it, back in the day. Respectable businessmen and city councillors were rumoured to be caught up in laundered money and unrecorded imports of exotic animals and hard liquor.

Those days were long past. Most of the shipping freight now bypassed Glaxxon and went to the harbour at The Dryans instead. The great warehouses were abandoned and given over to squatters and criminal gangs. Glaxxon was the distribution point for the powders and pills that made their way from backroom laboratories to the noses and gullets of men in tailored suits who worked in bright city offices.

But for all its signs of decay, Jonathon intuited, Glaxxon

was on the cusp of a radical reinvention. He saw that within a short space of time underground clubs would spring up in its obscure laneways, the kind of clubs that were popularised by word of mouth. Dimly lit bars with gorgeous, unsmiling staff and an impossible-to-pronounce signature dish would open their discreet doors beside tiny shops of curios and collectibles. Glaxxon's unsavoury reputation and its history of faded glamour would twin into a new cool. Jonathon had a good nose for that kind of thing. He could practically smell the money waiting to be made in the furtive streets, and he wrote a mental note to talk to Adalia about investing in a warehouse.

His GPS had difficulty locating The Arbour Room. The prim voice kept announcing 'arrived' in front of what looked like an abandoned factory. Jonathon cruised up and down the street a few times, looking for a shingle or a street number, but the road was blank, anonymous. Finally he parked his car, clicked it locked and walked slowly between the factories, warehouses and blocks of flats. He took a closer look at the abandoned factory and saw that an old-fashioned fire escape ran upwards along its side. Where the stairs ended he couldn't tell because it was obscured by a black, scalloped awning on which 'The Arbour Room' announced itself in faded silver letters.

A shiver of anticipation ran through him. What *was* Adalia planning?

He mounted the stairs at a clip, then slowed when he felt them reverberating. At the top of the stairs was a red door, closed, with a gleaming brass knob. He reached for it but the door opened inwardly as if by magic.

A man's baritone floated from the gloom. 'May I help you?'

'I'm The Fox. I'm here for The Redeemer.'

'Right this way, sir.'

The door opened wider and Jonathon stepped into an anteroom lit almost entirely by candlelight. He was in a place of shabby grandeur that might once have been a gentlemen's club. Floor-to-ceiling bookshelves, crammed tightly with hard-bound books, ran along one wall. Claret-coloured leather couches, deflated and frayed but still beautiful, invited one to sit down. Ashtrays were discreetly placed on the marble and timber surfaces. Jonathon expected a butler to bring him a brandy balloon and a cigar.

'The Redeemer is waiting for you, sir. Right this way.'

The concierge had the fluid, unobtrusive movements of a man who knew how to make himself invisible. Jonathon followed him up a narrow, winding staircase to what appeared to be a garret. Through the filth-encrusted window, he could just see the street below. He noted, with some annoyance, a couple of youths in hoodies idling near his car. The concierge unlocked the door and stood back to let Jonathon pass. The door closed and locked behind him.

Adalia was there, in the middle of the small room with an apex roof. An attic room, then. Behind her, intriguingly, was an ornate, heavy velvet curtain that divided the room. She was bundled up in a coat, belted at the waist. He began to salivate at the idea of what she was wearing beneath. The ambience suggested a corset. Perhaps a maid's outfit.

She drew her finger to her lips and indicated that he be silent, then ushered him towards a straight-backed wooden chair next to her. He sat down then reached for his wife's waist, but she slapped his hands away. With a secretive smile she pulled a pair of handcuffs from her coat pocket. They were heavy, the real thing: not some flimsy erotic fakery purchased from the sex shop. He briefly wondered where she had sourced them as she cuffed first one wrist, then the other behind the back of the chair. The cuffs pulled at his shoulders slightly.

Wordlessly, Adalia sashayed from him to the curtain. She drew on the plaited black cord, and the plum-coloured curtain pulled back. She ran the cord slowly through her hands, revealing the scene an inch at a time. Jonathon first made out a pair of red shoes, blue jeans and hands clasped tightly in a lap. Then two women on either side, both seated, one leaning forward eagerly; the other with her arms folded, her legs crossed, and her ankle jerking up and down. Another pull on the cord, a swish of the curtain, and a fourth woman materialised.

Adalia gave one more tug then looped the cord around a hook on the wall. She joined the women, taking a seat on the far right of the group. The fronds of the curtain whispered as they settled.

Jonathon's mouth fell open. In front of him were five women. His wife. Jureece. Clara. A woman whose face he recognised but whose name he couldn't quite recall. (Honour? Anna?) He hadn't seen her in years, since before he and Adalia were married. Finally, the tanned and bouncy intern whose breasts were a wonder for the ages, Yasmin. His cock sprang up against the press of his pants, demanding release. He looked in wonder at his wife, whose face was curiously blank. How had she known? How had she possibly arranged this delectable smorgasbord?

A shaft of sunlight prised its way through the grimy window, slicing the room into a triangle of sparkling dust motes. Jonathon could barely breathe for anticipation.

Adalia cleared her throat and tucked her hair behind her left ear, the distinctive gesture that preceded a discussion she expected to be difficult. 'Thank you for coming, Jonathon.' Her voice was cold, impersonal. 'Do you know much of the history of The Arbour Room?'

He shook his head, slowly.

'Back in its heyday, The Arbour Room was the club of choice for gentlemen of means. They'd come here after a day at work, overseeing their clerks and dealing with the harbour masters and the customs minions that stood between them and their freight. They'd come here to read the papers and mingle with other great men. Drink brandy, smoke cigars, talk about politics and terms of trade. There was a dining hall where they could take dinner unmolested by the petty concerns of women.'

His wife was using what he thought of as her 'official' voice, the one she broke out for public speaking and community events involving journalists.

'Of course their dinners and their brandies and their ironed newspapers were all prepared by women.' Adalia swept her arm in front of her, sending the dust motes dancing, and looked around. 'This was where they slept. This was the female servants' quarters. There was one for the butlers and club manager, of course. Much larger, better equipped. You can see it later if you like.'

Where, Jonathon wondered, *is this going?*

'Care to take a guess as to how many women called this little garret home?'

Jonathon looked around. The room was probably no more than ten square metres, fifteen at most. He shrugged, making the handcuffs rattle against the wooden backing of his chair. 'Three? Maybe four?'

'Twelve. Twelve women. Four beds, three to a bed. No plumbing. No heating. Crappy ventilation, as you can see. There's a story that one night the club manager and the butlers were bribed to leave the door unlocked. While the women were asleep, totally exhausted after a hard day's labour, a group of club members climbed the stairs, came uninvited to this room and took it in turns to rape the women. Some of them went to the police, but what chance did they have against all these respectable and powerful men? The whole thing was hushed up, though you can find traces of it in the papers. So the law let them down. The cops didn't want to know. The doctors who treated the women called them sluts and refused them even basic pain relief when the inevitable babies made their way into the world.'

Adalia laughed — a hard, nasty laugh. Jonathon felt the first finger of panic poke into his breastbone.

'You have to understand that most of these women were either new to this country, boat-fresh, with no connections, no family. Or they were orphaned. Or women whose husbands had run off to god-knows-where, leaving them destitute. So what choice did they have but to come back here, to this squalid little room, and go on serving and feeding and wiping the shitty arses of the bastards who had violated them?' Adalia paused. 'Can you imagine that, Jonathon? Can you?'

She let the question hang in the air. Five pairs of eyes looked at him.

'What is this about?' Jonathon said quietly.

Adalia appraised him with an expression he didn't recognise. 'What do you think?'

Jonathon hesitated. Some part of him wanted to believe, still believed, that Adalia had brought them all here for a delicious afternoon, and he didn't want to make a misstep that might jeopardise that. 'I don't know.'

Adalia took a deep breath. She was gathering herself, Jonathon knew, marshalling her forces. In a steady, controlled voice, she said, 'Clara, honey. Would you like to start?'

Jonathon hadn't seen Clara since the end of her internship, but he'd thought about her often. She looked different. Thinner. Older. Her hands trembled slightly as she reached behind her chair and took the jacket that hung there. As she twisted around, her shirt collar slid, revealing the wine-stain of her birthmark.

She held the jacket out in front of her, uncertainly, as if it might assume a different form. 'Do you recognise this?' She looked at the jacket rather than Jonathon.

He nodded. 'Yes, it's mine, but how ...?'

'The morning after the Christmas party, when I woke up, this was in the room. The Quiet Room. Along with my clothes. The ones that had been ... taken off me.'

Jonathon drew in his breath sharply, but the air would only go so far. A metal plate seemed to have sliced into his upper ribs and lodged there. He rattled the handcuffs and rocked, outraged, in his chair. 'Get these off me. Now! Adalia – what is this? This is bullshit. Get these off me right now,' he commanded.

None of the women moved. Clara continued to thrust the jacket towards him as if she expected him to take it. Jureece looked at the ground. Yasmin and the woman whose name he couldn't remember looked frightened.

'You,' Adalia said crisply, 'are not going anywhere. You are going to sit there and listen to what these women have to say.'

'The fuck I will. You lure me here under false pretences, for what? Some psycho-feminist pity party? Seriously, what the fuck do you think you're doing, Adalia? Have you lost your mind?'

'Have you?'

He grappled with the chair and the cuffs and succeeded only in toppling himself over. He landed on his side. The fleshy pad of his shoulder took most of the blow but there was still a crack as his cheek made contact with the floor. He was shocked at the pain of it. He imagined his cheekbone fracturing – cartoon-like – triggering a zigzagging faultline through his skeleton until he collapsed, a pile of bone fragments.

Tears pricked his eyes. Adalia had passed the handcuffs through a slat at the back of the chair so he couldn't move without taking it with him. He was almost immobilised. He lay there, gasping for breath as the pain subsided only to make way for a morbid, profound embarrassment. He hadn't felt like this since he was an adolescent at summer camp, and even as he lay there flushing red from scalp to toe, he registered the novelty of it. This unfamiliar scale was interesting to him and, he assumed, everyone else. *I will tell Adalia*, he thought, before the absurdity of that notion caught up to him.

He heard the scrape of her chair as she stood and the soft clack of her heels as she walked towards him. He watched her approach — sideways — and thought, *She's going to kick me.* He braced himself, and closed his eyes. But she didn't. She bent down beside him and investigated his crashed-up cheek with her fingers. 'I don't think it's broken. But you're going to have a bruise.'

'Adalia, please,' he implored her softly, so the others couldn't hear, 'untie me, for god's sake. Whatever it is you want to talk about, whatever point you're driving at, let's just deal with it on our own. This is nuts, this is crazy. Baby, please.'

Adalia spoke over her shoulder. 'I'm going to need some help to get him upright.'

The woman whose name he couldn't remember came towards him with Clara. The three of them manoeuvred him and the chair back up, then resumed their seats.

'The next time you throw a tantrum and end up on the floor,' said Adalia, 'you're staying there. Understood?'

He didn't answer. A sort of numbness was stealing over him. He couldn't believe — didn't believe — that this was happening. He was trapped in an unusually vivid dream. Or deep under an anaesthetic for an operation he didn't remember needing. Maybe he was dying, or already dead. He felt himself drifting away from his body and looking down on the scene from the tip of the A-framed roof. He saw a man tethered to a chair wearing an expression of glazed shock, purple blood flooding a spot on his cheek. Five women were arrayed before him; one of them his wife. A silk-inlaid, tailored grey jacket heralded the women like a standard. They rode chairs like horses into battle. Words floated towards the ceiling and seemed to echo there. It was only on the rebound that he caught them.

'When I woke up I didn't know where I was. I was in a room I didn't recognise. It was dark but oddly luminous, too. I could hear this *swish-swishing* noise and a low hum, like from a fan or something. I lay there very still trying to work it out. I heard a splash and that's when it came to me. I was in The Quiet Room at work and the noises I could hear were the fish swimming about in the aquarium. I felt this rush of relief.' Clara's words stopped collecting at the roofline, replaced by a shrill peal of laughter. Below him, the other four women flinched in shock at the sound. 'Sorry. I know it's not funny, yet somehow it is funny. That I felt relief at realising where I was. That's the last time I remember feeling happy. The last time I remember feeling safe.

'I just lay there, putting the pieces of the night together in my mind. I remember going about with Jureece with the Christmas decorations and making the punch. I remember talking to you and Arie and a bunch of other people from work. I remember drinking lots of punch and doing some coke in one of the boardrooms. Then everything gets really hazy. I remember being led down a corridor at one point. Jureece told me later that was you and her leading me towards The Quiet Room. I know I vomited.

'Then I remember lying down in the glow from the aquarium and going to sleep. Or passing out. But I woke up a few times.' She paused. 'I saw you. And Jureece.'

Jureece stopped jiggling her ankle up and down and became very still, her eyes on the floor.

'I don't remember you leaving The Quiet Room. I must've gone back to sleep. When I woke up there was someone sort of scrabbling on top of me, pulling at my clothes. I thought it must be Jureece trying to get my coat on and get me out and into a cab to go home. I remember saying, "Don't worry about my coat. I'll be fine." But it didn't seem to make much difference because the person kept tugging at me, so I kept saying about the coat but then I realised they were pulling at my trousers and they were pulling them downwards and I remember thinking that was really odd because you don't put your coat around your legs and then my legs were sort of pushed up against my chest and I was trying to get off the couch but there was someone above me blocking my way and then the next thing I knew I became aware that the person was, was fucking me and I remember thinking, *There must be some mistake*, and that I was confused because I was so drunk and thought the sounds were coming from Jureece and Jonathon who were fucking again on the floor so I thought, *I'll leave the room*, but then I couldn't because there was this person on me and it was me being fucked and the grunting was coming from this shadow above me and it was his cock that was in me and I didn't want it but I couldn't move and I couldn't get my thoughts together and I kept screwing up my eyes tight then springing them open like I could throw myself out of a dream but it didn't make any difference and then I must've passed out again and when I woke up the fish were splashing around and my trousers and my underwear were on the floor and there was this raw feeling between my legs and I felt flattened out somehow like I'd been run over and it took me a long time to dress myself and when I was gathering up my clothes I found this jacket bundled up with them and it's your jacket and I know it's your jacket because you used to leave it behind your chair and I always admired it because of the blue and gold swirls on the lining, and so I'm asking you if it was you.

'Did you rape me?'

It seemed to Jonathon that it took ages for all these words to make their way to the ceiling and assemble themselves into the right order. His wife was weeping, quietly. She had her hand around her mouth as if she feared what might come out and the tears were spooling from her eyes, down her cheeks and over her hand, dripping onto her coat. The sight of his wife in such distress, and his laboured comprehension of the question that was being asked of him, tore him from the roof. He crashed into his body and felt the swelling along his left cheekbone and the burning in his shoulderblades from the pull of the handcuffs.

'No,' he said; and his voice was clear and strong.

Clara dropped the jacket to the floor as if its weight was too much for her. Her eyes welled with tears. 'I went to the hospital and they did a rape kit. Do you know what a rape kit is?'

'No, Clara. I don't.'

'It's this cardboard box no bigger than this,' she mimicked its shoebox shape with her shaking hands, 'and it has lots of plastic envelopes in it with different swabs. They comb through your pubic hair and extract material that's not yours – and that's what they call it: "material" – and that material goes in one of the envelopes. Then they do a swab around your vagina. Then you have to lie back and they open you up with a speculum and poke around inside you looking for somebody else's DNA, and the whole time you just want to run out of the room and get into a shower as hot as you can stand it and scrub at your skin because you think that you will never, ever feel clean again.'

'Clara,' he said softly, 'I'm so very sorry.'

'So you admit you did it?'

'No. It wasn't me. I would never, ever do something like that.'

One of the women made a scornful noise.

Jonathon ignored it and continued. 'I'm sorry about what happened to you. I'm sorry that I didn't stay with you after –' He stopped. Was he going to admit to his infidelity while his wife was sitting right there? He felt assaulted by crosswinds of confession and rebuttal, guilt and innocence.

He looked at the young woman in front of him, so changed from the perky girl who had stencilled snowflakes on the glass doors of the offices. She kept her eyes on him, her mouth a thin line of pain. Her hands shook in her lap.

'I'm sorry that I didn't stay with you after I'd ... after I'd been intimate with Jureece.' Jonathon did not look at his wife. Could not look at his wife. 'I put my jacket on you to keep you warm. For what it's worth I felt terrible about what happened. I *feel* terrible about what happened.'

'You feel terrible,' said Clara flatly. 'Did you offer to make a statement to the police?'

'No, but no one asked me to. If I'd been asked I absolutely would have.'

'Did you instigate an internal inquiry? You've got the power to do that. I know you have.'

'No, but –'

'Did you go to HR with your concerns? Did you raise them in a meeting, tell your colleagues and your fellow executives that what happened to me is unacceptable and there needs to be changes?'

'No, but you can't go randomly accusing people or upturning an entire organisation because of one,' he was about to say 'unfortunate', but stopped himself, 'because of one horrible incident.'

'It's called rape, Jonathon.' It was his wife who spoke. He turned to look at her. She didn't seem angry, just sad. Unbearably, inconsolably sad.

'Yes.' He nodded. 'Yes, it is.' He turned his eyes back to Clara. 'What happened to you is unforgivable, Clara. For what it's worth . . . for what it's worth it did change things. For me, I mean. I've been looking at everyone at work with suspicion, wondering, *Was it you?* So I don't blame you for wanting to know if it was me. I'm happy to take a DNA test so you know I'm telling you the truth. I will help you. I'll do whatever you need me to do. If you want to press charges I will support you.' He meant it, and he felt good that he meant it.

'Why didn't you quit?'

'What do you mean?'

'If it affected you so much and you didn't know who to trust at work anymore, why didn't you quit? Why didn't you storm out of there in disgust? Find a new job? Go to the media? Raise a fuss?'

Jonathon thought about that.

The woman whose name he couldn't remember answered for

him. 'It's because it's all the same, isn't it? You leave one firm, you go to another, but it's all the same. Same culture. Same expectations. Same bullshit. Different poodles, though – that would have to be a plus.'

He started at the word 'poodles'.

'What? You thought we didn't know that's what you call us? Cute and decorative and great fun at the Christmas parties, after which you move us on and get a fresh, unsullied batch. Isn't that right?'

'What does any of this have to do with you?'

'Do you remember me?'

'Yes.' *Oh god, what was her name?*

'We were graduates together. Actually, we were the star recruits that year, the ones who all the top firms wanted. I remember thinking, *This is it. I've made it. All that hard work and now . . . now I've arrived.*' She smiled wistfully. 'And now here we are – you're one of the masters of the universe and I'm . . . I'm doing okay. Well, even. But I pay the vagina tax. And you don't.'

'I've worked fucking hard for everything I've achieved. Everything. It wasn't just dropped into my lap through sheer force of my magnetic penis so –'

She waved his words away as if they were an irritant. 'You're smart, you're motivated. You work hard. All true. But you know what? Those things are true of everyone in this room. It's a slow and painful process, learning that you'll never be quite good enough. You'll never have the goods, or rather, you're a different type of goods. One that gets served up for men like you.'

'That is such bullshit. I've never forced myself on a woman in my life. I find the idea repugnant. I've promoted women. I respect women. Jureece,' he turned from Anna/Honour to Jureece, 'you and I know what happened between us.' He wouldn't look at his wife. Jureece continued to look at the floor. 'Can you look at me, please?' She dragged her eyes from the floor to him, reluctantly. 'Did I force you to have sex with me?'

She shook her head.

'Did I threaten you in any way? Use a knife or drug you or tell you that if you didn't have sex with me then there'd be no job for you?'

She shook her head again.

'I'm a shitty husband,' he said, and his tone had the ring of a man used to having the floor. To being listened to in meetings and having his ideas attributed to him and no one else. 'I've been unfaithful to Adalia. But I've never, *EVER* had sex with a woman without her consent.'

'What do you know about consent?' Adalia spat the words at him. She appeared to him suddenly accipitrine, primed and ravenous. 'A girl comes into a firm like yours after years of study and slog. She's special. Different. She's one of the chosen ones. Her friends know it and they resent her a little. Her parents are bursting with pride. She's become a person apart, alienated from where she came from, not quite sure-footed in this new world she finds herself in. So when she finds out what's expected, what's *required*, how much choice do you think she has, Jonathon?' Adalia raised her hand to stop him speaking. 'And don't tell me that she can say no. She can say no to you, maybe. But what about the next one? And the one after that? How do you say no to a whole culture? A whole history?'

'That. Is. Such. Bullshit. You want me to carry the can for every shitty thing every man has ever done?'

Yasmin spoke softly, almost inaudibly. 'I didn't want to have sex with you.'

Jonathon flinched, remembering her naked from the waist up in the photocopy room. How her tanned, unblemished skin and impossibly round, inviting breasts had seemed so bountiful. He'd gone to the photocopy room because he was retracing his steps, trying to find a file that he'd misplaced. He found Yasmin instead – petite, golden and compliant. He'd unwrapped her like a rare and precious object, assuming all the while that she was aware of the worship he brought to her body.

'I have a boyfriend. We're faithful to each other. Well, we were. You just … You just.' Her voice tapered off and she seemed suddenly childlike, lost. 'You didn't give me space to say no to you in a way that wouldn't do either of us any damage.'

'I don't know what you mean.'

'You were so sure of yourself, so confident. Like it didn't even occur to you that I might not want to. As if such a thing was impossible, like, like … like water flowing upwards or the sun staying up for three days. And that made me worried that you'd get angry if I said no and then you might freeze me out and all of it would have been for nothing. So I tried to, you know, laugh about it when you kissed me, and I picked up my file and made busy noises but it was like you didn't register that, and then I just sort of … froze.'

Jonathon tried to remember their encounter, any noises she'd made or words she'd spoken. But all he could recall were those glorious, glorious tits and the colour of her, so even, like she'd been dipped in toffee.

'So now I just, I avoid you. I try not to think about it. Some days I'm mad with myself for not slapping you and storming out of there. Other days I just feel tired, like I'm in a fight that's too big for me and it makes me exhausted just thinking about it. My boyfriend broke up with me, by the way. When I told him. About what happened. He called me a slut.' She couldn't quite get this last word out, so all Jonathon heard was 'slu' before her whisper faded.

He could think of nothing to say. Literally nothing. He was a man adept at silences. He could drop them in meetings, let them fatten and grow portentous. He could do warm silence and icy silence, and a silence that was neither and discomfited people with its ambiguity. But this – this blankness, this absence – was new.

Again, he thought how he would like to tell this to Adalia, and that's when it hit him: he would be telling Adalia nothing anymore. Adalia was leaving him. Their marriage was over. The shock of this realisation made him momentarily forget where he was. He tried to lean forward and put his head in his hands before he remembered that he was handcuffed to a chair and could go nowhere until someone unlocked him.

So deep was his torpor that he barely noticed the women preparing to leave. There was a shuffle for coats and the silent, prolonged embraces of people who've been through something together that they will never speak of again. The door opened and closed a few times, and then there was just him and Adalia in the room, his jacket crumpled on the floor between him.

Adalia cleared her throat. 'I've arranged for your clothes and toiletries and papers you might need to go to your parents. I'll have the rest of your stuff boxed up. Let me know where you want me to send it. Or I can put it in storage. We can sort out the property and money issues later. Just so you know, I don't plan any funny business: fifty-fifty like we always agreed.'

'I was never unfaithful in my heart, Adalia. I've never loved anyone else.'

She was quiet for a few moments, mashing her knuckles into her mouth and trying not to cry. Her words, when they came, were cracked and hollow. 'It's not the infidelity, Jonathon. You can get over that. You can even maybe accommodate that. But what you're capable of. What you can ignore.' She shook her head. 'I don't know who you are.'

Me neither, he thought miserably.

'There's one other thing.' She stood up from the chair and unbuckled her coat. She dropped it onto the chair and took a step towards him, flattening the fabric of her dress around her chest and stomach. Her belly was taut and hard, her breasts fuller than usual. She let this new fact drop into the heaving wash of Jonathon's brain, then retrieved her coat. 'The concierge will be up in about ten minutes to remove the cuffs. Don't contact me, and don't come to the apartment. I've had the locks changed.'

Her heels echoed along the corridor, away from him. Of all the things he could have thought in that moment, he remembered his former colleague's name. Anya. Her name was Anya.

Jonathon thought about all of this as lay in his burrow of sticks and leaves. His masjythra was cinched around him, buttoning down against the autumn chill. He couldn't stay there, and there was nowhere he could run. He crawled out on his hands and knees. He pierced the side of his face on a thorn as he emerged. It was a deep cut; the blood ran warm along his face. He stood up in front of his hide-out and brushed the leaves and dirt from his arms and legs, then he swabbed at his face with his hand.

He trudged down the hill towards his quarters, expecting at every moment to be apprehended by a party of Vaik or red masjythra sent to cuff him. But the grounds were empty. A presentiment crept over him that everyone was gone. Some catastrophe had unfolded in his absence and he had shuffled out of the copse to find himself the last man alive at The Fortress. He pushed the thought away from himself and picked up his pace. Even when the quarters and the bathhouse came into view he saw no one, and the only antidote to the silence was his footfall on the darkening grass.

Relief flooded him as he entered the quarters and began to climb the ramp. Although it was quiet, it was a habituated quiet. There were others nearby, breathing, thinking. Yet no one had come to apprehend him. Why?

He entered his room and saw Mandalay sitting on the bed. Straight-backed and rigid, she was carved sharply in profile against the stone. He took up a position opposite her, his back to the wall. Her gaze moved deliberately from their abeyance in the middle distance, along his torso to his face. Her eyes were aflame with rage. The gold flecks in her irises had the molten glow of liquid metal about to be poured.

'You,' she said acidly. 'How dare you? How dare you?'

'She's a child,' he said. 'A child, Mandalay.'

'She's Vaik. And she's been raised to believe that pleasure is her birthright. This was a big day for Ulait, for all of her mothers. And I approved her choice.' Mandalay shook her head. 'Do you think I came to your bed because I find you irresistible?'

Jonathon was dumbstruck.

Mandalay laughed – a hard, nasty laugh. 'I was vetting you. For some reason Ulait likes you. I wanted to be sure you would bring her pleasure. To make her first time something she would look back on with pride and satisfaction. Not the furtive, awkward first fuck most girls out there,' she gestured at the window, towards The Dryans, 'have to endure and spend the next ten years getting over before they figure out how their bodies work. Ulait chose the food. We spent two days cooking. She poured the verrglet into the decanters herself. We all helped with preparing the room, her make-up. You are despicable.'

He wanted to know if Ulait was all right, but he knew he daren't ask a question. Mandalay was shaking slightly, from rage.

'I accept the punishment, Mandalay.'

She rose from the bed, erect and intentful, and stretched her hand towards him. With the hard, filed fingernail of her thumb she slowly sliced open the cut on his face that had closed in the gelid wind. He winced, then felt the weep of blood along his skin. She placed her palms on either side of his head and drew towards him, so close he felt her breath on his face.

'It's not for you to accept anything. You have no say here. You neither accept nor refuse. You are emptied out, ego-less. But you are such a giant to yourself that you don't know how to give yourself away. The only eyes you have are your own, so you're sightless.'

He shrunk into the wall behind him. Was he to be taken to The Great Hall again? Would he be brought before The Woman? Part of him didn't care. He'd done the right thing, and that was all.

Mandalay pushed off from the wall beside his head and clapped her hands, loudly, in front of his face, making him start. 'I wash my hands of you, Jonathon Bridge. I relinquish you from my assignment.' She lowered her voice. 'If Ulait is scarred by this, I'll kill you myself.' With that she turned on her heel, strode to the doorless door and clicked her fingers. 'The reds will come for you now.'

Then she was gone.

The red masjythra entered his room and wordlessly took him by the arms. They led him down the zigzagging ramp and towards the bathhouse. He was expecting to be taken to The Great Hall, but they came to a halt at a low stone building adjacent to the bathhouse. The building was small and compact, no larger than his room. He had always assumed it was a storehouse.

One of the men held the door open and Jonathon was marched inside. The room was vacant and airless, its only contents a desk and an intercom. It took him a moment to notice the dark rectangle sliced into the floor and the stairs winding down beneath it. He was sandwiched between the reds – one in front of him, one behind – and escorted underground.

The air in the stairwell was close and damp. The hood of his masjythra snaked upwards and tightened around his head, chin and cheeks, leaving only a thin sliver for his eyes. The walls were carved from the earth and marbled like cake. Had he been marched down those stairs when he'd first come to The Fortress, his legs would have trembled and buckled from the unfamiliar exercise. Now, standing in front of a square, barred cell – as a red punched a code into a keypad, making the door glide silently open – they shook from fear, not fatigue.

'How long will I be here?'

The men didn't answer. One jimmied his fist into the small of Jonathon's back until he shuffled into the cell.

'Wait. Just wait.' His mind raced. A lawyer. Could he speak to his lawyer? Get a message to her somehow?

One of the men punched in another code, and the door whispered shut. The men did not make eye contact with Jonathon. Silently, they disappeared back up the stairs and into the world on the surface.

'Wait,' Jonathon shouted after them. 'Wait, please. You need to tell someone I'm here. People need to know I'm here. My wife needs to – Come back!'

This wasn't happening. They couldn't just lock him up and walk away.

'Come back,' he demanded. He gripped the bars and screamed, 'Get the fuck back here *RIGHT NOW* or I won't be answerable for the consequences. I'll have this place shut down.'

He yelled his threats and demands until he grew hoarse.

This simply wasn't happening. It couldn't be happening.

And yet it was.

These contrary facts from opposing universes collided and brought on a kind of fit. His whole body shook under the pressure of it. The fine muscles under his eyes bunched and shivered, and his teeth chattered. Blood, warm and salty, filled his mouth from his punctured tongue. Electricity crackled through his hair. He gulped at the fetid air, but it dissolved before the withering branches of his lungs. His rapid-fire heart discharged into its chambers.

The ground rushed towards him.

He opened his eyes and took in the slantwise cell. He had landed on the same cheekbone he'd cracked at The Arbour Room and it was throbbing against the stone floor. Luckily, his masjythra had protected him from further injury. He pushed himself to a sitting position and nursed his cheek in his hands.

The cell was devoid of natural light, but a dull orange flickering along the walls told him a fire burnt in a drum nearby. Directly opposite him was another cell, empty.

'Is there anyone there?' he asked the darkness, his voice raspy. 'Is anyone else held here?'

His voice didn't echo, so the underground chamber was large. He'd heard stories of vast subterranean networks at The Fortress. They'd been built, the stories went, during the time of the civil wars, before his city and the Vaik agreed they could live, segregated, with one another. The tunnels had served as supply routes and escape hatches.

Jonathon willed himself to his feet and walked unsteadily to his bunk. The walls were bare earth, perfunctorily sealed. The floor was roughly paved. There was a drinking fountain built into the back wall and next to it a hatch – for food, he surmised. A clean, chemical toilet was built into the corner furthest from the bed. The mattress was clean and firm, the quilt freshly laundered. So even here, he thought darkly, a Vaik might want to fuck him.

He vacillated between fury and torpor.

Periodically, outrage would flood him and he'd stand railing at the door, demanding release. He indulged long and complicated fantasies whereby Mandalay got her comeuppance. He knew people. If only she knew how he knew people. He would have Adalia write an exposé; engage the best lawyer; take Ted – his MP – to dinner and tell him of the gross violations taking place not ten kilometres from where men made laws. He'd have The Fortress stormed, torn down beam by beam. He'd see Mandalay in the dock if it killed him.

The fury sustained him for a time, then it ebbed and he was left frozen by the reality of his incarceration. At such times he couldn't move. Couldn't talk. Could barely think. In his somnolence, the curtain between sleep and wakefulness drew aside until he was no longer sure of the difference between them. In his dreams he was awake, but lying on the mattress in this very cell. When he was awake he would remember nights spent in other beds – the hard, narrow bunks at Lake Wykaita and the scuffle of boys returning from or venturing towards night raids. Adalia's bed in her old apartment, fluttering with silver chocolate wrappers. His bed at his parents' house, the one he'd returned to – dumbfounded – when Adalia left him.

Time was the binding of his life. He had accreted milestones with the avarice of a hoarder. School, university, first job, post-graduate studies, promotion, promotion, executive, marriage, partner. Even his year in The Fortress as a supplicant had been roped off by temporal buoys: fifty-two weeks, at which point he would emerge as a husband and father and assume his trajectory. He had a horror of timelessness, those marshy spaces between deadlines. He must always be attaining the next goal or he felt himself dematerialising, a science-fiction character stuck in a malfunctioning teleporter.

In his tiny cell, time ceased to be linear and became at times circular, at others stuck fast. Food would appear at odd times in the hatch. But who brought this food? Why did he never see anyone? The dishes would gather and he would decorate the floor with them, arranging the smaller and larger plates in a model of the solar system. Then, suddenly, the plates would be gone and he would wonder: *were they ever there?*

He tried to pin time fast by visualising where his urine came up to in the chemical toilet. If it emptied then he would have a sign – proof – that change was going on around him. That people came in and out of his cell and he hadn't fallen into a cosmic anomaly. But even as he stared at the bowl, denying the urge to urinate, he was never sure if this was the first time he was about to urinate; that those previous times were figments or rehearsals for this moment.

His mind slipped sideways. Coronas burst in his cell and rearranged the marbled slices of earth into swirling kaleidoscopes. Ulait would tell him stories about what the shifting patterns in the soil meant.

Sometimes his father sat on the edge of his bed, ill at ease as he had been when Jonathon returned to his parents' home after Adalia left him. 'Well, well,' his father would say, as if preparing for a conversation that never came. Whenever he found himself alone in a room with Jonathon, he left hurriedly, summoned by an urgent task that could brook no delay.

Jonathon had long conversations with his mother in which he told her just how much he had hated summer camp. When she shrugged or made to contradict him, he'd reach out to shake her to attention, and she would glitter and disintegrate and re-form in another space in the cell.

Mandalay would come sometimes, slicing open the cut on his face again. Her words ricocheted off the cell walls: *Do you think I came to your bed because I find you irresistible?*

The words poured through the bars of his cell like water, rushing at him. They seeped out of the clay, and then out of his pores. *Do you think I came to your bed because I find you irresistible?* The sentence multiplied and played on different frequencies at once, until he was bombarded. It was a mocking whisper at his water fountain and a scream beneath his bed. When he clutched the bars so tightly that his knuckles whitened it was a chill, slow verdict incanted by a universal council. At night when the reflection from the fire in the drum was strongest, it was a children's singsong chorus.

At one point he fell asleep (or woke up) to find three girls sitting on his bed. They surveyed him politely. He shrunk into the bedclothes till only his eyes and forehead poked out. All of the people who had drifted in and out of his cell during his incarceration were known to him. He did not recognise these girls. Who were they? What did they want with him?

They would appear and disappear at odd intervals. When they were absent he would look for them, inexplicably worried for their welfare. When they appeared he would hide under the bedclothes waiting for them to be gone. They mostly perched on his bed. They were straight-backed and fresh-scrubbed, their hair swept into neat ponytails. They had the air of well-bred school students waiting for class to begin. On some level he knew that it was up to him to initiate an exchange with them, but his mind was blank, then it slid into panic.

Always the cell played its multi-track soundtrack.

Do you think I came to your bed because I find you irresistible?

Do you think (Do you think I came to your bed because I find you irresistible?) I came to your bed because I find (Do you think I came to your bed because I find you irresistible?) you irresistible?

Only Adalia never came to his cell, and he understood by this that she still did not know who he was. He called out to her, or thought he did, but he was too indistinct for her to locate.

They were there again, the girls. Two sat cross-legged; one dangled her legs by the side of his bed. She was strong, athletic. Good health radiated from her. Perhaps he could ask her to help him escape. But he stayed where he was, the blanket covering most of his face, staring surreptitiously at them. He'd never heard them speak, though they always seemed poised on the brink of it.

He longed for words, for anything other than the snaking chorus in his cell. He opened his mouth to speak but the language escaped him. How did speech happen? Of what did it consist?

I'm losing my mind.

At first, this realisation didn't cause him a great deal of pain. He viewed it dispassionately, the way he viewed profit-and-loss statements. He moved inexorably from the numbers to redundancies and restructures without sentimentality. When the facts spoke, they must be answered.

But then he understood that if he was insane his child was lost to him. The Vaik would hand him over to Adalia (assuming they ever planned on letting him go) and she would take the steps to have him dealt with 'appropriately'. He didn't doubt she would do this. Their baby came before either of them, a hierarchy of importance that he fully endorsed.

Something in him stirred. Some flicker of the boy who knew he didn't want to go to Lake Wykaita. The man who couldn't quite let go of whatever had happened to Clara in The Quiet Room. The father.

Slowly, he drew back the bedsheet until his face was visible. What must he look like? Cachexic and hairy like a starving madman lost in the wilderness.

The girls looked at him. Polite. Expectant.

'Hello,' he croaked.

They smiled at him, showing white, even teeth.

When the reds came to lead him out of the cell, he paid them only cursory attention. It wasn't until he stood outside, blinking in the feeble light with the wind raising goosebumps on his legs, that he began to suspect he was no longer in his cell. The reds wandered a few metres distant and politely looked away.

He dug his toes into the lush grass. There must have been rain in his absence, lots of rain. The grounds were a vast green canopy. After being enclosed with only the swirling browns and irons of earth colours, he found the emerald was almost painful to the eye. Tall reeds were licking at the side of the bathhouse and the low, tinny *whoosh* of water running through pipes echoed around him.

He kicked first one leg then the other in front of him. He jumped, tentatively at first, feeling the impact spread across his knees and feet. Then with real gusto, as high as he could. His body felt different. Slacker. Weaker.

How long had he been underground? Why had he been released?

The air, pure and fresh after the miasma he'd been breathing, bleached his lungs. His stay underground had refined his senses. Chlorophyll, sea salt, soil litter, wet bark — he detected them all on the rushing breeze. He dropped to all fours and curled like a cat, arching and flattening his back. His muscles twitched at the unfamiliar motion and his masjythra snaked around him.

He lay on his stomach, then rolled over, surveying the sky. Clouds rushed past so fast he thought they couldn't possibly be real and his mind was playing tricks on him again. But then the clouds opened and the rain fell, making his masjythra coil tighter around him. He stuck his tongue out and felt the raindrops splash into his mouth, and the certainty grew within him that he was outside and he was free.

The reds hovered nearby. Jonathon turned his face to the side and observed. A couple of them were conversing intently, their voices too low for him to decipher their words. They were clearly waiting to take him somewhere, some assignation. So why were they permitting him this indulgence? He turned his face to the sky again and pushed back his masjythra so he could feel the cool, clear water on his skin.

One of the reds tentatively approached him. 'Jonathon Bridge. We've orders to take you to your assigned Vaik.'

He didn't say anything, just lay there as the rain fell.

The red looked at the others, seeking assistance. 'She's waiting,' he said.

'Let her wait.'

He enjoyed their collective intake of breath at his insolence and spread his arms wide across the grass, as if settling in.

'If you don't come voluntarily we'll have to carry you.'

'Carry away.'

He made himself a dead weight as they lifted him by the wrists and ankles, his bum sagging towards the grass. Grunting, they manoeuvred him along.

'That ramp is going to be fun,' he said; then, as they all locked eyes at the thought of how to leverage him up the zigzag ramp, he began to laugh. The whole thing was suddenly, unbearably funny. Once he started laughing he couldn't stop. His body shook with it. The reds grappled with him as with a slippery fish. One lost his grip on Jonathon's wet ankle and his leg fell to the grass, making him laugh even more uncontrollably.

'You fucker,' a red swore under his breath.

Jonathon raised his hand and kept it up while he struggled to surmount his hysterics. 'Just – give – me – a – minute.'

They dropped their hands from his limbs and stood back as he laughed himself out.

'Whoo.' He breathed slowly and purposefully, gathering himself together. 'Okay.' He got to his knees, paused, then stood up. His abdominal muscles ached from laughing, and tears leaked from his eyes. He fought down one last wave of hysteria, then indicated that the reds should proceed.

He wanted to see Mandalay after all.

Mandalay was waiting for him in his quarters. She stood at his window, her eyes sliding from him to the horizon, her fingers thrumming against the stone sill. He looked around his room as if seeing it for the first time. It was larger than he remembered, the bed more luxurious, the floors and walls cleaner and brighter. He checked for strange hairs on his pillow, for dust accumulating in the corners – something to fix how long he'd been gone.

Mandalay gave him a single, searching look then turned again to the window. 'You are all right,' she said.

He was riled by the assertion, was ready to give her both barrels, but she spoke again.

'Ulait has disappeared.' She spoke to the perimeter wall, the sky, the air. 'No one has seen her for two days.'

Mandalay stayed like that, peering out the window, while he tried to comprehend the import of her words. He remained on the precipice of delirium and could easily fall into it. He would enjoy Mandalay's fury at his insensibility, his refusal to be reached.

But.

Ulait. Gone.

He commanded his thoughts to come to order. 'She's thirteen, she's a teenager. She's probably playing hooky with one of her friends, listening to music and –' he was going to say 'talking about boys', but stopped himself. 'And drinking verrglet.' He was startled by the sound of his own voice. Was he always so loud?

Mandalay's fingers fluttered from the windowsill to a pendant at her throat. She ran the pendant back and forth along its silver chain. 'When we were approaching The Great Hall there were two olöcks foraging in the undergrowth. Do you remember?'

Jonathon wondered what this could possibly have to do with Ulait. Now that he'd pushed back his hysterics he found he needed to sit down, to get his head together and embed himself once again in the ebb and flow of time at The Fortress. To feel normal. Once he'd achieved that he'd understand better what to do about Ulait.

'The olöcks are usually ground dwellers. They make their nests in the hollows in the downs. They feed on worms and bugs they find in the undergrowth. They don't have natural predators here, so they've fallen out of the habit of flying. But earlier this week, there were two reports of olöcks flying. The general consensus is that they're checking the air pressure. They're remarkably sensitive to changes in the weather. The olöcks disappeared two days ago. It all points to one thing: a sestyatesh.' She took a deep breath, steadying herself. 'I need to ask you something, and I need you to think very carefully about your response.'

'All right.'

'Did Ulait ever confide in you, mention a special place or a hideaway?'

He saw that it cut Mandalay; the idea that Jonathon, an outsider, might have a connection with Ulait from which Mandalay was excluded. He was pleased. He hated her. (*You frightened me.*)

'No. I think you've overestimated our intimacy. Look, Mandalay, I'm sorry but I'm going to have to sit down.' He dropped onto the bed. He felt not faint exactly, but as if the floor was unsteady and might give way beneath him.

'You've had weeks to do nothing but sleep,' she snapped. 'I command your attention. In the Story-Keeping House, what did you talk about?'

'Fuck off.' (*You frightened me.*)

Mandalay seemed to be struggling to retain her composure. He wondered if this was the first time he'd seen her authentic self. The self she inhabited when she wasn't playing chess with men like him. She took several deep breaths before she spoke. 'You feel hard done by. Very well. That is a discussion for another time. Please understand. Ulait is missing and we are on the verge of a terrible storm. If you know anything that might help us locate her —'

Beg bitch, he thought. (*You frightened me.*)

'It would be helpful if you shared what you and Ulait talked about in the Story-Keeping House. The information might seem innocuous or unimportant to you, but it might give us a clue.'

'Mostly we talked about how she wanted to create her own drawings, use her own imagination without having to rehash stale Vaik myths all the time.'

Mandalay's eyes darkened, and Jonathon rejoiced to find he'd provoked her.

'She asked me to draw a picture.' He smiled at the recollection of Ulait's expert mimicry and her encouragement of his inept scrawling. 'I was rubbish.'

'And when you broke your vow and humiliated Ulait – she didn't make any threat to run away?'

'When I refused to be a paedophile, no. No, she didn't make any threat.'

Mandalay and Jonathon looked narrowly at each other across the room. He'd been marched to The Great Hall for arguing with a man declared isvestyii for raping children; then marched underground for refusing to have sex with a child. He remembered the way Mandalay had sliced his face open with her nail. The sardonic smile playing about his lips spoke plainly: *Go fuck yourself*. The old, familiar pleasure in skirmish returned. It was a warm, piquant bloom in his belly, the same bloom as after the first glass of good red wine.

'She might have mentioned something, but I'm half-starved and exhausted.' He feigned yawning. 'It's hard to remember.'

'I can have a tray sent up if you like.'

'And I'm cold.'

The words came strangled out of her throat. 'I will arrange a warm bath.'

He felt the silken slipknots of power between them disentangling.

'I'll have some food prepared for you.' Mandalay strode towards the door, her shoulders squared and tense.

Do you think I came to your bed because I find you irresistible?

Now she did need him, needed him unfeignedly. He would not make this easy for her. The sensation of resuming power was intoxicating. There was a low hum in his body, reminiscent of the sound the light panel in his office made when he flicked it on first thing in the morning.

Mandalay was already out the door when he found himself speaking. 'Wait.'

Her footfall slowed.

'Wait,' he said again.

She appeared in the doorway, her expression wary.

'There is something. When Ulait and I were drawing, she talked about one of her heroes. Eshta? Eshta-something? A Vaik who swam among enemy ships and converted foreign women to the Vaik cause. Ulait spoke about one of the ships being preserved on the grounds somewhere.'

'Thank you,' said Mandalay wearily, fiddling with her pendant again. 'Eshtakai. Yes, I know the ship. Ulait was always fond of that myth, even as a small child. We've checked the ship several times, but she hasn't shown up there.'

'The Story-Keeping Houses, then.'

'We've checked them all. There's no trace of her. It's like she's just,' Mandalay dropped the pendant and swam her hand through the air, 'vanished.'

Jonathon recalled his own semi-frequent 'disappearances' as a child: days when, infuriated by his mother's version of history or being ignored by his brothers, he would take a packed lunch and his schoolbooks and climb into the canopy of a favourite tree. Most of the time his absences had gone unremarked, and he never drew attention to them in the interests of keeping his powder dry for the next time.

'I know you're worried.' He chose his words carefully, screening them for resentment before he spoke, 'but this is pretty normal teenage behaviour, at least where I come from. Teenagers get sulky and moody, and they act out.'

'Things are different here. You decide you want sex, no one contradicts you. You want to try sterysh, no one will stop you. You want to go to the outside, off you go. But even supposing you're right and Ulait is acting out, there's a sestyatesh coming. We need to account for everyone before we go into lockdown. Ulait knows this. She knows how important it is. The fact that she hasn't shown up at one of the sentry posts makes me afraid that she's injured herself. Fallen into a quarry or wandered off into the interior. If she can't get to shelter before the storm comes ...'

Daidd swung into the room, breathless and agitated. Even the waxy scars on his face were red. He placed his fists against his knees and bent over to recover. 'The isvestyii ... He's gone ... broke curfew ... I've sent the reds out to check the northern and eastern sector, but –'

'The sestyatesh,' said Mandalay.

'Yes.'

Jonathon looked past Mandalay to the sky framed by his window. Clouds had amassed in such numbers and at such speed that the air was a rippling pewter. The wind whistled like an aircraft through the doubled grasses and the waves crashed at the rocks of the perimeter wall. Jonathon understood Mandalay's dilemma. The Vaik promised that no immoderate physical force would be used against the men at The Fortress; it was part of the deal. If she sent the reds out to find Ulait and recover the isvestyii, they'd be heading into an uncertain fate.

'I'll go after them,' Jonathon said.

Mandalay looked at him – hard – for a few seconds. 'That's noble of you, Jonathon Bridge, but I cannot guarantee your safety. The Vaik cannot ask this of you.'

'I know. I'm going anyway.'

'Me too,' said Daidd. 'We can divide up the grounds beyond the buildings. We can cover more ground if we split up.'

Mandalay was silent for a moment, again weaving the pendant back and forth along its chain. 'It's too much. It defies our covenant. We have responsibilities, to you, to your families.'

'The Vaik are my family now,' said Daidd. 'They have been for a long time. You know this, Mandalay.' He spoke in a low voice and held her gaze. Jonathon looked from one to the other, and back again. There was an intimacy between them he hadn't noticed before.

'Jonathon Bridge,' Mandalay said, 'I cannot allow you to embark on this so soon after your release. You need some time.' But her eyes told another story. Go, they said. *Go.*

He was still angry with her and wanted to make her suffer. But not at Ulait's expense. 'I feel all right. I'm going.'

'Wait here,' said Mandalay. 'I'll be back shortly.' She left the room, glancing Daidd's fingers with her own, leaving him and Jonathon alone.

Daidd moved to where Mandalay had stood at the window, looking out at the gathering storm. 'The isvestyii can't have gotten too far yet. He's maybe an hour ahead of us, two at most. My guess is that he's not after Ulait at all, he's just using the storm as a cover to make a break for it.'

'But it makes no sense. There's nowhere for him to go. He can't scale the wall, he can't hide indefinitely. If he makes it – god knows how – to the city, they'll hand him straight back.' Jonathon bent his mind to a question. 'Does he know that Ulait is missing?'

Daidd stood very still, his unscarred profile towards Jonathon. 'I don't know. I doubt it.'

'Daidd. You and Mandalay ...?' He let the implied question fill the room.

'I love her,' he said simply.

Mandalay returned, bearing boots and maps. Other Vaik

hurried in and out piling backpacks, flasks, tarpaulins and blankets on the bed. Mandalay handed a pair of boots each to Jonathon and Daidd; they were scuffed and rigid and the laces didn't match. Jonathon perched on the side of his bed and pulled the boots on. Over the months his feet had callused and toughened until he barely noticed cold or heat under them. He wriggled his toes in the boots and stomped his feet. He felt clownish. He remembered what it was to feel the pinch of cufflinks at his wrists, the cinch of a tie at his neck. His gullet instinctively constricted and the masjythra twitched, anticipating the knot of his tie that he had perfected at high school.

He was into his third season at The Fortress but, beyond fatherhood, had barely considered what shape his future life would take. Now, imagining his body encased in a business suit, he realised that he would not be returning to his old job at the firm, would no longer issue decrees from his office and feel the world moving around him like a masjythra. It was both a welcome and a terrifying thought.

'Thank you.' Mandalay took a steaming silver jug from a Vaik and poured cups for Daidd and Jonathon. Instinctively, Jonathon recoiled, but Mandalay pressed it on him. 'It's a strengthening brew,' she said. 'It will revive you and sharpen your senses.'

Daidd took it without question and began to drink. Jonathon remembered how eager Daidd had been to drink the sterysh the day Mandalay fed them to the crones. He wondered if that was part of why Daidd stayed – the promise of a chemical high as reward for his obeisance. He felt a surge of anger towards Daidd. Hated his docility, his compliance, his love for his captor.

Daidd's eyes met and held Jonathon's across the room. *He's scared.* Jonathon's anger dissolved at once. The storm that was upon them was no inconvenient downpour – it was a sestyatesh. The storm of legend that flattened towns and placed the whole province on emergency alert. There'd been one in Jonathon's living memory. He and his brothers had been excited by it, huddling against the reinforced glass windows of their parents' home with bowls of popcorn. They'd exclaimed at the debris tossed through the ravening skies, their own boats and bikes and gazeboes securely tied down.

Now Jonathon was about to step into one, his body weaker than it had been in months and his state of mind precarious.

He sniffed the tea. It smelt of blood and bone, his wildman face reflected in the dark liquid. Steeling himself, he drank it down in several gulps. It tasted of salt and earth and left a mineral fuzz on his tongue. An acute warmth stole across his abdomen and then along his chest and extremities. Daidd's working pupil bulged, contracted and bulged again. Jonathon's ears buzzed, and the particulate nature of the storm became suddenly evident. Each raindrop was distinct from the rest, each tree buckling at its own frequency. Daidd and Jonathon glanced covertly at each other. What were they ingesting?

Then the world settled. Jonathon felt strong and centred, but slightly hyped. He wanted to run, box, fly.

Mandalay did not drink the tea. She smoothed a large map out on the bedspread. Jonathon's eyes instinctively moved to the black dot that enclosed his home; the patchwork chair where Adalia would sit to breastfeed their daughter, her feet resting on the purple ottoman she'd won in a raffle. Jonathon was not afraid for them. Their home was strong and secure.

Mandalay's hand was slightly a-tremble, but her voice was strong and clear. 'We'll split up, each of us taking one of three routes in broadly concentric arcs. I'll take the outer arc here.' She traced a wide semicircle from their living quarters inland then back towards the final sentry post close to The Dryans.

Daidd followed the sweep of her hand then shook his head. 'That could take you five or six days in these conditions, and there's almost no shelter.'

'You question me, Daidd?' A look passed between them, palpable as a shove, but Daidd held her gaze. It made Jonathon flinch, and he was relieved when Mandalay said in a softened tone, 'There's a cave system along here.' She pointed to some triangles tipped onto their side. 'If the way becomes impassable I can take shelter.'

One of the Vaik, a nuggety woman with cinder-grey hair, spoke. 'The isvestyii won't take the inland route, Mandalay. It's too remote and unfamiliar. He'll stay close to what he knows and risk the shortest route to The Dryans along the sentry posts.' She traced the line of the perimeter wall.

'I think you're right,' Mandalay said. 'But Ulait. What will Ulait do? Where has she gone?'

The hum of activity sheared away, making the storm seem abrasively loud. Thunder, hail and rain clambered over one another like drunk and belligerent members of an orchestra. Jonathon felt the room's attention triangulate around him. *He* was the reason Ulait had run. *He* was a vow-breaker, and this was the consequence. He looked at the ground, heat rising in his face.

'Daidd, you'll take the inner track through the north-western sector. You know the huts and the way stations along there — check them all.' Mandalay paused. 'The wells too,' she said, barely audible.

Jonathon sucked in his breath, his eyes still on the ground where a vision of Ulait, blue-lipped under dark water, had materialised.

'Jonathon Bridge, you will take the perimeter wall as far as you can. You will stop at all the sentry posts. It may be that Ulait has taken refuge there, or that one of the sentries has seen her. If the way becomes impassable, you are to remain at a sentry post. That is an order.'

'The isvestyii —' Jonathon began, then stopped, unsure how to frame what he needed to say without making it a question. 'We all suspect that he's most likely to follow the established tracks to

The Dryans and try to pass over there. That makes it most likely that me or Daidd will find him.'

He waited for the Vaik to respond to his unstated plea: what do I do if I find him?

Mandalay's gold-flecked green gaze was steady. She seemed as stoic and remote as the statues he'd seen in museums on long-ago school excursions.

'I repeat again what I said before. You are under no obligation to undertake this. I tell you frankly that the Vaik cannot guarantee your physical safety and we are thereby breaking our covenant with you. You are free to remain here and no blame will attach to you. Indeed, I advise it.'

'I'm going,' he said. He still did not know if he could have behaved differently, made a different decision where Ulait was concerned. But he accepted that he had hurt her, and he would make reparations if he could.

Mandalay slipped a pack onto her back. A couple of Vaik helped Jonathon and Daidd to do the same. The packs were heavy, and would grow heavier still.

'You've provisions enough for three days,' said Mandalay, 'four if you're careful. Let's go.'

IV **CEB**

THEY TOOK the ramp to the front entrance and stepped into the wind. It caught Jonathon off guard. He staggered a few steps backwards, then righted himself by bending at a sharp angle into the gale. The masjythra took the tenor of the air and sealed around him. It covered his face, leaving a thin slit for his eyes and a baggy pouch around his mouth.

The three of them took the path as far as the orchard beyond the bathhouse, then diverged. Daidd placed his hand on Jonathon's arm, then was gone, the silver of his masjythra dissolving into the air. Mandalay said something to Jonathon that he couldn't hear above the din of the storm, then she too was gone, leaving him alone on the path that led to the perimeter wall and its sentry posts.

He adjusted his pack and bent for the wall. The path twisted and turned to avoid clusters of trees, so sometimes the storm pushed him from behind and sometimes belted him in the face. Visibility was so poor he could just make out his hand at full stretch away from his body. He paused every few steps to make sure the path remained under his feet and he wasn't wandering blindly, and probably fatally, off course. The boots felt alien — hateful, weighty clods that slowed him down; he thought about taking them off.

Although he could not yet see it, Jonathon knew that the wall was approaching because the storm sounded different, a great force that was encountering like resistance. Then the wall was there, barely centimetres in front of him. He reached out and touched the rough stone, craning his neck to see if the top of the wall was visible. From the city, The Fortress wall seemed white and even, like teeth. In fact it hugged the contours of the sea and land, low where jagged rocks or deep ocean made escape impossible, high near The Dryans and the city. The rain struck the wall slantwise, then slingshot into the exposed parts of Jonathon's body, stinging his fingers and lower calves.

Most of what he knew about the wall he'd gleaned from Ulait and the reading he'd done before he came to The Fortress. Parts of the wall were nearly a thousand years old. It was constantly re-fortified by stone from the quarry. This indiscriminate mixing of the old and the new had at first struck him as odd, as insufficiently reverent of the past. Now he understood that the fountains and statues of his city were preserved precisely because they were relics. A living culture has no need to petrify itself.

Jonathon knew that the sentry posts started about two kilometres from the cluster of quarters and buildings where most of the Vaik and their charges lived. The posts grew more frequent the closer the wall came to The Dryans.

He stayed close to the wall and trudged forward, stopping sometimes to huddle against the stone when the wind grew too fierce. After a while, the ceaseless thud of the rain and the *whoosh* of his breath — loud within the bubble of the masjythra around his mouth — assumed a hypnotic rhythm. Ensnared in fog and unable to see much in any direction, he began to wonder if he was still underground. Perhaps he remained in the cell, and his search for Ulait was merely his mind enacting a sentence of judgement and amends.

The idea grew into a certainty. He was imagining this: all of this. The thunder, the lightning, the pack gnawing on his shoulders. He was conjuring it all from his subterranean prison. The Vaik, masters of potions, had doctored his tea to summon precisely this hallucination. The thought then came to him that if he was the architect of this hallucination, he could be the architect of *any* hallucination. He could render any thought, any fancy, as real as this one. He could preside at his own sentencing.

And so he began to imagine that he was in The Quiet Room at work the night of the Christmas party. He had not fucked Jureece. Instead, once they had helped Clara to the sofa he had asked Jureece to find a bottle of water, a face washer and a bucket, but to do it discreetly. He also asked her to keep an eye out for Adalia and let her know where he was when she showed up.

With Jureece gone, Jonathon placed his jacket around Clara and brushed her hair back from her waxen face. He wiped the vomit from her mouth with his handkerchief, forcing down his revulsion at the smell. His plan was to let her throw up the worst of it – then, with Jureece and Adalia's help, manoeuvre her through the stairwell (where there was the least chance of being seen) and into a taxi, away from the main entrance.

He switched off the overhead light and told Clara to rest, settling himself on the carpet beside the sofa. In the luminous blue of the tank and the rhythmic swish of the darting fish, he began to feel drowsy. He must have dozed for a while, for he was awoken by a scuffle. He thought Jureece must have returned, but when he spoke her name she didn't say anything. Clara emitted a low, strangled growl from deep within her throat, and Jonathon turned to reassure her. That was when he made out a dark figure clambering on top of her.

Jonathon sprang to his feet and grabbed the man about the shoulders, but he clung fast to Clara. Jonathon kneed the man in the side of his ribcage – hard – then, feeling his grip on Clara slacken, Jonathon pulled him to the floor. The man rolled over as he fell and sprawled at Jonathon's feet, staring upwards. Jonathon retracted his foot to kick the man in the face, then stumbled in recognition. The face staring up at him was his own.

Tea, thought Jonathon. *The Vaik have doctored my tea. Every thought I have, every imagining, every daydream is going to end here: with my guilt.*

So it was that sometime later, he was not surprised when there was a lull in the storm and he saw the isvestyii ahead of him. They had arrived at a stretch of wall that came only to about chest height on the land side then fell in a sheer drop towards the water. Below them the sea heaved over the rocks.

The isvestyii was staring intently at the water, his hands balled into fists on top of the wall, his knuckles white. Rain streamed off his masjythra. The look on his face was one of utter desolation. *If I didn't know him*, Jonathon thought, *I would feel sorry for him.*

'You'll never make it,' Jonathon said, raising his voice to be heard over the rain.

The isvestyii, intent on the grey sea below, seemed not to hear him.

The storm had retreated, and in the heightened light Jonathon could just see the outline of a sentry post along the curve of the wall. It was five, maybe six hundred metres away. Perhaps a Vaik had the two of them in view down the barrel of her binoculars and would soon be marching out from her lowered drawbridge, ordering them to take shelter. But maybe not. Jonathon looked around for a weapon of some kind, a rock or a sheared bough. *If none of this is real*, he told himself, *I don't need a weapon.* So why did he feel such fear?

He bent, slowly, to pick up a flat slab of rock bleached white by the sun and rain, then took a tentative step towards the isvestyii.

'You'll never make it,' Jonathon repeated. 'There's no point.'

The isvestyii's eyes slid from the sea and rested, vacantly, on Jonathon. Jonathon pushed his masjythra back from his head so the isvestyii could see him plainly, but even then his presence seemed barely to register. *Perhaps*, Jonathon thought, *we're both hallucinating*. He flinched at the thought of the nightmares the Vaik would send after the isvestyii. What horrors could equal his guilt?

The clouds rolled back in the ivestyii's eye and Jonathon felt his pupils locate him. It was like being caught in a crosshair.

'You.'

'Me.'

The isvestyii's gaze shifted to the rock in Jonathon's hand. 'Are you going to kill me?'

'If I have to.'

'The Woman has decreed that you will judge in this matter.' The isvestyii repeated Laliya's words in a dull, flat monotone. 'Will that make you happy? To fulfil a prophecy?'

Jonathon shrugged. 'Can't say I care much for prophecy.'

'Then why are you here?'

'Did you think the Vaik would just wait the storm out while you stalked Ulait?'

'Who?'

Jonathon tested the heft of the stone in his hand. 'Don't bullshit me. You know what I'm talking about.'

The isvestyii shook his head slightly, a dismissive gesture as if Jonathon was distracting him from something important. He turned back to the pitching sea. He unclenched his fists and flattened his hands on top of the wall, bent his elbows, then sprang up. He hung there, struggling to find a toehold, then hoisted himself onto the wall, lying flat against it.

Jonathon dropped the rock and launched himself at the man's torso, trying to tip him back towards land. *It's my dream*, Jonathon thought, *back in The Quiet Room where I pulled the man who was me off Clara*.

The isvestyii kicked his legs and thrust his arms out to shake Jonathon off, but he was at a disadvantage on his belly, flailing like a turtle. Jonathon held fast, pressing his knees against the wall. The isvestyii stopped kicking and hugged the wall tightly. They were at an impasse; the meeting point of their twinned nightmares.

'There's nowhere for you to go,' Jonathon insisted. 'You can't climb down to the sea, and even if you jump and somehow live, you can't swim in that wash. You wouldn't last a minute.'

Jonathon felt the tension leave the man's body, and he thought that the isvestyii saw the sense in his words and was about to roll onto the ground. Instead, the isvestyii carefully rose to a sitting position, one leg on either side of the wall like he was riding a horse. He held his palms up towards Jonathon in a gesture of surrender. 'I'm not trying to escape.'

'Then what are you –?' Jonathon looked again at the pounding sea, the drop to the rocky outcrop, and understood.

'Can you imagine what it's like,' the isvestyii said quietly, so Jonathon struggled to hear him, 'to want what I want?'

'I'll never feel sorry for you.'

'Then you can help me.'

Jonathon almost laughed aloud. 'Why the fuck would I help you?'

'Because you hate me. I've been staring at this water for what seems like hours. A few seconds. A minute at most and it would be over. All over. I want nothingness. I want the absence of this,' he slapped his head, 'what goes on in here. In my body. But I can't jump. I just can't do it.'

'You don't deserve death. You don't deserve suicide, at any rate. A slow death being quartered by a Vaik blade, maybe. You owe pain to your victims.'

The isvestyii's eyes were wild, his face a shadow play of hollows and rings. 'Pain. What do you know about pain, Suit boy? For years I fought. Every day since I was thirteen at least I've had this in me. Always pushing it down. Drinking it down.

Piling normality onto it. A wife, a job, my own kids, a backyard with a basketball hoop. A car in the driveway that I washed by hand on the weekends. Took my kids to football practice. And I loved those kids. Like, normal love. They were the best thing about me. I thought they'd saved me, I really did. Because the idea of anything happening to my kids was just –' He shook his head. 'It was more than I could imagine. So how could I be a man who could do that to someone else's child? But all the time there was this . . . this thing festering in me. Bleeding out in my dreams until it got so I was scared to go to sleep.

'I felt it spreading, infecting. I closed the door on it, but it oozed out the sides. I was hosting my kid's birthday party and handing out lollybags with a party hat on and I wanted to scream, "Run children, run along home!" And they left but they came back in my dreams and in the dreams they wanted me, too.

'And I started to think . . . it wouldn't be so bad. There's worse things. Maybe it would be like lancing a boil. Do it once and get it out of my system. Make myself whole again.'

The isvestyii's body shook, a tremor that ran from his legs to his neck. The hands he'd been holding outwards, supplicant, shot upwards and ripped at the roots of his hair.

'It won't stop. It will never stop. You think I care about being made isvestyii?' Something low and guttural moved out of his mouth, bearing a thin line of drool. 'It was a mercy. A mercy. The idea of blankness. Of nothingness. Absence of wanting, resisting, wanting all just . . . gone. But being named it doesn't make it so.' He ran his shaking hands down the sides of his face, his nails drawing blood along his cheeks.

'Wake up,' Jonathon shouted. 'Wake up!'

He yelled it into the wind, as loud as he could. He slapped himself, hard, with an open palm on his vulnerable cheekbone. But he didn't wake up. The layer-cake walls of the cell did not swirl before his opening eyes. He remained there, by the perimeter wall of The Fortress, where a child rapist begged him for mercy in the eye of a storm.

'You have a child don't you, Suit boy?'

The isvestyii pushed his tongue through his clenched teeth. It protruded – pink, meaty and glistening – between the wet, yellow slabs. Jonathon shuddered and fought down nausea. Slowly, very slowly, the isvestyii drew both feet onto the wall, keeping his eyes on Jonathon. When Jonathon did not react he steadied himself, crouching, then drew himself to standing position. He threw his arms out for balance, a cross swaying in the wind. Jonathon felt the primeval attachment to breath, the evolutionary ballast holding the man's feet to the stone. Jonathon squeezed his eyes tight shut, and opened them.

Then he reached out and shoved the isvestyii off the wall.

There was a falling shimmer, then nothing. Just the regathering clouds and the dark line where the sea met the sky. Jonathon forced himself to look down. The wall dropped about fifty metres. There was no beach, just fangs of rock bared and unbared with the surge of the sea. He lingered long enough to be sure, then turned away and trudged on towards the sentry post.

Part of Adalia's job at the paper was to cover the high-profile trials. She would come home at night and splay her notes and transcripts on the coffee table in their lounge room. Jonathon would ring for takeaway and pour glasses of red wine. Adalia sipped it as she read, occasionally muttering to herself as she circled words and highlighted passages. Jonathon would crib space from the papers on the table for the food and sit on the floor to eat, propped up against a beanbag.

'Mentions ... summary proceedings ... recklessness as to intent,' he read at random from one of the transcripts, 'vicarious liability ... strict liability ... Is this even in English?'

'A very particular English with a very particular intent.'

'What's that? Bamboozle the punters so they feel like they're getting their money's worth?'

'Partly,' Adalia nodded as she forked noodles into her mouth, 'but there's something deeper going on.' She chewed vigorously, excited as the ideas took shape in her mind. 'These legal words and concepts, they've been refined over centuries. What might have started out as a rock five hundred years ago is now agreed, by a painstaking process of elimination and taxonomy, to be a grain of sand. People, when they come to the courts, get to feel like they're in the flow of centuries of accumulated wisdom. Everything's been codified, from the greetings to the seating to the gowns to the order of events. It gives comfort to people, it really does. Even those who are found guilty get something out of the ritual.'

'Like what?'

'A part in a familiar play where everyone takes their role seriously. A chorus, an audience.'

Jonathon now understood what Adalia had meant. He felt entirely alone. Atomised. For the rest of his life he would carry the image of the man clawing against the pewter sky and the grey sea that closed over his head. The isvestyii bobbed up once, managed a lungful of air, then was yanked downwards as though by a giant hand. He disappeared from view, and Jonathon thought it was over, but then the sea offered him up – alive – on the hand of a wave, then curled and dragged him down again. Jonathon kept seeing this offering and retraction as he splashed towards the sentry post.

He didn't feel pity for the isvestyii, and would not have wished him alive again had he the power to do so. But how to assimilate what had happened? Jonathon wanted to be called before The Great Hall to account for himself. He wanted to hand himself over to The Woman so she could compartmentalise his innocence and his guilt, then unify them into a neat and authoritative judgement.

Yet, instinctively he knew that he would not be summonsed, and he alone would have to preside over the day's events. When The Woman had said he would judge, this was what she'd meant.

In The Arbour Room, ten minutes after his inquisitors left, the concierge came to Jonathon's rescue just as Adalia had said he would. If he was surprised to find Jonathon shackled to a chair, he did not show it. He inserted the tiny key into the handcuffs and then, while Jonathon stood up and shook his arms to restore feeling, he asked, seemingly without irony, 'If sir would care for a brandy?' Sir drank the brandy, then staggered outside to find his car. Barely considering where he was going and why, he drove to his parents' home.

Jonathon killed the engine and looked up at the imposing house where he had grown up. Through the open curtains he watched his parents entertaining their guests. 'We are entertaining this weekend,' his mother would announce when he was a boy, as if she and his father shunted from dull to amusing at precisely 6 p.m. on a Friday evening. Watching a waiter edge around a guest with a tray of canapés, Jonathon felt fury savage him, all bared teeth and ragged claws. Fury at Adalia for the outrageousness of what she had done. Fury at Clara's and Yasmin's accusations. Fury at the realisation that his child was being carried in a body that wanted nothing to do with him. Fury at biology, fury at the world. Fury that he found himself, at the age of forty-two, sitting in his car in his parents' driveway on a cold autumn evening.

He let himself into the house and took a glass of wine from a circulating tray. He noticed the ridges on his wrists from where the handcuffs had been. He downed the wine within three steps. He took another one and headed for the kitchen where he knew he would find whisky. He was riffling through the cupboards when he felt his mother's eyes on his back.

'Good evening, Mother,' he said, without looking up.

'Jonathon. What a lovely surprise.'

'Is it?' He took the bottle to the sideboard, found a glass and ice, and poured five generous fingers. He was mesmerised by the slow turn of the ice in the amber liquid.

'What's happened?' his mother asked.

'Adalia.' Jonathon took a slug. 'Adalia, she ... she ...'

'Adalia what? Jonathon, what is it?'

He stared at his mother, erect and immaculate in her frosted-pink twinset, and realised that Adalia had snookered him. How could he tell anyone – let alone his mother – about what had happened to him that afternoon? That he had been expecting a saucy rendezvous with his wife, but instead found himself handcuffed to a chair and interrogated about his adultery, his workplace practices and his possible complicity in a rape. That he had been kicked out of his own home and advised of his impending fatherhood in virtually the same breath. There was no way to package up the event that left him free of ridicule or suspicion.

'Adalia has left me,' he stuttered.

'I see.' His mother's expertly made-up mouth drew into a thin, crimson-coloured line.

'I need a place to stay.' He raised the glass to his mouth again, his hand shaking. 'Temporarily.'

His mother's appraising gaze moved from him to the kitchen doors and the sound of tinkling glasses and conversation on the other side. 'You're welcome to join us, of course, but no doubt you wish to be alone at this,' she paused, 'difficult time. I'll have one of the guestrooms in the new wing prepared.'

Jonathon was about to ask why he couldn't just go to his old room when he realised that this would require re-entering the party to take the stairs to his former bedroom. His mother was hiding him. 'Thank you,' he managed.

She nodded. 'I'll have a tray sent up.' She reached out and tentatively touched Jonathon's arm; her mouth twitched, as if she were about to say something but then thought better of it. She disappeared through the swinging doors and Jonathon heard her remark to a guest that this was 'just one of his impromptu visits'.

Jonathon took the whisky and the ice bucket to his room, shattering sparks of rage as he went. He stood by the window and looked out at the blue shimmer of the pool, drinking, as a maid fussed about with pillowcases and fresh towels behind him. She left the room and returned with a tray of food purloined from the party. 'Your mother says to eat something,' she said. Jonathon looked at the maid, remembering how he had profited from his Uncle Jasper's liaison with one of the staff years before. Could it have been this woman? 'An extortionist,' Adalia had called him, though not unkindly. 'A maximiser of opportunity,' he had countered.

He wondered now, about that woman. His Uncle Jasper was a fat, sweaty big-noter. It was hard to imagine that the woman had given way to him in a fit of passion. Had Jasper promised her something – a better job, perhaps? Or had he found her out in some misdemeanour and used it to bargain his way down her pants? Jonathon recognised Adalia in the direction his thoughts were heading, bringing on a fresh fit of rage. Not only had his wife tricked him and dumped him, she was colonising his thoughts, taking him over.

In the days that followed, rage shadowed Jonathon. He felt electric with it, as though if he clapped his hands sparks would fly. His mother began shaping his silence about the separation into a palatable narrative. When boxes of his clothes and paintings arrived in a van, he had done 'the gentlemanly thing' and left Adalia the apartment. The pregnancy shocked his mother at first, but soon became the plausible instigator of the separation. 'What you're prepared to put up with for yourself, you draw the line at where a child is involved,' though what precisely Jonathon was not prepared to put up with she did not say.

His workmates treated him with caution, taking care not to fuel his anger. He emitted blasts of pre-emptive aggression into the most innocuous encounters, until people began to avoid him. Colleagues made excuses not to attend one-on-one meetings. He imagined that the poodles, who would once have taken every opportunity to attract his attention, tossed coins to see which of them would have to take him his coffee. He noticed the way conversations tapered off when he entered rooms, and he became convinced he was the subject of gossip. Fear of ridicule stoked his anger higher.

He was at work when Adalia made the first contact since their encounter at The Arbour Room. Her name flashed up on his desk phone and all the air quit his body. He reached for the handpiece, watching his fingers closing on it in slow motion. 'Hello?'

'Hello, Jonathon.' She sounded tense, distressed. 'Look, I'm sorry to call you at work and without any warning. I just didn't want you to hear it from anyone else.'

'Hear what?' Silence on the other end. 'For god's sake, Adalia, hear what?'

She drew a breath. 'Jonathon, I've just heard from Jureece. She told me … she told me that Clara has died.'

'What? What happened?'

'She died by suicide.' A long pause down the phone. He listened to Adalia breathing on the other end, picturing the oxygen flowing into her, across the barrier in her belly and towards the fledgling lungs of his child. 'Jonathon? Jonathon, are you there?'

'Yes, I'm here. How did she … How did she … exit?'

'She hanged herself. I thought you would want to know.'

'Thank you for telling me.'

'Of course.' There was warmth in her voice. He wanted to

pour himself down the phone, along the wires and into her arms. 'I'll email you the details of the funeral. I mean, not that you have to go. I just thought –'

'I'll be there. I'll let everyone at work know, too.'

'Okay.'

He cleared his throat. 'How are you? How's the pregnancy?'

'I'm doing all right, all things considered. I didn't exactly plan on single parenthood.' Jonathon squeezed his eyes shut and gripped the phone tightly in his fist. 'The morning sickness is a trial. My complexion has this attractive radioactive-green hue until about eleven every day.' She attempted a laugh.

'We will need to talk, Adalia. About the baby.'

'I know. I know we will. I'm nearly there, I just need a little more time.'

'When you're ready.'

'Okay then.'

'Okay.'

'So I'll send through the details about the funeral now. I'll see you there. I'm sorry to be the bearer of bad news. I just thought … I thought it would be even worse if you had to hear it from someone else.' Despite everything, he realised that Adalia was trying to spare him the terrible shock of hearing it from one of his colleagues, someone who might pass over it with an off-colour joke.

'I'm glad you told me, Adalia. Take care. We'll talk soon, yeah?'

'Yes. Bye.'

The phone clicked and the receiver buzzed. Jonathon returned it to its cradle and mechanically opened his emails. He jotted down the details Adalia sent him, picked up his files and phone, and headed for his next meeting. Hearing from Adalia had quelled his rage and left a terrible emptiness in its place. He felt voided. In the meeting he clicked his pen, opened his notepad and gave every sign of being attentive as his colleagues relayed the monthly results. He nodded at the appropriate times, and looked as if there was much he could say when they discussed rumours of insider-trading at a rival firm.

'Well, that about wraps it up for the formal agenda items. Is there any other business?'

Jonathon waited for Arie to remind his colleagues about the end-of-financial year bowling event being hosted by Finance, then said, 'I have some news.' The table turned to him. 'You will remember Clara Fitzgerald; she was one of last year's graduates.' There was a ripple in the room, as if everyone was trying to move out of the channel of a noxious fart without drawing attention to its presence. 'I'm sorry to have to tell you that Clara is dead. She committed suicide. Her funeral will be held on Friday morning. I'll provide the details of the service to HR.'

'That is sad news,' said the head of Legal, 'very sad news. I'm not sure, though, that we should make a public comment about the deceased.'

'Who's making a public comment? I'm merely advising you that a former colleague has passed away in the saddest of circumstances and that her funeral is on Friday for anyone who wants to pay their respects.'

'That's all well and good, Jonathon, but given the circumstances in which Ms Fitzgerald left the firm, the presence of any of our staff at the funeral *will* be taken as public comment. Any official correspondence from Human Resources to the office about Ms Fitzgerald's death may well be subpoenaed if there is any … any unpleasantness surrounding her death.'

'Clara hanged herself. I think we've reached peak unpleasantness, don't you?'

'Don't be such a cretin, Jonathon. You know how these things get out of hand.'

'Have we considered, though,' it was Alexandra, the director of HR and the only woman in the room, 'the optics of not having a presence at the funeral? That might play even worse.'

'The optics?' Jonathon asked. 'Jesus Christ, Alex, *the optics?*'

'Yes, Jonathon, the optics.' She met his gaze across the table. 'Clara Fitzgerald was a fine young woman who made a solid contribution during her year here. I'm sorry to hear of her death. But there is precisely nothing we can do to change it. What we can do is manage the fallout from her passing in a way that protects this firm and Clara's memory.'

'I'm sorry, but perhaps you can explain to me what Clara's memory needs to be protected from exactly?'

His colleagues looked at him with a mixture of pity and contempt. They were trying to be tolerant and patient with him, he knew, because of his recent separation. But at the same time that tolerance had a limit, and he was discovering its precise location. Clara had interrupted *how things are*. Dropped a pebble in their collective shoe. This was so self-evident that Jonathon's obtuseness bordered on facile.

Jonathon was early to the funeral. He parked his car and waited. It was a cold, dull day, threatening rain. Several times he reached into his inside pocket to be sure the envelope was still there. He watched Adalia's car drive in: an orange retro number he had bought for her birthday several years ago. She had offered it to him on the inventory of their shared goods through her lawyer, but Jonathon had refused. It was a gift.

Adalia left the car and began walking to the church. A tightness spread across Jonathon's chest. She looked very much the same and yet entirely different. Her gait had changed to accommodate the growing life within her. She seemed more flat-footed. Her hair was mostly hidden under a luxe blue scarf but he could tell she had stopped dyeing it. For the baby, he assumed.

He quickly exited his vehicle and stepped nimbly across the car park. He didn't want to startle her unduly so stopped shy of the entrance where she was sure to see him.

Adalia gripped the handle of her bag a little tighter as she approached. That she was stressed was clear, but she attempted a smile. 'Hello.'

'Hello.'

They stood there, each at a loss, as mourners began to file into the church.

Jonathon cleared his throat. 'Adalia, can I have a word?'

She glanced towards the church, her fingers still clenched around her bag strap. 'I think the service is about to start.'

'It won't take long. It's important.'

She hesitated, glancing again at the church. Jonathon resisted the urge to take her by the elbow and usher her a little further from the entrance.

'Please.'

Adalia nodded and he gestured for her to follow him. By the side of the church was a laneway of close trees that gave them some shelter from the congregation. Each tree had a little plaque in front of it, commemorating the lost and valorous of some far-flung war.

Jonathon reached into his jacket pocket and pulled out the envelope. 'I wanted you to have this.' He passed it to Adalia.

'Jonathon, this really isn't necessary. I'm fine for money. I do earn a wage, you know.'

'It's not money.'

'Then what? Divorce papers?'

'What? No!' His heart shook at the thought. 'No. No, Adalia, it's a DNA test. I took one. It shows that I wasn't the one who —' His voice faltered. 'It shows that I'm not Clara's rapist.'

'Oh, Jonathon,' she said softly. 'Is that what this is about?' She shook her head, her expression incredulous. 'How can you be so smart and so dumb at the same time?'

'I don't understand.'

'Do you really think I would have engineered The Arbour Room if I thought you'd raped Clara?'

'What?'

'Of course I knew. If I thought you were guilty we would have had a very different conversation. And I would have gone to the police.'

Jonathon felt off balance. Outmanoeuvred in a game where he had misunderstood the rules. 'But I . . . I don't understand.'

'I know,' she said sadly. 'That's the problem.' She handed back the envelope, unopened. 'We'd really better go in.'

He followed her towards the church and into a pew near the back. As she sat down, Adalia's bump was visible. Jonathon disciplined himself not to stare, forcing his gaze forward. The service was well attended, and he could clearly differentiate between people who had known Clara before and those who'd known her after her move to the city. The afters wore muted suits and spoke softly among themselves; the befores were overweight and sobbed voluptuously. Jonathon noticed Alexandra and the firm's CFO taking a seat towards the front with the other afters. There to keep an eye on him, he suspected.

He was keenly aware of the letter in his jacket, close to his heart. The brief, impersonal analysis of his DNA indicating a less than 0.0003 per cent match with the semen collected in Clara's rape kit. He'd thought it was absolution.

The service began with a blare of music, a sentimental anthem attached to a football team that all of the befores knew. They sang with gusto, some of them standing to punch the air during a line in the chorus. Embarrassed for them, Jonathon looked down at the program.

He was overwhelmed by Adalia's presence, by the knowledge that his baby-to-be was within reach. He hadn't expected that the test results would effect an immediate reconciliation, but he had thought they would clear some debris from the road. Reveal the path. Adalia's proximity overwhelmed him.

When Clara's father — a small, dignified man with the strained posture and large hands of a physical labourer — took to the podium, Jonathon tried to focus his attention. Clara's father spoke in a halting voice about his winsome child, her childhood obsession with ice-skating and, later, with statistics. Pictures of Clara were projected onto a screen and the sobbing grew louder. A gap-toothed child, reserved and quizzical, slowly assumed the shape of the woman Jonathon recognised. A short, mousy blonde with a pronounced birthmark — attractive in her way but plain next to Jureece. He remembered with shame the dismissive comments about 'the runt poodle' that he had not corrected, had barely registered. Jonathon began to cry.

He could not recall the last time he'd cried, but it must have been when he was a boy. He wept openly, surrendering to the physicality of it. He cried great ratcheting sobs, a painful clutch in his chest. He heaved for breath through the narrowing tunnels of his nose and throat. The water astounded him. There was so much of it. Adalia handed him tissues. Why was he crying? He hadn't known Clara well, and his few engagements with her were meshed with shame. Her not being there didn't rip a Clara-shaped hole in his life. But he was stricken. Stricken by his wife's presence and by an overpowering regret. By the sense of what he had lost and would yet lose.

Adalia stood by him in the fine drizzle as the coffin was laid into the ground. He didn't drop a handful of earth with the other mourners, feeling he'd no right to it. The priest intoned the formula, reminding them that, in the end, this fate awaits us all. When the priest had finished speaking and offered what solace he could to Clara's immediate family, the mourners began to disperse. The family handed Jonathon a card that thanked him for coming and invited him to a wake to be held in The Dryans that afternoon.

'Are you going?' Adalia asked.

He shook his head. 'I'd feel like an intruder. Are you?'

She nodded and he could tell by the set of her teeth that she was steeling herself for it. 'I promised Jureece. Besides, I feel like I owe Clara something. I know that doesn't stand up to reason. But there it is.'

It began to rain in earnest. Jonathon and Adalia took shelter in his car. She wiped her damp face with her scarf. Water beads glistened in her hair, her regrowth light at the roots.

'I don't think you should drive, Jonathon. You're in no fit state.'

He let the latest wave of sobs move through him. It was like having diarrhoea. He just had to let it run its course. He rubbed his thumb against a smudge on the steering wheel, waiting until he could talk. 'Have you noticed how when shit goes wrong or bad things happen, people say "There was nothing I could have done" or "I didn't see it coming" and most of the time that's probably true. There's some comfort in that lack of power. But I actually could have done something here. I actually have power. Some real power. And I didn't use it.'

'I don't think you can hold yourself responsible for Clara's suicide. The reasons people kill themselves are complex. Jureece told me she thought Clara was doing well. Happy in her new job. Getting over … what happened. You're not perfect, Jonathon, but you didn't kill her.'

'No. I know that. But I sure as fuck didn't save her either. At every step along the way since what happened happened, I could have made a material difference. That's the thing, Adalia. I could have pushed for an internal inquiry like Clara said. I could have made a fuss and people would have had to listen. I'm a director and a shareholder. They wouldn't have liked it but they would have had to listen. Clara was easy to ignore. I'm not but I still just,' he waved his hand, as if reaching for something in the air, 'just sleepwalked through it.'

'Maybe that's better,' Adalia said in a low voice. 'I accuse myself of the opposite. Clara didn't want to be involved in my little set piece at The Arbour Room. Said she just needed to put the whole thing behind her. I convinced her otherwise. How articulate I was, how fulsome on the topic of justice and responsibility and taking back control. Of what we owe to other women. But really, was I just out for revenge? Was she just useful to me as someone who could help me hurt you?'

'You're not a vengeful person.'

'Not usually, no. But I think I went a bit mad for a while there. Jureece told me, you know, about what happened between the two of you. She was so young and so guilt-ridden, I think she just needed someone to confess to. When I found out about Clara, the whole thing became a crusade.'

He smiled wryly. 'Well, crusades *are* your thing.'

'I know, right?' She laughed bitterly. 'I'm the proverbial dog with a bone. Refugees, hunger, exploitation in The Dryans, give me a hint of injustice and I'm away. The intrepid journalist on the case. I just couldn't admit to myself that this was personal. That you'd broken me.'

He sucked in his breath. 'Please don't say that.'

'I'm not ashamed of it. It's a risk you take when you love someone. You can't be in love and keep your power. It doesn't work that way. I'm putting myself back together. Slowly. I just hope bubs isn't imbibing all this trauma through the umbilical cord.' She spoke to her belly, 'You doing okay in there, kid?'

Jonathon's heart lurched again. He kept his eyes on the rain through the front windscreen and asked what he needed to ask. 'Is there any hope for us, Adalia?'

He could feel her concentration from the seat next to him. Empires rose and fell in the seconds before she answered. He held himself very still, anticipating a tip into grief that would swallow him whole.

'I don't know what to tell you, Jonathon. I'd like there to be. For me and for the baby. But I don't trust you.'

'What happened with me and Jureece … and Yasmin. It will never happen again. I promise you.'

She waved the words away. 'It's not actually the physical stuff, the sexual stuff, that's the issue for me. Although I won't pretend I have a lot of trust in that regard. It's something else. It's got to do with you, Jonathon, with who you are.'

'I'm the same man you fell in love with.'

'I know. It's not as if I didn't know about the … the less savoury elements of your personality. I thought I was the woman to tame you.' She laughed. 'God, I'm such a cliché.'

'You're anything but a cliché, Adalia.'

'I was fascinated by you. Your stories. Beguiled by the entree you gave me to your world. But I think there's something in you that's faulty, or just not there at all. Like some empathy gene is missing. Sometimes I've wondered if I were to cut you open, if there'd be … blankness. A lot of energy, yes, and electricity and anger … but no – I don't know how to put this without sounding like a cheap pop-psychologist – no core. No furnace where all this energy is coming from. I don't think you deliberately set out to hurt me, or Clara or Jureece or Yasmin or anyone, really. But there was nothing in you stopping it, either. I'm not making much sense. I'm trying to articulate something I'm only just beginning to understand.'

He was silent for a moment, still feeling himself teetering on that precipice. 'You're right. Or, at least, you're in the ballpark of right. I've often felt like there was something missing. Some switch or valve. Most people I know are missing it too, but they don't know it. Or they don't care. I *do* care. I just don't know what to do about it. One thing I do know. I want to be a good father to this baby. Whether we're together or not, I want to be – I will be – a good father.'

'And what's that, Jonathon? What does a "good father" look like?'

'He's present. He's hands-on. He understands that the child is a unique little individual, not some extension of himself. He loves his child fiercely. Primally. But he holds himself in check because he knows the child has to find their own way.'

'God.' Adalia wiped a tear from her cheek. 'When you get it right, you really get it right. How can you be so great and such an irredeemable shit at the same time?'

'Tell me what to do, Adalia. Anything you want, I will do it. You see something in me, you know you do. I want to dredge that part of myself up to the surface, feed it and make it bigger. Tell me what you want me to do, how to fix this.'

'The Fortress.'

'What?'

'You could apply to go to The Fortress as a supplicant.'

He burst out laughing. 'You can't be serious.'

'Why not?'

'I just … It seems – bizarre. Under the circumstances.'

'What do you mean?'

He cleared his throat. 'I would be required, at The Fortress to, you know, go to bed with the Vaik. Since infidelity is part of our problem, it just seems bizarre to go somewhere it would be a requirement.'

Adalia shook her head slightly. 'You still don't get it, do you? You need to learn insignificance, Jonathon. You need to know what that's like. How it feels.'

He rubbed his thumb against his temple, trying – genuinely – to understand what Adalia meant. 'You know, I don't actually go through my life meditating on my own spectacular importance. I don't really think about myself much at all.'

'I know. You just exist. A priori. Beyond examination. The Vaik could change that.'

He held his thumb at his temple and considered the wan, desultory day. A nothing day. Drizzle and greyness that won't dignify itself with a storm.

'I'll think about it.'

'Thank you.'

That night he found the Department of Justice website and, with some difficulty, navigated his way to the Vaik page. It was largely blank: just a link to an application form.

While he waited for the form to download, he poured himself a generous whisky and watched the last of the day drop over the horizon. He was in the large kitchen at his parents' home, the one that pumped out the industrial-sized catering for their soirees. As a child, he and his brothers had loved this room. It was a ship: the octagonal window bay the prow, and the gleaming oven-hoods the flues atop the coal fires. They'd run the taps for the sound of water and shipwrecked themselves on the ocean-blue tiles.

Jonathon felt his body tilting, reorienting. Adalia had thrown him a buoy and he would cleave to it. He sat down, gulped whisky and surveyed the form. Disbelieving, he read again. The first field did not ask for his name, address or date of birth. Instead, stark in Times New Roman, was a question.

Are you a good man?

A strange sound escaped his throat, something between a snort and a guffaw. He stabbed at the tab key but the cursor did not move.

Are you a good man?

And there, beside it, check boxes next to 'yes' and 'no'.

This time he laughed properly and stood up to give full vent to his mirth. He moved again to the prow of the ship and surveyed the night sky. He wondered what Adalia was doing. Probably making dinner. He wanted to call her to tell her about the question on the form, but he doubted she would find it as funny as he did.

A blank resistance rose up in him – a choking, indignant feeling. What a ridiculous question. An absurd, unanswerable question.

But are you?

He heard the question in Adalia's voice, barrelling at him as if from across a vast plain. He downed the whisky, poured another one and sat down again.

The cursor blinked at the end of the question, waiting. He pressed the tab key, but he could not progress without providing an answer. He opened a new tab and typed in 'Vaik history'. He began to read, keeping to the sites that Adalia had told him were credible.

The night blackened and thickened and the bottle shallowed as he read. The outline of the information was more or less familiar to him from school: one civilisation coming across the sea – his ancestors, you would call them – to take possession of Vaik land. And why not? The land was fertile and rich in natural resources. To tussle over such things was inevitable.

The Vaik had inhabited the land for thousands of years, securing their civilisation with 'reproduction treaties'. The Vaik traded crops, animals and minerals for access to men. Twice a year an assortment of men from the surrounding territories would be granted safe passage across the patrolled borders. In those days, Vaik land was not fully enclosed and included all that Jonathon thought of as his country. Incursions into Vaik territory were answered with swift and deadly force. They did not happen very often.

The men who came to the Vaik were carefully selected. Only

those who had produced healthy children, and were themselves physically and mentally sound, were eligible. Farmers and musicians were favoured over tradesmen, sailors and nobility, and each man had to be able to trace their maternal lineage for at least four generations. Fourteen years after he was first selected, a man was exempt because of consanguinity. Historians differed as to whether the men had volunteered for the task or were nominated by a council. Choice or force. Desire or duty. Or perhaps neither one nor the other, just a tradition. A seasonal practice like thatching a roof or ploughing a field.

What struck Jonathon as he read was how sanitised his high-school version of events had been. His textbooks had suggested a short skirmish between the invaders and the Vaik with minimal loss of life. The victors were magnanimous and allowed the Vaik to retain a reduced parcel of territory. But that wasn't how it was.

The colonists arrived in an armada and tried to take The Fortress by sea. The Vaik had the advantage of higher ground and cannons and were able to repel the enemy. They were also cunning, infusing mutiny among the women of the ships, something that the invaders were slow to recognise. The invaders were pushed back many times, retreating to their country of origin to lick their wounds and stockpile. They stopped bringing women with them. Eventually they took the long way, bribing, threatening and entreating the people of the land south of the Vaik to grant them passage from which to mount a ground assault.

But why, Jonathon wondered, *did the people who had lived more or less peaceably with the Vaik enable the invaders?* He swirled the amber liquid around his glass, tinkling the ice cubes. Greed, he supposed: the prospect of getting their hands on the fertile fields and a sea port. But he suspected something more than this. It sounded great on paper to be the fuck-thing of an army of horny Vaik twice a year, but what man really wanted to be reduced to an object of trade?

Or perhaps it had not been the work of the men, but the women. Were they resentful at giving up the strongest and most beautiful of their men to a season of pleasure? Did they want to see the Vaik reduced and connive with the invaders to bring it about?

Both sides suffered heavy losses – thousands were slaughtered. Each side outdid the other in escalating acts of cruelty. The treaty that was finally drawn up saw the Vaik territory radically reduced. They lost their harbour and were walled in on three sides, the sea forming a natural barrier on the fourth. The treaty included a clause on what was rather primly called 'biological guarantees', whereby the Vaik were granted access to men and sperm. The details on this access were vague, but it evolved over many years into the present-day arrangement of national servicemen, supplicants and permanent residents.

Jonathon drummed his fingers on the table, thinking. Something was missing from the history. Some vital piece of information glossed over or elided. He'd read many a prospectus where words were piled up and arranged so as to hide a blankness. He himself had plastered over craters in due diligence with diversions and near-truths. For all its blood and mortality, the account the victors had written was too neat, too clean.

He thought, suddenly, of Clara. Alone in her box in the cold, damp earth. The idea of her spending her first night in the ground was unbearable. He considered the glass in his hand. He felt utterly, depressingly sober but knew he must be well over the limit.

He shut down his computer, the Vaik question unanswered. He found his greatcoat, scarf and gloves, and pulled a blanket from a hallway cupboard. The night air was cold but the rain had stopped. He swung his car from the driveway and drove carefully to the cemetery. The grounds were poorly lit, but he found Clara's fresh-dug grave without difficulty. He spread the blanket beside her headstone and sat down. The air smelt of rain, grass and churned mud. He had the feeling that there were others, unseen, holding vigil through the trees. He wished he'd brought the whisky.

Was he a good man?

The Vaik were tricky to ask such a question. Did anyone fall clearly on one side of the ledger – and by whose accounting?

Jonathon paraded the people he knew through his head: his mother, father, colleagues, friends, brothers. They seemed good enough to him. They made generous donations to their favoured causes. They bundled last season's clothing into charity bins and paid what the law required of them in taxes.

He knew no actual evil of them ... but then, one of his colleagues had violated the woman beside whose grave he now sat. Someone he said hello to in the kitchen. Maybe someone he'd had dinner with.

'Were you a good person, Clara?'

The dead woman kept her own counsel, and maintained it throughout the night.

Jonathon left the cemetery just before dawn. He was stiff, cold and groggy. He blasted the car heater, waiting for his animal heat to be restored before driving to his parents' home. He let himself in quietly, not wanting to disturb the household.

His mother met him in the hallway. 'Where were you? I was worried.'

'I'm fine.'

'You look like hell. I'll fix you some coffee.'

He followed her into the kitchen where his computer still sat, waiting for him to complete the supplicancy application. His mother heaped coffee into a glass jug and set the old-fashioned kettle she refused to part with on the stove.

'I've come to a decision,' he said.

His mother looked at him expectantly.

'I'm going to The Fortress for a year.'

Her expression barely changed. Only a slight thinning of the lips indicated that she'd heard him.

'Mother – the kettle.'

Its shrill whistle filled the space between them. She slowly turned and lifted the kettle from the stove then poured the boiling water into the jug.

'The Fortress,' she said dully.

'Yes, as a supplicant. I'll be gone for twelve months.'

'I see.' She put a steaming mug of coffee in front of him, her nostrils flaring. 'You don't smell very good.'

'I'll take a shower after my coffee.'

'You need to sleep.'

'Probably.'

'Hopefully then you will see how tasteless your little joke is.'

'I'm curious – why do you think I'm joking about this?'

'Why? Why? Because there are two types of people who go to The Fortress: hardcore sociopaths whom our own courts can't deal with, and misguided hippies who think they can be bossed into enlightenment.'

Jonathon wanted to laugh in spite of himself. 'I'll pay you the compliment of having a neat turn of phrase, Mother.'

'I'd rather you paid me the compliment of being sensible.'

'I'm trying to save my marriage, to be a good father. That's about as sensible as it gets, isn't it?'

His mother's eyes sparkled. 'Adalia's put you up to this, hasn't she?'

'She suggested it, yes, but –'

'You need to be very careful, Jonathon.'

'About what?'

'Oh, darling, can't you see? Adalia gets you locked up and out of the way for a year. You come out of there expecting to play happy families and instead you find she's claimed abandonment, you've forfeited your right to the child and all your assets have been liquidated.'

'You make Adalia sound like a conniving mastermind.'

'People do strange things when love goes wrong. All sorts of things get twisted, corrupted.'

Jonathon looked past his mother to the cold, indifferent morning that hulked behind the soft lights of the patio. 'Do you remember the summer camp you used to send me to when I was a boy?'

'Lake Wykaita? Of course I do. What has that got to do with you going to The Fortress?'

'Did you know I hated that place? I don't just mean I was occasionally bored or homesick, I mean I really fucking hated it.'

'No you didn't, you –'

'Stop. Just stop. You don't get to do that. You don't get to tell me how I felt about something. You've been doing that all my life – taking things and repackaging them so they make life more comfortable for you.'

'Fine.' She planted her feet wider apart and folded her arms across her chest. 'Tell me then. Tell me all about why summer camp was a blight on your childhood and I'm to blame. Someone hit you? Abused you? Starved you?'

'No, it was nothing like that.'

'You're damn right it was nothing like that. I vetted that place to within an inch of its life. If I thought for one second there was anything unsavoury about it I would've hauled you out and served a writ on them in the same visit.'

'People don't have to be starved or hit to be miserable.'

'I know you struggled to adjust there sometimes. I'd call the camp leader a couple of times a day the first week just to see how you were getting on. When I came to pick you up you were always full of stories about your adventures, what you'd done, what one boy or another was up to. It just took you a little time to warm up to it.'

'There you go, Mother, you're doing it again. Stitching up the narrative.'

She sniffed a little. Good god, was she about to cry? Jonathon was fascinated by the prospect.

'Yes, I encouraged you to go to summer camp. Yes, I chivvied you into it sometimes when you said you'd rather stay at home. I gave birth to three boys in seven years, Jonathon. Have you got the first clue what that's like? While you're so keen to forensically examine your miserable childhood, you might pause to reflect that you didn't have a nanny. How many of the kids you grew up with can say the same? That was my choice. I wanted to be present for my children in a way my parents weren't for me. In a way none of your friends' parents were for them. So yes, I sent you to summer camp for four glorious weeks every year because I was fucking exhausted and needed a break. When you're in The Fortress for the first year of your child's life I look forward to learning all the things you've learnt about parenting.'

And with that she turned and left the room.

They barely spoke in the weeks leading up to Jonathon's internment.

He spent the time reading all he could on Vaik culture and history. He became attentive to the traces of Vaik in his city, pausing before statues and plaques that marked treaties and truces. There was one statue that particularly intrigued him. He'd walked past it hundreds of times without giving it much thought; now, he studied it almost every day.

It was of a Vaik general – Lezah – who'd led the defence of the city two centuries before. (The Vaik and the city had long since established their accord, part of which involved a mutual defence pact.) General Lezah was presented in full warrior pose: a gun slung across one shoulder, her finger pointed at the marauding hordes. Yet something about the sculpture wasn't quite right. Some failure of proportion or execution made it an oddity.

It wasn't until Jonathon was at The Fortress that he realised the sculptor had been in conflict with his creation. Valour and power and breasts had unmanned him. He had been commissioned to honour the Vaik, but could not do so without making himself smaller. Another thing Jonathon realised: General Lezah looked like his mother.

He'd answered 'yes' on the form.

The second storm front barrelled across the sky, operatic in silver and indigo. The clouds massed and detached at such speed the universe seemed to be forming around Jonathon. Trees bent over themselves, sheaving leaves that blurred past him. The masjythra cleaved so tightly it pinched his eyebrows and chest hair. He huddled against the wall, feeling his way inch by inch, willing himself towards the sentry post he knew was there but could no longer see. His impulses had concentrated to a single point: forward. Even so, the wave kept revealing its quarry then snatching it down, down to the grey, cold seabed.

The wind turned on itself and was suddenly behind him. He used it as a fist at his lower back. Sometimes he found it easier to spin along the wall, shoulder by shoulder, fists at his sides, than to try walking. He dervished in this way, taking skin off his nose and hands as he flew against the rough bricks.

He was lucky to notice the grey smudge that moved haltingly across the plain at right angles to him. His first thought was that it might be a vehicle, a small agricultural cart or trolley. But it was flailing and erratic and seemed to have sighted him. His stomach iced over at the thought of a Vaik spirit weaving through the storm in search of unsheltered men.

It raised a hand and waved it manically. Jonathon peeled the masjythra from his head and shielded his eyes from the rain with his hands. The smudge clarified into Daidd, his masjythra now shimmering, now dull, in the storm. Jonathon jumped up and down in answer, waving his own arms about. He used the wall as a launching pad into the flooded plain, splashing in his cloddish boots towards Daidd.

Even taking the ferocity of the storm into account, Daidd moved strangely. At first Jonathon thought he was injured. Then he realised that he half-carried, half-dragged something – someone – with him.

Ulait! Jonathon's heart lurched with joy and relief.

Daidd reached out for him with his free hand; the other was clutched around Ulait's waist. As Daidd wilted against him in exhaustion, Jonathon reached around her back. Her body was slack, but she was conscious.

'Careful,' Daidd yelled above the storm. 'She's hurt.'

Ulait smiled weakly. Her skin was ashen and her lips blanched white. Jonathon drew her closer, then bundled her into his arms. 'Easy,' he said. 'We're almost there.'

Daidd positioned himself behind Jonathon, his shoulder pressed into his back to keep them from blowing off course. Although Ulait was heavy, Jonathon found it almost easier walking diagonally into the storm with the extra ballast. They were only metres from the sentry post but progress was hard won and came in inches. Finally, the door was visible ahead of them.

Jonathon huddled under the eaves, hugging Ulait to him, as Daidd banged his fists on the sentry door. They waited. No one came. Daidd banged again.

Jonathon leant towards him and yelled, 'Perhaps this post is inactive. We might have to move further down.' How would Ulait manage the two, perhaps three kilometres?

She lifted her head weakly from his shoulder and looked up. 'No. This post is active. Try again.'

Daidd raised his fist to the door when it opened. A woman's head emerged. She looked in silent astonishment at the three of them, as if disbelieving what she saw.

Then she flung the door open and rushed to Ulait, cupped her face in her hands, and kissed the girl's forehead. 'Inside. Quickly.'

The woman assumed control of Ulait, guiding her into the post. Daidd and Jonathon followed. 'Close and bar the door,' the woman instructed.

Jonathon shut it against the storm and lowered the latch, then turned and leant against it. The rectangular room he found himself in was spare and dark, but it was warm. An open fire burned in a stone hearth at the far end.

The Vaik deposited Ulait into a chair near the fire and mopped at her hair and face with a cloth. 'Come. Warm yourselves.'

Daidd and Jonathon moved gratefully to stand with their backs to the fire as the Vaik attended to Ulait. Their masjythras almost sighed against the heat, releasing clouds of steam, swathing them in fog.

'Where does it hurt, child?' the Vaik asked.

'My ankle. I fell.'

The Vaik carefully removed Ulait's boots and socks to reveal an ankle twice its normal size and purple like a norsling. The Vaik clucked her tongue and ran her hands over Ulait's foot and calf. 'How came you to be outside in the storm?'

'It was an accident. I was following the olöcks. I wanted to see where they went when the storms came. I realised I wouldn't make it back before the sestyatesh so I decided to take shelter. I had some food with me and I found a good spot to wait it out. I got a fire going and was quite snug. Then I found Daidd.'

'What do you mean?'

'I looked out during the eye and saw him on the plain. You can imagine my shock that a man would be out in the storm. He shouldn't have been there. I thought he must be lost. So I set off after him. I thought we'd both shelter in case there was a second front. But the visibility was so poor I fell in this sort of a ravine and hurt my ankle. We decided to make for the sentry post.' Ulait paused, and closed her eyes. Her skin was waxy with pain. 'I think I've broken my ankle.'

The Vaik clucked her tongue. 'Yes. This will need to be set. You need mistaelnet. Here.' She held out the towel to Jonathon. 'We need to get her warm and dry.'

He wrapped the towel around Ulait's head and gently massaged her scalp. She felt hot. She looked up at him, her eyes glazed. Beads of sweat ran along her upper lip and hairline.

'We swam under the boats,' she mumbled. 'Fish like rainbows. Knives in our mouths.'

'Shoosh, shoosh now,' Jonathon crooned.

Opposite the fireplace was a kitchen area where the Vaik pulled jars from cupboards and spooned seeds and pods into a mortar. In the opposite corner was a bed, neatly made and heaped with cushions and pillows. Crude shelves along the walls held books and candles. The other corner was taken up by a wooden ladder lashed to the wall by tough leather straps; it disappeared into the ceiling and the post at the top of the wall.

Jonathon dabbed the towel over Ulait's neck and arms.

'I poured the verrglet myself,' she muttered. 'I wore red silk.'

He recognised the word picture she was painting and blushed red, the heat rising all the way to his scalp. 'Hush now,' he said.

The Vaik drew up a low stool and sat next to Ulait, who occupied the only comfortable chair in the room. 'Open up for me. That's the girl.' The Vaik spooned a green paste – mistaelnet – into Ulait's mouth, then held a glass of water to her lips. 'Swallow it down for me. I know it tastes bad.'

Ulait's face puckered in distaste. She shook her head to avoid another spoonful.

'Come on, one more for me.'

But Ulait pressed her lips tight shut and craned her head away.

'Hold her head for me,' the Vaik instructed Jonathon.

Reluctantly, he kept Ulait's damp head trapped in his hands until she was still. The Vaik knuckled a point near where her ear met her jawbone, forcing her mouth open, then dropped a blob of the green paste on her tongue and pressed her mouth shut. Ulait made a half-strangled sound and screwed up her eyes and cheeks.

'Open your mouth for me.'

Ulait opened her mouth, revealing that she'd swallowed the mistaelnet. 'Good girl.' The Vaik stroked her cheek, then held the water glass to her mouth again. 'A few sips for me ... a few more ... there. You'll start to feel better very soon.'

The Vaik manoeuvred Ulait's chair closer to the fire. Steam rose from her clothes in ghostly white waves then dissolved into the darkness.

'Self dissolving to nothing,' Jonathon murmured.

Daidd looked at him questioningly.

'The isvestyii –' Jonathon began, but the Vaik shot him a warning look.

'This is not the time or the place for that.' She turned to Daidd. 'Do you know how to make a plaster to set Ulait's foot?'

Daidd nodded.

'You'll find the materials in the kitchen. There are bandages in the cupboard below the sink. There's hot water in the pot above the fire.' Daidd moved to the kitchen and began preparing the plaster. The Vaik bent towards Ulait's foot and examined it closely. Softly, so as not to be heard by Daidd, she said, 'He is dead?'

Jonathon nodded. 'I found him by the low point in the wall, near the sea. He was –'

The Vaik shook her head. 'It's finished now.'

'But I want to tell you, Mistress,' Jonathon whispered. 'I need to tell you.'

'It's for you alone.'

Daidd handed the wet plaster and the bandages to the Vaik, and she deftly layered them from Ulait's toes to her ankle.

Ulait barely stirred as the mistaelnet took effect. The first flush of colour returned to her cheeks and her lips. Jonathon was mesmerised by the steam leaving her body and drifting to the fire. He felt there was a message in it for him, but he couldn't decode it. Without warning he pitched forward towards Ulait's chair as a wave of exhaustion tackled him.

'Come,' said the Vaik, 'you need to sit. And eat. You both must be starving. Can you finish this?' She left Daidd to bind Ulait's foot and picked up a chair from across the room, setting it down next to Ulait by the fire. 'Come. Sit yourself. Your name?'

'Jonathon Bridge.'

'You are a supplicant?'

'Yes.'

'How long is your tenure?'

'One year.'

'Of which you have served?'

'About ten months. I think.'

Daidd, she seemed to know already.

The fire flickered and glowed, casting ghostly shadows on the walls. Jonathon's eyelids twitched with fatigue. The storm still raged, but the fall of the rain on the thick stone walls was almost homely, comforting. Daidd finished binding Ulait's foot then knelt by Jonathon and pulled his boots off. He held a pitcher of water to Jonathon's lips. Until it hit his tongue, Jonathon had no idea how furiously thirsty he was. He gulped it down.

'Easy, easy,' cautioned Daidd. 'You'll make yourself sick.'

Jonathon fell back in his chair and reached for Ulait's hand. The mistaelnet had broken her fever and her hand felt cool in his.

The Vaik returned with a tray of food that she placed on a

rough wooden box. 'It's not much, I'm afraid. The storm has affected our supply lines.'

'We have supplies,' Daidd said. 'At least Jonathon does. I lost my pack somewhere.'

It took Jonathon a moment to comprehend, but he was still carrying the pack on his back. He stood up and sloughed it off, handing it to her, and she thanked him.

A few moments later she gave Jonathon a plate of dried fruit, sausage, cheese and chewy brown bread. There was also a nutty paste that he guessed to be a high-calorie invention of the Vaik. He could almost feel it doubling the marrow in his bones. Sitting before the crackling fire, he felt euphoric: the kind of lazy, sleepy euphoria he remembered from the strong headache tablets he'd pilfered from his mother's bathroom cabinet when he was in his teens. He wavered between asleep and awake as he ferried the food to his mouth. The mallow root sweet on his tongue, the cheese strong and bitey. He had half an idea to climb the ladder to the Aeraevest to watch the storm spending itself out to sea, but the chair was like a warm, loving hand that embraced him. He set the idea down by his side and thought of it no more as he drifted into sleep.

He woke wrapped in the same peace that had transported him to sleep. The fire had burnt low. The charred logs flared red when the wind whistled down the chimney. The ferocity was gone from the storm, but still the rain came down. Ulait remained asleep in the chair beside him, her head tucked on her shoulder, her mouth slightly ajar. In sleep she looked a child still; her eyelids full, her skin poreless. Her fringe had dried in sticky triangles against her forehead. Across the room, Daidd and the Vaik shared her bed. Jonathon wanted to freeze the moment, to hold it perfect and unchanged for a while yet. He feared Ulait's wakefulness. Her anger.

There was a scattering sound as drops of rain flew down the

chimney, hissing at the logs. Ulait stirred and opened her eyes. She looked at the fire, then turned her gaze towards Jonathon.

'Good morning, Mistress.'

She yawned, pink-mouthed like a kitten. 'Good morning.'

'We're in a sentry post along the perimeter wall. You set out after Daidd and fell and hurt yourself.'

She nodded. 'I remember. How did you come to be here, Jonathon Bridge?'

'I set out after you. Me, Daidd, Mandalay, we all took different routes.'

Ulait frowned. 'A supplicant and Daidd authorised to look for me in the middle of a sestyatesh? That doesn't make sense.' She wrinkled her brow, then drew the blankets tighter across her shoulders.

The Vaik hailed Ulait from across the room. 'How are you feeling, darling girl?'

'Okay, I think.' She wriggled her toes, the only part of her foot not encased in plaster. 'My foot hurts a bit. It's throbbing.'

'It will hurt for a few days yet. Stay here again tonight, then we'll get you home tomorrow.'

She threw back her covers, stood up and stretched. She was completely naked, and rather short for a Vaik. Climbing up and down the ladder to the Aeraevest had roped her quadriceps and calves into thick knots of muscle. She drew her yellow hair into a rough ponytail on top of her head, revealing sculpted biceps. Her skin was dark and glossy. Jonathon looked at her admiringly. She dropped a silky green gown over her head, then washed her hands and face in a bowl of water.

Daidd too was naked, his long penis hanging slackly against his thigh. Jonathon was slightly awed by the man who had become his friend. Last night he'd been so exhausted in mind and body he would have been incapable of satisfying any Vaik commands, probably earning himself another term in the subterranean prison. Had Daidd nobly assumed the task, recognising Jonathon's incapacity? Or had the Vaik not thought of Jonathon when Daidd was in the room? Was Daidd superhuman?

The Vaik danced merrily across the room and placed her palm on Ulait's forehead. 'You're still a bit warm, but you're doing well. Eat something, then you'll need another dose of mistaelnet.'

Daidd dressed in his masjythra then bent to tend the fire. His waxy profile and milky eye were turned towards Jonathon and Ulait as he coaxed flames from fresh logs and kindling.

'Daidd, what happened to your face?' said Ulait.

Daidd didn't pause in his task as he answered. 'I was burnt with acid.'

'Was it an accident?'

'No, Ulait' – Jonathon noticed that she had given Daidd permission to use her name – 'it was a punishment. I wronged a woman, and she was entitled to Vaik justice.'

'She chose acid over having you declared isvestyii?'

'Yes.'

'Did she pour it on you?'

'Yes.'

'Did it hurt?'

'It was agony,' he said simply.

Jonathon was shocked. How could his gentle, patient friend have done something so terrible, so brutal to warrant such punishment? To potentially be declared isvestyii?

Daidd turned from the fire, replenished now, and focused his good eye on Jonathon. He read Jonathon's expression. 'The punishment was just.'

'Come,' said the Vaik. 'Let's check the Aeraevest.' She rearranged the blankets around Ulait. 'You will be all right for a few minutes, darling?'

'Of course.'

The Vaik nodded towards the ladder near the bed. Daidd

ascended first; Jonathon followed. He climbed towards the open air moving above them. He stepped out onto a narrow landing and gripped the railing. His masjythra snaked around him, closing out the cold. The sea — calmer now but still in the after-burn of yesterday's fury — circled him. There was nothing between the Aeraevest and the grey-blue line of the horizon. He tried to imagine the time when flotillas had sped across that line to capture The Fortress. Tried to imagine the omnipresent state of siege and vigilance that the Vaik must have felt, but mostly he just felt small. Small and insignificant in the grey-blue vastness. It wasn't an unpleasant feeling, exactly.

The Vaik climbed over the railing and sprang onto the roof. Jonathon heard her clunking above him and watched the debris she tossed over the side fall into the ocean. He thought of the body of the isvestyii suspended in that same ocean. Nothing. Nothingness.

'Did you ever see anything like this?' he asked Daidd.

Daidd smiled. 'I know this vista like the back of my hand. Better.'

'How?'

'I spent seven years in an Aeraevest much like this one, but closer to The Dryans. Even more remote. Even now when I close my eyes at night I see the ocean.'

'I've worked beside you almost every day for nearly a year and I know virtually nothing about you.'

'You know why I'm here and why I stay. Everything else is just a footnote.'

'Mandalay isn't — can't be — yours. Exclusively. Can't be ... I'm struggling for the right words ... wedded to you. Nor you to her. That must hurt. Badly.'

'You've gotten better at framing questions as statements.' Another flurry of debris flew past them to the water. 'Yes, I hurt. But I own that pain. I honour it.'

The Vaik swung back onto the landing and picked stray leaves from her dress. 'There's some damage. Some holes that will need to be tarred over. Nothing too dramatic, though.' She placed a fond hand on one of the posts. 'You've done well. Sound and true.' She opened a strongbox tucked into a corner and removed some fishing pots. She dropped three of them carefully into the sea then secured them on hooks. 'With any luck we'll have fish for supper.'

The three of them stood there for a few moments, staring out across the dark ocean.

Evening came and there were, indeed, fish in the pots. The Vaik skinned and filleted the fish and dropped their white flesh into a pot hanging above the fire. A strong smell of herbs suffused the space, making Jonathon slightly light-headed. Ulait had dozed for most of the day, still tired after walking so far on her injured foot and lethargic under the sway of the mistaelnet. Jonathon surreptitiously watched the Vaik as she went about preparing the meal. She exuded an air of quiet capability. From her colouring and bearing, Jonathon assumed she had been born and bred at The Fortress: a woman whose birthright included power and belonging. He realised he envied her.

They ate the fish stew out of wooden bowls and sopped up the juice with chewy, slightly bitter bread. They didn't talk much, but the silence was companionable. The fire flickered brighter as the evening set in. Daidd brewed tea for them all and spooned another dose of mistaelnet to Ulait. Soon, she was dozing. The Vaik collected up their plates and cups and deposited them in the kitchen area. She returned to the fire with a large bowl of water.

'Come.' She gestured to Daidd and Jonathon. They stood in the middle of the room as she dipped her elbow into the water. Satisfied with its temperature, she dropped a cloth into the water. 'Take off your masjythra.' Jonathon did as he was bid, dropping the garment onto the floor beside him. 'Bend a little lower.' He dipped his face towards her and she gently ran the cloth over his face and neck. It was warm and smelt like one of the flowers from the shaenet. The Vaik stood behind him and sponged his shoulders. A drip of water ran down the furrow in his back and into the crease of his buttocks, making him shudder. The Vaik dipped the cloth into the bowl again and cleansed his arms and torso. Her ministrations were gentle and thorough.

When she had finished with Jonathon she brought a fresh bowl of water and bathed Daidd. She took special care around the puckered, scarred skin on his face, neck and pectoral, at one point leaving a soft kiss on the damaged tissue before moving her sponge to his stirring penis. When he was clean she lay down on her bed, her head propped up on her hand, looking at the two of them. Her instruction was brief, polite: 'Please,' followed by a wave of the hand indicating they had the floor.

Jonathon and Daidd looked at each other in the flickering shadows. Jonathon was not revolted by the idea of touching Daidd. He respected him, had come to feel admiration for him even if there was much he didn't know about his history. Nor was Daidd's body alien to him. Having bathed with him almost every day since he arrived at The Fortress there was only his own and Adalia's bodies that he knew better. What Jonathon felt was physically inept. The Vaik may as well have asked him to perform a lyrical dance piece. He didn't know the steps, and didn't know how to imagine himself into them. There had been furtive experiences with boys at Lake Wykaita, but they'd come about after hot-breathed leering at big-busted women in porn magazines – a kind of hydraulic release that used whatever method was at hand. This Vaik wanted a spectacle, a performance.

Daidd stepped towards Jonathon and placed his large hand around the back of his neck, drawing him closer. His mouth opened under the pressure of Daidd's and he flickered his tongue tentatively in the other man's mouth.

Jonathon closed his eyes and tried to imagine that Daidd

was a woman, but the evidence was too contrary to enliven the fantasy. The sheer bulk of Daidd, the musky smell of him evident even under the Vaik tincture, the sensation of butting rather than melding stomachs and hips permitted no conclusion other than that Daidd was a man. Jonathon thought of Laliya, how powerfully attracted to her he had been from first sight before learning that she was once electii. Mandalay had grabbed his penis, threatened to tear it from his body with her teeth to prove that womanhood was not an absence, a lacuna.

'Relax,' Daidd whispered into his ear. 'Clear your mind. Don't think about anything.'

Jonathon tried to vacate his mind but all it left was the strange reality of Daidd's hand gripped behind his neck, the rough tongue in his mouth, the fingers moving down towards his buttocks. He opened his eyes and looked at the Vaik. She remained propped up on the bed, watching them intently. If only she would remove her dress: give Jonathon the physical stimulus of her lithe legs, the narrow vortex of her waist, her proud breasts, that sweep of impossibly blonde hair. But she didn't.

There was a shuffling noise behind them as Ulait stirred in her sleep. He worried about the girl waking up to the sight of two men making love, then realised it would be neither prurient nor strange to her. There had never been any evidence of a physical relationship between his parents when he was growing up. He had assumed their sex life was effectively over, but perhaps they'd simply taken care to hide it from him and his brothers. He tried to imagine the scene through Ulait's eyes; to be a teenager for whom sexual expression was no more mysterious than seasons passing and new crops being sown in the soil.

He allowed an experimental hand to drift along Daidd's shoulders and torso. He felt the puckered skin and winced slightly at the thought of the pain the acid must have caused. He willed his hand further, to the trail of wiry hairs between Daidd's belly button and his pubic bone. He flattened his hand against the taut plane of Daidd's belly. It was like and unlike touching himself. Familiar yet strange.

Daidd pulled him down onto the threadbare rug. Jonathon felt its roughness on his skin as Daidd stretched himself out on top of him, a crush against his rib cage. Was this what Adalia felt under his weight? Daidd found his mouth again. Jonathon ran his hand down the furrow of Daidd's back and across the upturned flank of his bottom. The curves were not unlike a woman's, and Jonathon felt a momentary reprieve of familiarity. But the curves were hairy, and not the soft downy fur of golden hairs on Adalia's body, but wiry.

Jonathon looked again towards the Vaik. Perhaps she intended to join them at some point. But still she reclined on the bed, clothed and watching.

Daidd's breath was hot against his neck. A hand closed on his penis and began to gently massage it. He sucked in his breath as the blood ran to his cock, an involuntary movement like a tide. Daidd coaxed him to a full erection, then planted a line of kisses along his chest towards his groin. He sucked in his breath again as Daidd's hot mouth closed over him. The gasp was one of surprised pleasure as sensation and thought collided: *a man is sucking my dick.*

The Vaik stirred and Jonathon felt her concentration double. She was enjoying this. The thought gave him pleasure. He grasped Daidd's hair between his fingers and held him against his groin. Daidd held Jonathon tightly around the base of his cock with his thumb and forefinger, then pressed the head of his penis to the roof of his mouth and moved up and down the shaft, licking him. Daidd's touch was expert; a polymorphous master in the art of pleasure. The Vaik changed her position slightly to see better, and Jonathon was overcome by his climax. He shuddered against the floor and made an inarticulate strangling sound.

'That was lovely,' said the Vaik.

Daidd sat up and wiped his mouth. The Vaik offered him a mug of water, which he accepted.

'Was that your first time with a man?' she asked Jonathon.

'Yes,' he said somewhat breathlessly.

'I love watching men,' she said. 'They become so beautiful here at The Fortress. All earth and muscle and concentrated energy.' She rose from the bed and Jonathon expected her to join them. Instead she walked towards the kitchen cabinets and took a jar from a shelf, paused to check on Ulait, who was sleeping soundly, then returned.

'Here.' She handed the jar to Daidd. He removed the lid and dipped his finger inside. It emerged shiny and redolent. The scent was familiar, but Jonathon could not immediately place it. Daidd ran the oil along the length of his penis.

He raised his eyes to meet Jonathon's. His expression was apologetic. 'Roll over, Jonathon.'

The smell. He remembered. When he'd first entered The Fortress, the electii had conducted a cavity search. The slap and stretch of the glove exploded in Jonathon's ear canal.

He had never experienced anal sex. Once, he and Adalia had purchased a vibrator. 'I am so fucking you up the arse with this!' she had said gleefully. They'd tried, but his anus was having none of it, and they'd descended into a fit of giggles, silver lolly wrappers floating from the bed. It had become a running joke between them. Whenever Jonathon had done something to annoy Adalia, she had grabbed a salt shaker or a candle – anything vaguely phallic within reach – made a buzzing noise and directed it at his bum.

Jonathon rolled over, feeling the rough weave of the rug scratch his belly. Daidd began massaging his lower back and buttocks with the oil. His thumbs came closer and closer to the entrance to Jonathon's body, and with each concentric circle Jonathon tensed up. He did not want this. He profoundly did not want this. Yet this would happen. He was underground again, two impossible worlds colliding.

Daidd ceased kneading his buttocks and laid himself over Jonathon's back. Daidd's penis pressed against the crevice between his butt cheeks. Daidd gently entered Jonathon's body.

'Breathe, Jonathon. You need to breathe.'

He closed his hands over Jonathon's and was still. Jonathon breathed in and out as Daidd had instructed him, trying to relax. Jonathon knew that Daidd would not intentionally hurt him, but he was sick with panic. If he tried to fight Daidd off, he would anger the Vaik and expose himself to further pain. If he tried to fight Daidd off, it would be futile; Daidd had the advantage in height and power. If he tried to fight Daidd off, it would only serve to prove how powerless he was.

Jonathon pressed his forehead against the rug and closed his eyes as Daidd entered him a little more. It hurt and it was strange and it was also ... good. He bucked involuntarily, his body responding. That his body would do this, produce pleasure in the midst of his fear and confusion, seemed traitorous. Tears leaked from his eyelids. His body had robbed him of the certainty of victimhood. He had a sudden, unprecedented urge to pray but did not know how, or to whom. Instead, he ran Clara's name through his mind, over and over again. He had never doubted that what had happened to her was awful, but until this moment he hadn't understood how self-reproach and confusion did the violator's work for them.

It was over. Daidd eased himself off and sat beside him. Jonathon didn't move. He simply lay there, tense and rigid, waiting for further commands from the Vaik.

'Jonathon,' Daidd whispered. 'She's asleep.'

Jonathon looked up. The Vaik's head was on her outstretched arm, her mouth slightly ajar, her chest rising and falling. Jonathon felt a surge of fury. In his mind's eye he saw himself belting her across the face with an open palm, squeezing her bulging throat till her eyes popped. He lay on the rug, unmoving.

'Are you hurt?' Daidd asked tenderly.

'I don't think so.'

'Would you like some water?'

'No. Thank you.'

Jonathon didn't know what to do, where to look. He felt ashamed. He closed his eyes. He thought about asking Daidd to fetch him some of Ulait's mistaelnet paste, but didn't trust himself to speak. He would cry, and this seemed a terrible thing. The final debasement.

Daidd began to talk. He spoke in a low voice, the sort of voice you would use to coax an injured animal towards shelter. Jonathon lay there, his face pressed against the scratchy rug, his heart aflame, and after a while he began to listen.

Daidd's family were quite well-to-do – not establishment like the Bridges, but three or four generations out of The Dryans. Daidd's father was a municipal councillor, his mother an art teacher. When Daidd was growing up his father was engaged in an endless, tortuous battle with banal things. Zoning and by-laws and fire hydrants. His mother's nails were always smudged with paint and she collected glass jars from the neighbours to wash paintbrushes in. These were the things Daidd remembered. It had been a long time since he'd had any contact with his parents.

Daidd met Naomi at university. He had taken his usual seat in the semicircular lecture theatre – eight rows back and slightly left of the middle – when he saw her. She sat forward of him in the extreme curve of the semicircle near the door, so he had a clear view of her profile. In the intensely stratified world of university life in which he had struggled to find a firm footing she was just so … normal. Nice and normal.

Her hair was long and dark. She pulled it loosely back from her face and tied it with a purple ribbon. Her cardigan was wheat-coloured, soft and feminine. Daidd felt that he might reach out and touch it, pluck the nodules of fluff from her shoulder and drop them to the floor. She unzipped her bag and removed a spiral notebook and two pens: one black, one red. How his heart leapt at that detail. It meant she was ordered, like him. He used the black ink for the things he understood, having already gleaned them from the pre-reading, and red for the things he would follow up on later in the science library.

She placed her bag beneath her seat, squared her chair to the front, then turned and surveyed the lecture theatre. She had a high, wide forehead where the soft down of her hair collected at her temples. A small, snub nose with a light spray of freckles across the top. Dark, almond-shaped eyes and small, white, regular teeth. Daidd had the stunning realisation that time, which he had always considered uncompromisingly linear, ran on a multitude of tracks at different speeds. He had proceeded in an orderly fashion to this moment, which stretched longer than moments do, and in deep, ineffable silence. Time would run differently when the moment finally tapered, and in a different channel.

It was love. It had to be.

Later, Daidd would look over the notes he had made in that lecture – foundations of quantum mechanics – and marvel at them. He had no memory of anything the lecturer had said. No memory of writing anything down. Yet there were the notes in his square, legible hand: black ink for what was known, red for what was not.

Daidd was wholly unprepared for the physicality of love. It made him seasick and put him off his food so that he was six kilos lighter by semester's end. The mere sight of her constricted his throat and dumped sweat from his armpits so that his shirts were always damp and, frankly, stank.

That love was such a time-thief stunned him. He'd sit down to his books, determined to brush up on formulas and theorems, only to realise that half an hour had gone by in which he'd done nothing more productive than imagine conversations with her. In some of these conversations he was arch and debonair, in others shy and tender.

Sometimes, before an exam or when an assignment was due, he'd feel a flash of irritation at the girl for consuming him so entirely. His future was by no means assured. He didn't have a family name to rely on so he needed a good degree and glowing references from his tutors.

Once, exasperated at his inability to concentrate, he yelled at her image to go away. His mother knocked at the door of his room, poked her head around it and asked if he was all right. She had globs of grey paint on her forehead.

'I'm fine,' he assured her, 'just struggling with this paper.'

His mother smiled. 'You work too hard. Try not to take it too seriously.' He knew this was something she could afford to say precisely because he did take it seriously.

The girl colonised his dreams, his airways, the tubes of his vas deferens. *Imagine*, he thought, *how unbearable unrequited love would be*. As it was, *this* was barely tolerable.

Daidd learnt her name the next term when they were allocated to the same tutorial group. Naomi. Her name was Naomi. Daidd took to scribbling it on the corners of his lecture pads. He twinned it with his own name. Naomi and Daidd. Daidd and Naomi.

Being in tutorials with her created an atmospheric pressure that could be unbearable. Their proximity caused a strange friction, like a scientific anomaly he couldn't yet explain. Too much red ink on the page. Like those moments when the tutor would hand back their assignments and Naomi would score better than him. Quite considerably better. He watched the coy drop of her head as she read the commendation inked on her title page. How, he wondered, had she focused her concentration like that; unshackled herself from the time-theft that was ravaging him? It was a question that made the lining of his stomach freeze.

It wasn't just the marks, either. Sometimes, after class, he and Naomi would go for a coffee in the cafeteria and three or four of the other students would tag along. One of them, a boy named Marek who wore a green trench coat and had long, foppish hair, offered her a cigarette. To Daidd's astonishment, Naomi accepted it. Marek leant over and offered her a light. She cupped the flame in her hands and inhaled.

'I didn't know you smoked.' Daidd spoke so abrasively, so accusingly, that the table stopped. He laughed to break the tension. 'Sorry, I'm a reformed smoker,' he lied. 'We're incorrigible.' The table laughed with him, glad to have a satisfactory explanation, but still Naomi had given him a look that unsettled him. It was a wary, hesitant look as if she'd caught the first whiff of an incipient danger.

Daidd wanted to establish himself in a job before they married, but he felt that the right thing to do would be to announce their engagement shortly after graduation. Nothing too big and frilly. Just a few friends and family, champagne, a string quartet, speeches that were warm, witty and short. 'Intimate and elegant' was how he thought of it, a riposte to the mortifying, exclusionary proms and dances of his high-school years. Intimate and elegant. He could see the font in which this would be printed on the invitations.

Not that he would object if Naomi wanted to do things differently. Girls, he knew, had firm and inflexible views on weddings and suchlike. He pictured himself good-naturedly humouring her in all the particularities of the planning. Still, he liked to scroll the 'intimate and elegant' across his mind's eye. His desire to simultaneously control and relinquish the engagement became twinned with a certain preening satisfaction he felt about resisting the 'sowing of his wild oats'. This was another phrase he pictured in a very particular font on the flyleaf of his inner eye. Not that he wasn't tempted sometimes. Not that he didn't consider it might even be for the best, in the long term, if he did. He jumped over the glaring realities of this sowing – the lack of offers, the singular and unwavering disinterest girls before Naomi had always shown in him – and repackaged it as an offering. He would resist, and give himself pure and unhandled to Naomi, a noble sign of his devotion and self-sacrifice.

Intimate and elegant   Sow his wild oats

The depth of his investment in the fantasy made what came later even more of a shock.

It was a Thursday, Daidd told Jonathon, a month out from final exams, and everyone was feeling the pressure. The mood in the lab was tense and claustrophobic, a feeling that the most threadbare triviality would push someone into tantrum and tears. Daidd was trying to concentrate on the beaker in front of him, his notes and the promptings of his lab partner. But he felt a strange suspicion, mounting to conviction, that signals of secret understanding were passing between Naomi and her lab partner, the same boy who had given her the cigarette – Marek. They didn't say much to each other, in fact they were the least verbal of any of the partners in the lab. The myriad tasks of the experiment were divvied up between them by way of nods, half-smiles, hand semaphore and once a light bumping of shoulders. Gestures of collusion. The sort of intimacy, like his and Naomi's, that operated on a higher plane than words. Was Naomi two-timing him?

Intimate and elegant

    Sow his wild oats

        Intimate and elegant

            Sow his wild oats

Daidd's beaker dropped, smashed and splattered alkaline solution over his shoes and onto the floor. He looked at his wet sneakers, the puddle, the glass fragments – but it took him a moment to piece together the cause and effect. He had dropped the beaker. The beaker had smashed. His shoes were wet … A throat-tickling, sulphurous smell permeated the air.

The tutor rushed over and placed his hand on Daidd's shoulder. 'Daidd. You've gone completely white. Are you all right? What happened?'

Daidd didn't reply; he was intent on the broken beaker, trying to figure out how it had come to be in pieces on the floor.

'Come outside. Come get some air.' The tutor led him out of the room, leaving the door propped open to air it out. He held up his hand to the group, indicating he'd be five minutes. 'Don't anyone touch the glass, okay? I'll worry about that when I get back.' He gently pushed Daidd along the corridor towards the swinging doors of the building. Daidd could tell that the tutor was genuinely alarmed. Daidd felt older by the second; when they reached the front doors, he thought, he might well be an old man.

Once they emerged onto the lip of the always fresh-cut oval, Daidd sank to his knees and hands before retching a thin stream of green bile onto the close-cropped grass. His tutor rubbed his shoulderblades encouragingly and said something about going for medical help if Daidd needed it. Daidd's thoughts divided into distinct bubbles that jostled against one another, sometimes merging and sometimes bouncing apart. *It couldn't be. I'm imagining it. I'll kill her. I'm feverish, hallucinating. I'll kill him. Flings aren't insurmountable. Pre-wedding jitters. Sauce for the goose. I'll kill myself.*

Pieces of his flesh went skipping off after his thoughts. He felt himself disintegrating, imagined the university's maintenance staff collecting clumps of his hair, a bloodied ear, his still-beating heart from the oval.

He concentrated his will on one thought, surely the correct thought, and in so doing began to draw the pieces of himself back together. He had imagined it, conjured his deepest fear and given it life, aided and abetted by the fatigue and stress that came with exams. He repeated the thought to himself over and over, until the pieces stirred, twitched and rolled back to Daidd like iron filings to a magnet. He began to feel the coarse grass under his hands, smell the sharp chlorophyll, feel the sun on the back of his neck. He collapsed onto his stomach and then rolled over onto his back, his arm slung across his eyes to keep the sun out.

'I'm all right,' he managed after a moment.

'What happened?' the tutor asked.

'I felt sick all of a sudden. It's gone now.'

'I need to get back. Will you be all right for a minute? I'll send someone out with water.'

Daidd nodded.

When he saw Naomi emerge from the doors with a glass, the relief was an opiate flooding his body, bursting a clear wall that had stood between him and a hitherto unrealised, unknown realm of bliss. Of course she had come to check on him. Of course she was concerned. What a fool he was. He dashed the tears from his eyes, embarrassed, and pulled himself up to a sitting position. Later (years later and in a different body in a different country) he realised that the tutor had sent Naomi out because she was the only girl in the lab.

'Hey, Daidd,' she said as she dropped to the grass beside him. 'Sorry you're not well. Do you want some water?'

He took it from her, his hand trembling. Their fingertips brushed as they exchanged the glass, kicking the opiate in his blood even higher and bucketing the tears from his eyes.

She looked at him with concern. 'It's the stress, isn't it? It's getting to everyone. I think we're all on the verge of a major freak-out. Drink some water and take deep breaths.'

He did as she suggested. He drank a few mouthfuls, wedged the glass into a tuft of grass and brushed the tears from his eyes again. He smiled at her then opened his mouth to tell her of the green serpent that he'd conjured from sleeplessness and worry, when the lab class poured out of the building.

Marek came bounding towards them and dropped down beside Naomi, throwing two backpacks onto the ground. 'They let us go early to clean up and air out the room. Sorry you're crook, Daidd, but man I'm seriously grateful you got us out of there. That was one dull tute.' And then he leant over and kissed Naomi softly on the lips, raised a hand to brush back some hair that had come loose from her ponytail and said, 'Ready to go, babe?'

She nodded. 'You'll be okay, Daidd?' She stood up, took the backpack that Marek had retrieved for her, reattached it to her back, gave Daidd a wave and walked off towards the car park, hand in hand with the green-jacketed cigarette boy.

During the trial Daidd's lawyer described what happened next as a period of temporary insanity. Daidd remembered little of it. What he did remember came to him in flashes, unexpectedly, as though he was plucked out of time and dropped into a cinema where events rolled randomly and out of sequence.

He was labouring against Goosen's Trial during the first season he spent in The Fortress gardens when the warning on the label came to him, rising up from the field like a vengeful ghost. It levitated for him to read: the red label, the white lettering, the skull-and-crossbones symbol. 'Dangerous chemical. To be used under supervision. Not to be removed from the lab.' He didn't remember stealing it. Didn't remember throwing it at Naomi, didn't remember her screaming, though the witnesses testified that the sound would stay with them forever.

Naomi had wanted judgement by the Vaik, as was her right as a female citizen. In his fevered and furious state Daidd took this as further proof of the inherent treachery of women. Naomi had made him feel these things, encouraged them, let him plot his life around her then casually pulled a thread that unravelled the entire edifice and sauntered off into a future in which he had no part. The acid was a poor attempt at evening the score, at giving her a taste of the corrosion she'd unleashed on him. It seemed to him a kind of justice: to contort that face with its mask of innocence and ordinariness and force it to assume its true shape. False. Cruel. Monstrous.

That he was committed to stand trial, and under Vaik statute, when all he had done was right a wrong, disgusted him. This wasn't justice. He'd *served* justice by delivering the restitution. When the presiding Vaik delivered her sentence – that Naomi could choose between Daidd being declared isvestyii or being doused in acid then sentenced to The Fortress for seven years – he spat on the ground. It was so unfair. He cursed Naomi. He cursed the Vaik. He cursed women.

He was escorted to an Aeraevest at the furthest end of the perimeter wall. The wall ran for nearly fourteen kilometres from the main buildings in one direction and just over sixteen in the other. One curve of the wall met a mountain range that served as a natural defence for the city nestled on the other side of it. The jagged teeth of the range made a landing from the water virtually impossible. Where the mountains gave way to a gentler undulation of hills and a small, natural harbour in The Dryans, the perimeter wall cut inland to keep a watch on any craft that might try to make land. All this had made sense two hundred years ago when any attack would have come from the sea, but who was going to invade them now? What enemy would announce themselves in a sailboat? Wars now came through fibre and cables, invasions of data and diseases of zeroes and ones.

It was ridiculous, his sentence. To keep watch from an Aeraevest looking to the sea and the harbour for twelve hours at a stretch, then to shimmy down the wooden ladder to his quarters and write his daily report: 'Nothing sighted', and send it through the shunt up the line to the Aeraevest ahead of him and from there to the nerve centre of The Fortress. Two pointless words telling the Vaik what they already knew, of no use to anyone, while he rotted away in his stone quarters.

He climbed the ladder and took up his post every day, not out of a sense of duty or obligation but because the confines of his quarters pressed in on him. His heart sped up and a tightness spread from the centre of his sternum outwards, a radial of pain and pressure so intense he felt his heart and lungs would, literally, burst within him. His palms grew clammy and little crosses sparkled at the edges of his vision – clear on his right side where his eyesight was unimpaired, blurry on his left where the acid had taken seventy per cent of his vision. Less than he had taken from Naomi, the Vaik reminded him when she had tended his wounds after Naomi inflicted them. Naomi would never see again.

The panic attacks forced him out of his quarters and there was nowhere to go but the sentry post above. The maze of underground tunnels and shunts that connected each Aeraevest were kept locked, opening every three days to bring him more food and water, writing materials, medicines if he needed them.

To escape he would need to find a way down the wall. One side was a sheer drop to the sea; it was far too high to leap from, and the sea was ferocious until it flowed into the harbour. Daidd was a reasonable swimmer but by no means a strong one. The drop on the land-side was higher but less sheer; it might have been possible for him to slowly, carefully pick a path downwards through the jutting stone. But even assuming he could do so without being seen, the path would drop him in The Dryans – the steaming, impoverished underbelly of the city's high-tech, high-gloss topcoat. The acid burn would mark him as a Vaik prisoner, and they would hand him straight back. He could try to make his way along the top of the wall between sentry posts but he'd have to do it under cover of darkness. It was unlikely he'd be able to make it between sundown and sun-up. Once he hit the wooden ramparts the boards would squeak, alerting the people – either prisoners or Vaik – keeping watch in the other Aeraevest. Escape was impossible.

Even then Daidd did not consider suicide. His slow-burning sense of indignation and injustice kept him from self-harm. For seven years his world consisted of the three square metres of his quarters and the tower of the sentry post. He learnt to recognise the book-end of the seasons by the changing concentration of salt in the air; the colour of the sky; the seeds tossed up on the tide below his Aeraevest. For three of those years he went up and down the ladder between rock and sky, collared by sea and dirt until he realised that the enemy the Vaik had set him to watch was himself.

There were no intimations that he was approaching this revelation, no slowly evolving sense of understanding that delivered him, gently but inevitably, to the truth. Instead it burst on him all at once, the way a thunderclap will erupt from an invisible cross-current of air and shake the gods themselves. Naomi had never loved him; she'd barely noticed him. He'd felt for her and – in the usual way of male sensibility that credits itself with neither fancy nor entitlement – attributed the genesis of that feeling to her. Something she had created or willed. Something for which she was responsible.

He'd poured acid on a girl for whom he had barely existed.

The next day, the sestyatesh was over. The skies cleared and a tepid sunlight lazed to the ground. A fresh, clean smell was in the air as if it had been rinsed and polished.

Ulait was propped up on a low trolley, the blanket by her side if she needed it; Daidd gripped the trolley handle.

The Vaik leant towards Jonathon and surprised him by settling a gentle kiss on his cheek. 'Goodbye, Jonathon Bridge. You won't be with us much longer. Remember us on the other side.'

It hit him like a cold blast to the belly: he would be leaving soon. When the spring came, Mandalay would collect him from his quarters and lead him back the way he had come, through The Veya Gate and into the outer quarters where the electii lodged. They would take his masjythra and he would dress in the clothes he'd left in the basket. Adalia and his child — his child! — would be waiting for him on the other side of the wall. Would he be ready? He didn't know.

'Goodbye, Ulait,' said the Vaik. 'Take care of that foot — no more hiking during storms.'

Ulait smiled sheepishly. 'I won't.'

They set off along the track running by the perimeter wall. It was littered by debris from the sestyatesh, so they had to stop every few metres to bundle up boughs and sticks and palm fronds to clear the way. They passed clusters of workgroups patching up the low stone walls that bounded the fields. Other groups hacked at boughs fallen across roads. Jonathon wondered how the Vaik coped with natural disasters. Did they buy in supplies from the outside world when required? How did they raise capital? Who did their banking? The first gleam of an idea flashed for what he might do as a free man.

Ulait seemed to have divined his thoughts. 'Will you be glad to leave us, Jonathon Bridge?'

He stooped to pick a bike wheel from the path and propped it against the gate to a neighbouring field. 'Not to leave you, but to be with my wife and my baby, yes. To be a father.' He paused. A workgroup of silver masjythra shouldering shovels and hoes crossed a distant field. In the weak sun their garb was dull and unreflective. 'To be a father, Mistress. I long for it.'

Ulait wrinkled her nose. 'The Vaik have no use for fathers. I'm trying to imagine what a father is. What he does. Is it the same as being a mother, do you think?'

'I honestly don't know, Mistress. Perhaps carrying a child and giving birth to it makes a difference to how you love. But I can't imagine that I could love my baby any more than I do. It's the biggest thing I can imagine. The most powerful.'

'Will you cry, do you think, when you see the baby for the first time?'

The tears rushed into his eyes at the thought. He laughed as he dashed them away. 'All the evidence would suggest yes.'

And he cried some more at the realisation that this moment, which had seemed so remote, both temporally and spiritually, was nearly upon him.

'Come, my turn,' he said to Daidd as he assumed control of the trolley. They trundled on for a while, then Jonathon said, 'I will miss you, Mistress. I will think of you often.'

Ulait's mouth twisted. 'And yet you defied me. You insulted me. You insulted the Vaik.'

'Yes. I was wrong. Forgive me.'

She seemed to think on this. He saw, then, the woman she would become. The sharp cheekbones that would be left behind when the last of her girlish roundness dissolved. The gold-flecked green eyes that would oversee these fields and their workgroups for the rest of her days.

She smiled, the elastic face of adolescence returning. 'I forgive you.'

They turned into the orchard where a party of Vaik were awaiting them. Mandalay broke into a run towards them and fell to the ground, throwing her arms around Ulait. 'My darling girl,' she sobbed. 'My darling girl.'

'I'm all right, I'm all right,' Ulait crooned, soothing her.

Mandalay held the girl's face in her hands and looked at her earnestly. 'I was afraid, Ulait. I thought I'd lost you.' Mandalay rested her high, wide forehead against Ulait's.

Ulait took Mandalay's hand from her cheek and pressed her lips against her palm. 'I was never in any real danger. I simply couldn't walk well. I would have ridden out the storm even if I hadn't found Daidd.'

Mandalay looked up at Daidd, her eyes tearing over again. 'You got my girl to the sentry?'

Daidd nodded.

'Thank you.' Mandalay stood up and embraced Daidd, then she turned to Jonathon. 'I thank you too, Jonathon Bridge.' She held him close.

He took the opportunity to whisper into her ear. 'Mandalay, I must speak with you. The isvestyii —'

'Not now.' She drew away. 'Come, you must be cold and hungry.'

They set off, the Vaik fussing over Ulait and giving their voluble thanks to Jonathon and Daidd. They were upon the footpath leading to the verandah when Jonathon was able to draw Daidd a little away from the others. 'Daidd. I need to know. Ulait.'

He shook his head. 'Those of us who make our home here, the permanent residents, we can't. It's taken care of. For consanguinity reasons. Only supplicants and national servicemen can impregnate Vaik.'

'You have no children.'

Daidd ran his hand over his stubbled chin, his eyes dark with fatigue. 'No.' He turned from Jonathon and walked wearily up the stairs and along the verandah, a strange and solitary figure among the rejoicing, weaving Vaik.

On the first fine half after Ulait's ankle had healed, she and Jonathon set off from the men's quarters towards the Story-Keeping House. Both had packs slung across their backs. Most of the storm damage had been cleared away, but still they came across felled trees and crumbling stone walls. The skies were dull, and a fine mizzle hazed the air. There were rumours that returning olöcks had been sighted on the far side of the downs, and Ulait was excited at the prospect of seeing them.

'I'm surprised you're still keen on olöcks, Mistress. Given what happened last time you went looking for them.'

'I'm even *more* keen on them.' She lifted her foot from the ground and wriggled her ankle. 'I'm physically invested now.'

'If you lived in my city, you'd probably go and get a tattoo of an olöck and some foreign word meaning "kindred".'

'What would be the point of that?'

'No one knows.'

Ulait planted her foot and set off again. 'Sometimes the people in your city don't sound too bright.'

'With that, Mistress, I would have to agree.'

They trekked purposefully over the countryside, canvassing various spots.

'Could this be it?' Ulait asked. They had come to a tumble of boulders within which was a mossy hollow.

'No. There weren't boulders. Not that I remember. Just lots of branches and leaves in a thick tangle. I don't think you could tell from the outside that there was a clearing within.'

Ulait pursed her lips and paused. 'It's possible that whatever was there was blown away in the sestyatesh.'

'Yes, I know.'

She scanned the landscape. 'This way,' she said. 'I have another idea.'

They passed over the rise and into the dell on the far side. They were trying to find the copse where Jonathon had hidden when he'd run from the Story-Keeping House. He'd described it to Ulait and she had some notion of where it might be. They marched up another hill and tacked diagonally across it until they came to a semicircle of imposing trees. The trees bent towards one another, conferring.

Jonathon poked into the tangle of branches, sheaved bark and leaves collected around the trunks. 'I can't be sure,' he said. 'But I think this is the place.'

He was surprised how far it was from the Story-Keeping House, five or six kilometres at least. In his memory he'd run only a short way. He held the curtain of foliage back while Ulait scrambled under it. He followed, careful to keep the thorny twigs from his face. They slid off their packs and sat cross-legged in the clearing, facing each other. The air was damp and vegetative. Jonathon pushed back against his fear of being enclosed underground; he was determined to do this. The masjythra expanded around him like a blanket.

He opened his pack and removed a roughly fashioned wooden cross. He'd made it in the shed at the back of the shaenet from branches brought down by the storm. He'd sanded the wood back, treated it, then painted it blue. Blue like the water Eshtakai had swum in. In a strong, clear hand he'd painted 'CLARA' in claret-coloured paint. Ulait dug a hole with a trowel, spooning out tree litter, then filled it in while Jonathon held the cross upright.

'I don't know what to say,' he admitted. 'My family weren't churchgoers so I don't know any prayers. And the Vaik don't have any.'

'Just say what's in your heart, and make the offer.'

He nodded.

'Clara.

'Clara.

'It's Jonathon Bridge here. I'm not a religious man, or even a spiritual man, but I believe that, wherever you are, you can hear me.

'I'm sorry I didn't make the effort to know you better. I'm even sorrier that I didn't help you when you needed me on your side. I don't think I really got it. My sense of innocence got in the way of me really understanding. I am a giant to myself, and sightless. I hope you can forgive me.

'We'll never have the opportunity to be friends now.

'My friend Ulait is here. She is Vaik and she has authorised me to offer you sanctuary here. Your spirit is welcome at The Fortress. Come rest here with the people who will honour you.

'Work. History. Sex. Justice.

'Amen.'

Ulait and Jonathon sat silently for a while. He thought back to his encounter with Daidd at the sentry post. (He didn't know what to call it. 'Sex' implied consent, but he had not wanted it. 'Rape' wasn't accurate either. 'Encounter' it was, then.) At first, he had thought of Clara's suicide as the logical endpoint of her rape. She may have stepped into it, but her rapist had tied that noose, and Jonathon and his colleagues had helped her to slip it over her head.

Lately, though, he had begun to wonder if her suicide was better understood as an act of defiance. The rape was an incursion, her body a white flag. Clara was obviously tough. She'd gotten out of The Dryans and into Jonathon's world, so he couldn't believe that she hadn't tried to wrestle her body back. When that proved impossible, was death a final act of defiance? A flight from her flesh?

It was late when Mandalay appeared in his doorway. He'd been struggling to sleep again; every time he closed his eyes he saw the wave holding the isvestyii and dragging him down into the grey deep. The noise of the returning seabirds then kept him awake. He lay very still, watching her. Her red hair fell down her back, her luminous skin a profound contrast against her dark green gown. He did not recall that the first time they'd met, in the antechamber where she'd recited the terms of his confinement, he had not found her attractive. He desired her now, in the way he desired all powerful things.

He was afraid of her, too.

She stepped softly on bare feet into his room and relaxed against his window.

'You can feel the season turning. It's always a strange time for me. All the new supplicants are locked in, the national servicemen signed up. We prepare to say goodbye to the men we've come to know. We decide on the new plantings. There's a spate of pregnancies and passings. It's the season of opposites.'

Jonathon understood this. He both wanted and did not want for her to slip out of her gown and join him in his bed.

'You understand what is required,' she spoke to the night air rather than to him, 'with Ulait?'

'Yes,' he said softly.

She pulled a string on her gown and it fell in lush folds to the ground. He threw back the bedclothes for her and she slid beside him. He did not understand why she was in his bed. She had already vetted him for Ulait and made it clear that she didn't think much of him as a human being. Perhaps his endeavours in the sestyatesh had softened her heart towards him. Perhaps it was no more than a way to pass the time.

She made him nervous. Even when she was tracing her fingers down his back, he was thinking, *Those claws.*

He also thought of Daidd, who loved this woman; had chosen to hold his will in permanent abeyance to remain close to her. There had been a time when Jonathon relished the idea of cuckolding other men. Now, Daidd's longing just made him sad. Or perhaps Daidd had truly surmounted possessiveness. Jonathon could not bear the idea of another man touching Adalia and acknowledged his own hypocrisy in this.

It was impossible for him to reconcile his various fears and desires so he shut his mind off, focusing only on Mandalay's body. He approached her as a cartographer might. He committed to memory the pearly claw marks around her hips, the knuckles that seemed too large for her long fingers. He studied the arch of her foot, her faceted ankle. The milky skin overlaid on taut muscle. He listened intently to the precise way she enunciated his name. *Jonathon Bridge.* The way an admiral might address a sailor who'd seen the same action, even though their lives overlapped in no other way.

When it was over, and before Mandalay's breathing steadied and she stood up to leave, Jonathon tried to raise the subject of the isvestyii, but she cut him off.

'I'm not your confessor,' she said. 'You need to learn to carry it.'

Jonathon thought this unfair. After all, the Vaik had promised that an isvestyii would 'dissolve to nothing'. But he had not. His death was lodged in Jonathon's body: behind his eyelids and in the hands that had shoved the man from the perimeter wall.

If the isvestyii had been electrocuted in a state prison or lanced with a Vaik blade and left to drown, it wouldn't have cost Jonathon a moment's concern. But he couldn't place the thing apart from himself. He would have to craft a narrative to make sense of it, integrate it. The Woman — whoever or whatever she was — had said he would judge. Despite the horror of what he had seen and continued to see, he thrilled to the idea that he had a part in Vaik cosmology.

'I contain worlds,' he said in the darkness. Mandalay wrapped her arms around him and pulled him towards sleep.

V ANIN

H E KNEW that after what happened last time there would be a big performance. The world needed to be righted, precedent asserted, the future written. He arranged his face to blankness so the Vaik might project what they needed there, hiding his horror deep within himself.

Four Vaik entered his quarters after lunch on the half. They were high-spirited and fey, laughing among themselves as they removed his masjythra and escorted him, naked, down the zigzagging ramp and onto the path to the north-eastern sector.

Jonathon tilted his head to the sun, enjoying the feeling of warmth on his skin. The gardens had recovered well from the sestyatesh. Buds were springing up in the mild weather, and everything wore an expectant, hopeful aspect. The light caught in the fine gold hair of the Vaik as they led him into a part of The Fortress where he had never been before. He squinted, and it seemed he was orbited by four glowing suns.

This had to be a residential district because, as they made their procession, women and girls appeared at windows and threw petals towards them. Jonathon did not understand the words they spoke, but there was no missing the ribald nature of the raillery. His Vaik escort laughed, springing into the air to catch the flowers and dropping them atop his head. The women wore loose, white gowns that flowed like water as they slipped along the path.

They stopped at a blue building festooned with red window boxes. The Vaik led him in, their touch warm and soft. They were excited, chirruping like birds. They came to a three-walled room that opened onto a lawn. The room was tiled in whites and blues and bathed in light. Incense burned from delicate glass jars but still the scent of the garden – fresh-washed and cut – permeated the room. Jonathon breathed it in and felt slightly light-headed.

One of the Vaik led the way towards a perfect blue slab of water, a narrow rectangle slicing through the room. She stepped nimbly down the marble stairs, still robed. 'Come here, Jonathon Bridge.'

He followed her into the water. She took a sponge and wiped his hair, his face, his neck. She worked methodically and gently, cleansing him in slow, concentric circles. The water was warm and rose-scented. Her wet gown clung to her breasts and hips, her brown nipples perfectly visible through the white material. Jonathon's penis stirred. Smiling, the Vaik reached for it and gave it a wash. 'Lucky Ulait,' she said, and winked at him.

Jonathon kept his face determinedly blank, but he was imposing the image of this nubile, rose-scented Vaik on his retina. He would carry whatever he could into the bedchamber with Ulait, determined not to fail her.

'Close your eyes,' whispered the Vaik. She sponged his hair, and the rivulets ran warm along his cheeks.

There was a slight splash and, when he opened his eyes, Mandalay was sitting on the side of the bath, her bare legs swinging in the water. Next to her was a tray bearing an intricately carved silver jug and half a dozen small red glasses.

'Hello,' he said.

'Verrglet?' she asked.

'Yes, please.'

She poured the fizzy green juice into the glasses and handed them around. The other Vaik came and sat on the rim of the bath, too.

Jonathon took his glass from her hand. 'Thank you.'

She had an air of mischief about her he had never sensed before. It made her impossibly beautiful. He had an urge to reach for her and pull her into the water with him. But he stayed where he was, sipping his verrglet.

'I'm wondering about the beard,' said Mandalay. 'Should he keep it, do you think? Or should we shave it off?'

The Vaik in the pool with Jonathon reached out and bunched the wiry, salt-and-pepper beard that framed his face. The men had been given shaving equipment in the bathhouse, and Jonathon had used it during the summer when the salt gnats gave him such grief. But in the colder months he'd let it grow.

'I like a man with a beard,' said the Vaik, and she leant in and kissed him on the mouth. She tasted of ginger and the berry, tingly aftertaste of verrglet. 'But,' she drew back, his face in her hands, and considered him, 'there's the scratch factor. Best it goes, I think.'

She spoke matter-of-factly, in the prosaic way of the Vaik when dealing with sex, but Jonathon's stomach iced over. He turned away as if to cough, then downed the rest of his verrglet. This would happen. He could do this. He scrunched his eyes tight and opened them rapidly a few times. Then settled his features and turned back around, serene.

Mandalay nodded. 'Bring me the razor. Come, Jonathon Bridge, let's see what you look like under that foliage.'

The Vaik led him out of the bath. He hung back a little to watch the undulating bottom swathed in white cloth ahead of him. Mandalay wrapped a large, soft towel around him then motioned for him to take a seat. He took the chair she offered, faced towards the lawn. The birds chirped in the soft blue sky and something scurried in the undergrowth nearby. He wanted to be out there with the sun on his back, pruning the leaves and watering the flowers. Or just flopped on the cool green grass, unmoving, letting the sun dry him and enjoying the play of light within his lashes.

Mandalay prepared the lather and set a long blade to warm in a bowl of water. She towelled his beard off and applied the lather with a small brush. The smell of pine and spruce filled his nostrils. Mandalay worked quickly and without hesitation, planing the blade along his cheeks and chin. He was acutely aware of her proximity, could feel her breath warm on his skin, the tickle of her red hair along his temples. Her tongue protruded a little as she concentrated, working around the cleft in his chin. She wiped the blade clean on a towel and stood back to check her handiwork. He didn't relax until she'd put down the blade.

'You look – different.'

Jonathon ran his hand along his face, feeling the unfamiliar smoothness.

'Here.' She handed him a jar and helped him to apply the moisturiser.

'I will miss these smells,' he said, inhaling the scent. 'The shaenet smells. Mistaelnet balm. Norsling. I don't remember what the outside world smells like. If it smells at all.'

'More verrglet, I think,' said Mandalay.

'One only for you, Jonathon Bridge,' said the Vaik who had bathed him, crooking her little finger. The others laughed.

They all sat around the edge of the azure pool, their feet in the water, drinking. He sipped the bubbling tea, enjoying the warmth of it coursing through his chest and along his limbs, while letting his mind wander freely, though the blankness of his naked face never wavered.

He wondered about the Vaik who had brought him here from his quarters. Despite the wildly random chromosomes that produced them, they barely wavered from the essential prototype:

fine hay-coloured hair; high, wide foreheads; dark skin; and heavy lids over almond-shaped brown eyes. Mandalay, who looked so different — did she truly feel one of them, even after more than twenty years at The Fortress? She had an authority here, that much was obvious, but the physical fact of her difference was undeniable. He remembered the first Vaik who had come to his bed and left her blood on him. *The Vaik don't trust bridges*, she'd said. *Things of difference should keep their own kind.*

But the paradox of Vaik civilisation was that without the supplicants and national servicemen it would all end. Whatever boys were produced by the union of the Vaik and the men did not live here. Was it possible that the Vaik had evolved to a point where they produced girl-children only? Or did they do ... something else? The vision of Mandalay holding the hot, sharp blade rose before him.

Did they?

He became aware that Mandalay was studying him. Was she committing him to memory? He chided himself for the thought: he was one of dozens, perhaps hundreds, to flow through her hands. He remembered what Daidd had told him, that nothing was spontaneous. The Vaik choreographed every encounter. But how many men, he considered darkly, did Mandalay permit to sleep with her daughters?

He met her gaze. She was flushed, perhaps from the verrglet, and holding a hand protectively over her belly. 'Come. A toast.' She stood and held her glass aloft. 'In the beginning there was nothing, and the Vaik were not afraid.'

As Mandalay spoke, the revelry of the group subsided and the women bowed their heads. Jonathon bowed his also.

'They fashioned themselves from the state of nothingness and devised four pillars so that they might take shape and form.'

'Work. History. Sex. Justice,' the women incanted as one.

'A moving body is a creative body. It produces the food on

our plates, the walls that protect us and the art that delights us.

'We created and recreate ourselves by standing apart. We honour they who won us our solitude, but we are not petrified.

'Pleasure consists in the freedom to, and the freedom from, and every Vaik will herself determine in what measure these things are best.

'We are instruments of the sovereignty of all women, and do not shrink from the sacrifice this entails.

'Work. History. Sex. Justice.'

'We are Vaik,' they all said as one.

'Come,' Mandalay said abruptly, 'it's time.'

The Vaik wrapped him in a silken robe – 'for Ulait to unwrap' – and led him to the bedchamber.

He lay in bed watching the light creep through the window and into his room. The sea whispered below the perimeter wall and the seabirds began their chorus. He threw the bedcovers back and let the fresh air magnetise his body. He splashed water on his face and leant out the window. He filled his lungs with the salt sea air then turned back to the room that had been his for the past three hundred and sixty-five days. He wouldn't sleep here tonight and soon, very soon, all traces of him would be erased. Daidd and Mandalay would carry him for a while, then gently let him go. Ulait might remember him. He hoped so.

Instinctively his body tensed for the chime of the bell, then he began his last walk down the zigzagged path, along the verandah and to the dining hall. Daidd hailed him from their usual table near the alfresco area where the Vaik were assembling. He sat next to Daidd, who reached for his hand and closed his fist over it. 'Soon you will have coffee.'

'Coffee,' Jonathon repeated. Then he laughed. 'Man, I was in bad shape those first few days.' The blue masjythra ladled fruit and porridge into his bowl. He sipped the astringent tea he'd grown used to. 'I won't miss this,' he said, nodding to the tea. 'It's an abomination. Tastes like grass.'

'You don't know yet what you'll miss. It might surprise you.'

'Yes, thank you, Master.' He felt uncomfortable. Overfull. As if he might burst into hysterics or start a fight because there was too much to contain within himself. He wanted to be both in and out. With Adalia and his daughter outside, out there. But also in the shaenet tethering the vines to stakes and pressing mistaelnet. The twilight between them both was unbearable.

'I'll miss you,' said Daidd.

Jonathon swallowed a sob. He concentrated on chewing his food until the impulse passed. 'If you leave, Daidd, you can stay with me and Adalia. For as long as you like. Mandalay knows where to find me.'

Daidd nodded. 'Thank you, my friend. But I can't leave. You know that.'

'Things change. All things change. I just want you to know you have options.'

'What will you do now?'

'Change nappies. Learn to make bread. Take my daughter to the park. Talk to my wife. Beyond that, Daidd, it will be one day at a time.'

'You won't go back to your old job.'

'No.' It was one of the few things about which Jonathon was certain. That time was past. 'I do have an idea.'

Daidd raised an eyebrow, curious.

'The Vaik must need intermediaries with the city. Someone to do their banking, ensure supply lines in the event of a storm. Recruit supplicants.'

'Yeah. I suppose.'

'I meant what I said, Daidd. You can come to us if you leave.'

'I can't leave. I can't leave her.'

After breakfast, Jonathon followed Daidd to the foot of the stairs where the assignment assembled for the day's task. A few of the men shook his hand and wished him well.

Daidd hugged him tightly. 'It has been a privilege knowing you, Jonathon Bridge. I think you may be Mandalay's masterpiece.'

'Thanks. I think. Remember, my offer stands.'

Jonathon turned and walked to his room. He swung between an almost unbearable anticipation and paralysing dread. In a matter of hours he would pass through The Veya Gate. He would see Adalia. He would hold his child. The idea of his child had changed him, the way a strong wind will bend a tree. That he would look into his baby's eyes, hear her sounds, feel her soft, warm body against him ... That this would be a reality.

His sensitivity was heightened with each passing minute. Every follicle was upright in the breeze. The nerve endings in his tough, callused feet started working again. The grains of sand on the polished boards of his room felt like golf balls. The sea beneath his window was especially salty. He opened his mouth to feel the sodium crystals stick to his tonsils.

When it seemed he might snap under the strain, fear flooded in. It made his knees buckle and he had to sit on the bed, drawing air into his lungs.

He knew that he and Adalia were different people after this past year. Would they be different in complementary ways, with new channels opening up between them that they could explore at leisure? Or would the way back to each other be closed?

It was a risk they had taken with their eyes open.

'May I come in?'

'Of course.'

Mandalay sat next to him on the bed, smiling. 'I've come to escort you, if you are ready.'

Jonathon nodded. They were silent as they took the zigzag ramp through the residential quarters and followed the path towards The Veya Gate. He'd been drugged when he first passed through it, and felt he may as well have been so now. Everything seemed hyperreal: the green shimmer of Mandalay's gown, the pink buds waking from their winter hibernation, the bleached white of the clouds lazing overhead.

He paused as they came to The Gate. It was a curved, pearlescent structure, dazzling in the weak sunlight. It seemed to wear a halo.

'I can ask questions on the other side of this,' said Jonathon.

Mandalay laughed. 'One. I'll permit you one.'

He inched forward, ruminating on what he would ask. He longed to know how much of what had passed between him and Mandalay was real, though he understood that each of them would have different conceptions of what constituted 'real'. But for the physical changes in his body he might have believed he'd dreamt the whole thing, psychically guided by the Vaik while he lay drugged and inert on a camper bed for twelve months.

He wanted to know about The Woman: whether she had ever been a real person and was now an idea, a Vaik bogeyman wheeled out to ensure compliance.

Had the Vaik known he would say no to Ulait that first time and, if so, why hadn't they prepared her for that eventuality?

When he had pushed the isvestyii off the wall, was that what Mandalay had intended all along? If he hadn't done it, would the Vaik have leapt from boltholes in the ground and done it themselves?

He was now moving so slowly he was barely moving at all. Mandalay passed through The Gate ahead of him. It was the way that she held her hand on her rounding belly as she waited for him that decided Jonathon. Really, there was no other question to ask.

He took one last look at the fuzzy, gleaming structure that connected his past and his future selves, and walked through. On the other side, he took Mandalay's arm, drawing her close.

'I know you're pregnant,' he said. 'I don't ask if the child is mine. I want to know, if it's a boy, what will happen to him?'

'This is your question?'

'Yes.'

'The boys live in a sequestered part of The Fortress – though, as you may have guessed, the Vaik don't conceive boys at the same rate as they do girls. Perhaps every tenth child is a boy.'

'That doesn't seem possible. Biologically.'

'What do you know about the treaty between our peoples? About the biological guarantees?'

'I read about that before I came here. When the war ended there was an agreement that men would be provided to the Vaik.'

'Before the war there were rules about the men the Vaik were sent. Only men who'd conceived children and were sound mentally and physically. They also had to be able to prove their maternal line. Those rules were supposed to continue under the biological guarantees. Instead, your people sent us your lunatics, your prisoners. Inbred, deformed, violent, deranged. That was our stock.'

Jonathon remembered when he'd read about the treaty, the powerful sense he'd had of a key piece of information withheld. Now he understood. 'They tried to breed you out,' he said. 'A form of biological warfare.'

'But here we are, centuries later. Barely altered.'

Being Vaik is a state of mind, she had told him once. He could almost believe they had willed their DNA into an immutable state; men contributing nothing but the enlivenment of the egg. In such circumstances, birthing few boys seemed entirely possible.

'I never saw a Vaik boy the whole time I was here. Never heard a boy's voice. They don't live here.'

'They do, but we keep them confined. They are not free to move around the grounds like their sisters. They can leave if they wish. Most choose to stay.'

His child with Mandalay – if he was a boy – might come to him. Come to his world.

'If he leaves, will you –'

But Mandalay cut him off. 'One question only.'

Jonathon wasn't sure that he believed her, about the boys. He remembered the day of The Great Hall when he'd upturned the tiny bones in the soil. He was almost certain they hadn't been bird bones.

Whatever the truth was, Mandalay would give him no comfort. Fatherhood was something she could not conceive of. He had to trust her, for his own sanity. One day, years from now, he might be walking down a city street and a young man would brush past him and Jonathon would know that this was his boy. It was the sort of thing that Adalia would believe possible, even likely.

'Goodbye, Jonathon Bridge.'

'Goodbye, Mandalay.'

How did you take leave of such a person, under such circumstances? Jonathon briefly considered kissing her, or shaking her hand. But none of that would suffice. Now they had passed through The Veya Gate, there was no language between them. She turned, and was gone. He felt a strain at his heart, as of a cord at maximum tension, then a snap and relief.

'This way, please, Mr Bridge.'

The electii had appeared as Mandalay left. This was not the one who had inducted him. As the two of them wound their way through the rabbit's warren of corridors and anterooms, Jonathon wondered what had happened to the first electii he had met. Was that electii still here, welcoming supplicants like him? Or had a decision been taken at The Great Hall that the electii was now Vaik?

Finally, he and the electii came to a bare, square room with a wicker basket in the corner.

'In the basket you will find your clothes and personal effects.

Place your masjythra in the basket when you're done. I will be waiting outside the door for you. Take all the time you need.'

But Jonathon had no wish to linger. His child – his child! – was waiting for him. He pulled the masjythra over his head and unpacked his clothes from the basket. The fabric was strange in his hands, dull and lifeless, after the gown he'd grown used to. His fingers were clumsy at the buttons of his shirt and the cotton felt scratchy. His underwear felt tight and restrictive. Unnecessary. He took the jocks off and balled them up into his jacket pocket. His pants were far too big; he had to cinch them at the waist with his belt. At the very bottom of the basket was his wedding ring, also too loose for his leanness. He placed it on his index finger. He dropped the masjythra in the basket and called out to the electii that he was ready.

The electii opened the door and stood aside to let Jonathon pass. 'Follow the corridor until it diverges. On the right is a staircase, on the left another corridor. Take the left. This will lead you to the grassed enclosure and then the iron gate. Goodbye. And good luck.'

'Thank you.'

Almost jogging now, Jonathon followed the corridor until it stopped at a wall painted with trees bent double in the wind. He turned left, his heart pounding, and ran for the rectangle of sunlight where the door opened to the small, grassed enclosure. It took a moment for his eyes to adjust. Birds pecked at the grass, undisturbed by the wheeze of the iron gate.

He walked through the gate to the outside. Then there they were on the steps leading down to the car park. His wife's hair had grown, and she hadn't started dyeing it again. It fell in a two-toned wave to her shoulders. Her cheeks were as ruddy as he remembered, her smile as infectious. The baby she held was curious about her unfamiliar surroundings, looking about – wide-eyed – from a head determined to support itself.

'I brought you coffee,' said Adalia, nodding to a plastic cup by her feet.

'Adalia,' he said. 'I don't think I can stand up.' But he was already down, his legs buckling. He landed, hard, on his bony bottom. Adalia laughed, and he closed his eyes to drink in that rich, cheeky cackle that had lured him, siren-like, on the night they'd met.

'Sit on the step,' she said.

He shifted along on his bottom to the step, dangling his legs over the side. Adalia lowered herself to be next to him and handed their baby to him. He placed her in the crook of one arm and circled her with the other. He gazed at the baby, at her molten grey eyes exploring his, silently. She felt in his arms just the way she had felt in his dreams. As if he hadn't known what his arms were *for*, until now. Adalia reached across for the coffee, placing it on the far side of him, then leant into him. She rested her head on his shoulder so he could smell the minty fragrance of her shampoo.

They remained like that, all three, for some time.

GLOSSARY

Aeraevest — watchfulness of self. Also the name for the sentry
posts at The Fortress that face out to the sea.

Anin — spring.

Annod — summer.

Ceb — winter.

The Dryans — the poorer area of the city at the back of the
valley near the pass into the mountains.

Electii — transgender individuals who serve the outer perimeter
of The Fortress. Some enter The Fortress as women.

Eshtakai — a Vaik who features among the foundation myths of
The Fortress. Eshtakai fended off a maritime attack on The
Fortress by winning over the women onboard the ship. The
women poisoned the men and threw them overboard. Those
who survived were taken as prisoners into The Fortress.

Ettëvy — autumn.

Goosen's Trial — a tenacious weed common to the gardens of
The Fortress. It has thorns that, if they pierce skin, release a
toxin that causes a burning rash.

Isvestyii — the unredeemed; literally 'self dissolving to nothing'.
These men can never leave The Fortress. The Woman has
the power of life and death over those declared isvestyii.

Masjythra — the robes worn by the men at The Fortress. The
different colours serve to differentiate their roles.

Mistaelnet – one of the herbs grown at The Fortress. It has multiple medicinal applications.

Norsling – a plant with purple fruit grown in the shaenet. Used for bringing on contractions.

Olöck – a ground-dwelling bird at The Fortress, known for its ability to sense changes in atmospheric pressure and predict a sestyatesh.

Oorsel – a bean grown in the fields at The Fortress.

Sestyatesh – literally 'seventy-year wind': the powerful, destructive storms that happen a handful of times in a generation.

Shaenet – the 'body garden' where medicinal herbs and recreational drugs are grown at The Fortress.

Sterysh – a drink made from crushed mistaelnet seeds. It induces feelings of euphoria.

Vaik – the native women of The Fortress. Also the name of the language that they speak.

Vaikray – literally 'speaking blackly of the Vaik', Vaikray means to criticise Vaik ways and laws, to attempt to usurp or overthrow Vaik power and authority, or to speak in ways that demean or belittle the Vaik. In the past those found guilty were strapped to a mast at low tide, cut with a Vaik blade at the nipples and left either to the sharks or to drown. The law against Vaikray has been repealed but a cultural hangover of sorts remains.

Vende – a plant grown in the shaenet. The peppery-tasting stalk is used in cooking. It strengthens the immune system and promotes blood flow to the genitals.

Verrglet – a Vaik drink of celebration, reserved for the most special occasions.

Vest – the Vaik word for 'self'.

ACKNOWLEDGEMENTS

My gratitude to the following people who, in one way or another, are present in this book:

Jo Case, Rochelle Siemienowicz, Rebecca Starford, Jenny Ackland, Bec Jones, Alan Brown, Claire Baker, Karen Scoble, Yvette Farran, Donna Vyse Hamilton, Nina Crowe, Melanie Williams, Susan Gontaszewski, Clare Hennessy, Sarah Thorpe, Sarah Eccleston, Ben McMillen, Fiona O'Dougherty, Angela Meyer, Jacinta Di Mase, Hazel Jones, Stephen Jones and Tessa Bex.

And, of course, Jason Johnston.